**Praise for Cressida M**

'One of our favourite wome

***Heat***

'Hopeful and hopelessly romantic. . . A gorgeous, sweep-you-off-your-feet slice of escapism'

***Red***

'A warm and wonderful read'

***Woman's Own***

'Cressida's characters are wonderful. A delicious summer treat!'

**Sarah Morgan**

'Evocative and gorgeous'

**Phillipa Ashley**

'Uplifting, heartwarming and brimming with romance'

**Cathy Bramley**

'Gorgeously romantic . . . forced me to go to bed early so I could read it'

**Sophie Cousens**

'I just LOVED this story. All the characters are wonderful'

**Isabelle Broom**

'Real heart and soul'

**Sarra Manning**

'The most gorgeously romantic, utterly perfect book'

**Rachael Lucas**

'A triumph. Breathlessly romantic, it sparkles with wit and genuine warmth'

**Miranda Dickinson**

'So many perfect romantic moments that made me melt. Just gorgeous'

**Jules Wake**

'A wonderful ray of reading sunshine'

**Heidi Swain**

'I fell completely and utterly in love . . . it had me glued to the pages'

**Holly Martin**

'A total hands-down treat. A book you'll want to cancel plans and stay in with'

**Pernille Hughes**

'Sizzlingly romantic and utterly compelling, I couldn't put it down'

**Alex Brown**

'Bursting with [Cressida's] trademark warmth and wit'

**Kirsty Greenwood**

'Funny, sexy and sweep-you-off-your-feet-romantic'

**Zara Stoneley**

'Perfectly pitched between funny, sexy, tender and downright heartbreaking. I loved it'

**Jane Casey**

'As hot & steamy as a freshly made hot chocolate, and as sweet & comforting as the whipped cream & sprinkles that go on top'

**Helen Fields**

'Just brilliant. Sweet, sexy and sizzzzling. It was a pure joy to read'

**Lisa Hall**

'A little slice of a Cornish cream tea but without the calories'

**Bella Osborne**

'Perfect escapism, deliciously romantic. I was utterly transported'

**Emily Kerr**

'Utter perfection . . . a total gem'

**Katy Colins**

'Sexy, sweet, and simmering with sunshine'

**Lynsey James**

# The Cornish Cream Tea Holiday

Cressy grew up in South-East London surrounded by books and with a cat named after Lawrence of Arabia. She studied English at the University of East Anglia and now lives in Norwich with her husband David. *The Cornish Cream Tea Holiday* is her twelfth novel and her books have sold over half a million copies worldwide. When she isn't writing, Cressy spends her spare time reading, returning to London, or exploring the beautiful Norfolk coastline.

If you'd like to find out more about Cressy, visit her on her social media channels. She'd love to hear from you!


/CressidaMcLaughlinAuthor
@CressMcLaughlin
@cressmclaughlin

Also by Cressida McLaughlin

Primrose Terrace series
*Wellies & Westies*
*Sunshine & Spaniels*
*Raincoats & Retrievers*
*Tinsel & Terriers*

*A Christmas Tail* – The Complete Primrose Terrace Story

The Once in a Blue Moon Guesthouse series
*Open For Business*
*Fully Booked*
*Do Not Disturb*
*Wish You Were Here*

The Canal Boat Café series
*All Aboard*
*Casting Off*
*Cabin Fever*
*Land Ahoy!*
*The Canal Boat Café Christmas*

The House of Birds and Butterflies series
*The Dawn Chorus*
*The Lovebirds*
*Twilight Song*
*Birds of a Feather*

The Cornish Cream Tea Bus series
*The Cornish Cream Tea Bus*
*The Cornish Cream Tea Summer*
*The Cornish Cream Tea Christmas*
*The Cornish Cream Tea Wedding*
*Christmas Carols and a Cornish Cream Tea*

*The Staycation* – a standalone novel

# The Cornish Cream Tea Holiday

Cressida McLaughlin

HarperCollins*Publishers*

HarperCollins*Publishers* Ltd
1 London Bridge Street,
London SE1 9GF

www.harpercollins.co.uk

HarperCollins*Publishers*
1st Floor, Watermarque Building, Ringsend Road
Dublin 4, Ireland

First published by HarperCollins*Publishers* 2022
1



A catalogue record for this book is available from the British Library

ISBN: 978-0-00-850366-6 (PB)



Typeset in Birka by Palimpsest Book Production Ltd, Falkirk, Stirlingshire

Printed and bound in the UK using 100% Renewable Electricity by CPI Group (UK) Ltd

MIX
Paper from
responsible sources
FSC™ C007454

This book is produced from independently certified FSC™ paper
to ensure responsible forest management.

For more information visit: www.harpercollins.co.uk/green

To Sheila Crighton

xoxo

# Chapter One

The whitewashed, semi-detached cottage could not have said 'summer holiday' any more boldly if it had been wearing a floppy hat and a pair of shades. It glistened in the early June sunshine as Thea Rushwood stood looking at it, leaning against the car from which she had just extracted her stiff body, enjoying a breeze that was unmistakably seaside. The wafts of salty freshness inhabited all of her senses and sent her excitement up a notch.

She was finally here.

The drive from Bristol had been a lot longer than Apple Maps had first suggested, due to it being Saturday – change-over day – the beginning of June, and perfect weather. If any combination of things pointed firmly in Cornwall's direction, then it was those three. Thea felt a stab of unoriginality at her holiday destination, and rubbed the back of her neck, which was tense from hours in the driving seat, the traffic jams, the complete standstill when she'd reached Exeter that was due, the signs told her, to a charity rugby match.

She should have been sharing the driving. She should have spent the journey chatting and laughing with her best friend Esme, anticipation building between them, instead of listening to the radio and eating a duck wrap from the services one-handed so she ended up getting plum sauce on her chin. But. *But.* She was here now, with three whole weeks ahead of her where she need do nothing but tick off the items on her and Esme's bucket list, a lot of which involved lying on the beach and reading book after book, eating fish and chips, drinking cold beers, and not answering emails or dealing with any customer queries at all. Ha! Take *that*, Esme.

Turning one hundred and eighty degrees, Thea put the white cottage behind her and looked out over the Cornish coastline. It was inconceivable to her that the sea could glitter quite so much, as if someone had chucked the world's supply of diamonds across a floor of sapphire-coloured marble. The breeze wasn't strong enough to put crests on the waves, but there were jaunty little humps, the tide ambling towards land in a welcoming sort of way.

Port Karadow: a bustling, cheerful seaside town, if one long-ago memory and her research were telling her the truth. Here, on the edge of it, were these two cottages, attached down the middle, a mirror image of each other, as if they might have once been a single house. They were longer than they were tall, generously sized, and had uninterrupted views of the sea. A paved walkway ran in front of them, then there was a wide gravel space with room to park several cars, and beyond that, sloping grass ran down to a hedge dotted with starbursts of little white flowers.

Then it was the coast road, then the clifftop heathland that ended abruptly, with a significant drop down to the sea below.

The most popular beach, she and Esme had been told when they had booked the cottage, was back towards town, where the tall cliffs fell away, just before the quaint, cut-out harbour in the centre of Port Karadow. There were other, more secluded coves along this stretch of coastline, and Thea was looking forward to exploring them.

She watched, already feeling more carefree, the stress of the long drive sliding off her, as a red car turned into the driveway that led up to the cottages. Mrs Harris, Thea decided. Sure enough, a woman who looked to be in her early forties, with a neat bob of ash-blonde hair, got out and strode over, her arm outstretched and a smile on her face, wearing green wellies despite the dry, sunny day.

Thea felt a familiar tension return to her shoulders, her usual urge to clam up, but she forced herself to match the woman's smile.

'Theophania, I assume?' the woman said loudly.

Thea tried not to wince. 'Thea is fine,' she replied. She had to learn to ignore the *full name* requests on registration forms and just call herself Thea. 'Are you Mrs Harris?'

'Yes, but do call me Mel. Welcome to Port Karadow! Here's your key.' She held out a single key on a keyring, a photo of a Cornish beach stuck inside a see-through plastic frame dangling below.

'Thank you,' Thea said as she took it.

'Usually I would have left it in the lock box,' Mel went on. 'But I thought it best to come and greet you in person, so I could explain.' She glanced at the houses.

'Is that a holiday cottage too?' Thea asked, peering beyond Mel to look at the second house, to see what was making her brow crinkle. Mel had tanned skin and freckles, fine lines around her eyes and mouth that suggested she was always outside, that she had a healthy, invigorating lifestyle.

Thea wondered if her own pale skin could ever become freckled, or whether her dark, wavy hair – that she wore long enough to brush her shoulder blades – could develop lighter strands after regular exposure to sun and coastal winds. Mel also had a bright, no-nonsense approach that Thea couldn't help envying. Confidence was clearly not a problem for her.

'Not a holiday home,' Mel said now, her tone hardening slightly. 'It used to be, when we bought Sunfish Cottage, but the owner sold it at the beginning of the year. It's a private house now, which is what I wanted to mention.' Mel touched Thea's arm lightly and drew her towards Sunfish Cottage's ocean-blue front door, until they were sheltered by the shallow porch, the panes of coloured glass in the decorative door panel lighting up the sides of their faces.

Thea bit her lip. She thought Esme would have loved this low-level subterfuge, a mystery before they'd even got inside their cottage. She would have to tell her about it later.

'Everything OK?' she asked lightly.

'The new owner,' Mel said. 'He's doing some work on the house, on Oystercatcher Cottage – though I don't know if he'll keep the name.' She shook her head. 'We had some complaints from our last guest about the noise. Some banging and sawing sounds. The house needs some modernising, it's true, and it's his right to do whatever he wants, but . . .'

'You're worried it'll disrupt my holiday?' Thea asked. So far, she hadn't heard a peep from the house next door, but there were no cars parked in front of it. The builders probably weren't working on a Saturday.

Mel sighed. 'I had hoped it might have stopped by now, but I heard hammering as recently as yesterday, so I wanted to come and meet you, to mention it in person. It's not ideal, when you've come for an idyllic Cornish holiday. And on your own now, too.'

'Oh that's fine,' Thea said breezily, even though it wasn't. 'My friend had a work emergency at the last minute. It'll be lovely, being here alone, with nobody to argue with about what to do. I'll have free rein for the entire time, and when does that ever happen?'

Mel brightened. 'Too true. I have three children, and the eldest just moved up to secondary school. You wouldn't believe how many sports clubs and extra-curricular activities she needs dropping off at. Free rein sounds like another planet at the moment.' She smiled. 'I'm glad you're looking forward to it. Would you like a tour of the cottage?'

'Yes please,' Thea said, and there was an awkward moment where they both stood in the porch, waiting, until Thea remembered she had the key. She unlocked the door and stepped inside.

It opened straight into an airy living room, the walls white and slightly uneven, with dark wooden beams bisecting the ceiling and matching, solid-looking furniture. The open fireplace would hold real fires when the weather was cold enough, an empty basket positioned next to it waiting for logs. Two squashy turquoise sofas faced each other over a low wooden tea chest that served as a coffee table, a small, flatscreen television in the far corner clearly an afterthought. The ceiling was higher than Thea had anticipated, and the sea-facing windows let in acres of sunlight. Glass ornaments in swirling pinks and blues, their abstract shapes indefinable, added a shimmer of colour on the windowsills, and the thick carpet was a soft blue. On the right-hand wall, between two wooden doors, there was a low bookcase filled with paperbacks.

'This is the main space,' Mel said, all efficiency now the unpleasant business of next door had been dealt with. 'Nice and cosy, but with lots of room for lounging or entertaining.'

Thea nodded. She didn't anticipate entertaining anyone, but the sofas looked comfortable, and there were books: so many books. This place, she decided, was perfect.

It wasn't as if she didn't have a whole electronic library in her bag – her Kindle was close to its storage limit – or that she didn't live her life surrounded by books working at Bristol library, but neither of those things were the point. Books were an essential part of her life, and a new bookshelf, somebody else's curated selection of stories, was to her what a new dig site was to an archaeologist. You could find a new author or novel you'd never heard of, but, once you read a few pages, wonder how you'd ever survived without.

'This is the kitchen,' Mel said, walking through the nearest door on the right. Thea followed, stepping into a room with cream cupboards and pine work surfaces, a breakfast bar running along the front-facing window, two stools placed below it. She could drink coffee looking out at the sea, she realised with a skip of excitement. 'Dishwasher, coffee machine, oven, microwave,' Mel ticked off on her fingers. 'A washing machine concealed here, if you need it.'

'Brilliant,' Thea said. 'It all looks so lovely.'

Mel grinned. 'I like to think so. Let me show you the bedrooms and bathroom, and there's a downstairs loo too.'

The stairs were soft and uneven, as if the wood beneath the thick carpet had started to warp with age. Mel showed Thea the two double bedrooms, and the large bathroom that was clean and colourful, with blue, pink and turquoise tiles interspersed with the white, a deep bathtub, and a rainfall shower in a separate cubicle.

'At least you won't have to pick straws for who gets the master,' Mel said, as Thea stood, looking out of the window in the bedroom at the front of the house. A floor up, the view over the coast was magnificent, the stretch of deep blue sea beyond the clifftop so vast and overwhelming that she felt as if she could fall straight into it from where she stood. The bed was wider than she was used to, with a dark wooden head and footboard, and there was a small, fabric-covered bench at the end of it, like something out of a country house hotel. It was touches like this that tipped the cottage from lovely into luxurious.

Thea thought she might have cried if she hadn't had this bedroom; if Esme had found a way to convince her that she needed it. For the first time, she was glad her friend had bowed out of their holiday, but that thought was chased down by a twinge of guilt at her selfishness.

'It's glorious,' she said, turning to Mel. 'Three weeks here isn't going to be a hardship at all.'

Mel clapped her hands together. 'I'm so glad! There's a folder downstairs with all the useful information you might need, along with my mobile and home numbers if you run into any problems. We're only five minutes down the road, in the town itself, and always happy to help if we can.'

'Oh no,' Thea said. 'I'm sure I won't need to call you. This place is going to suit me so well.'

'It is a beautiful spot. Not just here,' Mel flung a hand towards the window, 'but the whole area. The town has a lot of character, and obviously there's the surrounding coast and countryside. Beaches and coves and endless walks you can go on.'

'Would you say Port Karadow's a lively place?' Thea asked, running her hand over the light blue fabric of the bench at the end of the bed. It felt velvety against her skin.

'Oh yes,' Mel said, folding her arms. 'It's got a real creative energy to it: lots of independent places, still, which isn't always the case, and there are always events happening. I think there's a sand sculpture competition taking place while you're here, actually.' She took her phone out of her pocket and started scrolling.

'Sand sculptures?' Thea asked with a laugh. 'That might be fun to watch.'

'Yes, here we are.' Mel held her phone out, and Thea looked at the page, which seemed to be a list of events on a community website. 'I'll send you the link.'

'That would be great, thank you.' This was exactly what her research had told her – though she hadn't come across the site Mel was showing her – and to have it backed up by a resident gave her an additional glimmer of hope.

Mel showed Thea the heating controls, reiterated that if she had any problems she shouldn't hesitate to call, then got in her car and drove away. Thea stood in the doorway and watched until she was out of sight, as if they were best friends rather than two near strangers who'd met for the first time half an hour ago.

Then it was just her and the gentle shushing of the sea, and no noise at all from the cottage next door. It was so *quiet*, she thought, as she slipped off her sandals and padded into the kitchen. She examined the welcome hamper that she'd noticed when Mel had been showing her around. There was a box of Cornish teabags, a bottle of white wine that Thea put into the fridge – where, she discovered, there was also a pint of milk – a packet of chunky biscuits, and a bag of fudge with an attractive label that said it was from somewhere called *Cornish Keepsakes*.

It was the middle of the afternoon, and she would have to go to the supermarket she'd passed on her way in, but half an hour's rest would revitalise her before she got back in the car. She made a cup of tea and put two biscuits on a plate, their chocolate chips glistening.

The sofa she chose was as comfortable as it looked, and Thea drew her legs up under her. There wasn't even the ticking of a clock to break the quiet. She could hear the drift of wheels on tarmac as cars passed on the road, and beneath that the constant, gentle thrum of the waves. She had already decided she would leave the window open at night to let the sound of the tide creep into her bedroom.

Three weeks here, all on her own. Could she do it? No, that was the wrong question. Of course she *could* do it, but there was a difference between hiding in this calming room with coffee and an endless supply of books, and actually getting out there: doing all the things that she and Esme had planned. They had drawn up a holiday bucket list, and now Thea was going to be doing all those things by herself because, even though Esme had bowed out at the last minute, she was still going to hold Thea to it.

As if connected by some psychic bond, her phone pinged, and Thea saw it was her friend.

Are you there yet? I need photos! Ex

Thea was tempted to send her zero photos, and only the briefest reply. Esme continued to be the busy, optimistic whirlwind she always was – which was one of the reasons Thea loved her, except she was struggling to love her right now, because she was acting as if nothing had happened.

Esme was one of the library managers, while Thea was a library assistant, and she understood that her friend's hands were tied, she really did, but it didn't make her irritation and hurt much easier to bear. They had been planning this holiday for two whole years. Three weeks of leave was a rare enough occurrence as it was, and the fact that they'd been able to get the time off together was a minor miracle. Esme had found someone to cover the library's annual summer festival – Jane, one of the other managers, who was competent and reliable – and had made back-up plans of her back-up plans, and everything was under control.

But then Jane had been in a freak accident involving her daughter and her dog, a TikTok dance routine and a spilled jug of lemonade, and had broken her leg. The summer festival was a busy, frenetic event at the best of times, and when Michael Morpurgo confirmed, Esme had been left with no other choice than to take over the festival's final preparations and stay behind.

She had apologised, had taken Thea out to dinner to make up for it, and since then had acted as if the slate was wiped clean. They had put down a significant deposit on the cottage, and Esme had said she would still pay her half, as long as Thea still came, on her own, to Cornwall, and had the holiday they had both dreamed of, while she stayed behind with the writer of *War Horse*, and Alex Marchant.

Alex was the operations manager for the council with responsibility for the library, taking care of everything from procedures and protocol to health and safety. Thea and Esme had agreed, on countless occasions, that Alex, with his easy smile, blue eyes and ability to make manual handling training fun, was the least stereotypical operations manager of all time.

Esme and Alex and Michael Morpurgo were all in Bristol, and Thea was here.

She gazed at her new surroundings, the bookshelf heavy with stories for her to explore, and felt the comforting warmth of the tea through her mug. Mel had left the window on the latch, and the outside was drifting inside, surrounding her with a fresh breeze.

She had three weeks of peace and calm, and if she didn't want to fulfil the bucket list, then so what? She could take a few photos, fool Esme into thinking she'd been to more places than she had. Besides, she had her own agenda. One that was looking even more hopeful after her chat with Mel.

She smiled and polished off the first biscuit, then replied to her friend.

I'm here! Will send photos in a bit – I'm just having a cuppa. P.S. the view is amazing! xx

She closed her eyes and rested her head against the sofa, thinking how quiet, how tranquil, it was.

And that was when the banging started.

# Chapter Two

The bed was incredibly comfortable. With the window open, the sounds of the sea had lullabied Thea off to sleep, her head sunk deep into the pillows, the hotel-style duvet feather-light, providing just enough warmth. Her belly was full of fish pie, and even though it had been a supermarket ready meal rather than something crafted by a chef at a local pub, it had still given her Cornish seaside vibes.

By the time she'd got back from the supermarket, the banging that had briefly disturbed her had stopped, and as she'd parked her Renault Clio in front of the two houses there had been no other vehicles. She was completely alone, and it was a strange feeling. She never felt alone in Bristol.

She and Esme had exchanged a few messages, and then she'd ended up watching the Saturday night entertainment shows on BBC One, having to angle herself oddly on the sofa to see the screen properly. Even though Mel hadn't said so explicitly, the cottage's aesthetic said, 'This is not a place for boxsets or the BBC: you're in Cornwall for God's sake, so get out and enjoy it!' But, Thea had told herself, it was her first night. She had been driving for a lot of the day, and she had three weeks to explore.

First thing on Sunday morning, she made herself a milky coffee and heated up one of her supermarket croissants, then took them, along with her book, and went outside. She had, with immense self-restraint, saved the latest Elly Griffiths novel for this holiday even though it had been released in February, and she was looking forward to starting it.

There was a set of wooden garden furniture on the gravel in front of the living-room window, which seemed an unusual place for it until you considered the view, and Thea took one of the cushions from the under-stairs cupboard and put it on the chair facing the sea.

There was a blue Ford Transit van parked in front of Oystercatcher Cottage now, but no other signs of life: no lights or twitching curtains, no more banging or the squealing of drills. Would builders want to work on a sunny Sunday in June when there were umpteen more pleasurable things they could be doing? She was pretty sure the answer was no.

And it was already shaping up to be a glorious day, the early sun pale milk rather than vibrant orange juice, its rays shifting the blue sea to the high-sparkle setting, a few wispy clouds drifting gently overhead. It was achingly beautiful, and for a second Thea wondered how anyone got any reading done in the face of such a view. But if there was anyone who could ignore distractions and fall completely into a book, it was her – especially when that book was the latest Ruth Galloway mystery.

Half an hour later her croissant was cold, her coffee had been neglected, and the sea was still shimmering away, though she hadn't spent a minute watching it. She put *The Locked Room* down and tore her croissant in half, her phone buzzing as the pastry flakes stuck to her fingers. She glanced at the screen just as the sound of a door opening resonated in the quiet.

She glanced at the message from Esme:

What are you up to? Any pics to send me yet? xxx

God, her friend could be demanding. But her request wasn't as demanding as the need for Thea's eyes to focus on the man who had just stepped out of Oystercatcher Cottage and was stretching his arms towards the sky, as if he'd been hibernating for the last six months and all his limbs were crackling and stiff. *Lying torpid*, Thea thought, happy at the choice of phrase, except now, she realised with a hard swallow, he looked the opposite of torpid.

He was tall, with wide shoulders, his arm muscles well-defined beneath the sleeves of a faded blue T-shirt. His pale jeans were slung low on his hips, and he was wearing a pair of scuffed brown boots. With his back to her, Thea could only see that his walnut-brown hair was short and neat, revealing a long, tanned neck. He was proportioned like a builder; his frame was strong, his limbs long, his arms golden brown, as if he worked outside a lot. He pressed his palm between his shoulder blades, pulling his elbow in tight with his free hand, then repeated the stretch on the other side, letting out a low groan. *Crepitus*, Thea thought absently, though she didn't know if he'd appreciate her giving a name to the way his joints cracked like that.

She couldn't take her eyes off him, her coffee mug hovering close to her lips, as if it was no longer liquid she needed to sustain her, and she could instead just drink *him* in all day. The cheesiness of this thought was not, sadly, enough to stop her gazing at him. He wasn't like the grizzled foreman who had been in charge of her neighbour, Helen's, extension, with his stomach hanging over his waistband like a cushion, his greying chin fuzz almost indistinguishable from the hair on his head. No, this was a Diet Coke Break builder, and Thea thought that if she snapped a photo of him and sent it to Esme, then her friend would declare their bucket list null and void, because Thea would have already won at her holiday without moving from the cottage.

She pictured Esme working closely with Alex to get the festival risk assessments completed: Alex, who could make something that dry and relentless a fun task, with his twinkling eyes and easy smile. The thought made her uncomfortable, though she didn't quite know why. To banish it, she held her phone up in front of her.

The builder was still facing away from her, his hands on his hips, the breeze tugging his T-shirt against him so that she could see the shape of his back, the peaks of his shoulder blades. His brown hair tufted up on top, where it was slightly longer. She opened the camera, angled herself so that if he happened to turn around she could claim she was taking a selfie – vanity was a lesser vice than spying, surely – and snapped a photo. The artificial camera click sounded embarrassingly loud, and he turned, but as her heart lodged in her throat she realised she wasn't the object of his interest.

No, that was the large dog that had just trotted out of Oystercatcher Cottage. It was long-haired and shaggy, its fur mostly white, but with a few black and pale brown smudges. It looked like a drawing one of her Young Readers class at the library might do after reading *The Hundred and One Dalmatians*. The dog approached the man and he crouched, running his hand over the animal's head.

'Decided to finally wake up, have you?' he said in a soft voice. 'You lazy sod.' There was an acre of affection in his words, and Thea was treated to a view of his profile: dark brows, a square jaw, cheeks with a tinge of pink showing through the tan.

The dog raised his head, accepting the attention, then turned in Thea's direction. The man followed his pet's gaze, and Thea sucked in a breath as their eyes met. His were brown, but not dark: somewhere close to hazel, she thought.

'Hey,' he said.

'Hi,' she replied. Her voice was a squeak, as it often was when faced with strangers outside the safe confines of the library, where knowledge of her job gave her a confidence that wasn't always present in other areas of her life.

'Staying in the cottage?' He nodded at the house behind her.

'I arrived yesterday,' she said. 'Are you . . . working on the house alone, or waiting for your colleagues to turn up? You must have a hard taskmaster to be working on a Sunday.' She was pleased she'd got the words out, and that she was no longer squeaking.

This man, who was crouching in front of her, holding onto his dog's collar to stop it approaching her, was not Thea's type of person. He was too handsome; too coolly sure of himself. She was 28, a decade removed from school, but her time there had given her a mistrust of people like this that she hadn't, despite common sense and all the logical arguments she'd levelled at herself, been able to banish.

'The hardest taskmaster,' he said, agreeing with her assessment. She could already see the glimmer of amusement in his eyes. She'd managed two sentences, and he was already laughing at her.

Something deflated inside her, and she picked up her book. 'Well,' she said, turning back to the pages, 'he's probably paying you double time, so there's that.'

He laughed abruptly, then muttered, more to himself than her, 'I'm not getting paid anything.'

Thea was intrigued – and shocked, if he really was having to work for free – but she wasn't going to bite. She also wasn't going to give him the satisfaction of going back inside, even though her mug was empty. This was her outside space as much as his.

'You know,' he said, standing up slowly, 'I've heard that every time you take a selfie, it steals a part of your soul. Take too many, and there'll be nothing left.'

Thea clamped her jaw shut to stop it from gaping open, like a fish. 'Is that so?' she ground out. 'Good thing I wasn't taking one, then.' She realised, a second too late, what she'd just admitted to.

Surprise that he'd been the subject of her photo flashed across his face, before he schooled his features and raised a supercilious eyebrow. She thought he straightened slightly, too, but decided she'd imagined it.

'Enjoy your book,' he said. And then, 'Come on, Scooter. Let's go and find you some breakfast.' He gestured towards the cottage and the dog obediently led the way, with him following behind.

'Shit.' Thea flopped her Elly Griffiths onto the table, then realised she'd left it open, stretching the spine of the hardback, and carefully placed the bookmark inside and closed it properly. Already, this man was unsettling her to the point of carelessness. She should have gone inside the moment he appeared.

She made herself a fresh coffee, then returned to her seat and the story set in windswept Norfolk, which was doing a good job of taking her away from the beautiful view and the sun warming her legs. There were a few bangs from Oystercatcher Cottage, she thought she heard a shouted swear word, but she ignored the noise and was soon lost in the pages again.

'Hello!'

Thea started, almost dropping her book, and looked up, into a pair of very blue eyes. This blond, smiling man didn't look like a builder, in his pale green shirt with the sleeves neatly rolled up to the elbows and dark jeans, his hair tightly curled. He was tall, but his frame was leaner than the builder's, and while he was undoubtedly handsome, his expression was immediately welcoming, rather than closed-off.

'Hi.' Thea closed her book and slid her feet off the chair she'd been using as a footstool.

'I'm Finn,' the man said, holding out his hand.

'Thea,' she replied, shaking it.

'You're here on holiday?' he asked. 'It's a lovely spot.' He glanced around him, as if he was seeing the cliffs and sea for the first time.

She nodded. 'Three weeks. I'm on my own, though, so—'

Finn looked horrified. 'Are you? I'm so sorry. Unless that . . . unless you planned it that way? That sounds terrible, doesn't it? Let me start again.' He grinned, and Thea couldn't help laughing.

'It wasn't planned,' she admitted. 'I was supposed to be here with a friend, but a work thing came up and she had to stay behind.'

Finn blew air out through pursed lips. 'Now that is something I know a little about: work getting in the way. Or I used to, anyway. At least it's not because you've had a horrible break-up,' he added, but then his horrified expression was back. 'Unless—'

'No, I haven't,' Thea said quickly. 'Not at all.'

'Thank God.' He smiled, relieved. 'Foot-in-mouth disaster number two averted. Have you met Ben yet?'

'He's Ben the builder?' Thea asked, and was rewarded with a chuckle from Finn.

'Now why didn't I think of that? So you *have* met him.'

'And his dog. It seems a bit unfair of the owner to make him work on a Sunday. And he told me he wasn't being paid anything, but I can't believe *that's* true. That would be outrageous!'

Finn narrowed his eyes as he turned to look at Oystercatcher Cottage.

'Oh shit,' Thea muttered. She said to him, '*You're* the owner, aren't you?'

'What?' Finn turned back to her. 'No! Not me. I live with my girlfriend in town. Ben's the owner.'

Thea frowned. 'He's . . .'

'Doing the place up himself, so that comment about not being paid . . .' Finn shook his head. 'I must apologise for my friend. He occasionally has a less than sunny disposition, but he's generally a great guy. I'll go in and drag him back outside, because it's obvious that he didn't introduce himself properly, and if you're going to be rubbing along next to each other for three weeks, that has to change.'

'He told me that whenever I took a selfie, I lost a bit of my soul,' Thea admitted, because unlike Ben, Finn didn't make her feel remotely self-conscious.

'Did he really? Well, then. I'll be back in a few minutes.'

'You honestly don't have to—' Thea started, but Finn was already striding in through the front door of Oystercatcher Cottage without knocking, calling out for his friend. She heard the dog, Scooter, barking, then a conversation she couldn't make out. She felt inexplicably nervous at the thought of Finn bringing Ben back outside to speak to her. There was no need: they might bump into each other occasionally while she was here, but it wasn't as if they were sharing a house.

She fidgeted, silently cursing herself for allowing such a simple situation to overwhelm her. She was a grown woman with a good job and a fully fledged life plan – a *business* plan, that she was going to start implementing over the next few weeks, all being well – and yet the thought of having a conversation with an attractive, oblique man was making her palms clammy. Did she have croissant crumbs around her mouth? A dribble of coffee on her chin? Should she go inside and check? What would Ben think if he came outside with Finn and she wasn't there? Would he think she'd run away? Why was she even worrying what he thought: what *either* of them thought?

She realised she could check her appearance in her phone camera, and that was what she was doing, pushing a strand of hair off her forehead, when Finn reappeared with Ben behind him, Scooter bringing up the rear.

Thea hurriedly put her phone down, but it was too late. Something like satisfaction flashed in Ben's eyes: that he had caught her at it, she supposed.

'Just losing a bit more of my soul,' she said, trying for jaunty, and achieving, she thought, slightly manic.

She saw Finn elbow Ben in the side, and after a moment he strode forward, holding out his hand. 'I'm Ben, the owner of Oystercatcher Cottage.'

Thea grasped it. It was warm, his grip firm, and he met her gaze as they shook. Those two points of contact, after his earlier evasiveness, made her cheeks heat up.

'Thea,' she said quietly. 'Nice to meet you.'

'Likewise.'

The dog nudged his nose into her lap, and Ben started to pull him away.

'No, it's fine,' she said, stroking Scooter's head. She noticed the animal had very pale eyes, his stare somehow more intense because of it. 'He's beautiful.'

'He's an Australian Shepherd,' Ben explained. 'Very loyal.' There was a slight edge to his voice, and Thea glanced up, noticing the way his jaw was set firm. 'Not so good at helping me plaster, though,' he added, with less bite.

'You're fixing it up by yourself?'

'That's the plan. Finn's a painter, but more seascapes than ceilings.'

'I have offered to help,' Finn said, picking up Thea's book and scanning the cover. Rather than be offended, she wanted to ask him if he'd heard of Elly Griffiths, what he thought about her, what his favourite crime series were. Her love of books surpassed all other concerns.

'Yes, but I want plain walls, not murals,' Ben said. He shook his head, and Thea couldn't tell if the exasperation was feigned, or if this was old ground and he was tired of going over it. Finn, she could tell, had an oversized personality.

'I know,' Finn said lightly, then added, 'did I mention the bit about Thea being on holiday for three weeks, all on her own?'

Ben glared at his friend. 'You did.' He glanced at Thea. 'Look, all that stuff about selfies stealing your soul . . .'

'It's fine,' Thea said.

He winced. 'It wasn't, but I—' He ran a hand over his head. His hair was thick on top, and a few strands were left ruffled by his fingers, making him look softer, less intimidating.

Finn stepped forward. 'I've actually come here to convince Ben that he doesn't want to spend the day sandpapering walls or ripping up floorboards or whatever he's got his heart set on, and to come to the beach with me and Red – Meredith, my girlfriend – instead. There's Scooter, and Meredith has a beagle called Crumble, and I'm aware you don't know us from Adam, Thea, but if you wanted to come with us, you'd be very welcome.'

Thea's gaze immediately flitted to Ben. His jaw was set, like marble, and while his expression wasn't exactly warm, she was drawn to his eyes. Close up, they were a mix of brown, green and blue: a whole watercolour landscape in his irises.

'I'm actually . . . going for a walk.' It sounded lame. 'Along the coast path.'

'Oh, of course,' Finn said. 'It's a good day for it, as long as you take a big bottle of water.'

'Definitely,' Thea said, laughing as if the mere suggestion that she might not have thought of that was ludicrous; as if she went on long walks along clifftops all the time. 'It was lovely of you to offer, though. You should have a great time at the beach, with the weather like it is.'

'Should do,' Finn agreed. His perkiness seemed entirely genuine, while hers was taking a lot of effort. Ben offered the weakest of smiles, and even though she hadn't warmed to him, she had to applaud him for not even trying to fake good humour. Here was a man who didn't care what other people thought of him.

'It was nice to meet you,' she said, gathering up her cup and her book. 'And I'm sure I'll bump into you again, Ben. Have a good day.'

'You too, Thea,' Finn said.

She bent to pat Scooter, the dog's nose angled up towards her, displaying all the friendliness his owner was lacking.

'Bye then,' she said, giving them a little wave with her hardback.

Finn waved enthusiastically back. Ben raised a static hand, then dropped it at his side.

As she turned away, she could hear his low voice as he murmured something to Finn. Probably: *What on earth were you doing inviting an annoying, selfie-obsessed stranger to come with us to the beach?* But she couldn't worry about that now, because she had something much more pressing to cope with: the fact that she had no idea when Finn and Ben would be leaving, or when Ben was likely to return, which meant that, now she had said she was going on a walk, she had to at least give the impression that it was really happening.

She sighed as she washed up her crockery. It was Esme who had added a long, limb-punishing hike to their bucket list, not her. But Esme was at home with Michael Morpurgo and Alex, and Thea was here, doing what she'd been instructed, with Mr Sunshine and Mr Grumpy hanging about next door, and she had well and truly shot herself in the foot.

She trudged upstairs to take off her skirt, change into hiking gear and walking boots, and try to remember where she'd put her water bottle.

# Chapter Three

Port Karadow, Thea's home for the next three weeks, was a place that she held close to her heart, despite having only been here once before. As she walked into town, it shone with charisma, as if preparing to do battle with the clouds that were now racing overhead; as if it knew how much it meant to her and was showing off in her presence. Its cobbled streets and quaint seaside houses – many of them in soft, pastel colours like a display in an ice cream shop – were welcoming in a way that made the knot in her neck loosen.

She'd changed into shorts and T-shirt, and had a small rucksack containing her phone, a light jumper she was positive she wouldn't need, and the bag of fudge from the hamper, her full water bottle secured in the side pocket. Her walking boots, bought specifically for this holiday and not subjected to enough wearing-in, were already pinching her heels. She had a tendency to be unprepared for things she was reluctant to do, in some vague hope that before she had to do them the plans would change, and today this approach was biting her on the bum.

There had been no sign of Ben or Finn when she'd walked out of Sunfish Cottage, though both the Ford van and a grey Alfa Romeo, which she presumed was Finn's car, were parked outside, so they could have been watching from the windows. Her plan was to buy a sandwich and set off along the coast path, take in the sights and enough photos to satisfy Esme. Then, by the end of her first whole day, she would have ticked off an item on their list.

She turned onto a steep, gently cobbled street with shops running down either side. This was an item on her own, personal to-do list: exploring every corner, every alleyway, of Port Karadow, to see if it was suitable for life beyond a three-week holiday – if it was everything she'd remembered and dreamed of.

A glance down a side street showed her a glint of blue water, which must be Port Karadow's picturesque harbour: there were photos of it on every website that mentioned the Cornish town. Thea didn't know if all the shops and cafés would be open on a Sunday, and she needed to see it at its busiest and quietest, in sunshine and in rain, and find someone who could tell her what it was like during the winter months, too. Her thoughts tripped back to Ben and Finn, and she thought that Finn, at least, wouldn't mind her asking some questions.

'No, leave all that now!' said a loud voice, startling Thea out of her daydream. She noticed a man with dark, thinning hair, wearing a suit, shirt and tie despite the heat, backing out of a doorway. The shop's name was Cornish Keepsakes – the place her fudge had come from – but the sign on the door said *Closed,* despite the door itself being open.

Thea approached, the man still talking to someone inside. He stopped mid-sentence and glanced at her, his smile widening. 'Hello,' he said. 'I'm afraid we're not actually open right now.'

'Ah, no problem,' Thea replied, glancing through the doorway. There was a display of hampers in the centre of the space, the shelves against the walls holding candles, trinkets and boxes of edible goodies. 'It looks like a lovely shop. My welcome hamper had some of your fudge in it.'

'Excellent! I hope you enjoy it.' The man rubbed his hands together. 'Where are you staying?'

'Not too far from here, a place called Sunfish Cottage.'

'Oh, I know it: one of Mel's properties. Are you having a good time?'

'So far,' Thea said. 'I only got here yesterday.'

The man nodded in response, like one of those toy dogs that couldn't stop. 'You'll have a grand time. And don't worry about the clouds; the weather here changes as swiftly as a . . . summer swift, I suppose. The sun'll soon be back.'

'Good to know,' Thea said, her voice weak as she thought of the walk ahead. 'I don't want to keep you. Especially not if you're off to . . . church?'

The man chuckled, rocking back on his heels. 'No, not church. My wife and I have a lunch to go to.' He smoothed down his tie, which was pale pink with bold white daisies adorning it. 'You know, we will *soon* be open on Sundays,' he added, his tone suddenly conspiratorial. 'My colleague is intent on bringing us screaming – well, laughing, hopefully – into the modern age, and Sunday openings are part of that.'

Thea smiled. 'A tourist town like this, I'm sure you'll be busy. It's fairly hectic now, and it's still early.' There was a steady stream of people passing them from both directions, a few throwing frustrated glances their way as they had to change course to go around them.

'That's what Meredith keeps telling me. I have to get going, I'm afraid. Come on, Enzo, we can unpack the delivery on Monday,' he called through the doorway. 'You don't want to be inside for much longer!'

There was a shouted response from the bowels of the shop, and Thea took a step back. 'Nice to meet you,' she said.

'Oh, you too!' the man called. 'Enjoy your holiday.'

Thea found a café next door, a pretty place called Sea Brew, with gingham tablecloths and old-fashioned, illustrated postcards in frames on the walls, that offered sandwiches to take away. She ordered a cheese and pickle baguette, hoping it wouldn't wilt too much in the heat, and waited by the window while it was prepared. It was the perfect place for people watching, for eavesdropping; it had an intimate, small-town feel, tourists mingling with locals who all knew each other. In fact, the man with the daisy tie had mentioned Meredith: wasn't that what Finn had said his girlfriend was called?

She remembered Alex's reaction to her and Esme's planned holiday when she'd told him about it a few weeks ago. He had been outside the library, assessing an uneven paving slab that was causing him concern.

'Cornwall?' he'd said, his curly hair ruffling in the breeze while he crouched in his grey suit and peered at the slab, which was sticking up at a jaunty – and dangerous – angle. 'So this is the start then. You're really doing it?'

Thea had swallowed, wondering why it felt so terrifying admitting it to the one person who knew what she was planning. 'I'm going to look at some properties while we're there,' she had said.

'And Esme knows?' He'd raised an eyebrow, his blue gaze fixing on her with its usual intensity. It was one of the things she liked most about him, except at that moment.

She had shrugged. 'There's no point mentioning it when it's still just an airy fairy dream. I'm going to tell her when we're there, in Cornwall. Get her to come with me to the viewings.'

Alex had pressed his lips together, and even though she was almost certain that he wouldn't tell Esme if she didn't want him to, it had still felt precarious. 'You know,' he'd said casually, getting out his tape measure and the slim camera he carried with him, 'Bristol could withstand another independent bookshop, and the library offers so much more than the book loaning service. You wouldn't be competing with it if you chose to open your business here.'

'I know that,' Thea had replied, glancing around her to check her colleagues weren't looking for her. 'But I want the whole dream, Alex. A bookshop by the sea. It's what I've been working towards, what I've saved up for, for all these years. I'm not going to be half-hearted about it.'

It had felt both scary and empowering to say it, to tell her friend that she wasn't compromising on the plans she'd had for over a decade. Determination wasn't her default position: she didn't think anyone who knew her well would ever accuse her of being too forthright, and some people

– her mother included – would surely say the opposite. But on this one thing, her dream of opening a bookshop close to the sea, she wasn't going to waver.

She had never intended to tell Alex what she was doing – she hadn't known him that well, when it had happened: when he'd surprised her on her lunch break, seen her working studiously on something on her laptop, and coaxed the truth out of her. Since that day, he'd offered her advice, his business degree putting him in the perfect position to assist her in the areas where she lacked knowledge and experience.

As they'd spent time together, she and Alex had got closer, and that had inevitably, eventually, included Esme, too. Now the three of them had an easy friendship that didn't often, but occasionally, broke through the confines of work. Thea hadn't admitted to anyone that she also felt a tug of attraction whenever she thought about Alex. He had said she could call him about the bookshop whenever she had a question, and a couple of times she had taken him up on the offer, not wanting to examine her feelings too closely when both business and friendship were involved.

Now here she was, in the Cornish town that was at the top of her list of potential bookshop locations, all the gaps from her one, childhood memory recently filled in by online research, and she was charmed by it. The last bookshop in the town had closed down not that long ago – a fact that both encouraged and concerned her – which meant it was hers for the taking. It *could* be hers, if she was bold and savvy enough, if she found the perfect home for it.

She collected her sandwich from the friendly man behind the counter and strolled down the cobbled street, looking in shop windows at greetings cards and delicate sea glass jewellery, inhaling the scents of frying dough and sugar from a bakery as she passed. It was easy to imagine her bookshop nestled here, alongside the other retailers, fitting in with the holiday vibe. She hesitated in front of an empty shop, metal shutters pulled over the door, the picture window foggy with lack of care and cleaning, a few bits of torn paper left where the poster glue had been too stubborn.

She had a meeting on Tuesday with a landlord who was going to show her this very property – and any others that had come up for rent since they'd spoken – and her blood pulsed every time she thought about it. She knew that the sense of her destiny looming, the importance she had given to that meeting, would be even stronger now she'd seen the town again; now she'd confirmed it was everything she had hoped for.

She wanted to spend a whole day here, wandering every street, soaking up Port Karadow's unique atmosphere and imagining it as her home. Right now, though, she had a date with Cornwall's wild glory. If she could write an entire business proposal, plan and save for ten years to get to this point, then she could go on one clifftop walk on her own and survive it. After all, it couldn't be *that* hard, could it?

Two hours later, grasping her nearly empty water bottle with sweat-dampened hands, Thea sank gratefully onto a bench that looked out over the most awe-inspiring coastline she had ever seen. The tide was out, the blue-green of the calm water and soft gold of the sand HD bright, the beach dotted with giant, prehistoric-looking rocks that, from her precarious position high above them seemed small, but which she knew were actually gigantic.

Finally, she could appreciate it.

The blisters on her feet were throbbing in time to some beat that had started annoying her over an hour ago, the seam of her shorts was rubbing against the inside of her thighs, and she only had a few drops of water left. At least she had remembered her hair tie, allowing her to sweep her dark hair into a high, messy bun and save her neck from melting quite as much as the rest of her.

'Afternoon!' called a man who looked to be in his sixties, striding past her refuge point, his long legs eating up the uneven path.

'Hello,' Thea replied, aiming for bright.

'Lovely day, isn't it?' said the woman with him, who seemed equally chipper and unflustered. They had hats pulled low over their brows, and sticks that, Thea supposed, they could use when the terrain got too rough.

'Very lovely,' Thea replied. 'Just taking a little breather!' She hoped she didn't look too much like a wilting daisy.

'Good on you. We're powering through: there's a cream tea with our name on back at the hotel.'

'Sounds delicious,' Thea said, imagining the luxury of a simple cup of tea, the way it would coat her throat as it went down; the sweet, sensuous sugar rush of a warm, crumbling scone with jam and cream dolloped high.

'You need to get a hat on you,' the man called behind him, only slowing slightly. 'The sun's unrelenting.'

'I should have thought—' Thea shouted back, but they were already out of earshot, almost galloping down a bit of the path that she would have hesitated to attempt at a snail's pace. She should have worn a hat, but when she'd left the sun had been fractured by cloud, and it hadn't seemed quite so necessary. She could feel that her cheeks and forehead had tightened, and laughed humourlessly as she remembered her desire for a few, charming freckles. Now she would have peeling skin and an unattractive fuchsia hue, if she even made it back to the respite of the cottage, and didn't fall to her death on the way.

She burrowed in her rucksack for her phone, and saw that Esme had responded to the photos she'd sent her, all those hours ago when she had still felt good about the walk: before encountering perilous paths that seemed far too close to deadly drops to be safe, and sections that were so steep she was panting like her mum's ancient cat, who was sixteen years old and chronically overfed.

She had watched other walkers, wearing their confidence proudly, traversing the crumbling track as if it were a Bristol pavement. She wished she could be a gazelle on these clifftop paths, rather than a lumbering panda, even if pandas were cute in other ways. She thought longingly of her Elly Griffiths book, waiting for her at Sunfish Cottage, where there would also be a cool glass of lemonade.

The sustenance she had with her consisted of the last, very melty piece of Cornish Keepsakes fudge, and those remaining, precious drops of water that she could only get by tipping her head right back and upending her bottle, as if she were a starving person stranded on a desert island.

If her mum could see her now, she'd laugh – and not in a kind way. Even Esme would struggle to hide her smile. Kind, generous Esme, who had rescued Thea from a very particular kind of social torture at secondary school, involving a girl who Thea had thought was her friend but had turned out to be anything but. Since then, the two of them had been inseparable, staying close even though they went to different universities, supporting each other through Esme's various break-ups and Thea's two.

At first, Thea had balked at the idea of a three-week holiday without her friend, but now she was here, she wanted to show Esme – who had always been protective of her, in some ways like a big sister – that she could flourish on her own. After all, she would have to do that if she was going to move here for good. She couldn't be put off by vertigo-inducing stretches of terrain or a few awkward encounters with the locals. She had to put her fears aside and embrace every moment of it, regardless of how hard it was.

Her thoughts tripped back to cool, handsome Ben, and she wondered what he would say if she took a selfie now, with her sunburned cheeks and her hair plastered to her sweaty forehead. He'd probably make a smart comment about how, looking as she did, her soul was already long gone. The thought made her fuzz with annoyance, and she realised she wanted to prove him wrong, to show him she could get past her fear of heights, and all the many other ways this foray into the countryside made her uncomfortable.

She took the squashed fudge out of the bag and put it in her mouth, listening to the sound of the waves sliding effortlessly onto the beach far below her. She pictured Port Karadow with its trinket shops and snack stalls, the smell of warm, sugary dough and chips – the essence of summer holidays – and the empty property that could soon be transformed into a new independent bookshop, and her irritation fizzled away like the clouds had done earlier.

She rolled her shoulders and stretched her legs out in front of her, and realised she was smiling. A couple of years ago, a meditation coach who she had booked to run an 'Empowering Women' course at the library had talked earnestly to Thea, Esme and her colleagues about the power of visualisation. Thea had dismissed it at the time, but right now, after picturing her bookshop nestled alongside Cornish Keepsakes on Port Karadow's Main Street, her blisters didn't seem quite so painful, the return walk wasn't looming ahead of her in quite such a daunting way, and she thought she might even enjoy her hike back to the cottage, with the promise of a soothing bath and an ice-cold glass of lemonade dangling in front of her like the world's most welcome carrot.

Thea's sigh was more like a huff. She had been dissuaded from her good mood the moment she set off walking again, the heat closing in on her like an unwelcome blanket. Her blisters screamed at her from inside her boots, and her route back along the pathway seemed a lot more terrifying than it had on the walk out.

There was one point where the track narrowed and steepened, the way ahead looking like a short skip to instant death, where she gave in and sat down, scooting along the dusty ground on her bum. She didn't have vertigo, exactly, but she had never loved heights, and this pathway was extreme; she couldn't imagine Esme or Alex relishing it either. She was encouraged that, in this, at least, she wasn't alone, but then a group of three friends, two men and a woman, passed her – actually *passed* her – while she was sliding along, offering her cheery hellos, as if using her bum instead of her feet was entirely normal. That, she decided, had to be her lowest point: it could only get better from there.

But then, only a couple of hundred metres from where the craggy path met genuine road, with smooth tarmac, a gentle gradient and the promise of Sunfish Cottage in her near future, she didn't notice a small boulder protruding from the shaggy grass at the side of the track, and she stepped on it, twisting her ankle. It wasn't bad enough that she couldn't walk; not bad enough to cause anything other than a limp and an additional throb to add to all her existing throbs, but it startled her enough that for a few minutes she was close to crying, and subsequently, felt a hundred per cent pathetic.

She watched a bird in the hedgerow, flitting from one branch to the next, its melodic call sounding bright in the still, summer air. Once it had flown out of sight, she spurred herself onwards. She couldn't worry about what she looked like: limping because of her blisters and her ankle, her progress further stymied by how uncomfortable her shorts had become. Maybe past selfies *had* stolen her soul, and this was what she looked like without it: a hunched, stumbling monster, with raw, sunburned skin and sweat dampening her T-shirt. God, she hoped Finn and Ben would still be at the beach when she got back. She couldn't bear it if they saw her like this.

She took the route that would lead her along grassy tracks at the edges of the fields surrounding Port Karadow, rather than cutting through town and walking along the harbour. It would take her longer, but she looked a state, and the town would be busy in the afternoon sunshine. Besides, on higher ground, the wind was keener, cooling her hot skin, and if she kept the sea glimmering away to her right, she would get back to the cottages soon enough.

She saw a junction up ahead, a wooden signpost typical of the countryside indicating where each trail would lead her, and one of them announced it would take her to *The Old Post House*. Someone had painted an illustration of a childlike house next to the words, a glossy smudge suggesting a postbox red front door. Despite all her aches and grumbles, Thea wanted to see if the house matched the depiction. Besides, if it was open, it might have a cool drink to fuel the rest of her journey.

Her new route was lined by seven-foot hedges thick with buzzing insects, chirping birds and lacy clusters of delicate purple flowers. The end of the trail was soon in sight, but before she saw the building, she was presented with its outlook: Port Karadow spread out in front of her, rooftops sliding down towards the glistening harbour. It was postcard beautiful, a premium viewpoint, and she realised the Old Post House must be a prominent building in the town, looking over it like a monarch surveying his kingdom.

Thea took a few more steps, emerging from the hedge's shelter, and turned towards the building on her left. She couldn't help smiling.

The Old Post House looked like she did: hiding a whole lot of potential behind a less than groomed exterior. Before she'd had a chance to take in any of the details, she heard a loud, shrill creak, and then a voice called down to her from an upstairs window.

'What is it you want, standing outside my house looking like you've gone eighteen rounds with old Marty's biggest bull? Come closer so I can get a proper look at you!'

Never able to ignore a direct command for fear of something worse coming if she did, Thea stepped forwards and raised her head, meeting the gaze of the person who had spoken to her.

# Chapter Four

The woman leaning out of the upper window was in her seventies, at least, with a narrow face and white hair cut into a short, wispy bob. Thea couldn't see the colour of her eyes, only that they were pinning her in place with a bold, curious look.

'I didn't mean to disturb you,' Thea called up, because customer service training – and her own dislike of confrontation – had taught her to always defuse a situation if possible.

'You didn't! I was waiting for the post.'

Thea smiled, because wasn't that ironic, that she was in the Old Post House and had to wait until mid-afternoon for her own mail to be delivered?

'Yes, yes, I see you laughing,' the old woman said. 'Things are very much not what they used to be, young lady, and I don't mind using the cliché because it's true.'

'Does the post often come so late?' Thea shouted, then cleared her throat. She was parched already, and this yelled conversation wasn't helping.

'No,' was the reply. 'But I am a study in optimism over reality. I'm waiting for something, and I was assured by my solicitor that it would turn up today.'

'Oh. OK, then.' Thea didn't want to be drawn into an in-depth conversation, discussing a stranger's private matters at such a high volume. They might have been in a quieter part of town, but they must be disturbing at least ten sparrow families with their bellowing.

'What are you doing here, anyway? Hiking by yourself doesn't seem so wise.' The older woman clearly didn't share her concerns.

Thea huffed. The sun was slowly baking her, and she could feel her thigh muscles stiffening up, her ankle throbbing gently, as if to remind her that she was *so close* to a cool drink, a long shower and a comfy sofa. She licked her lips and tried not to whimper.

'Do you want to come down?' she called up.

'No! It will take me at least ten minutes with my creaking joints.'

'I could . . . come inside, then? Come up to see you?'

The old woman was already shaking her head. 'I won't have you traipsing through the disaster zone that is the lower floor, then breaking your ankle and suing me when I'm weeks away from escaping.'

Thea wanted to tell her she'd already hurt her ankle, that she didn't have the energy to sue anyone, but she was too intrigued by the hints she'd dropped. 'You're leaving?' she asked. 'It's such a beautiful building.'

She inspected it more closely, noticing that behind the tangle of ivy consuming it, the brickwork was honey-coloured. There were large windows either side of the front door, though the frames around them, and the lattice between the small panes, were far from white, and the red paint of the door was cracked beyond what could be considered vintage charm. Thea peered in through the glass, trying not to start at her reflection – the dark hair that had gone to frizz in the heat, pulling haphazardly away from her makeshift bun; the shiny pink of her cheeks; the sweaty sheen on her collarbone.

Ignoring her own image and stepping closer, she could see the dark, hulking shapes of furniture – a table and a heavy wooden chest pushed to the back of the space, a high desk that might once have been a counter, and, along the left-hand wall, bookshelves. They were grey with dust, and she didn't want to think about how many spiders used them as walkways, but they still whispered at her, gleeful in their possibility.

'Had your fill?' The woman was resting her forearms on the windowsill, leaning out so she could look down at Thea.

Thea shrugged. 'It needs a bit of work, but—'

'But I need more,' the woman finished. 'I can't stay here any more. Not with the narrow stairs and the steep hill down to the centre of town. My daughter's waiting for contracts to be exchanged, then she's having me in with her, once she's in the new house. Lots of room so we don't murder each other, apparently. And hopefully, once I'm gone, the Old Post House will be transformed from its current disaster zone.'

'Are you selling it?' Thea asked.

'It belongs to the town,' the woman said. 'Some complicated arrangement, I didn't pay much attention when Eric was in charge. But they'll have some use for it, no doubt.'

'Can't they spruce it up now, so you can stay in it?' Thea asked. She was drawn back to the window, noticed a stand of discarded greetings cards in one corner.

'I didn't want to let them, before.' The old woman sniffed. 'My Eric only died last year, and I know the old shop is in a state, but I haven't had the energy, or the spirit, to clear it of everything it used to be. The townsfolk rallied round, of course, but I was a moody old goat. Grieving, I suppose. Now my mobility's too bad to stay here, so it's going back to Port Karadow. It feels wrong to hand it over to them like this, but it's too late to do anything about it. They'll just have to make a go of it once it's back in their hands.'

Thea nodded, a lump in her throat at the thought of this woman, who seemed so mentally robust, grieving alone in this beautiful but decaying old building, too stubborn – or just too heartbroken – to accept help.

'I'm sure if you wanted to—' she started.

'I was asking about you, anyway. I've not seen you before. Even in the sunshine, that bit of coastline's a treacherous place.'

'I was fine,' Thea said sharply, even though she had thought exactly the same thing. She didn't quite understand how she had got embroiled in this conversation.

'You don't look it.'

'I'm hot and thirsty. I'll be OK once I get back to the cottage.'

'On holiday, are you? Of course you are.' She shook her head, and her neat hair danced gently in the breeze. 'Too green to be a local. Have you even got suncream on?'

Thea bristled. 'I should be getting back.'

'Indeed you should, before you spontaneously combust.'

Thea turned to go, then realised the old woman, stuck upstairs and as stubborn as a Cornish cliff face, might have shouted down to her for a reason. 'Can I get you anything? From the shops? I could pick up milk or bread, or go to the pharmacy if there's anything you need.'

Thea saw a flash of something – a glimpse of vulnerability, perhaps – in the old woman's eyes. Her shoulders dropped. If she could help her in some way . . .

'You know, even with my creaky old bones, I'm not nearly as much of a state as you are.' Thea was stunned into silence, which left room for the other woman to continue. 'I reckon, right this moment, I could get down and up the hill as quickly as you.'

'OK then,' Thea said, unable to feel anything other than a bone-deep weariness. Let this woman tease her if it made her feel better; more connected to the world.

The older woman chuckled. 'I'm only joking.'

'Fine.' It came out as a sigh.

'Want me to call a big strong man to come and take you home?' There was a gleam of amusement in her eyes now, and Thea was close to walking away. But curiosity won out again, as it so often did.

'Know many of those, do you?'

'I have one on speed-dial who would be only too happy to help a damsel in distress, and I'm sure he'd much prefer tending to your needs than mine.' The old woman smiled, the change of expression transforming her from cantankerous to kind.

Thea thought of Finn, and how unabashedly helpful he'd been; his obvious ability to charm the socks off anything that moved.

'I'm OK, really,' Thea said, softening, because even though she'd said it in a very roundabout way, it seemed this older woman was looking out for her. But then she realised that was because she looked like someone who had, quite possibly, escaped from a hole that she'd fallen into weeks ago, who had been living on grass and rainwater, and had had to claw her way out in order to survive. Her reflection had suggested as much.

'Get yourself home then, girl,' the woman said. 'What's your name?'

'Thea.'

'You don't look like a Dorothea. Are you – wait, don't tell me. You're a Theophania.'

Thea stared up at her. 'How did you guess?'

'I went to school with a Theophania. She was a horrible creature, kept throwing my textbooks in the toilet.'

'I've never done anything like that,' Thea said indignantly. She didn't add that she'd been on the receiving end of similar treatment during her own school years.

'I don't doubt it. Now, off you trot. I hope you've got some aloe vera, because you'll be needing it for your burns.' With that, the old woman disappeared inside and pulled the window closed, her movements gentling, as if any sort of force would lead to the thin glass falling out of its frame.

'Bye then,' Thea muttered, and then, baffled and wearied and wondering why, of all the people out walking today, these bizarre encounters had to happen to *her*, she stepped close to the building again. A bee drifted lazily out of the thick ivy next to her head. Its buzz startled her, but not enough to distract her from the bookshelves she'd been coveting earlier. Despite the dust, they were undoubtedly solid, and they were a good indication of how much space the building had – not to mention the history that came with it. She wouldn't think about the spiders, the possible rats, dry rot and mould. Everything had its issues, you just needed to look past those to the steady – and in this case charming – core.

She wondered what the old woman had meant when she said the building belonged to the town, and what they would do with it when she had moved in with her daughter. She caught sight of herself again, the way her hair was sweat-dampened in places, dry and frizzy in others, the glowing pink of her cheeks and nose, the general air she gave off of a woman who had given up on anything approaching self care. A headache was pulsing, from not enough water and too much sun, and she knew that the old woman was right, and she would have to get some aloe vera. She didn't think she'd even remembered to pack Aftersun. She would have to go into town again and, despite her plan to explore it, right now all she wanted was the cool hideaway of Sunfish Cottage.

She turned away from the Old Post House, and began her trudge down the hill. She realised, as she was reading the signposts to find out which direction she needed to go in, that she hadn't even found out the old woman's name.

Thea dragged herself up the last bit of hill, along the path to the right of the coast road that, unlike earlier, was far enough away from the cliff edge to feel safe. She could see the cottages up ahead, just over the road, and tried not to whimper with relief. *Home sweet home.* The bottle of aloe vera infused aftersun felt heavy in her rucksack, and she'd almost finished the two-litre bottle of water she'd bought, even though she knew she was supposed to sip it, rather than glug it all down in one go.

The Alfa Romeo was gone from outside the houses, but the van was still there. Thea would not be seeing Ben like this: no way. She climbed the stile set into a gap in the hedge, waited for a space in the Sunday afternoon traffic, then crossed the road and limped up the driveway. Then, keeping the van and her car between her and the houses for as long as she could, so as to shield her from anyone who happened to be looking out of the window of Oystercatcher Cottage, she made a beeline for her front door. She hurried past the table and chairs where she'd spent a pleasant few hours – had it only been that morning? – then hauled her rucksack off, unzipped it and searched for the key.

She couldn't find it, because the Gods of the Universe had decided that today was to be her darkest day. She took out the aloe vera cream, the empty sandwich and fudge packaging, and had kneeled down because that felt better than standing up any longer, when something cool nudged her leg. She jumped, then turned to find Scooter gazing at her balefully.

She sent a silent curse up to the Gods of the Universe – though she was honestly not surprised – and stroked the Australian Shepherd. His fur was so soft, and he came closer immediately, nuzzling her hot neck. Even though it meant that Ben wasn't far away, Thea couldn't help but be comforted by the simple affection. The dog knew she was knackered and frustrated, Thea was sure of that, and didn't care that she looked like a fright fest.

'Scooter?' Ben's deep voice was laced with irritation. 'Scooter, where have you— oh.'

Thea raised her head to see him standing on the path, halfway between their two front doors. He was staring at her, and she couldn't tell whether he looked surprised, horrified or worried, or a combination of all three.

'Hello,' she said, and when her knees protested at kneeling for so long, she thought *what the hell*, and sat down fully, her back against her front door. Scooter shuffled closer and laid his head in her lap.

'Are you . . . is . . . did you—?'

'I'm fine,' she said. 'Fine as a dandelion.'

He frowned, and she did too because that wasn't the expression. *Fine and dandy*, that's what she should have said.

'Did you have a nice walk?'

Thea couldn't detect any sarcasm or humour in his voice, though she thought he must be laughing at her. She didn't have the energy to fib.

'Not really,' she admitted. 'It was way too hot and I forgot to take a hat, I didn't have enough water and that coast path is really scary in places, don't you think? Properly, genuinely terrifying. And then, on the way back, I . . .' she thought of how to explain her encounter with the old woman, but it seemed too difficult. 'I twisted my ankle.'

Ben's brows lowered, and he took a couple of steps towards her. 'You walked here on a twisted ankle?'

'I'm exaggerating, I think.'

'But it hurts?'

'It's uncomfortable, but then all of me is uncomfortable. You should probably leave me alone so I can grumble and ache in peace, because this is . . . I'm not at my best.'

For the first time, she saw a glimmer of warmth in Ben's expression. He was wearing shorts, she noticed now, and had on a different T-shirt from earlier. This one was apricot, and it made his skin look even more tanned, highlighted the pink of his cheeks that suggested sunshine, exertion and all-round good health. She noticed a tiny spot of white in his hairline, which proved that *he'd* been sensible enough to wear suncream.

To her surprise, instead of nodding and walking away, he stepped closer and held out his hand.

Thea paused for a moment, then lifted her arm and let Ben take hold of her. His pull was gentle, but got her effortlessly to her feet. She put her weight on her ankle, and the spark of pain made her yelp. Scooter cocked his head on one side.

'That doesn't seem like exaggeration,' Ben said.

'I think I have a really low pain threshold.' Thea watched his gaze roam over her face, now she was closer to his level.

'Have you got any aloe vera?' he asked, and she laughed.

'I'm a walking poster about the perils of too much sun, I know.' She pointed to where the bottle rested on the step at her feet.

Ben looked at her a moment longer, then bent to pick it up. Then he picked up her rucksack, and the plastic wrappers that Scooter had begun to sniff.

'You don't have to—' she started, but he'd already found her key and was leaning over her to put it in the lock. He smelt of suncream and sugar, and he radiated warmth. She thought she would have had enough heat by now, but the warmth Ben was emitting was moreish.

'Here,' he said. He waited for her to stop leaning on the door. When she stood up straight, he pushed it open, then turned towards her.

'Thanks,' she said, taking the rucksack, holding it open so he could drop the other items into it, one by one.

'Put some cream on after your shower,' he said. 'More than you think you need. Believe me, I misjudged the strength of the sun when I first moved here, and you can . . .' his words drifted away. 'Sorry. You don't need me telling you what to do.'

But she found she was touched by his concern, especially after earlier, when he'd seemed almost allergic to her. 'No, but thank you,' she said. 'I feel like an idiot, for—' she gestured at herself, and his hazel eyes flickered down to her walking boots, up her bare legs and sweaty torso, then met her gaze again. His cheeks seemed pinker now, a muscle ticking in his jaw. 'It hasn't been my finest hour,' she added.

'It can't be that easy,' he said, after a beat. 'Coming here on your own, even if it's what you wanted to begin with. Sometimes, even if you're determined to make a go of things, all the bravado in the world can't make up for having someone else to talk to, or . . .' He shrugged, glancing away from her. 'I don't know.' He cleared his throat. 'Have you got peas for your ankle? If you need some, knock on my door. I've got frozen hash browns, which won't be as good, obviously, but they're better than nothing.'

'Thank you,' she said sincerely, hoping she was conveying how much she appreciated his words. What had made him friendlier? Had Finn given him a talking to, or was there something about her forlorn, lonely state that he identified with? Awkwardness radiated between them, a palpable force that was as strong as the sunshine. 'Do you want to—'

'I'd best be getting on,' he said, talking over her. 'Come on, Scooter.' He clicked his fingers and the dog trotted from her side to his. He started to walk away, then turned. 'If you need anything, just knock. I'll be in.'

'OK, thanks,' she said. 'This was really . . .' What? He'd helped her up and opened her door for her. It was a small thing, but he hadn't needed to do it. 'Really nice of you,' she settled on, and he nodded once, quickly, as if he'd already had enough of talking about it. He led his dog back to Oystercatcher Cottage, and Thea finally, *finally*, stepped into the cool, airy embrace of her holiday home.

Thank God that was over. Maybe she wasn't cut out for solo adventures after all.

# Chapter Five

Thea stayed in the cool shower for a long time, and though the water pattering against the tender skin of her face, arms and knees was sometimes uncomfortable, it was mostly glorious. She dried herself, slathered on a generous helping of aloe vera cream – remembering Ben's words – and dressed in her comfiest cotton dress. The sun was still strong, but the cottage was big enough that sunlight filled the rooms without bringing its scorching heat to every corner.

She made a cheese salad sandwich and a pot of tea, and sat on the sofa, scrolling through the photos on her phone. They didn't do justice to the magnificence of the coastline, and already, it felt unreal that she had been there just a few hours ago. She sent them to Esme, and three minutes later, her phone rang.

'God, I *so* wish I was with you,' Esme said, after Thea had given her an edited version of her walk. She left out the despair, but did include her fear of the precarious drops, and the encounter with the woman at the Old Post House.

Thea tried not to go on the defensive, because she knew, logically, that the festival mess hadn't been her friend's fault. 'Yeah,' she said, rubbing her leg where some of the aloe vera hadn't absorbed, 'but you've got the festival, and I know it's important to you. How's the prep going?'

'Oh, great,' Esme said, her brightness sounding forced. 'It's mostly done, but you know Alex: we're dotting the 'i's and crossing the 't's, then going back to the beginning, re-dotting and re-crossing everything.'

Thea knew her boredom was feigned, because they both loved working with Alex. She felt a pang of FOMO, a twinge of envy that Esme had him to herself, which must have been why she blurted out her next words. 'The man next door offered me frozen hash browns for my twisted ankle, even though I'm sure it isn't twisted, just twiddled a little bit.'

'What man next door? Who is this?'

'He owns the cottage next to mine, and he's renovating it himself. He's gruff. Cantankerous and irascible,' she added, because she loved words, and tried to exercise her mind with lesser known ones on a daily basis.

'Irascible?' Esme asked. 'And yet, he offered you hash browns.'

Thea's stomach rumbled, because she'd burned off a lot of calories that day. 'He did. He's . . . I don't know. Anyway. It was a good walk,' she lied. 'Something to tick off the list.'

'Great,' Esme said, and Thea could tell she'd become distracted. 'Tick it off on our shared note, so I can stay up-to-date. I have to go now, because I just realised I haven't sent the refund and returns policy to Wendy. I promised her I'd—'

'It's Sunday night,' Thea cut in. Her laugh was forced, because even though Esme hadn't had a choice, she still felt a sense of abandonment it was hard to quash. She loved the library, but she didn't want to hear about the returns policy from Esme, when she should be sitting next to her on this squishy sofa so they could compare sunburns and share a bottle of wine.

'I know,' Esme said. 'There's just so much to do!'

'I'd better let you get to it, then.'

'Thanks! Oh, and please take a photo of Mr Irascible Hash Browns for me.'

Thea laughed as if it was a ridiculous request, and didn't mention that she already had a photo of Ben, because it had been a little bit stalkery and she wasn't proud of it.

They said goodbye and hung up, and Thea was left alone with her thoughts.

She felt bad that she hadn't told her friend about her other reason for picking Port Karadow as their holiday destination, although, she told herself, if Esme had been with her, then she would know everything by now. Esme knew that running a bookshop by the sea was her lifelong dream, because they'd been friends since secondary school, but she didn't know how serious that dream was, because they'd always talked about it in fantasy terms. She didn't know that Thea had a business plan, or that Port Karadow was at the top of her list of locations: that it had gone from a: *One day, when the stars align, what I'd love to do is—* to: *I'm actually making this happen.* Esme's absence meant that she was still in the dark, and Thea trusted that Alex wouldn't reveal her secret.

It felt strange, she thought, as she poured herself a glass of wine, to be keeping something so big from the one person who had always been on her side, even when everyone else was laughing at her: who she trusted without question. But she couldn't help holding her dream close; keeping it safe from prying eyes and other people's judgement. She was afraid that the moment everyone knew – the moment it stepped from dream-land into real possibility – it would disintegrate. On Tuesday, two short days from now, she might be a step closer towards real possibility. She tried to ignore the way her heart sped up at the thought.

She went to bed early, changing into her summer pyjamas and turning off the light, then opening the curtains and the window. The night-time breeze was soft and cool, ruffling her cotton top as she looked out over the flat, still water, a midnight blue glossed in silver from the crescent moon. She drank it in, a sense of calm washing over her, and was about to climb into bed when a loud, rhythmic banging started up from next door.

Thea slumped onto the mattress, and there was a loud, splintering crack beneath her. She jumped up again, glared at the bed –which seemed exactly as it had done a minute ago – and tried not to wail. It was a huge, solid piece of furniture, but there was no escaping the fact that something had just broken. It was Sunday night, too late to call Mel, and she didn't have the energy to investigate it. She walked around to the other side of the bed and slid gingerly beneath the lightweight duvet, hoping that whatever had happened was minor, and easily fixable.

Thea stared up at the darkened ceiling, listening to the

banging from next door, and prayed that tomorrow would be a better day.

When she woke up the following morning, her legs ached from her long walk, and her neck felt knotted from trying to lie very still so as not to cause more damage to the bed.

She got up and hauled the mattress over to the side, revealing the wooden slats underneath. One of them, near the middle, had cracked at the place where it joined the frame. Not a fatal wound in itself, but the more she slept on it, the worse it would get.

It was just after eight, and Thea knew she should call Mel and tell her what had happened, but she was worried the owner would blame her. Perhaps she would imagine Thea had had a guest to stay – which of course was up to her – but she didn't want to make a bad impression, come across as a disruptive tenant, so soon into her holiday.

She listened carefully, but all was quiet next door. Maybe Ben was a night owl, rather than a morning person. Still, she could remember exactly what he'd said to her: *If you need anything, just knock. I'll be in.*

She pulled on a skirt and a T-shirt and went downstairs.

The day was already bright and cloudless, and she could see several small boats dotted on the water; this early, she assumed they must be fishing boats. She squinted against the brightness, glad that the aloe vera had settled her skin to a pinkish sheen, and that even though it still felt tight, she was no longer Day-glo.

Before she could talk herself out of it, she walked up to Oystercatcher Cottage and knocked on the door. She heard Scooter barking, followed by a low murmur. Footsteps approached and her pulse kicked up, then the blue door swung inwards.

Ben looked early-morning rumpled in loose jeans and a white T-shirt, his hair tufty on top, a pillow crease down the side of his face. When he saw that it was her, his gaze dropped to her ankle, then came back up.

'You OK?' he asked.

'I hope I didn't wake you.'

He shook his head abruptly. 'No, you're fine. How's the ankle? You didn't come for hash browns last night.'

He almost, *almost* sounded disappointed.

'A fry-up would be lovely,' she mused, and then, when he frowned, added, 'my ankle felt much better once I took the weight off it, but I really appreciated the offer.'

'It wasn't a problem,' he said.

Thea bit her lip. It had seemed such a good idea, back in her bedroom with the ruined slat, to ask Ben to have a look at it rather than trouble Mel. But now she was here, faced with all his stoic solidness – his impenetrability. And she knew now that he was kind – he had been *so* kind to her yesterday – but she could almost taste the awkwardness that still lingered between them. He was just so . . . *there.* In his white T-shirt, with his tanned, muscled arms, his wide shoulders, his swirly, green-brown eyes scrutinising her. She could see he was about to ask if there was anything else, or if she'd just come to gaze at him, so she blurted, 'You said if I needed anything, I could knock.'

He leaned against the door frame. 'I did, and I meant it.'

'Thank you for that.'

He nodded, the corner of his mouth lifting now, with that same hint of amusement she'd seen yesterday. She knew she deserved it this time for her woeful conversational performance, but it didn't make her feel any better.

'What can I help with?' he asked.

'My bed,' she said.

His eyebrows rose up to his hairline.

*Crap.* 'My bed's broken,' she clarified. 'One of the slats has splintered.'

'You didn't look like you had much energy left after your walk,' he said, and when their eyes met she saw his cheeks colour at the same time she felt hers redden. 'I mean, for jumping on it. The bed. I was trying to make a joke that you must have been jumping . . .' He shut his eyes and squeezed the bridge of his nose. 'That's not – I'll get my tools.'

'Are you sure?'

'Isn't that why you're here?' He opened his eyes again. 'You haven't just come to tell me your bed's broken; it's not really something to brag about. Or maybe, under some circumstances, but—'

'No,' she said hurriedly: her cheeks were on fire, now. 'No, I was hoping you'd help.'

He reached out and touched her arm, just a brief brush of his fingertips. 'Of course I will, if I can. Give me two minutes.'

She stayed on the doorstep, trying to settle her pulse as she peered into his front room. She couldn't see anything except the edge of what looked like a large metal toolbox. Scooter padded to the doorway and nonchalantly nosed her hand, as if they were old friends. Thea smiled, stroking the silky underside of his jaw.

The door opened wider and Ben had – not a smaller version of the toolbox, but a tool*belt*. It was mustard-coloured and looked soft, as if it was made out of suede, and it was slung low on his hips, the polished handles of various tools poking out of the pockets.

Thea chewed the inside of her cheek. Was he aware how much of a hot builder poster-boy he was? She was sure he wasn't. After her original assessment yesterday, that he was coolly arrogant, she had decided she'd misjudged him. He seemed reserved instead, awkward in some social situations, which made him a kindred spirit.

'Let's see what we're dealing with.' He gestured for her to lead the way.

She led him through the living room and up to the bedroom, where the mattress was still half off the bed, exposing the broken slat. The open window had freshened the room, and her belongings were all arranged neatly. Still, she couldn't help but try to picture it through his eyes: the make-up and skincare on the chest of drawers, her book and water glass on the bedside table, a small cuddly book-worm that Esme had bought her, and who she called Bert, sitting next to them.

Ben stood for a moment, his eyes assessing, then he knelt down in front of the bed.

'Is it fatal?' she asked, after a few moments' silence. Scooter was standing next to her, and she was glad she'd remembered that dogs were allowed in the cottage if arranged beforehand. This short visit surely wouldn't upset Mel.

'I can shore up the break temporarily or replace the slat,' he said, 'but you should speak to Mel first. I can do a patch job if she's happy, then replace it with another slat as soon as I can find one.'

'I don't want to hog your time,' Thea replied.

'It's no problem.' Ben sat back on his haunches. 'Give her a call, see what she wants to do.'

Thea nodded, but didn't reach for her phone.

Ben's gaze turned curious. 'What is it?'

'What if she thinks I *was* actually . . . jumping on it? That I caused it?'

'Did you?'

'No! I mean, technically, yes. I sat on it and it cracked: I heard and felt the moment it happened. But I haven't been doing anything untoward on it.'

'Double beds in holiday homes should be able to withstand a lot more than one person sitting on them,' he said.

Thea's mind immediately went to other, more vigorous, activities. 'Yes. Well . . .' She averted her gaze.

Ben cleared his throat. 'Sorry. I wasn't trying to imply—'

'No, it's fine.'

'All I'm saying,' Ben went on, 'is that you shouldn't feel guilty. Tell Mel the bed broke, and ask her what she wants me to do.'

'Right. You're right. Of course.' She found the number, and waited while the phone rang and rang and was eventually answered by a harried-sounding Mel. She explained the situation, treading carefully over the words, ensuring the other woman knew she *hadn't* been doing anything other than sitting and sleeping. She made the mistake of glancing at Ben while she spoke, and saw one side of his mouth lift again, even while he peered closely at the damaged slat.

To her relief, Mel apologised, and said that if Ben could do a temporary fix she'd try and track down a new slat from the bed manufacturer. It had been a recent-ish purchase, and she prided herself on keeping her cottage to high standards. That led to her apologising again, and Thea saying not to worry, and apologising for having troubled her in the first place, until it turned into a circular conversation of sorries and reassurances, and when she finally said goodbye and hung up, Ben was leaning against the bed, watching her with an amused expression.

'You have nothing to apologise for,' he said.

Thea shrugged. 'Saying sorry always seems like the easiest thing to do. That way everyone knows you're not mad with them.'

'I disagree.'

'About which bit?'

'About it being easiest,' he said. 'Especially if you don't mean it or you've no need. It puts you on the back foot, gives the other person the wrong impression, tells them they can get away with whatever it is.'

'I guess,' she said. 'I'm sorry, I just—'

He glared at her, and Thea laughed.

'Right.' She looked at her toes so he wouldn't see her smiling. 'No sorries.'

'Mel wants me to fix it?'

'She's going to try and get a slat from the bed manufacturer, so it matches.'

Ben nodded and pushed himself to his feet. 'I'll go and get some wood to strengthen it in the meantime. I'll be back in a jiffy.'

'This is so kind of you.'

'It's no problem,' he said, in the doorway. 'Can't have you worrying when you *do* get to the bed-jumping stage of your holiday.'

Thea laughed again. 'Is that a regular stage that I don't know about? Do I need to add it to my bucket list?'

Ben shrugged. 'Not sure. I haven't ever thought about it, apart from in the last ten minutes. Now it seems like fun.'

She wouldn't have immediately put Ben and the word 'fun' together. She tried to imagine him jumping up and down on the mattress, like an over-excited toddler. 'You'd better do a *really* good job of fixing the slat then,' she said, to stop herself from grinning at the mental image she'd conjured.

'Oh, I will,' Ben replied, and she was treated to a moment of a real, unrestrained smile; she even saw a flash of white teeth before he schooled his features again. 'Scooter, come on.'

Scooter responded by lying down in front of Thea, like a guard dog.

Ben rolled his eyes. 'Fine. Stay there, then.'

'Do you want a tea?' Thea called after him.

'Coffee?' he called back. 'White, no sugar.'

'Coming right up!'

As Thea followed him downstairs and busied herself making their drinks, she realised she was humming.

Ben came back with some slender planks of wood and a small toolbox to go with his belt. Thea brought the drinks up to the bedroom and, not wanting to either crowd him or abandon him, sat on the bench at the end of the bed and tried to appear entirely relaxed. She was searching for something to say when Ben broke the quiet.

'Your sunburn doesn't look too bad after yesterday.'

'Aloe vera saved the day.'

'And your ankle's better?'

'Much,' Thea confirmed. 'Though I did dream about hash browns. With fried eggs and crispy bacon, a couple of grilled tomatoes. Some baked beans in a little pot, so the sauce doesn't mingle with the egg yolk.' She sighed.

'Not had breakfast, then?'

'No, sorting out the bed was top of my list.'

'Right. Well, it's still early.'

'It is, and there must be a café around here that could satisfy my breakfast needs.'

'It's more a place for artisan coffee shops,' Ben said, and she thought he sounded slightly scathing.

'There must be *somewhere* I can get a good holiday fry-up.'

'There is,' Ben said, but didn't tell her where that might be.

Thea chewed her lip while he measured and assessed and started to secure a piece of wood to the frame, underneath the broken slat.

'Tell me about your terrible walk,' he said eventually, the words bursting into the quiet as if he'd been dying to hear all the details.

'It wasn't *terrible*,' she said. 'I mean, it wasn't *that* terrible. It was . . . I wasn't as prepared as I should have been, despite Finn's words of wisdom.'

'He does tend to stick his nose in.'

'Have you been friends long?'

'We met soon after I moved here in February. He's a really good guy – he and Meredith are both great, even if their friendship keeps waylaying me.'

'With your house update?'

'I thought saving the work until summer would be easier, so I could avoid the worst of the weather and all the problems that comes with, but it's got a lot hotter, a lot sooner than I expected. I can't seem to win.'

'Is that why you do most of it after nine o'clock at night?'

He looked up sharply. 'Shit. Sorry. I'm so used to being here on my own, and I . . .'

'It's fine,' Thea rushed. 'There were other things that got in the way of me sleeping last night, and you're sorting that for me, so it evens out.'

He turned back to his work. 'So what happened on your walk?'

'I almost fell off the cliff,' she said, and there was a clatter as Ben dropped his screwdriver and looked up at her, alarmed.

'No no,' she rushed, instantly feeling guilty. 'I didn't – not really. I just meant that it's terrifying up there. It feels so precarious, like you could just go *whoosh* off the side at any moment, and nobody would know you'd disappeared. At least,' she added, 'nobody would have known if *I'd* gone over the edge.' She'd started off trying to be funny, but it suddenly felt anything but.

Ben kept his gaze on her as he reached out to stroke Scooter, who was splayed out on the carpet between them. 'It doesn't sound like you wanted to be there on your own. Finn mentioned a friend who was supposed to come with you? On holiday, I mean.'

Thea sighed. 'Esme. There was a disaster at work, which meant our festival suddenly had nobody at the helm, so she stayed. I came here anyway, because . . . for all sorts of reasons, so I'm having to adjust. Clearly I haven't done a good job so far, considering I almost fell off the cliff – sort of – got sunburned and dehydrated, then accosted by an old woman who seemed intent on telling me her entire life story even though I had *no* clue who she was, and—'

The sound of Ben's laughter jolted her out of her rant. It was a lovely laugh, deep and warm and unexpected. She couldn't help smiling in response.

'Anyway,' she said.

'What woman?'

'In the Old Post House. I came past it on my way back.'

'Sylvia.' Ben shook his head.

'You know her?'

'Everyone knows her,' he explained, as he bent over the bed frame. 'She makes sure of that.'

'I don't feel quite so idiotic, if everyone gets the same treatment.'

'You know,' he said, as if he hadn't heard her, 'if you wanted to try another walk, one where you felt less out on a limb, where you were properly prepared and had a guide, someone who knew the area quite well and could show you the best spots while ensuring you didn't fall to your death, then I could always go with you.'

Had she misheard? Had taciturn Ben just offered to hike along the cliff path with her? Except he wasn't as taciturn as he had been yesterday, and now he was in her bedroom, kneeling over her bed, and – he was fixing it, obviously, but the realisation still brought a flush to her throat, and—

'What?' she blurted.

'You heard me, I think. And I know how I come across, sometimes – how I can be. I get it. But I will do, if you want – go with you. If your ankle's up to it, and you haven't got other plans.'

'I just . . .'

He looked up at her, his hands resting on the bed frame. 'I'll be done in ten minutes, then I'll fix you a fry-up in your kitchen, if you'd still like one, and you can decide whether you want to go. No pressure, of course. But the offer's there if you want it.'

He bent his head again, getting back to work, and Thea exchanged a look with Scooter. She was obviously reading too much into it, anthropomorphising the dog, but she was almost convinced Ben's pet looked as incredulous – his blue eyes wide and staring – as she felt.

# Chapter Six

Thea stepped outside, glanced up at the open bedroom window, then hurried across the gravel and onto the grass that sloped down towards the road. She heard a cry, and looked up to see three black birds – cormorants, maybe – flying overheard, beaks trained on the crisp, sparkling blue of the sea.

She had fled the bedroom, explaining that she needed to wash up their mugs, even though she'd had to knock back half her drink to make it seem remotely plausible, and had left Ben's with him when she realised it was too close to his tanned arms and his strong torso and his warm, sunny smell for her to dare go near it.

She pressed the speed dial number that would connect her to Esme, and waited while it rang.

'Thea?' her friend said, her voice light with laughter, and Thea heard a familiar, male chuckle in the background. Not even ten o'clock on a Monday, and Esme was already with Alex. She felt a familiar pang of jealousy, then realised she couldn't afford to be jealous when there was important panicking to do instead.

'How are you?' she asked, because it was ingrained in her to be polite.

'I'm good! What's happening with you? What are you up to today?'

'Uhm, going on another walk, I think.'

'There's *loads* of stuff on our list, and I didn't think your walk was a huge success yesterday. Why not opt for the beach today, especially if you've got as much sun as we've got in Bristol? I'm worried our volunteers will get heatstroke if they're working next to the window.' Thea heard Esme turn away and say something to Alex, and she waited, pressing her flip-flopped foot into the long grass.

'Ben's offered to take me on a walk,' she said when her friend was back with her. 'No, that makes me sound like a dog. He's offered to *accompany* me on another walk. He knows the area, so he can show me the best sights.'

Thea thought Esme had drifted into festival preoccupation land, but after a moment she said, 'Mr Irascible Hash Browns?'

Thea laughed. 'The very same. He's currently fixing my bed, which broke, and I—'

'OK, you don't need our list any more, clearly!'

'It's all got a bit complicated, and I . . . what should I do?'

'What do you *want* to do?'

'I . . . uhm.'

'If you were totally against going, then you wouldn't be calling me,' Esme pointed out. 'You want to go, but for some reason you don't think you should.'

'He's too handsome,' Thea blurted.

'Oh, well then. Definitely don't go with him.' Esme's eye-roll was almost audible.

'He's just . . . he is way out of my comfort zone,' Thea explained, feeling a familiar churn in her stomach. Unlike Alex, who was all familiarity and kind, encouraging smiles, or her two previous boyfriends, Elias and Jon, who had been straightforward and predictable, in a way that had made her feel secure. It wasn't just that Ben was basically a stranger, it was that he had huge pockets of unknowability, a metaphorical sign that said, 'Don't come closer.' Because of that, she found that she already wanted to know more about him, to peel back his layers. But surely, like with so many things, where there was temptation, there was also danger.

The background of the phone call changed, and she imagined Esme moving away from the main area of the library, which would be a hive of activity in the days before the festival. There would be bunting going up; posters detailing the locations and times of the events; displays celebrating each author and their myriad books.

'Theophania,' Esme said, in that firm but gentle tone Thea knew so well.

'Esmerelda,' Thea echoed back, as she always did, even though it wasn't Esme's name.

'What makes you say that?'

'Because he just *is*,' Thea said, already tired of the conversation, even though she'd instigated it. 'He's confident and attractive and he's . . . there's something really remote about him. He offered to go on a walk with me, and he's been kind, gone out of his way to help me, but he's also a bit . . . unfathomable. Like he's at least fifty per cent secrets.'

'But you're still tempted?'

Thea looked back up at the bedroom window. She couldn't see him inside: he was probably still kneeling, fixing the new piece of wood to the broken slat.

'It's hard being here on my own,' she admitted, thinking of what Ben had said to her the day before, the way he had seemed to understand her contradictory feelings. 'I'm definitely tempted.'

'Good. And you know,' Esme added, 'a holiday romance wasn't specifically on our list of things to do, but that doesn't mean—'

'There's no way,' Thea said, laughing. She pictured Ben, working in her bedroom, with his tanned arms and his hidden thoughts, and she realised that she didn't feel threatened by him, put off by his looks or his presence in the way she had done yesterday. She still knew very little about him, but he'd come to her aid, offered her freezer items, not hesitating for a second when she'd asked him for help, and all those things had made him seem instantly softer, more approachable. She thought of how she hadn't been able to step close and pick up his mug a moment ago. She was still having a reaction to him, but it wasn't that she was feeling threatened – that had been something else entirely.

'No way means maybe,' Esme said. 'And you can't possibly know what's going to happen. It's only day three.'

'Technically it's day two,' Thea pointed out, 'because Saturday doesn't count.'

'You already love it,' Esme said. 'Especially now you've got Mr Irascible Hash Browns.'

Thea laughed. 'I doubt there's anyone else in the whole of history with that nickname.'

'That's because we're too creative for our own good,' Esme said. 'I have to go – there's a problem with our order of cuddly Gruffalos, and it's the *one* thing we need to get right.'

'The *one* thing?' Thea said, feeling a lot more settled now she'd spoken to her friend. 'Good luck with the Gruffalos, Es. And thank you.'

'Always,' her friend replied. 'Catch you later.' She hung up.

Thea's composure lasted as long as it took her to turn around and find Ben hovering in the doorway of Sunfish Cottage.

'Hi,' she said.

'All done,' he called. 'I put the mattress back on, made it as best I could, but you might want to . . .'

'Sure. Thank you so much.'

'So, how about breakfast? In your kitchen, because mine's a building site.'

'You honestly don't need to,' Thea said, walking back up the hill. 'After all you've done—'

'This is a one-time offer,' he said. 'Decide what you want to do, and do it.' She raised her eyebrows, and he shrugged. 'Indecision goes with apologies. If I wasn't happy to make you breakfast, I wouldn't have offered. All you need to do is decide if you want it. If you don't, just say so.'

Thea exhaled. 'You're very direct.'

'It helps,' he said simply. 'Don't forget I have hash browns in the freezer. Except . . .' he glanced at his watch. 'They're only there for genuine emergencies. I'll make them.'

'You'll *make* hash browns? For real?'

'For absolute real,' he deadpanned, and Thea, rather than feeling irritated, grinned.

'Yes, then. A big fat yes, with knobs on. What can I do?'

'Another coffee?'

'Simples,' she said, and watched as he took his toolbox back to Oystercatcher Cottage. When she went into her kitchen, she found Scooter waiting for her, as if man and dog had already decided it was a done deal. 'Emergency hash browns, eh?' she said, and the dog looked up at her, as if he knew exactly what she was talking about.

Half an hour later, as the kitchen filled with the irresistible smells and sizzles of a fry-up being made from scratch, Thea told herself that just because she'd agreed to breakfast, it didn't mean she had to say yes to the walk – Ben had already made that clear. Now he was moving around her kitchen as if performing a carefully choreographed dance. He made it look so easy, and he seemed relaxed – happy, even – while he grated potato and mixed it with herbs, got the eggs and bacon rashers ready, seasoned cut-in-half tomatoes ready to grill.

The conversation wasn't flowing like the coffee, however, and Thea knew she was responsible. She leaned against the breakfast bar, feeling useless but content to watch him.

'Do you do a lot of cooking?' she asked eventually.

He glanced up, a cracked eggshell in his right hand. He'd offered her a choice of eggs and she'd said buttery scrambled were her favourite. She'd always envied people who could crack eggs in one hand: her attempts always ended messily.

'Whenever I can,' he admitted. 'It's a hobby of mine.'

'Does that mean you're working on your kitchen first?' She wondered if she probed slowly, her questions small and incremental, she could crack him open like he'd just done with the eggs.

He ran a hand over the back of his neck, checked on the baked beans that were simmering in a pan. 'I've sort-of gone all in,' he said. 'I just want to get it done and dusted.'

'Sounds pretty clinical, considering it's your own house you're talking about. I could understand if it was a job that you weren't that keen on, but your new home?'

His sigh was quiet. 'I just want to get settled. The cottage needed some major renovations, and after moving here—'

'In February?'

'Right. After that, I gave it a couple of months to . . . at the beginning, I didn't really feel like it.' He turned away from her, separating bacon rashers, checking the sausages that were already under the grill. 'Then, when I did, I thought I could do it all at once, as quickly as possible. But I know that's not how it works: I'm a bloody builder!'

'What kind of builder?'

'Small-scale projects. Fitting kitchens, tiling, floors. I've done a few home renovations like I'm doing now, and I just assumed that without the added complication of having actual customers, who change their minds all the time and get overly protective about the smallest thing,' he gave her a look that made her feel included in his exasperation, 'that it would be a piece of . . .'

'Cake?' Thea finished.

He nodded. 'The point is, I was stupid. Now it's taking up every waking hour, the whole house is a nightmare, and I should be there right now, trying to make sense of it, but trips to the beach with Finn and Meredith, cooking breakfast for you, they're always going to be more appealing.' He whisked the eggs, his biceps flexing, and Thea turned her gaze to the window.

'So I'm a distraction?' she said.

'An excellent one,' he admitted, and when she glanced at him, his half-smile was back. It sent a shiver through her, and made her say something entirely out of character.

'So, what you're suggesting is that, if I were a good person, I would tell you that I didn't want to go on a walk with you, so that you would be forced to go back to your place and get on with your tiling or floor laying, or whatever it is you need to do?'

His smile widened. 'I'm hoping that, on this occasion, you're going to choose to be bad.'

Their eyes held, and it was such a flirtatious moment that Thea didn't know what to do with herself.

Usually, she would run from men like Ben, and that was partly because they didn't ever go for women like her. He might have a string of Cornish surfer girlfriends texting him every few minutes, or a boyfriend whose house he escaped to when his renovation project got too much. She knew so little about him, but she thought of what Esme had said, the mention of holiday romances, and wondered if she could lean into it.

She thought of her Elly Griffiths book on the bedside table, the hours she'd planned to spend reading it today. But she didn't want her lasting memories of the coastal path to be bad, and if she let them linger, they might dampen the holiday, and her impression of a place she hoped would be part of her future. Besides, it was clear Ben wanted this distraction: he was cooking her a breakfast that her local greasy spoon in Bristol could only dream of producing. Surely it was only fair, after all he'd done for her, that she help him out too?

'I did have a pretty rough night,' she said. 'What with broken bed frames and neighbours making inhospitable noises until late.'

'Which means?'

'I might well decide to be bad today.' She ran her hand slowly over the pine countertop, and then, when that seemed like a step too far, quickly added, 'Ready for coffee number three?'

'Always,' Ben said.

They moved around each other in a companionable way until the breakfast and coffee were ready, Scooter had been given a couple of sausages, and they were sitting side by side at the breakfast bar. Thea didn't know which she was more impressed with: the view, her breakfast, or the man next to her, slicing into a home-made hash brown with focused determination.

Already, this holiday was a completely different shape to how she'd imagined it. She knew things never turned out the way she anticipated them – that was just the nature of expectation versus reality – but it was already so far removed from her preconceptions. The hash browns, for example, were like nothing she'd ever tasted before.

'Wow, Ben,' she said, when she'd eaten a mouthful, then shovelled some of the golden, buttery scrambled eggs onto her fork. 'If cooking's only a hobby, then I'm excited to see your building work.'

'I've hidden it under the mattress.'

'Not the bed frame: your house.'

'My house is a tip, which is why I'm here.'

'Do you do this with all Mel's holidayers?'

He glanced at her. 'Do what?'

'Befriend them so you can use Sunfish Cottage as a refuge?'

He chuckled. 'No, this is the first time I've been inside. It's giving me some ideas, actually. She's kitted it out really nicely. Besides, you were the one who knocked on my door, remember?'

'I was.' She scooped up some baked beans. Despite the supposed chaos at his house, he'd brought around little pots to put them in, so they were kept separate on the plate. Was that just the way he did things, or had he remembered the details when she'd described her perfect breakfast earlier? 'And suddenly, you're doing everything for me. Bed fixing, breakfast making, walk chaperoning.'

'Only if you want to,' he repeated. 'This is your holiday, after all.'

She nodded, and there was a pause while they focused on the food. Scooter had finished his sausages within seconds, and was lying beneath their stools, his pale, handsome body stretched to its full length. Thea thought the tiled floor was probably a cool place for him.

'Can I ask why you still came here by yourself?' Ben said. 'Not that it isn't something people do, but if your friend had to cancel, and you'd been planning it together, wouldn't it have been easier to do it another time? You seem like . . .'

'Like I'm not that great at holidaying alone?'

'I wasn't going to say that.'

'No, but it's true. Esme and I had been planning this for ages: three weeks off in an idyllic Cornish village, doing a whole load of summery activities. But she *was* going to make me go coasteering, so there are some upsides to being here on my own.' She took a sip of her coffee.

'Coasteering?' Ben's eyebrows rose.

'You know, where you clamber over cliffs and then jump off them, into the sea. Using the wild, dangerous coastline like a cute little obstacle course. Can you really see me doing that? After yesterday?'

He opened his mouth, then chewed on his bottom lip in a way that made him look about twelve, and was far too adorable for such a solid man.

'I know,' she said, rescuing him. 'Me either. But other things, like lazing on the beach and going to festivals, trips to those lovely gardens along the Helford river, they're all on the list, and I was looking forward to them. And just having time together: hours away from work to catch up properly. It feels like it's been a long time since we had the opportunity.'

'Where do you work?'

'At the library in Bristol.'

'You're a librarian?'

She shifted in her seat. She loved everything about the library, the books and the events, and that it was a resource for tiny tots and their parents; teenagers; job-seekers and ninety-year-olds. But the word librarian always conjured up an image of a lonely, pedantic woman with unfashionable glasses and few friends. It was her own prejudice – she didn't see any of her colleagues like that at all – but she levelled it at herself far too often.

'I'm a library assistant,' she clarified, wondering why she couldn't own it. 'A total book nerd. And Esme is one of the managers. We've got a summer festival on, and the woman who was due to be running it broke her leg quite badly. She's going to be OK, but running that festival is busy and tiring, and you can't do it with a broken leg. So Esme's back there, working on it, and I'm here, getting all the benefits of our extensive planning.'

Ben's gaze on her was unwavering. 'There's a lot of Cornwall to explore, so you need to make the most of your time.'

'I will. I have a whole list. And I think . . .' Was she really going to do this? Go hiking with a man she'd met only yesterday? Maybe he was a serial killer who had a personal quota of pushing one person off the cliffs every month, getting away with it because tourists sometimes got into difficult situations, and those cliffs were bloody dangerous. But he'd done nothing to suggest he wasn't trustworthy. He'd helped her out a lot, so far. 'These eggs are so good,' she said instead. 'Do you put milk in them?'

He looked appalled. 'Definitely not! Philistine.' He softened his words with a smile, and Thea knew she was going to say yes.

She looked out at the Cornish vista that promised another perfect day, with no clouds and hot sun and breathtaking views. 'If it turned out that I'd forgotten my sunhat,' she said slowly, 'could I borrow something from you?'

He sat up straighter, and even though his smile didn't widen, she could tell that he was pleased. 'No problem,' he said, for about the fiftieth time that morning.

# Chapter Seven

Going on a walk with Ben and Scooter, Thea soon discovered, wasn't like going on a walk on her own, even though they took the same route she had taken, heading through Port Karadow and then out the other side, picking up the cliff path on the north of the small town. Man and dog had more energy and determination in their little finger and paw than Thea had in her whole body, and despite Ben having the biggest rucksack, with two large bottles of iced water and a bottle of suncream in, and Thea only having the sandwiches she'd insisted on making, it wasn't long before she was lagging behind.

Ben turned, seeking her out, and must have realised their strides didn't match, because when she caught up with him he slowed his pace, leaving Scooter to run on ahead, nose down, investigating the smells and sounds as he went.

It was even more beautiful than it had been yesterday, the sun so bright that it made the blues and greens, the aquamarine of the water, pop. But the breeze was also stronger, and the cool tugs of air stopped Thea being overwhelmed by the heat. She realised she was enjoying it more, taking in the views properly, knowing she didn't need to worry about getting lost.

'The beach down here is a prime spot for surfers,' Ben said, stepping closer to the cliff edge, the grass there tufty and uneven. Thea could hear the waves crashing far below them, and was happy to imagine the wetsuit-clad thrill-seekers without peering over to take a look. 'There are a lot out today. Here.' He held his hand out.

Thea shook her head. 'I'm good.'

'Come and see,' he said. 'You'll be fine.'

'I don't want to get too close. Heights and I aren't the best of friends.'

'I'll look after you.' He waggled his fingers and, reluctantly, Thea held her hand out. His grip was firm and warm, as it had been yesterday, but he didn't tug her forward. He waited for her to come to him, which she did in tiny steps, until they were standing side by side. Thea looked out at the endless blue, the shimmering peaks and troughs of waves heading in to shore, and gave a small nod.

'Lean over,' Ben said. 'You can't see them from there.'

She bent her upper body half an inch. She couldn't see any surfers, but she could see the white foam as the waves broke closer to the beach.

'Go on,' Ben said softly. 'I'll hold onto you.' She felt his hand grip her waist, the pressure enough to make her feel secure, but not enough to hurt. He moved so that he was behind her, the solid pillar of his body shoring her up. She took a deep breath to calm herself, to still her wobbling legs, and leaned forward. Ben's hand anchored her to him as she peered down at the beach, and there they were.

There must have been fifteen or twenty of them; shiny black figures with slashes of colour beneath them, heading into or out of the waves, some catching a large swell as it rolled in towards the shore, following it through and then falling, in a splash of foam, as the wave dispersed. It was hard to concentrate on them, though, when all her attention was focused on the spot where Ben's hand gripped her waist; the heat of him behind her, his breath feathering the back of her neck.

'Do you surf?' she asked, still staring at the people far below.

'No. At least, I haven't tried it yet. Finn and Meredith go sea swimming every day – even in winter – but I've been too busy. Or, let's face it, reluctant to get up at some ungodly hour to freeze my ass off in the water. But maybe one day.'

Thea straightened and Ben moved backwards, still holding onto her, until they were a few metres from the edge, then he let her go. Even though it was a warm day, she felt the absence of his touch like a cold brand against her skin.

'I'm planning on swimming while I'm here,' she said. 'But only because it's June, and the weather's already like August.'

'You have to pick the right beach,' Ben replied. 'Some aren't suitable for swimmers because of the currents. They all have signs though,' he added with a wince, as if realising he was being too domineering.

'Where did you move here from?' she asked.

'The Lakes. Near Ambleside.'

'Did it get too touristy for you?' she teased.

'Yeah. I wanted somewhere remote, untouched by visitors, which is why I picked the Cornish coast.' They exchanged a smile, but there was something in his expression, something guarded, that made Thea think she shouldn't press. Of course, that meant she wanted to even more.

'Is the work better down here?'

'There's work everywhere,' Ben said, then whistled loudly at Scooter, who was burying his nose in someone's discarded cardigan. The dog glanced at him, then trotted on. 'I wanted a fresh start,' he continued. 'I loved Cornwall as a kid, and I know it's full of tourists, and that incomers aren't seen as much better than the holidaymakers, but I like that it's rugged and rural, despite all that.'

'You couldn't live in a city, then?'

He shook his head. 'Not my scene. You like being in Bristol?'

'I do,' she said lightly. 'It's got the river, of course, but I love being close to the sea, too – terrifying clifftops aside – and I wouldn't be against living near it one day.' She wasn't ready to tell Ben about her bookshop, even though a part of her was desperate to: she would love to get the opinion of someone unbiased – especially someone as direct as Ben.

'It's good for the soul,' he replied, his gaze drifting out over the water. 'Good for everything, really. It's the same with the Lakes. There's something calming about being near water.'

'It reminds you how small you are,' Thea said. 'It puts everything in perspective.'

He nodded his agreement and they walked on, until they reached a fork in the path. 'I'm guessing you went this way yesterday.' Ben pointed to the route that angled inland.

'Of course I did,' Thea said. 'The other way has a sign that says: *Caution! Sudden drop*.'

'Come on, then.'

'Not a chance.'

'It's fine, I promise.'

Thea wondered if she could secure her walking boots to the ground, tie the laces to the surrounding undergrowth in undoable knots so she was stuck where she was. She shook her head.

Ben tapped the peak of her baseball cap. It was actually *his* cap, because he'd lent it to her, spending an inordinate amount of time fiddling with the adjustment so it fitted her better. It was dusky blue, had *Lakes for Life* embroidered in white across the front – she should have guessed where he'd moved from – and was so soft and comfortable that she never wanted to give it back. Him tapping it felt like an oddly intimate gesture.

'You need to trust me, Thea.'

'I do?'

'On this. I promise you, it'll be worth it.'

She nodded, her words getting stuck in her throat. She spent a few happy seconds imagining she was back in the fiction section of the library, replacing the returned Christina Lauren and Sophie Cousens books on the romance shelves, their bright spines always so pleasing, then brought herself back to the present. 'OK then,' she said. 'Let's do it.'

Scooter led the way, then Ben, with Thea going last, because almost as soon as they took the path it got even narrower.

Soon they were walking along a craggy, stone-littered track that dipped downwards, skirting along the very edge of the cliff, with only a couple of feet of unruly grass between them and the edge of the world. There was a makeshift wooden barrier, but it didn't look like it would take Scooter's weight, let alone hers or Ben's if one of them stumbled.

With every second that passed, Thea's throat felt tighter, while her legs seemed to get weaker. They came to a series of steps cut into the rock, and she gripped the back of Ben's T-shirt. As she did, her fingers brushed against the hot skin at the back of his neck, and for a moment her terror was replaced by the fizz of that contact.

'OK, Thea?' he said, half turning his head.

'Sort of,' she replied.

'Nearly there.' His tone was soothing, but she didn't feel soothed, because the fear was back, crowding her senses.

As they walked, she kept her focus on her feet, on making sure they were landing safely, and on the anchor that was her hand in Ben's T-shirt. When he came to a stop and said, quietly, 'There we go,' she almost bumped into him.

He stepped sideways, so he was under the shelter of the cliff face above them, and as he did, Thea gasped.

In front of them was a cutaway in the cliff, the sandy stone littered with crevices and crags, most of them full of seabirds. A lot looked like gulls, but there were some darker birds too, and the noise, now she was coming out of her fear fog, was loud: there was a *lot* of squawking and chirping going on. From their position – no longer on top of the cliff, but about a third of the way down – she could see the waves crashing against the rocks, the sea turned into a churning, frothing mass, with no hint of sand or pebbles.

It was like some kind of otherworld, something ancient and forgotten, with prehistoric creatures and a whirlpool beneath them, deadly and loud and inescapable. It was *preternatural*, she thought. Breathtaking.

'The tide's in, so it's at its most dramatic,' Ben said.

'It's . . . what are they?'

'Razorbills and guillemots, some different types of gull that I'm not clued up on yet. There might be some puffins, but without binoculars we'll be hard pressed to see them.'

'Puffins?' She almost squealed in delight. 'I'd love to see a puffin in real life.'

'We might have more luck on a boat trip.'

'A boat?'

'There are some rocky outcrops a bit further up the coast, which we could get closer to. You can't get a boat in here.' He gestured to the water, crashing and swirling in a way that was close to hypnotic, and wholly, indisputably terrifying.

'No,' Thea said faintly. 'I bet you can't.'

'If you're not a fan of boats—'

'Oh no, I love boats,' she said. 'I was just . . . you don't have to be tour guide for my entire holiday.'

He flushed: she could see his pink cheeks under his baseball cap. 'Of course not.'

'No, I didn't mean—' *Shit*. 'I just meant that you've got so much to do. I don't want to hog all your time, because as much as these distractions are nice, nobody else is going to do your renovation for you. I assume not, anyway.'

'No.' He sighed. 'You're right.'

The quiet between them was swallowed by the cries of the seabirds. They watched them flying in and out of the crescent until Thea felt a little dizzy, and a whole lot precarious, being so close to the edge. She put her hand on Ben's arm.

'Ready to go?' he asked.

'If that's OK?'

'Sure.'

The walk up felt easier, mostly because she wasn't staring into the abyss, but could gaze ahead at the path that led up to firm, solid land; to walking trails more than two feet wide; to benches and grass and safety. When they emerged onto the clifftop, she hurried forward a few steps and then dropped to her knees, just to feel the ground beneath her, to stop the swaying that had taken root inside her head. Scooter buried his nose in her neck and she wrapped her arms around him.

Ben gazed down at them, a look of amusement on his face.

'Thank you,' she said breathily. 'For showing me that. It was incredible and I loved it, and I'm very glad to have seen it.'

'Past tense being the important bit, right?' He took his cap off, and she saw that his hair was dark with sweat. He rubbed a hand through it and put the cap back on.

She nodded. 'I'm not ungrateful – in fact I'm *very* grateful, because there's no way I'd have gone there on my own, even if I'd known about it. But . . .' she pressed her hands, palms flat, into the grass and grinned up at him.

Ben laughed. 'Understood. Sandwiches?'

'Good plan.'

They ate their ham sandwiches sitting on a low wooden bench that looked days away from collapse. Thea was surprised, and relieved, that it had taken their weight. Ben had bought a bowl for Scooter, which he filled with water, letting his dog drink his fill before giving him a couple more cold sausages.

'What else is on your list?' he asked. 'Aside from hiking and coasteering? Is your friend a bit of an adrenaline junkie?'

Thea laughed. 'No, not at all. There's the Eden Project and Trebah Garden, a trip to Tintagel. We wanted to find a local fair or festival while we were here, and have a cream tea, because it has to be done – as well as trying some other local dishes. We were also going to have at least three long, uneventful days soaking up the sun at the beach. I'm still planning on doing most of those, and I've got a few things of my own, too. Now I'm going to add a boat trip to the list.'

Ben finished his mouthful. 'I know a guy who does day trips on his boat – that's how I found out about the puffins. He's a friend of a friend, and I'm sure he'd have the space for you to go while you're here.'

'That sounds ideal, thank you. I'm going to add that and scrub off the coasteering, which I would be more than happy to consign to the reject bin.'

'Remind me when we get back,' he said, 'and I'll give you his number.'

'Thanks, Ben.'

Thea wondered if he realised just how grateful she was that he'd offered her this trip today: that he'd shown her something so magnificent. Their apples were sweet and crunchy, the juice dribbling down Thea's chin, and for the first time since she'd arrived she felt like she was having a proper holiday. She grinned at Ben, and he gave her his half-smile in return. She was beginning to think that was as much happiness as he ever showed, but she couldn't say for sure.

It wasn't a surprise when, on the way back, they went past the Old Post House and Thea heard the window creak open. It was as if she was replaying yesterday's walk, but the universe was giving her another chance to get it right.

'Benjamin Senhouse,' said a familiar voice.

He looked up. 'Sylvia.' He sounded resigned and amused all at once.

'Who's that you're with? Take your hat off, girl!'

Thea did as she was told. 'It's me. Thea.'

'Oh, yes. Taken pity on this waif, have you, Benjamin? I told her she should seek out a big, strong man, and she found the very one I had in mind. When you've got a minute, could you check the boiler? It's on the blink, and I can't hand this place over to the town without any heating or hot water. This glorious summer means the winter ahead will be especially cruel.'

'I'll come and look at it tomorrow,' Ben said. 'Ten o'clock a good time?'

'Suits me. You can bring your new friend, if you like.'

Ben smiled up at her. 'She's on holiday, Sylvia. I'm not sure she's after a tour around your boiler.'

'This is a historic building,' Sylvia said. 'Even in its less than perfect state, anyone would be lucky to get a glimpse. Thea?' Her stare shifted focus, and Thea tried not to shrink back from it.

'I'm actually . . . I have an appointment tomorrow morning. But I'd love to come and see it some other time.'

'Excellent. I'll let Ben arrange it: he can show you around. Tomorrow then, Benjamin.' She pulled the window shut and the two of them stared at the place where she'd been, then Ben turned away, shaking his head.

'How did you meet her?' Thea asked.

'She's a bit of a legend in Port Karadow. Finn's aunt, Laurie, mentioned that she needed the gutter fixing – around March time, not long after I'd moved here, when the weather was still pretty bad. Since sorting that out for her, she's called me on a semi-regular basis.'

'So you've done a lot of work here?' Thea asked. 'Another distraction from your own project?'

His laugh was tinged with sadness. 'She only ever wants a few bits looking at. She's moving in with her daughter soon, but the Old Post House was her and her husband, Eric's, pride and joy. She can't bear the thought of letting it go, but she turns that into concern about handing it back to the council. She asks me to come and do small, pointless jobs, but won't let me tackle the real problems with the building, the safety issues – I think she should have moved out months ago, because there's some structural damage – or even clean up the shop downstairs. She's stuck emotionally, and I can only help where she wants me to.'

'That's so sad,' Thea said. 'It's very kind of you to help her.'

'People have been kind to me since I moved here, and I'm sure a lot of the time, she just wants the company. I'm trying to be a good member of the community, in the few ways I can be.'

'You've certainly been good to me,' Thea said. 'And obviously Sylvia, too. She doesn't come across as necessarily being an easy person to deal with.'

‘She speaks her mind,’ Ben said. ‘It’s refreshing. She tells you what she thinks, which is much better than hints and sly remarks.’ His tone had lost its gentleness, and Thea glanced at him, trying to read his expression beneath the baseball cap. She didn’t see the stone in front of her on the path and she tripped on it, heading for the hard, baked ground until Ben clasped her arm, hauling her back with a firm tug.

‘Careful,’ he said. And then, ‘Did I jar your shoulder?’

She hadn’t realised she was rubbing it. It was the surprise, more than anything. ‘No. No, I— thank you. Much better that than I face plant into a rock.’

He nodded, but she could sense a change in him, see the tension in his shoulders, and got the impression that he was elsewhere, all of a sudden: lost in thoughts of something far removed from Port Karadow and their sunny Monday afternoon.

Thea decided to take a leaf out of his upfront, honest book, and said, ‘This has been so good, Ben. So different to yesterday. I can’t thank you enough.’

‘No problem,’ he said; his standard reply. ‘What’s your appointment tomorrow? Unless you just wanted an excuse to avoid Sylvia and her boiler, which I wouldn’t blame you for.’

Thea chewed the inside of her cheek. She didn’t want to lie to him. ‘No,’ she said. ‘I do have an appointment. It’s . . . something I want to check out, while I’m here. But I don’t—’ she stopped, turning to face him. ‘I’m not ready to share it, if that’s OK? Part of me wants to, but it’s something I’ve held onto for such a long time, and—’

'It's OK,' Ben said, squeezing her arm. 'You don't owe me anything. You don't have to tell me anything at all.'

She laughed. 'I think, after everything you've done for me, I owe you a whole lot.'

He shook his head. 'I'm wiping the slate clean.'

They'd reached the last section of path, and would soon see the white beacons of Sunfish and Oystercatcher cottages, where Thea's cool living room and her beloved book would be waiting for her. This time, however, she was reluctant to go back to them. She wanted more time with Ben, but she knew he liked working later in the day, when it was cooler. It was funny that she already knew these little, habitual things about him, almost as if they were flatmates rather than temporary neighbours.

Scooter trotted ahead of them, no sign that he was flagging despite the hours they'd walked under the pulsing sun.

'I will ask you one thing, though,' Ben said after a moment, his voice serious.

'Anything,' Thea said with conviction.

'If you decide to go ahead with the coasteering, and your appointment tomorrow is to book it, will you tell me when you're going?'

She stared at him, surprised. 'Really? You'd want to come along?'

He shook his head, his half-smile kicking in. 'No way. I'm not throwing myself off rocks for anyone, but I would love to watch you give it a try.'

Thea burst out laughing, a warmth spreading through her that had nothing to do with the weather. She hit him on the arm, and he made a show of it hurting, rubbing the spot with an exaggerated wince.

'You sod,' she whispered.

They walked back to the cottages, the atmosphere between them easier than ever.

# *Chapter Eight*

They stopped outside Sunfish Cottage. The sun had lowered, slipping towards the sea as if it couldn't wait to take a dip in the blue water, and Thea catalogued her feelings. She was hot, sweaty and still a bit frazzled, but Ben's cap had taken care of her head and face, and she'd put plasters over yesterday's blisters and worn two pairs of socks, which had helped. The main difference, though, was her mood. Yesterday she'd felt defeated, today it was more like exhilaration.

'Thank you again,' she said, knowing the words would soon lose their meaning. She didn't know how Ben felt, his face so often impassive, his hazel eyes direct and calm, revealing little. 'I've had a great time this afternoon – today, in fact. The whole day.'

'It's been good,' he replied, his shoulder resting against the wall of the cottage. 'Much better than tackling the tiling in the bathroom, which is next on my list. I'll try to keep the banging down, though.'

'Thanks,' Thea said. 'But also, don't worry. You can't help making noise. I mean, sorry, I—'

'No apologies. What have you done wrong?'

'I—' she floundered.

'Exactly. So, catch you later, then?'

'Of course. It's not like there's miles between us, is it?'

'Not very far at all,' he agreed.

She turned away at the same time as he did, then glanced back to see Scooter hurry past him and stand in front of his door. She was unlocking Sunfish Cottage when she heard Ben call her name.

'Yup?' she called back.

'On Friday afternoon, there's a barbecue cook-off on the beach. It's the first time they're running it, part of the town's events programme, but . . .'

'You're taking part?'

He nodded.

'It sounds fun,' she said. 'And it's much more my thing than diving head first off cliffs. I'd love to come and cheer you on.'

'If you've got other plans—'

'I haven't,' she said. 'Not at all. Summer fairs are on the bucket list, and I've decided a cook-off competition counts.'

'There'll be food stalls, music, possibly. It should be a good afternoon.'

'I'm in.'

'Great.' His mouth kicked up. 'See you, then.'

Thea went inside and flopped onto the sofa, untying her boots and peeling off her socks, enjoying the endorphins coursing through her. Why did it feel like she'd achieved so much today, when yesterday had felt like a failure? Was it that she'd shared the experience, felt like she was living her best holiday life, rather than floundering alone? She didn't have the energy to examine her feelings too closely, so she went to have a shower instead.

As the cerulean sky turned to evening turquoise, and shadows shifted across the living room, Thea's focus on her book was interrupted by creeping thoughts of tomorrow. She was going to see a building that could, in the not too distant future, become the bookshop she'd dreamed of owning. She had spent hours – thousands of them, probably – imagining every square foot: the layout of the shelves, the different sections, the book-related gifts she would sell. Ideally there would be a café area, or at the very least a hot drinks machine and a squashy, inviting sofa for people who wanted to linger, to read the prologue of a book before they committed to buying it.

When the only limit was her imagination, it was the best bookshop in the world. It had been Alex who had honed her ideas, brought reality into it as he helped her with her business plan, and she was so grateful for his advice. She had a chunk of savings to get her started, and once she had the perfect property, she was going to apply for a business loan. Alex's expertise was in operations, but his parents were both accountants, and he had more business sense than anyone else she knew.

When she'd reached the denouement of her book, she realised she wasn't concentrating properly, and decided to save the conclusion for when her mind was quieter. She picked up her mobile instead.

Alex answered after four rings. 'Rushwood,' he said. 'What Cornish delights have you been indulging in today?'

'It's tomorrow, Alex,' she said, ignoring his question. 'My meeting with the landlord.' She could almost hear him dialling up his concentration.

'I know, and you're going to be great. Remember that it's the first visit to the first property. Of course it's significant, but if this place isn't right, then somewhere else will be. You don't have to prove anything to anyone. You're a businesswoman looking for a location for her bookshop, and you've done the background research, the planning. Focus, be calm, take the time you need. Don't let them railroad you into a decision. No rushing, Rushwood.'

Thea took a deep breath. 'You're right. It's just that it means everything to me, and to them I'm just one possible tenant.'

'That's good, though. You're not doing them a favour by taking it. It has to be right, that's the main thing. Ask all your questions. You've got your list?'

'I have,' Thea said. She had it in the notes app on her phone, along with her and Esme's holiday list, but she'd almost got it memorised. Questions about the conditions of the lease, what she could and couldn't do in the property, whether she could put fixed bookshelves up, the terms of notice. There were so many things to check, and in her limited experience, landlords and estate agents – people who wielded control over properties – had oodles of confidence, because they had oodles of power. When faced with those confident people, Thea was often the exact opposite.

'I'll be about,' Alex said. 'If you want to call me while you're there, just tell them you have to confirm something with your business advisor.'

'I will. I so appreciate this, Alex.' She hoped that, once she had found the right location, she could stop asking for his help so often. He was always so kind, always had time for her, but she needed to rely on herself more as her plans progressed, even though the thought of having fewer reasons to speak to Alex gave her a pang of sadness.

'Anything for you,' he said. 'Now, tell me all about your day.'

Thea leaned her head against the sofa. 'I went on my second coastal walk of the holiday, but this one was a lot better than yesterday's. There was a crevice in the cliffs full of seabirds, and the cacophony while they wheeled about and perched – nested too, I guess: I've never seen, or heard, anything like it.'

'How did you find that?'

'I had a guide,' she admitted. She could hear the soft shushing of the sea through the open window, but there were no sounds from next door. She wondered if Ben had given up for the day, or if he was measuring tiles, being quiet and industrious. 'Someone who took pity on my solo attempt.'

'That's great,' Alex said. 'And tomorrow, Rushwood, you'll ace your meeting, then you'll be one step closer to bookshop world domination.'

'I will, won't I? I can't quite believe it.'

They hung up, and Thea spent a few idle moments wondering what Alex was doing. Was he in his flat, watching

TV or reading, or had he just got in from seeing friends? She imagined him sitting next to her on this sofa, talking face to face rather than on the phone. She'd kept the main light off, the room lit only by lamps, the one on the table next to her bright enough to read by. But despite the shadowy corners, it felt cosy rather than sinister, the space calm and relaxing with its soft, neutral colours.

Her mind drifted back to Ben, and she wondered whether he had a clear vision for the improvements he wanted to make, or if he was deciding room by room, feature by feature. She tried to imagine living somewhere like this, with character and lots of space, the unbeatable view and the ocean scent on tap. To her, it was almost too good to be true, and yet Ben didn't seem overjoyed with his situation. She wondered why that was.

She had realised, soon after pulling off her boots, that he hadn't actually invited her to the cook-off on Friday. He'd simply mentioned it, and she had jumped at the chance. Was she coming across as too eager: a lonely woman on a solo holiday, clawing for scraps of company? She hoped not. She hoped that, when she told Ben about the other reason she was here, he'd be impressed.

With that thought, as much as Alex's reassuring words, comforting her, Thea closed the window, turned off the lamps and went upstairs to her freshly mended bed.

'What are you planning to do with it, then?'

Jamie Scable, the landlord Thea had arranged to meet, whose company owned the vacant shop on Main Street, had his hands on his hips and was staring out of the window, not looking at her. He was around mid-twenties, she guessed – a few years younger than her – and was wearing a shiny grey suit, white shirt and bright red tie, despite the heat. His dark hair was slicked into helmet-like submission by God-knows how much hair gel.

Thea felt unprofessional in her pink and white sundress, her dark hair pulled back into a simple ponytail, but when she'd looked in the mirror that morning she thought she'd struck the right balance between being businesslike and *her*, because Esme always told her that she shouldn't hide her true self behind a persona, otherwise every relationship would start off on the wrong foot. Now, though, Thea felt so wrong-footed it was as if the floor was unstable.

'I'm going to open a bookshop,' she said, clasping her hands in front of her.

He turned to look at her, his gaze sharp. 'Is that right?'

'It seems like a good match,' Thea said. 'Port Karadow and a bookshop, I mean: in keeping with the vibe of the town. I know there was one here until fairly recently, so I'm filling a gap in the market.'

Jamie nodded along, but she could see he wasn't convinced. He confirmed it when he said, 'It won't last. You've just mentioned the one that failed.'

Thea took a moment to find her voice. 'It doesn't mean that mine has to.'

'Port Karadow has a few independent places left, but the trend's the other way. People want to know what they're getting. The standard of Starbucks coffee, clothes from Primark. Gift places still do well with the tourists, if the stock's local and unique, but with Amazon dominating, books are one of the hardest sells these days. You'd be better off with an antiques shop, or one of those ninety-nine pence places.'

Thea couldn't think of anything worse. 'Everyone loves books,' she said.

Jamie chortled. 'Not everyone. Last book I read was some Dickens thing – *Bleak House*. We had to do it for GCSE. I just wait for Netflix to do them.'

*Then you're missing out on so much*, Thea thought, but out loud she said, 'Does it matter to you what kind of business I open?'

'Course it does.' He was walking around the shop like a billygoat unafraid of trolls.

The space was simple, clean and a good size, with a solid-looking floor and a generous storage room behind the main area. There was also a tiny office, kitchen and toilet. It was halfway down Main Street, not too far from an old-fashioned ironmongers that had a window bursting with tools, lights and garden decorations, proving that some independent places were thriving. Thea could imagine running her bookshop here, nestled amongst the other popular shops on the main tourist street. She wouldn't be far from Cornish Keepsakes, with its beautiful hampers. Books could easily be accommodated into hampers: they were perfect for them, in fact.

'Why?' she pressed, when Jamie didn't elaborate.

'Because if you fail in six months' time, then I have to re-advertise, re-let, and have a whole lot more paperwork to deal with. I want a solid tenant who will stay the course and cause me no trouble.'

Thea wondered if Ben would admire this man's honesty, or whether he'd think it was cruel and dismissive, like she did. She could feel her shaky confidence crumbling further, as if her skeleton were disintegrating. She thought back to Alex's pep talk and clutched her phone tightly, her list of questions open on the screen.

'You don't know I'm going to fail,' she said, but it came out wrong: defensive, as if part of her believed him, rather than defiant.

'I know this business, love, and the amount of pie-in-the-sky dreamers who've come through my properties and gone under swifter than a tanker with a socking great hole in it, you wouldn't believe.' He was staring out of the window again, as if she wasn't even worth looking at.

She ran through responses in her head: *And what about you – was your business an overnight success? Did you do anything to help these people: introduce them to other business owners in the community, champion them in your networking circles, or did you start off by telling them they'd fail, before they'd even signed a contract? What do you think your unfounded assessment did to their confidence, to their chances of success? Do you take any responsibility for it at all?*

She didn't say any of them, though.

'Do you have a business plan?' he asked.

She had spent so long putting it together: researching the market, consulting other independent shop owners, going over and over the financial projections until her head hurt. Mr Scable sounded slightly relenting, as if he realised he'd been harsh, but the damage had been done. She wasn't prepared to have him trash all her hard work in the same way he'd dismissed her dreams.

'Of course I do,' she said. 'But I didn't think I needed to bring it with me for this.'

He scoffed. There was no warmth in his dark eyes, and Thea decided that some time long ago he'd had it sucked out of him, by ambition or greed or some awful event that had made him focus on profit and nothing else.

She felt as if there was a pressure cooker building up inside her, and the thing that would burst out when the lid popped off wouldn't be anger, or righteous indignation, but tears. Jamie Scable was the kind of man who made her want to hide in a corner; who looked at her and decided she was nothing, and who had the ability to almost make her believe it.

She had thought that Ben was too cool and aloof for her, the type of person who would dismiss her instantly, but now, standing in this empty, echoing space that could have held her dreams, he was the person she wanted to run to. But, if she told him, it would give him the chance to see her the way Jamie did. He might agree with the landlord that her plans were the stuff of fantasy. She hadn't told Ben what she was doing while they were walking, and maybe deep down that was because she knew he'd think it was as pointless as Jamie did.

'I'll have to have a think,' she said now. She tried to sound businesslike, but her chin was aimed at the floor.

Jamie glanced at his watch. 'You do that. I've got someone else coming in five minutes, anyway.'

Thea walked towards the door.

'Oh, and love? Next time, if you're really serious, you might want to think about asking a couple of questions. If you want to make it look like you know what you're talking about.'

Thea couldn't get out of there fast enough, the fresh air a balm against her hot cheeks. She had imagined going to the café further up the hill and getting an iced mocha, or browsing the gift shop, perhaps finding something to give Ben as a thank-you gift. But now, all she wanted was to go back to Sunfish Cottage, shut the door and lose herself in the last pages of her book.

If she was honest with herself, she could easily do that for the next two and a half weeks, until it was time to go home to the safety of her flat and the library, to Esme and Alex, and her quiet, unambitious life.

But as she walked, her hard soles tapping out a rhythm on the cobbles, the gentle wind caressing her, listening to people laughing, discussing which flavour of ice cream they wanted, and whether to head to the beach now or after lunch, hearing the ping of a bell over a shop door, she remembered why she had steered Esme towards this particular town when they had been planning their Cornish holiday.

It was here, after a damp, dreary week staying in a faded guest house near Penzance when she was ten, her mum and dad arguing constantly, that their holiday had – in her eyes, at least – been rescued. Her mum had got a migraine less than an hour into their journey home and, in her usual, dramatic way, said she couldn't possibly sit in the car for another four. So they had stopped in Port Karadow, found a B&B with a vacant family room, and she and her dad had left her mum to rest, exploring the town on their own. There had still been a bookshop then, and her dad had known this was where Thea most wanted to go.

She had spent ages browsing, had chosen *Tiger Eyes* by Judy Blume as her prize, and then she and her dad had bought fish and chips, gone down to the harbour, and sat on a bench. The ground had been glistening after a heavy rain shower, the water grey-green and choppy, the boats bobbing and twisting, as if they were trying to outrun the weather. Thea had always felt calmer when it was just her and her dad, and she had soaked up the town's charm, the simple pleasures of the seaside view and the moreish, salty chips, and the haven of the bookshop, her new story wrapped in a paper bag and laid carefully on her knee.

Her parents had divorced not long after that, and now she kept in touch with them as separate entities. Her mum, always talking about her latest crisis, putting herself in the centre of every story, and her dad: quiet, gentle and practical. It was books that had got her through their divorce, hiding from the worst of it inside a different world, and she still had the copy of *Tiger Eyes*. She reread it once a year, using the faded receipt as her bookmark. She could still, just about, read the words, *Port Karadow Books* on the top. Even though the shop itself was long gone, the memory remained.

Thea watched a young boy waving a fishing net in the direction of the harbour wall while his mother held onto him, not letting him get too close to the edge, the dad helping a little girl pick up pebbles and put them in her castle-shaped bucket. Soon, Thea thought, it would be filled with sand instead, and upended on the beach. A fisherman was unloading crates from his boat a little way along the wall, and an old couple, arm in arm, said hello to him, then stopped to chat, as if they'd all known each other for years.

There was too much here, Thea realised, for her to let Jamie Scable dampen her dreams. She had picked Port

Karadow for a reason, and she couldn't let him dissuade her. There would be other options, other properties. She just needed to find out what they were, rebuild her confidence, and keep going.

The cottages were almost blindingly white in the sunshine, Thea squinting against the glare as she walked up the hill.

She was putting her key in the lock when she heard footsteps behind her.

'Thea.'

Ben was standing a few feet away. Had he been waiting for her to get back? She dismissed the thought immediately.

'Hi,' she said, trying her best to sound chirpy.

'You OK?' he asked. 'How did your appointment go?'

'It wasn't . . . I might have to rethink a few things. But it doesn't matter.' She forced a smile. 'How are you?'

He didn't answer immediately, as if he was weighing up whether to accept her change of subject. But then he said, 'What do you know about barbecue food?'

'I know that I like it. I'm not an expert, though.'

'I'd like your opinion, if that's OK?'

She nodded, noting that there was something new in Ben's expression, a lightness she hadn't seen before. It was almost as if he was giddy – as giddy as a serious, stoic, six-foot-something builder with wide shoulders and furrowed brows could be.

'Hit me,' she said. 'What do you want my opinion on?'

'The cook-off on Friday,' he said. 'Obviously, you have to make the best dish to win, and I wondered what you thought would impress the judges more: a rack of beef ribs with my own-recipe hot sauce and barbecued potato rösti, or I've got these, uh . . . they're like a barbecued chicken saltimbocca, chicken breasts wrapped in streaky bacon and seasoned with a herb and Prosecco rub – it sounds strange, I know, but it's delicious – with chips and a mustard mayonnaise.' He moved his hands while he spoke. The deadpan exterior she'd come to expect was nowhere to be found, and she laughed.

He frowned. 'You think they both sound terrible?'

Thea shook her head quickly, biting her lip at the way his eyes widened with hurt. She had found what made Ben tick: something he was really passionate about. She remembered the way he'd choreographed his way around her kitchen, making her one of the best breakfasts she'd ever eaten.

'They sound incredible, seriously. Can't you make both?'

His shoulders dropped, relief lightening his expression. 'We have to choose one meal.'

'And you really want to win?'

He shrugged, but it wasn't quite as relaxed as she thought he was aiming for. 'I'm a guy entering a barbecue competition: it's a cliché in so many ways, but of course I want to win.'

Thea leaned against her door, making a show of considering. 'I love the idea of the chicken wrapped in bacon,' she said eventually, 'and I'm intrigued by the Prosecco and herb thing, but if you've got your own hot sauce, and you're really proud of it, then I think go with that and the beef. Also, potato rösti on the barbecue sounds so good.'

'You really think so?'

'Oh yeah,' Thea said, nodding. 'My mouth is watering at the thought.'

'Great! Good.' His smile was wide and bright, and Thea wondered where she'd put her sunglasses, because that, along with the glare of the whitewashed houses, might permanently damage her eyesight. 'I think you're right.'

'Whatever you do, Ben, you're sure to do it well. I've had your breakfast, remember?'

'Yeah.' He ran a hand over the back of his neck. 'Anyway, I don't want to hold you up, so . . .' He pointed at Oystercatcher Cottage.

'I'm looking forward to seeing you win,' Thea called to his retreating back.

He laughed. 'We'll see,' he said over his shoulder.

Thea didn't want to wish away any part of her holiday, but already she couldn't wait for Friday afternoon.

It was after five when there was a knock on the door and Thea opened it to find Mel standing there.

'Hello,' she said, brightly. 'I come bearing news, though it isn't really relevant to you.'

'Come in.' Thea stepped back to admit her.

'I've ordered a new bed slat,' Mel said without preamble. 'I'm so sorry you had to deal with that. It's not going to be here for another few weeks, though, so as long as the job Ben did is going to last, then you won't need to worry.'

Thea noticed the way Mel's features tightened when she mentioned Ben, and felt a stab of protectiveness towards him.

'He's done a brilliant job,' she said. 'And he came to help me immediately.' She didn't add that he'd cooked her breakfast or taken her sightseeing, because neither of those things were relevant to the plan that had formed in her brain in the last few seconds. 'He's doing up his whole house by himself.'

'I'm aware,' Mel said wryly.

'And he's clearly good at it,' Thea went on, perching on the arm of the sofa.

Mel nodded and smiled. 'I am grateful to him. It would have taken me longer to arrange for someone to come and fix the bed. A few hours, at least.'

'Ben could help you out,' Thea said, keeping her voice light. 'I mean, he could be a contact for you. I don't know how many other holiday places you have, but—'

'There's four. All close to here, though this is the nearest one to town.'

'Ben would be ideal, then. I can vouch for his manner and his efficiency. It's up to you, of course, and I know him working next door has been a bit inconvenient, but I think it could, if you wanted it to, actually turn out to be the opposite.'

Mel folded her arms. 'Have you said all this to him?'

'No! I only just thought of it. But he's a good person to know, if your business is houses.'

Mel nodded quickly. 'Well, I'll definitely consider it. And thank you, for being so understanding with the bed.'

'No problem,' Thea said. The two of them exchanged a few more pleasantries before Mel said she had to go: she was picking up her middle child from football practice, and her youngest from her singing lesson.

Once Thea was alone again, she felt slightly sick. Would Ben want her interfering like that? Offering his services to other people? Still, it wasn't as if it was a done deal. Mel might not follow up on it, considering that she was already annoyed about his building work impacting one of her properties. But she had a strong urge to help Ben, to do something for him, in return for all his kindness. If he had a few more opportunities for once he'd finished fixing his own place, then that could only be a good thing, couldn't it?

# Chapter Nine

The following day Thea was woken by voices outside the open bedroom window. She was startled into sitting, thinking for a second that they were angry, heated words, until she heard a woman laughing and what sounded like, 'No, Crumble!' though it couldn't possibly have been that.

She got out of the – now very sturdy – bed and tiptoed to the window. Her eyes were drawn, as they always were, to the sea. Today it was a deeper blue, and there were clouds overhead: white, no hint of grey anywhere, but they were racing across the sky, the wind giving the sun's heat a run for its money. It felt like a more serious day, somehow.

Down below her, she could see Ben and Finn standing with their arms crossed, and there was a woman, too. About Thea's age, she thought, with mid-brown hair in waves over her shoulders, wearing a summery green dress. The three of them were watching Scooter and another dog – a beagle – dance around each other, the beagle's high-pitched barks peppering the quiet morning air.

'Crumble will never be outdone,' Finn said.

'Scooter's not trying to outdo him,' Ben replied. 'He's just being friendly, and Crumble's hysteria is confusing him. My dog likes the simple things in life.'

'Just like his owner, eh?' Finn nudged Ben with his elbow.

'Like that's a bad thing,' Ben said.

'How's prep for Friday going?' the woman asked. She was very pretty, Thea noticed, with freckles across her nose and an interested, open face. She remembered Finn mentioning his girlfriend the first time they'd met, and that eased something inside her; some ache she hadn't been aware of until it dissolved into nothing.

'I've got my menu sorted,' Ben said. 'Thea thought the beef ribs and hot sauce would give me the best chance.'

'Thea?' the woman asked.

'I mentioned her the other day,' Finn said. 'She's staying at Sunfish Cottage. Have you been fraternising, Ben?' Thea could hear the curiosity in his voice.

'She invited me on a walk with her,' Ben said, and Thea had the urge to shout out of the window that it wasn't true, that he was the one who had offered. 'We had fun.'

Finn raised an eyebrow, and the woman turned away from them, saying something to the dogs while she hid a grin.

This, Thea realised, was ridiculous. Moping about Jamie Scable and his lack of faith in her, eavesdropping on her neighbour's conversation with his friends. She pulled the curtain across very slowly, hoping they wouldn't notice the movement, and went to have a shower.

When she got down to the kitchen, the three of them were still outside, sitting in brightly coloured deckchairs and drinking mugs of tea, the dogs lying contentedly between them.

Thea made herself a coffee, and took it, and her book, outside. She was wearing a spaghetti-strapped green top, denim shorts, and pink flip-flops. Her dark hair was still wet from the shower and she'd tied it up in a haphazard bun, loving the way the softer water here made it feel. She would take it down later, when it had dried into messy waves in the sun.

'Thea,' Finn said brightly. 'How are you?'

'Good thanks,' she replied, her eyes drifting to Ben.

'Hey,' he said.

'Hi.'

'This is Meredith,' Finn said, standing up. 'My girlfriend.'

Meredith stood and held out her hand, offering Thea a full, warm smile. 'It's lovely to meet you, Thea. I've been hearing a lot about you.'

'A lot?' Her gaze returned to Ben, and he rolled his eyes.

'I told them about our walk, and that you helped me decide which dish to go for on Friday.'

'Which, coming from Ben, is close to a monologue,' Finn said, 'so I don't know what he's eye-rolling about.'

'It was nice of you to take pity on him,' Meredith added. 'Get him out of the house, so he doesn't suffocate in all that sawdust.'

'All I've been doing recently is getting out of the house,' Ben protested. 'I need to actually get on with something, or I'll never be finished.'

'And yet here we are,' Finn said, 'distracting you all over again.'

'Don't you have a masterpiece to paint, or something?' Ben narrowed his eyes.

'Probably.' Finn shrugged.

'And I've got a day off,' Meredith said.

'What are you up to?' Finn asked Thea, as she sat at her own table. 'Do you have any grand holiday activities you can steal Ben away on?'

'It wasn't actually like that,' Thea said. 'He took *me* along the coast, when my first walk didn't go so well. He showed me that incredible bit of cliffs with all the seabirds.'

Meredith and Finn both turned to Ben, who seemed fixated on the frayed hem of his shorts.

'And today I'm going into Padstow,' Thea went on. 'I want to look at the bookshop there.' It was part of her plan while she was here, to visit other independent bookshops in Cornish towns, to get inspiration for her own. She didn't want to admit what had happened yesterday, to tell these people – Ben especially – that Jamie Scable had been able to affect her so deeply.

'You only brought one book with you?' Finn asked.

'What? No!' Thea couldn't help but laugh. 'Are you crazy?' Finn's eyes widened, but she could see he was amused. 'Sorry, I—'

Ben cleared his throat, and she shot him a look which he returned unwaveringly.

'What I *meant* was,' Thea continued, 'I have two paperbacks and my Kindle. I have approximately five hundred books I can choose from after I finish this one.' She waggled her Elly Griffiths hardback.

'Five *hundred*?' Meredith said. 'Wow.'

'Then why on earth do you want to go to a bookshop?' Finn asked.

'I'm doing some research,' Thea said. 'For a project I've got on the go.'

'Thea works in the library in Bristol,' Ben explained to his friends. Then, to her, he said, 'Is this project something for work, then?'

'Sort of.' After yesterday, Thea felt as if there was a dent in her dream, a rupture that she would have to fix before she was back to full confidence. Visiting another bookshop in an idyllic seaside location, seeing what was possible for *her*, would help. 'So it's a fun visit, but it's work, too.'

'Do you want some company?' Meredith asked. 'I was going to take Crumble for a long, fortifying walk, but it's hotter than I anticipated, so a shorter walk around Padstow would be ideal.'

'You'd really like to come?' Thea asked.

'Only if you want me to. I don't want to muscle in on your holiday.'

'No, that would be great.'

'Excellent.' Meredith stood. 'I'm going to buy you a rhubarb and custard pastie.'

'A *what?*'

'You're in for a treat,' Finn said, standing and grinning. 'I'd best get back to my masterpiece.'

Ben stood too, though he managed to turn the simple act into the most world-weary thing Thea had ever seen. 'And I'd better get back to the shit-show that is my house.'

'You know,' Finn said as he closed his deckchair, then the one Meredith had been sitting on, 'if you didn't want to do it yourself, you could hire another builder to come and get it sorted for you.'

Ben took the deckchairs from his friend, hooking them over his shoulder as if they were shopping bags. 'Thanks, Finnegan, but I can manage. I've got some good ideas for the kitchen now, anyway. A breakfast bar looking out over the view.' As he said it, his gaze slid to Thea, and she gave him a small, encouraging smile.

'That sounds perfect,' she said. 'And I meant to say earlier, you left your ramekins at mine after breakfast the other day. If you wanted to come and get them, have another look around, then you'd be very welcome. Maybe when I get back?'

His mouth remained fixed, but warmth kindled in his eyes. 'That would be great. I'd forgotten about the ramekins.'

Thea noticed Finn glancing between them, wearing a puzzled expression. 'Is this some kind of code?' he asked. 'Are you communicating in another language?'

'Nope,' Thea said. 'We're talking ramekins, that's all.'

Even as Finn kissed Meredith goodbye, and gave Thea a quick peck on the cheek, she could see his mind was still working. He clearly didn't like having unanswered questions, but Thea loved that she and Ben could already understand each other in this way. She was actually making friends on her solo holiday, and that was something she had never imagined would happen.

Thea felt slightly self-conscious about being in the car with Meredith, with nowhere to escape to and small talk to make. It was like being at the hairdresser, which she hated, because she worried that silence made her seem grumpy rather than shy, but she could never think of what to say, her mind emptying the moment she sat in the chair.

She soon discovered that this was going to be a hundred times better than the hairdresser, though, because Meredith was intent on breaking the ice.

'I'm sorry about Finn and all his questions,' she said. 'I don't think he even realises he's doing it: he's just naturally curious. About *everyone*.' She laughed.

'Doesn't it get tiring after a while?'

Meredith thought for a moment. 'At the beginning, definitely. But he's so . . . he's so *lovely*,' she said, and gave a romcom sigh, her smile kicking up, and Thea felt a pang of envy. She would love to be in love with someone, to have that bond, that overwhelming feeling of togetherness. She thought of Alex, the kindness that came so easily to him, and pushed the thought away.

'How long have you been with him?' she asked Meredith.

'Since December. It was . . . all kinds of things happened, but he did this big, romantic gesture on Christmas Day, and—' she laughed again. 'He pretty much sold himself to me. And he's a wonderful artist. He's finding his feet, and it's so good to see, because he hasn't always found it easy to be himself.'

'What about you?' Thea asked.

'Me? I work at Cornish Keepsakes, a gift shop in town.'

'I passed there on Sunday. It wasn't open, but I'm going to go back.'

'It will be open on Sundays soon. My mission is to make it a fully modern business, while keeping its essential quaintness.'

'Is it really old, then? The whole street looks like something out of a Dickens novel, actually, so it makes sense.' She had thought her bookshop would fit right in – up until yesterday, anyway.

'It's not that ancient,' Meredith said, laughing. 'It's just my boss, Adrian. He's great, but he's got some old-fashioned ideas. I'm trying to blend them with some more up-to-date stuff, to make sure we stay relevant and optimised and all those other ridiculous buzzwords. What's your project, if you don't mind me asking? Padstow Booksellers is one of my favourite shops, and I'd love to know what you're doing.'

They were driving along the coast road, nearing Padstow, seeing flashes of the sea as they passed inlets and sandy coves, the power of the Atlantic obvious even from such small glimpses. Thea changed gear, peering at the signposts, and Meredith directed her, telling her the back road into town was easiest, and she nodded and took the turning, and then everything was quiet.

'I have this idea,' she started, then thought of Ben's insistence that she should be direct and unapologetic. 'I'm going to open a bookshop,' she said.

'In Cornwall?' Meredith squeaked. 'Really?'

'Really,' Thea confirmed. It felt good, saying it so definitively, and easier, somehow, to tell Meredith, rather than Esme – or even Ben. There was a freedom in it, because they didn't have any expectations of each other. 'It's been my dream for years. I've been saving up, I've put together a business plan, I know which loan to apply for when I find the right location.'

'You think Port Karadow might be that place?' Meredith asked. 'It had its own bookshop a while ago – before I moved there – and I know people have felt the loss of it. This is amazing, Thea. So this is more than just a holiday?'

'Well,' Thea said, buoyed by Meredith's enthusiasm, 'I'll have to go back to Bristol, whatever happens. It'll take a while, sorting everything out: finding somewhere to live in Cornwall, packing up my old life. And of course I have to find the right premises before any of that, secure the loan. It's not a done deal by any means, but . . .'

'But what?' Meredith asked, reaching between the seats to pet Crumble, who had woken from his slumber on the back seat with a cute, doggy yawn.

'But I'm determined to make it work,' Thea said, gripping the steering wheel tightly, thinking of Jamie Scable's hard eyes and his sneer. But he was just one man, she realised: one man who she could take completely out of the equation if she found somewhere else in Port Karadow to open her bookshop.

Padstow was sunny and alive with people, strolling through the streets and sitting outside cafés, buying ice cream from the shop on the harbour, where boats were chugging in and out, queues of excited tourists waiting for the day-trippers and sea safari launches to come back and scoop them up. Thea could smell fish and chips, the delicious tang of frying batter and vinegar wafting over to them as lunchtime approached.

'Oh God,' Meredith said. 'Maybe we'll have to save the pasties for another time.'

'We could get some to take back with us as dessert,' Thea suggested. 'I bet Finn and Ben would like one, after all their hard work.'

'Great idea,' Meredith said, and Thea could feel the other woman's stare on the side of her face.

Padstow Booksellers was a warm hug of a shop, its busy, colourful shelves and the cheerful hello from the bookseller welcoming her like an old friend, even though she'd never been there before. She examined the space critically, taking in its display stands, the way it compartmentalised the books, the front desk that was slightly chaotic but all the better for it. She saw books she'd already read, books she'd put out on display at the library, noticed that they had a 'Cornwall Stories' section with Daphne du Maurier, Winston Graham, Fern Britton and Phillipa Ashley novels, and an elegant display of signed hardbacks. Everything about it was enticing and desirable.

They had allowed Crumble in, and the beagle was being well-behaved, occasionally sniffing the shelves but staying close to Meredith's ankles, while Thea took her time inspecting it all.

'Can I help you with anything in particular?' the bookseller, a woman who looked to be in her early thirties, asked.

'We're just browsing at the moment,' Thea said, then turned to Meredith and added, 'unless you want something specific?'

'No, I'm good, thank you.' She was poring over a large hardback: seascapes on glossy pages. 'Finn would love this,' she murmured, and Thea left her to it.

There were so many things she liked about this bookshop, but it also helped her clarify what she would do with her own. Ideally, she wanted a coffee machine; the premises on Main Street hadn't been big enough for a café, but she didn't think a coffee machine was out of the question, or a couple of comfy chairs. She wanted, more than anything, for her customers to feel like they could browse: that they could take their time and not feel harried or rushed. She had been imagining a children's area with a beanbag, and possibly a small, raised section, somewhere she could host signings and poetry readings. Looking around Padstow Booksellers, she was worried she had been too ambitious.

'I'm going to get this,' Meredith said, hefting the art book under her arm. 'Do you want anything?'

Thea shook her head. She had her Kindle with her. But then there was the hardback she'd been eying up, Sarra Manning's *London, With Love*, released last month in all its pink and purple romcom beauty. She had been going to wait and borrow it from work once the initial flurry of loans had died down, but she was on holiday, and it would be a great addition to the romance bookshelf in her flat. Also, it was a momentous occasion: she would always associate it with coming here, looking at bookshops in Cornwall. A big step on the way to realising her dreams.

'Actually,' she said, picking it up, 'I might treat myself.'

'Good idea,' Meredith said, peering at the cover. 'A holiday book is an absolute necessity, and that one looks glorious.'

Thea grinned. She was starting to think she and Meredith could become good friends.

They sat in the window of Rick Stein's fish and chip shop, having decided to treat themselves to scallops to start with, followed by traditional cod and chips. Crumble was lying under their feet, his lead tied to Meredith's stool.

'I love Ben's idea of a breakfast bar,' Meredith said, drizzling soy sauce vinaigrette onto her scallops, which had been presented in their large, elegant shells. 'He needs to make the most of his ridiculous view.'

Thea sighed. 'It's *such* a good location. I leave all the windows open when I'm in the cottage, so I have the sea as a low-level soundtrack. I'm so envious of Ben, getting to live with it permanently.'

'I don't think he appreciates it quite yet. He's got so much work to do.'

'He doesn't seem that enthusiastic about it,' Thea agreed. 'If I had a whole house to renovate, and the skills and knowledge to do it myself, I think I'd be beside myself with excitement. He told me he's finding it more difficult than he imagined.'

'I don't know,' Meredith said, sighing. 'Maybe it's the wider picture he's struggling with. He's used to going into places and working to his customers' plans, and I'm sure they all have strong views about what they want. Maybe it's easier for him to take direction from other people, especially if, emotionally, he's not quite settled into his new place.'

'What do you mean?' Thea asked, then put a forkful of scallop into her mouth, chewing slowly so she could savour every burst of flavour it had to offer.

'He left the Lakes at the beginning of the year, and it wasn't . . . I don't think it was under happy circumstances. I mean, I *know* it wasn't, but—' she winced.

'That's OK,' Thea said, waving a hand. 'I'm not expecting you to share all your friends' secrets with me, especially not Ben's.'

'Why especially not Ben's?' Meredith asked, her tone unashamedly curious.

'He strikes me as a very private person,' Thea said. 'He's been kind to me, but he's not . . . ebullient. Effervescent. Irrepressible – except perhaps when it comes to cooking.'

Meredith laughed. 'So true. When you get to know him, though, he does come out of his shell.' She held up an empty scallop shell, and Thea joined in with her laughter. 'I'm glad he's been kind to you,' she added.

Thea felt a flush creep onto her cheeks. 'My first hike was disastrous. I'm not used to long tromps in the countryside, and definitely not solo, and he banished all my bad memories by coming with me, showing me things I wouldn't have found on my own, forcing me to challenge myself with the scary parts.'

Meredith's eyes lit with something new as Thea spoke. 'That's so good,' she said. 'For you *and* for him.'

Thea nodded. She was desperate to ask Meredith what she meant, but didn't want to put her in an awkward position.

'And he asked you about the cook-off,' Meredith went on. 'Does that mean you're coming on Friday?'

Thea hummed in happiness as her empty scallop shells were replaced with a box full to bursting with chips and a crispy, delicious-looking piece of cod. There was a parsley garnish, a lemon wedge, and a pot of garlic mayonnaise on the side. It smelled like food heaven. 'God yes,' she said, sticking her fork into the crispy batter, relishing the crunch. 'Ben's dish sounds amazing.' Her eyes widened as she tasted the fish, the melt-in-the-mouth texture, the seaside flavour. 'And he's already cooked me the best breakfast I've had in years.'

'He cooked you breakfast, did he?' Meredith raised her eyebrows. She looked full of energy, as if she was just about managing to restrain herself from bouncing up and down on her stool.

Thea sighed, making her expression serious even as the

smile threatened. 'It wasn't like *that*,' she protested. 'He came over to fix my bed, and – OK, that sounds wrong. It was entirely innocent, but he was kind, and generous. He stopped me from feeling lonely, and that's the part of this trip I've been struggling with the most.'

'How come?' Meredith asked.

Thea explained what had happened with Esme, about her staying behind to work at the festival – and spending time with Alex – and about her own reluctance to do all the holiday things they'd planned when there was nobody to share them with.

'In that case you're definitely coming to the cook-off on Friday,' Meredith said. 'We'll be your holiday buddies, if you can stand us for another couple of weeks. Me, Finn and Ben.'

Thea grinned around a chip. 'I would love that,' she said, when she'd finished her mouthful. 'And I was wondering if you could help me with something?'

'Sure,' Meredith said, drowning a chip in homemade ketchup and eating it slowly, her eyes closing in appreciation. 'What is it?'

'I want to get Ben a thank-you gift. I thought I could find him something barbecue-related. Some plates or a set of tools – though he probably has all those, so perhaps an arty dish or platter in one of the gift shops we passed? There must be something he'd like for his new kitchen.'

'I bet we can find the perfect thing,' Meredith said. 'And we mustn't forget the pasties, either. I'm not sure I'll have room for dessert, but Finn will be ravenous because he forgets everything while he's painting, and Ben will have burned off eight million calories with all his hefting and sawing, and seems to eat whatever he likes and still have a washboard stomach.'

'A washboard stomach?' Thea said faintly, trying to picture Ben – who was already too handsome for his own good – with the kind of body that would make the *Baywatch* cast envious. Of course, she'd already seen that he was fit, but she'd been trying very hard not to think about the bits he usually kept under wraps.

'Yup,' Meredith said, a note of glee in her voice. 'When we go to the beach, it's all on show. If I wasn't so hook, line and sinker for Finn, I would not be immune.'

'Right,' Thea managed.

'Does your Alex, at home, have a washboard stomach?' Meredith asked, all innocence, and Thea realised that despite describing her friendship with him in what she had hoped was a measured way, she must have revealed that she was attracted to him.

She resisted the urge to hit her new friend with her paper napkin, saying instead, 'I have no idea,' as if she didn't understand the dig Meredith was trying to get in. 'He's an operations manager at the council, so I don't get much opportunity to see his abs.'

Meredith shrugged. 'I bet we'll go to the beach before your time is up,' she said. 'I doubt they'll let the competitors barbecue topless on Friday, but there'll be plenty of other opportunities.'

'OK then,' Thea said quietly.

She had thought, up until this holiday, that all her affection lay at home, with Alex, though she had never really allowed herself to explore her feelings for him in any great detail: the triumvirate of her, Esme and Alex was too precious to be complicated by anything beyond friendship. But now Meredith had forced her to make a comparison, and the thought of Alex in a pair of swimming trunks wasn't having the same effect on her nervous system as the possibility of seeing Ben with his top off. Not at all.

Meredith must have seen something in her expression, or noticed the flush in her cheeks, because she started wafting at her with her wooden fork, her smile making her eyes sparkle. Thea was glad when a waiter came to clear their empty boxes and give them the bill, mercifully changing the subject before it got even more awkward.

# Chapter Ten

By the time Thea and Meredith got back to Port Karadow, they had formed a plan. Or, at least, Meredith had suggested it, and Thea had readily agreed to it, because it meant exploring a new part of the town and spending more time with people she was already starting to see as friends.

'Excellent,' Meredith said, hanging up the phone. 'Finn's on board, as I knew he would be. Now we just need to convince Ben.'

'You don't think that's going to be easy?'

Meredith shrugged. 'He's taking this cook-off on Friday seriously, so he'll probably want to spend the night before practising his dish. I think he needs the break, though. To empty his mind of it. I remember my favourite teacher at school, Mrs Sanders, saying just that before exams. You have to stop revising at lunchtime on the day before, give your brain time to rest before the real deal.'

'And you think Ben will see it as a rest, if we're going to the restaurant run by one of the judges for the cook-off?'

'It's had rave reviews since it opened, it's undoubtedly one of the best places to eat in town, and I think it will inspire him more than anything. A night away from his building site and his beef ribs will set him up for Friday better than any more practising could. If he's not ready now, then he never will be.'

'It sounds like you're rehearsing all the things you want to say to him,' Thea observed, turning onto the cottages' driveway.

'I don't need to, because you're here to charm him into agreeing,' Meredith said. 'I have faith in you.' She got out of the car when Thea cut the engine, not giving her a chance to protest.

Meredith knocked on Ben's door and he opened it, pink-cheeked and slightly out of breath. The neck of his old Beastie Boys tour T-shirt was loose, and there was a rip in the fabric near the hem, but somehow that scruffiness just added to his overall hotness. Thea dragged her eyes up to his face. How was it fair that he looked so amazing when he'd spent the day doing strenuous, sweaty work? She thought back to her state after her first walk, and resisted rolling her eyes.

'I've been moving cabinets,' he said, by way of explanation.

'On your own?' Thea asked, as Meredith thrust a paper bag containing a rhubarb and custard pastie into his hands.

'You need this, then,' she said.

'Thanks.' He opened the bag and glanced inside. 'I missed lunch.'

'And I got you something,' Thea added. Was it a step too far, buying him a present? It was a large serving dish they'd found in a quaint, backstreet gift shop in Padstow, where the soft, dove grey interior made every glossy item on display call out to her. The dish was white and blue ceramic, with a map of Cornwall in the middle and the names of the most well-known beaches around the edge. As soon as she'd seen it, she realised nothing else would do. She had imagined Ben serving up his beef ribs in it, or a giant portion of potato salad, or a Christmas roast. It would work for any occasion.

'What is it?' he asked, as she handed him the tissue-wrapped package.

'It's to say thank you, for all you've done for me.'

'I haven't done anything.'

'We both know that's not true,' she said. She glanced at Meredith, knowing her new friend would be intrigued about what that meant. 'I saw this, and I thought – once your kitchen's sorted – it might be useful.'

Ben unwrapped the paper slowly, revealing the glossy blue and white ceramic beneath. 'Shit, Thea,' he murmured, turning it over. He held it as if it weighed nothing, whereas when she had taken it from the display stand to the counter, she'd been terrified of dropping it. 'This is too much.'

'It's not. I wanted to get it for you, so you can't give it back.'

'But this—'

'Please accept it,' she said. 'And come out to dinner with us tomorrow.'

'What?' He looked up.

'Great manoeuvre,' Meredith murmured to her, then said, 'I've booked a table at the Happy Shack for tomorrow night.

For the four of us. And you know how hard it is to wrangle one, so you can't turn it down.'

Ben looked between them, and Meredith clasped her hands in front of her, a picture of sweetness now she'd said her piece. 'OK,' he said. 'Sounds good. Thanks for going to the trouble, Meredith.'

'It was my pleasure.' She gave him a wide smile. 'See you there, just before seven. Thanks for today, Thea,' she added, then hurried to her car, calling over her shoulder, 'I'd better take Finn his pastie before it becomes a soggy mush.'

When she and Crumble had gone, Scooter came to join Ben and Thea, sprawling on the doorstep and closing his eyes against the sun.

'Did you have a good time?' Ben asked. 'And do what you wanted for your project?'

'It was useful,' she admitted. 'It gave me some encouragement, which I really needed. And I got a new book, too.' She grinned.

'Success all round, then,' he said, returning her smile. 'Thank you again for the dish. I love it. It'll have pride of place in the kitchen, once it's finished.'

'It sounds like you're getting on well with it?'

He grimaced. 'Slow and steady wins the race: that's what I have to keep telling myself.'

'You'll get there,' she said, giving his arm a brief squeeze.

He nodded. 'See you tomorrow night, then.'

'Looks like it.' They exchanged smiles, and Thea went back to Sunfish Cottage with a spring in her step.

The Happy Shack was brightly coloured and weather-beaten, a mixture of fisherman chic and faded rainbows, the dining area surrounded by glass and opening onto a terrace that wrapped around the whole building. This was where the four of them sat, caressed by a gentle evening breeze, bottles of Sol, with fat lime wedges peeking out of the tops, on the table in front of them.

Thea pushed a strand of hair away from her face. She'd left it loose, and was wearing a purple star-print dress that she'd bought specifically for the holiday. She had anticipated eating out with Esme, trying the local restaurants and watering holes, and was happy that tonight she could tick another item off the holiday list: especially if the Happy Shack's claim of being committed to local ingredients was true. What she hadn't imagined was being out for dinner with a new group of friends she had met so recently. She had surprised herself by looking forward to tonight, not feeling any dread or anxiety about it – and mostly ignoring the fact that it felt a little bit like the four of them were going on a double date.

She had spent the morning in St Ives, looking in the shops, then she'd bought a fresh seafood salad, a banana milkshake and a bag of honeycomb, and taken them to the magnificent expanse of Hayle Beach, watching kite surfers and soaking up the seaside atmosphere.

'It's beautiful here,' she said now, her head swivelling, as if magnetised, towards the sea. The shack was on the southern edge of Port Karadow, the same side as Sunfish and Oystercatcher cottages, and overlooked the wide, popular beach where, Ben had told her, the cook-off would be taking place tomorrow. Even though there were a few buildings between them and the sand, the hill was steep enough that their view was magnificent. 'And the head chef is judging the cook-off?' she asked, turning back to the table.

She sipped her beer, and decided that a cold drink on a hot evening, with a view of the sea and a night of friendship ahead, had to be one of life's most pleasurable experiences.

'Marcus Belrose,' Ben said, breaking through her reverie. 'He moved down here from Liverpool a couple of months ago. He's already won awards for his food, but he obviously wanted a change of direction, a piece of the Cornish seaside scene.'

'It's not very original,' Finn said. 'A top chef opening a restaurant in Cornwall, the USP fresh fish, which, of course, isn't a *U* at all. It should be CSP: Clichéd Selling Point.'

'Which you're perfectly happy to say as you sit in his restaurant, preparing to eat his award-winning food and give him your money,' Meredith said with a grin.

Finn shrugged, sipping his beer before replying. 'I'm just commenting. Wondering. It's not a criticism.'

'Clichéd Selling Point doesn't *sound* like a compliment,' Meredith pointed out.

'Let's see how you feel after you've had his fish and chips,' Ben said. 'You can decide whether he's made the right decision after that.'

'And he's already in with the community,' Meredith added. 'He's judging the cook-off tomorrow, ingratiating himself with the great and good of Port Karadow.'

'By which you mean Adrian,' Finn said, and it was his turn to grin.

'It's a good move, is all I'm saying.' Meredith turned to Thea. 'My boss at Cornish Keepsakes, Adrian, is a little bit obsessed with the hierarchy in this town, singling out anyone who's rich, famous or noteworthy in some way. He sees himself as some sort of Port Karadow socialite, and even though that sounds pretty terrible, he's a genuinely lovely man, so it's easy to forgive his pretentiousness. Marcus Belrose getting involved in the cook-off so soon after moving here – and he's running a barbecue stall on the beach, just at weekends during the summer, I think – anyway, it shows that he's savvy.'

'You don't need to be here for very long to realise there's a tight community,' Ben said. Thea thought back to his comments outside the Old Post House: that people had been kind to him, and he was determined to repay some of that kindness.

A waiter brought a large platter of crispy-coated prawns to their table, alongside a dressed salad and a generous pot of mayonnaise that smelt so citrussy Thea could feel her taste buds coming to life.

'Wow,' she murmured, as they all reached for side plates and started dipping the golden morsels in the mayonnaise.

After a few moments of contented eating, Ben said, 'This is doing nothing for my nerves. His standards aren't exactly low.'

'But he knows he's not judging Michelin-starred chefs,' Finn said, serving salad onto each of their plates. 'And *you* know you're good enough.'

'When did you get into cooking?' Thea asked. 'Is it something you've always loved?'

'Not really,' he said, shrugging. 'I helped Dad out when I was growing up – he was the cook in the family, rather than Mum, and it was something we could do together – and then, when I got older, it made sense for me to do an equal share. I was good at it, and it was a lot more fun than homework.

'Then, once I'd moved out, a friend of mine opened a pub in the village I was living in, and employed this really great chef, Claude. I was blown away by the food, how he transformed traditional pub grub into original, creative dishes. I started testing out new recipes at home, teaching myself techniques. This is the first time I'm trying them out on anyone other than friends or family.'

'Is that because you're new here?' Thea asked. 'Something you wanted to do as part of your fresh start?'

'Something like that,' Ben said, turning his attention to his last prawn.

Finn clapped Ben on the shoulder. 'That whole community thing? He caught on quickly that you can't live in Port Karadow and keep to yourself. He would have been dragged into the town's clutches soon enough, so he took the initiative.'

Ben rolled his eyes. 'You make it sound like a cult.'

'Maybe it is,' Finn replied mildly. 'You've only been here four months.'

'And *you* only moved here permanently at Christmastime,' Meredith said to Finn. 'What if there's stuff *you* don't know about?' She raised a teasing eyebrow at her boyfriend, and then said, 'What made you pick Port Karadow for your holiday, Thea? As . . .' her eyes flicked to the two men sitting opposite them, ' . . . as the place to work through your bucket list?'

Thea gave her a grateful smile. She hadn't specifically told Meredith not to mention the bookshop, and appreciated her tact. 'I came here once before, when I was about ten. It was an unplanned stopover at the end of a longer holiday, and . . . I don't know.' She sighed. 'We'd been all over, visited Penzance and Falmouth and some of the smaller, pretty villages, but I loved Port Karadow instantly.

'My dad bought me a book in the bookshop, and we ate fish and chips on the harbour. It felt so welcoming. You know when you visit somewhere and the atmosphere is good, or . . .' she shook her head. 'It's more than that. It feels right for you? It feels like there's something personal, between you and the place.' She adjusted her cutlery, then looked up.

'But it was such a long time ago,' she continued, 'and this is the first time I've been back.' It was her turn to glance at Ben and Finn. They were both listening intently, and she felt a shiver of nerves, as if she was only wearing her underwear, rather than a pretty dress. 'When Esme, my friend, suggested a holiday together, and asked if there was anywhere I really wanted to go, I knew I had to find out.'

'Find out what?' Ben asked.

'If the place I remembered, that had seemed so welcoming, was just as I'd imagined it, or if it was one of those rose-tinted memories that dissolves when you try to recreate it: you know, like how tinned ravioli was the most delicious thing when you were little, but if you have it as a grown-up, it tastes horrible.'

'*Tinned* ravioli?' Ben said, aghast.

Before Thea could reply, Finn said, 'And what's your verdict?' A waitress came to take away their starter plates, put full beer bottles on the table.

Thea took a breath. 'It's perfect,' she said. It came out sounding slightly sad, because even though it was true, she couldn't help thinking about Jamie Scable, and the big hole he'd kicked in her plans.

'Perfect for what?' Ben asked. 'For a holiday?' The way he said it, she knew he'd realised there was more to it.

Their main courses arrived, and because Thea had had fish and chips in Padstow the day before, she had gone for a grilled pork chop with creamy horseradish mash. Meredith had chosen crab linguine, and Finn and Ben had opted for fish and chips. Thea took it all in: the bright pop of the slow-roasted cherry tomatoes on her plate, the sunshine joy of a basket of golden chips, the tantalising smells of well seasoned, cooked-to-perfection food wafting up to meet her.

There was a reverent silence as they gazed at their meals, and then, very quietly, Ben said, 'Fuck.'

'You'll be great tomorrow Benjamin,' Finn said. 'And I bet none of the other competitors are here tonight; you're ahead of the game.'

'At this point I think ignorance would have been a better tactic,' he replied, spearing a chip with his fork. 'I was nervous before, but . . .'

'Your food is *easily* as good as this,' Thea said, after she'd had a mouthful of tender, juicy pork and creamy mashed potato.

Ben raised his eyebrows. 'Really?'

'Oh yeah,' she said, and she meant it. 'I've eaten your hash browns, remember. I have a unique ability to give you honest, unbiased feedback, and I can confirm your food is as good as Marcus Belrose's.'

Ben caught her gaze, and despite the food that commanded to be eaten and enjoyed, the chatter and clink of glasses around them, the sun hovering above the clear line of the sea, turning it to liquid gold, she couldn't look away. She wanted Ben to see that she had faith in him, that she believed he could do anything he set his mind to. What would be less welcome, she realised, was if she also telepathically conveyed the way looking into his hazel eyes made her stomach feel almost too full of fluttering wings to admit any more of her dinner, or her urge to put her hand on his strong, tanned arm, and feel how warm his skin was. She cleared her throat and gave him a bright, unwavering smile.

'Thank you,' he said quietly, and at that moment Thea thought she could see the colours of the sunset in his irises, competing with the blues and greens that were already there.

'Unbiased, huh?' Meredith said lightly, and Thea knew she hadn't quite got away with it.

They declared themselves too full for dessert, split the bill, and then, after a round of thank yous and goodbye hugs, Meredith and Finn set off towards the town centre, walking back to Meredith's house that was on the north side. Thea and Ben turned in the opposite direction, their own walk to the cottages quicker, as they were already on the right side of Port Karadow.

The temperature had dropped, and Thea was glad she'd brought a cardigan with her. They passed houses with cosy lights filtering through thin curtains, outdoor lamps shining like torch flames against a sky that was inky blue high above them, a richer hue closer to the horizon, where the sun hadn't quite relinquished its hold on the day. Thea felt as if they were in a storybook illustration, the buildings dark silhouettes against a dreamy summer's night, the cobbled path they were on gleaming beneath the soft street lights, disappearing into nothing.

She had loved spending time with Meredith, Finn and Ben, and could see how, if her plans worked out, she would have friends in her new town, everything shiny and full of hope.

Ben's next words crystallised her thoughts, his voice sounding loud in the still night air. 'You said earlier that Port Karadow lived up to your memory of it: that it was perfect. Was that just about having a holiday here, or is there more to it?'

'There's more to it,' Thea said, after a moment. 'Something I've been planning for a while. A dream I have.'

'I like hearing other people's dreams,' Ben said. They were walking so close together that she could feel his warmth down her left side, and thought how easy it would be to slip her arm through his.

'I want to open a bookshop by the sea,' she said instead. 'I remember the one that used to be here, even though I only went there once. This has been my life plan, for a long time now. And Port Karadow has always been there, like . . .' she thought how best to explain it. 'Like the brightest star you see whenever you stop to look up at the night sky. You know it's there, but you don't really focus on it when there are a whole load of stars to take in. But now my business plan's finished, and I've saved up enough to take the first steps towards making it happen, I'm focusing all my attention on that bright star.' She took a deep breath. 'So here I am.'

Ben's easy stride faltered, and she felt his fingers brush against hers. She didn't know if he'd done it on purpose. 'You want to move here?' he said. 'To open a bookshop?'

'If I can find the right premises,' she replied. 'There are still a lot of hurdles and hoops, a whole obstacle course, really, between me and pulling open the front door to receive my first customers, but now I'm here, I want my bookshop to be here, too.'

'You're going to move here,' Ben said again.

'Possibly,' she admitted. 'But it's all – I haven't told very many people. I'm still feeling things out.' She thought of Jamie Scable and his blatant dismissal of her. 'There's a long way to go.'

'You can do it, though,' Ben said. They'd reached the edge of town, and all that was left between them and the cottages was the pathway on top of the cliffs. The sea was a huge, shadowy expanse, white where the moonlight skimmed it, the stars flickering high above them. 'If you want it enough, you can do it.'

'Like you and the cook-off,' Thea said, wanting to deflect attention away from herself. 'You can do that, too.'

Ben laughed, the sound low and warm, heating up Thea's blood. 'One cooking competition isn't quite the same as a whole life plan.'

'But every big thing starts with a single step, doesn't it?' she said. 'Just because this competition is one afternoon rather than the rest of your life, it doesn't make it any less important. I walked into a bookshop, smelled its wholesome, comforting smell, ran my fingers along the spines and picked out a story I thought I'd love. Now, I want to open my own. You don't know where things might lead.'

He glanced at her, but she couldn't read his expression in the moonlight. She gave a jolt of surprise when he flicked on a torch she hadn't known he was carrying, lighting the path ahead. 'Just thought we might want to see what's in front of us,' he said.

'Good idea.' She reached out and squeezed his fingers: just once, for no more than a second.

It wasn't until after they'd said goodbye, and she'd heard Scooter's jubilant greeting as Ben opened his front door, that Thea realised he hadn't questioned her plan. He hadn't asked her why she wanted to do it, or if she thought she was really capable, or whether she thought it might be better to set her sights slightly lower, be a bit more modest. He'd simply told her she could do it, if she wanted it enough. She realised it was a long time since she'd been aware of anyone having that much brazen faith in her, least of all herself.

# Chapter Eleven

There were ten of them altogether, lined up in a row. Six men and four women, standing behind charcoal barbecues that they had brought with them – gas barbecues weren't allowed on the beach – large cool boxes at their feet. They all looked incredibly focused, as if they were preparing for a World Championship 100-metre sprint instead of a friendly BBQ competition. The smell of charcoal tainted the warm sea air, and Thea's stomach rumbled in time to the background beat of music that added to the carnival atmosphere. Luckily, there were several food trucks lined up in the car park at the edge of the sand, because it was the judges who would get to taste the competitors' food, not the crowd.

The beach, the one the Happy Shack looked out over, wasn't that far from the twin cottages, and now that she was standing on it, Thea could see that it belonged on postcards and wall calendars. It was a long strip of golden sand, the sea a deep blue swell that came in to meet it, and on a sunny Friday afternoon in June, it was attracting the crowds. Not only was it bigger than many other beaches around here – this stretch of coastline mostly littered with crevices and coves – but the currents weren't as treacherous. Because of this, it also had a lifeguard station, so it was perfect for swimming, kite-surfing, and family days out.

When Thea had arrived with Meredith and Finn, she'd been worried they wouldn't be able to find Ben, but the cook-off had been easy to spot, the barbecues gleaming in the sun and an audience starting to gather.

'He looks very serious, doesn't he?' Meredith said.

She was standing between Thea and Finn, with Crumble at her feet. The beagle was exploring as far as his short lead would allow, while Scooter stood, poised and serene, at Thea's side. She had her hand on the dog's head, his soft fur filling the spaces between her fingers. She felt a swell of pride that he'd picked her to stand beside while his master was otherwise engaged.

'They all look like they're about to have a hernia,' Finn replied. 'Honestly, it's just barbecue.'

There was a gasp from behind them, a few whispered mutterings, and Meredith laughed. 'Way to make friends, Finn. And you know how much this means to Ben. If it was a painting competition, like those *Big Painting Challenge* things on the BBC, you'd be fully invested.'

Finn's blond curls ruffled in the breeze. 'I wouldn't be, because I know I'd win.'

Meredith's laugh was louder this time. 'Good to see you're so humble about it.'

'I'd love to see your paintings some time,' Thea said.

'There are a few on display in a local gallery,' Finn told her. 'They look much more impressive than the works in progress in my studio, but I don't mind showing you those, if you want. Lots of options.' He shrugged, giving her his easy smile.

'I'd be happy with the gallery or studio,' she said. 'Whatever you want me to see.' She turned back to the competitors, peering over the heads of the people standing in front of them. 'Who are the other judges for this competition, aside from Marcus Belrose, and when do we get to eat barbecue?'

Meredith grinned, gesturing to the food trucks that already had queues forming behind them. 'We're not going to miss out. And the judges are Max – he runs the Sea Brew café on Main Street, and was instrumental in setting up this whole thing. Then the guy on the end, the one with thick black hair and the designer beard?' Thea nodded. 'That's Marcus: he's the one everyone will be trying to impress.'

'Not surprising,' Thea said, thinking back to their food the evening before. She watched as the chef inspected the crockery and cutlery lined up on the long trestle table in front of the three judges. 'It looks like he's going to be a tough cookie.'

'I don't doubt it,' Meredith said. 'But Nick, on the end there, balances things out. He's my best friend's husband. Anisha works at the council, which is how he got the gig because he's not a food connoisseur – though he'll be very appreciative of everyone's dishes.' She raised a hand, and the brown-haired man on the end grinned and waved back. 'Anisha's around here somewhere, but she's got her two kids, Jasmine and Ravi, and they might have got bored already. I'll introduce you as soon as I can – she'd love to meet you.'

'That would be great,' Thea said. She was about to ask what Anisha did at the council, when there was a squeal from a loudspeaker.

'OK then, folks!' The compère was familiar, and it took Thea a moment to recognise him as the man she'd spoken to outside Cornish Keepsakes. He was wearing a white, short-sleeved shirt and dark trousers, and a tie with cartoon cuts of meat on it – ham legs, chicken thighs and steaks. He stood in front of the crowd, while the competitors behind him prodded at their charcoal, making sure it was hot enough, Thea supposed.

'Welcome to the Port Karadow summer barbecue cook-off!' he declared. 'We have ten eager cooks ready to wow the judges with their culinary skills, and we hope you'll all cheer them on while they barbecue their hearts out. The rules are simple: one complete dish, forty-five minutes to perfect it. You lot can enjoy the beach and the food trucks while we wait to see who will be crowned the winner!'

There were whoops from the crowd as he gestured to the competitors, and said, 'Ready, barbecuers?'

'Ready!' they chorused back.

'Excellent! Three . . . two . . . one! Happy cooking!'

'That,' Meredith said, 'is my boss, Adrian, who I told you about last night. I wonder where his wife, Tillie, is . . .'

While Meredith scanned the crowd, Thea watched as the ten hopefuls got to work. She had to acknowledge that it wasn't quite as exciting as runners sprinting off their starting blocks. They bent down, opened their cool boxes, and began to pull out ingredients, arranging them on the tables they'd been provided with. While they did that, Adrian explained the origins of the cook-off and introduced the judges – Nick Glynn, Max Holden from Sea Brew and Marcus Belrose, owner of the Happy Shack.

Nick and Max waved eagerly to the crowd, and Marcus gave a cool nod that suggested he knew just how good he was. Thea wrinkled her nose and crouched to check on Scooter, who nudged his wet nose briefly against hers. She stroked his ears, then turned to pat Crumble while Adrian introduced the competitors.

She stood up, slipped her feet out of her flip-flops so she could feel the sand between her toes, and was wondering if they'd have a chance to go paddling after the competition, when she heard Adrian say, 'And now we come to Ben Senhouse. A builder by trade, he moved to Port Karadow earlier this year, and this is his first time competing at a cook-off. We have been positively salivating at his dish: rack of beef with his own-recipe hot sauce, barbecued potato rösti and creamed spinach.' There was a smattering of applause and a few 'Oooohs' from the crowd. 'We asked each of our competitors for a little-known fact about themselves, and Ben has told us that he . . . ah . . .' there was a chuckle through the loudspeaker, and the sound of ruffling paper. 'It seems we're missing that bit of information. Never mind! We'll speak to our hopefuls throughout, just to put them off their stride, so we can get a factual nugget from him then.'

Thea smiled, thinking it was typical of Ben not to want to share a soundbite about himself. He was wearing a black T-shirt and long denim shorts with frayed hems, his hair ruffling in the breeze while he shredded potato and made sure his ribs were fully marinated. He moved between the table and the barbecue with easy confidence, as he had done in her kitchen. He looked tanned and healthy, tall and strong – *potent*, Thea thought – while a few of the other competitors looked like they spent more time eating their food than cooking it.

'I hope he wins,' she murmured. She glanced to the side and discovered that Meredith had slipped away, and Finn had taken her place.

'You know,' he said, 'I think he'll actually care, too.'

Thea laughed. 'Why do you say it like that?'

'Because Ben makes a big show of being nonplussed about most things, but it's a defence mechanism. This competition, though, he's definitely bothered about, but I think if he comes last, he'll shrug it off. Then he'll go back to his house and angrily saw some wood.' Finn turned to Thea. 'You like him, don't you?'

'We're friends,' she said quickly. 'As much as you can be with someone you only met a few days ago. But after last night . . . I'm really grateful to all of you – you, Meredith and Ben – for letting me attach myself to you.'

'You're not a stray orphan in need of adopting,' Finn said, then looked horrified. 'Unless—'

Thea laughed. 'No, my parents are still alive, but you're much more fun to hang out with. In the case of my mum, you're much calmer, too.'

Presley Rushwood, Thea's mum, waltzed through the world expecting everyone to pay attention to her, entirely confident that she was worth the spotlight. She was a publicist for a cosmetics company in London, but spent an equal amount of time promoting herself to whoever seemed influential at the time. Thea's introversions and insecurities partly came from not wanting to be like her, for resisting when Presley had tried to mould her in her own image.

'I'm calmer than your mum?' Finn raised an eyebrow.

'So far,' Thea said, and Finn laughed.

'I know a little about overbearing mothers,' he said softly, then, before he could say anything else, their attention was dragged back to the competition, because one of the competitor's barbecues had tipped over, spilling coals onto the sand, and there were cries of alarm from the audience. He rescued his chicken thighs just in time, but Adrian made the most of the drama, ramping up his patter like a commentator at the end of a horse race.

Through it all, Ben remained focused, though at one point he glanced up and caught Thea's eye. She smiled encouragingly, and he returned it, the simple gesture tugging at something deep inside her. It was a disconcerting feeling, and she chose to put it down to mild heatstroke.

Meredith returned with her friend Anisha, a polished, put-together woman whose large dark eyes were warm and intelligent, and who greeted Thea enthusiastically. She explained that her parents had taken her children back to their house, because they were full of ice cream and getting fractious. She smiled and waved at Nick, distracting him from the incredibly serious job of walking along the line of chefs, inspecting the food they were about to eat.

'He's trying to be like Paul Hollywood,' Anisha said. 'But he doesn't have it in him. He's far too nice.'

'He'll give everything a nine or ten,' Meredith added. 'Eight and a half for the inedible ones.'

Anisha laughed. 'Handshakes all round from my husband.'

'Hopefully he'll give Ben a ten,' Thea said. 'If – is he even allowed to judge Ben, if they know each other?'

'Everyone in Port Karadow knows everyone else,' Finn said. 'The only one who's new enough not to be influenced is Marcus Bellend, or whatever his name is.'

They all laughed, and got a sharp look from Adrian, who was gearing up for the five-minute countdown.

When the cooking time was up, there was a long period while the judges tasted every dish in turn, the crowd straining to get a good look at each one and – if they were anything like Thea – wishing they could try them all, too. There was a lot of deliberating while the competitors stood in their line, looking like naughty schoolchildren ready for a telling-off, and Thea saw Ben rub a hand across the back of his neck.

'Wonderful, wonderful,' Adrian said eventually, coming to stand in front of the crowd, clutching a piece of paper. 'I have the results! Congratulations, all of you, on an incredibly high standard of barbecuing. I've tasted a few, and I can safely say you'd all be invited to cater my summer party. The judges were very impressed, and it was hard to narrow it down to a top three, but they *have* made a decision. So, without further ado, here's the moment you've all been waiting for. In third place, we have Melvin Nungent, with his Cornish mixed grill. Wonderful effort, Melvin!' The man, who looked to be in his early twenties, greeted Adrian against a soundtrack of rapturous applause, collecting a trophy that looked plastic, and an envelope that Meredith whispered to Thea contained a voucher for the Happy Shack.

'Now, on to second place. It was a close-run thing between the top two, but as runner-up in the competition we're very happy to have the man of mystery himself, Ben Senhouse, with his beef ribs and hot sauce. Congratulations, Ben! Those potato rösti were something special.'

Thea watched Ben's expression go from tense to surprised, and then, when he stepped forward, into a wall of enthusiastic clapping, he was smiling. Thea applauded harder than anyone.

'Thanks,' Ben said to Adrian, collecting his trophy and envelope, posing with the judges for the local press photographer. When he was done, instead of returning to his barbecue, he came over to them.

'Well done my man,' Finn murmured, patting him on the back.

'Amazing!' Meredith hugged him, followed by Anisha.

Ben turned to Thea, and she tuned out Adrian's voice, feeling only slightly guilty that she wasn't paying attention to the winner.

'You were brilliant,' she whispered, wondering if she should hug him, too. She smiled, self-conscious, as Ben stepped closer and put his arms around her, making the decision for her, and she threaded her fingers behind his neck. He was much hotter than her, his nape damp with sweat, and he smelled of charcoal and beef and some cologne that was rich with spice and vanilla. Thea was slightly overcome by the assault on her senses.

'Ribs was the right call,' he murmured into her ear. 'Thank you.'

'I didn't do anything,' she said, laughing. 'It was all you. Congratulations, Ben.'

They broke apart to cheer the winner, a woman called Sally Bailey, who had made a fish feast of lobster, prawns, scallops and whitebait.

Adrian closed the competition with as much enthusiasm as he'd opened it, and the crowd and competitors began to disperse. Anisha joined Nick, and Ben went to clear up his workstation. Thea, Meredith and Finn followed him, as if they were band groupies with a new frontman to adore.

'What's this?!' Thea squeaked when she saw Ben's barbecue, which, far from being empty, had another rack of ribs on it, and a whole pile of golden potato rösti.

He grinned. 'I couldn't let you miss out, could I? There were no rules about only cooking enough for the judges, and I had some extra space and ingredients, so . . .' He pulled paper plates out of his rucksack, moved the ribs to the chopping board on his table and began portioning them up.

'You absolute legend,' Finn said, rubbing his hands together.

'My mouth is watering,' Meredith added, and Scooter, who had stayed so politely by Thea's side for the whole event, sprang up and put his front paws on the table. She just managed to pull him down before he got his nose in the food.

'Sorry!' she gasped, as Ben blinked in surprise. 'I didn't—'

'It's not you,' he said, his eyes trained on his dog. 'Scooter, what the hell? Was that really necessary?'

The dog dipped his head and put his paw over his nose in a comically repentant gesture. Thea laughed and crouched down to hug him.

'He's usually so well-behaved,' Ben said.

'Your hot sauce must be irresistible.' Finn gripped Ben's shoulder. 'Your dog hasn't been possessed by a demon, he's just after a bit of barbecue.'

Ben nodded, and Thea saw his chest rise and fall in a sigh. She stroked Scooter and whispered nonsensical things into his ear, and when Ben had served the food, he came around the table and crouched in front of them both.

'Hey,' he said, in the low, soothing voice Thea had come to recognise. 'Scooter.' The dog looked up. 'I'm sorry, OK? It was a surprise, that's all. I love you, dude, don't worry.' He ran his hand over the dog's head and down his back, and after a moment Scooter padded forward and pressed his nose into Ben's neck.

As Thea watched the exchange, her pulse quickened, and she thought her heart might be in danger of exploding because it was, hands down, the most adorable thing she'd ever seen. She stood up and stepped back, and Meredith gently nudged her ribs.

'Imagine if he'd done that with his T-shirt off,' she whispered. 'Mind you, black looks good on him, don't you think?'

Thea gave her what she hoped was a serene smile, and picked up her plate.

Anisha and Nick returned briefly to say goodbye, then went to collect their kids, and Thea joined Meredith, Finn and Ben on a patch of sand close to the gentle, froth-trimmed waves. They ate Ben's award-winning food, throwing plaudits at him between mouthfuls until he raised his hands and told them to 'stop now, please,' and Thea realised that there was nowhere else in the world she would rather be.

Then Finn shattered her happiness with one, simple sentence that made her question whether it had been a good idea to hook up with these people, after all.

'I hope this has put you all in a competitive frame of mind,' he said, around a mouthful of potato, 'because I've entered us as a team for the sand sculpture competition on Sunday.'

# Chapter Twelve

Thea discovered, that Friday afternoon, that Ben's stubbornness wasn't quite a match for Finn's. As the two of them had a verbal battle on the beach, she and Meredith had to avoid each other's gazes for fear of bursting into laughter that, she was sure, neither man would appreciate.

Ben said he categorically wasn't taking part in the sand sculpture competition, and Finn was adamant that he was, and Thea wondered how the two friends would compare in a game of Top Trumps: Ben, stoic and thoughtful, his kindness and loyalty running like an underground river, underpinning everything; Finn, generous and effusive, with charm in abundance and an ability to persuade. She had a soft spot for Ben, of course, but that was only because she'd spent more time with him.

Finn eventually won the argument by appealing to the other man's ego, suggesting they only had a chance of winning with a visionary builder on their team. Thea hid her smile behind her hand and Meredith guffawed into Crumble's fur.

When Finn went to get drinks from one of the refreshment trucks, Ben said, without any prompting, 'I only agreed to it to shut him up.'

'Not because he said you were a visionary?' Meredith asked sweetly.

Ben huffed. 'No, because I'm not. Anyway, you're both a part of this too, and I think we need to agree now that the best way to get through it is to do everything Finn says. Make what he wants us to make, take on the roles he assigns us. It'll be a few hours of torture, then it'll be done.'

'I'm bowled over by your enthusiasm,' Finn said as he returned, and Ben's cheeks coloured. 'But it's a good plan. I can come up with an idea before Sunday, think about what will give us the best chance of winning. I'll start working on it now.'

'It's just a friendly competition, Finn,' Meredith said, laughing. 'A bit of fun.'

'And if everyone else goes into it with that attitude, then we're even more likely to win,' Finn replied with a smile. Thea could see the glint in his eye, and realised he was as bothered about the outcome as Ben had been about his barbecuing.

They got back to the twin cottages late on Friday evening, the burning sun hovering above the calm shimmer of the sea. It would soon be the longest day of the year, Thea realised, her thoughts contentedly sluggish after hours outside and too much good food.

They reached Ben's door, and she paused. 'Congratulations again,' she said. 'Second place for your first cook-off is pretty incredible.'

'I'm pleased,' he replied, smiling. 'And look, about Sunday. You don't have to come if you don't want to. I know Finn can be . . .'

'Excitable?'

'Overbearing. And I get the sense that he's going to be unbearable over this.'

'I came here to have a proper holiday,' Thea said. 'But if it wasn't for you, Finn and Meredith, I would be reading out here,' she gestured at the garden furniture, 'going for long, hopeless hikes, and drifting through Port Karadow like a lonely ghost. I've had so much fun today, I've ticked another thing off my list, and sand sculpting isn't going to take me as far out of my comfort zone as coasteering would.'

'You keep telling yourself that,' Ben said gently, and when Thea couldn't hide her surprise, he grinned. 'Whatever mad suggestion Finn throws at us, we'll weather it together. You don't have to worry with me there to back you up.'

Later, when Thea crawled into bed, tired and happy, it was Ben's last words that kept going round and round in her head.

Thea allowed herself the laziest of Saturdays. She refused to let her thoughts drift to the unsatisfying meeting with Jamie Scable or the fact that, after his initial encouragement, Alex hadn't been in touch to ask how it had gone. The stubborn part of her didn't want to call him first, and the confident part told her she could do it all by herself anyway, so instead she spent her time sitting outside, reading *Book Lovers* by Emily Henry – she had finished the Elly Griffiths book – and researching sand sculptures.

It seemed all that was required was sand and water, though you had to be strategic about the water quantities and placement, and she couldn't imagine that the four of them would get anywhere close to the dragons and fairy-tale castles posted all over Instagram under the appropriate hashtags. If Finn was really expecting to win, then she was worried they were facing a day of stress followed by inevitable disappointment.

As Saturday afternoon shifted towards evening, the nerves started to creep up on her. Performing was very much not her thing: she was much happier standing on the sidelines or in the background, cheering people on as loudly as she could, or working behind the scenes, organising author talks and events at the library. The only time she made it to the front of a crowd was during the toddler groups. She never felt judged at those, because the toddlers were giddy at being read to, and the parents were grateful for an hour's pause in their busy lives.

Experience had taught her that she wasn't one of life's leaders, that her confidence lay with her knowledge of books and the library, and she would rather not put herself on show when someone might find a reason to laugh at her or mock her. Would there be a crowd watching on Sunday, like there had been on Friday? Would judges walk past, pensive looks on their faces while they scrutinised her efforts? Would there be—

She jumped as a door opened, and looked up from her book. Ben and Scooter were standing on the doorstep, the dog pulling on his lead to get closer.

'I'm taking Scooter for his walk,' Ben said. 'Do you want to come?'

Thea hesitated. She wanted to say yes, she realised. Except that she knew she would end up telling him how nervous she was about tomorrow, that she didn't think she could do it, even though it was a friendly, fun competition. But Ben wasn't an agony uncle, and she found it slightly disconcerting that she wanted to spill all her insecurities to him after only a few days in his company.

'Thanks,' she said, 'but I've got a lasagne in the oven.' It wasn't entirely true, but it would be the moment he walked away.

'You made lasagne?'

'No! I bought one of those ready meals from the shop. Sorry.'

'Ah.'

'If I'd made it, then I would have invited you round to show off,' she said. 'Except that I would also be a little bit worried about poisoning you.'

Ben laughed. 'If you made lasagne and invited me, then I'd gladly accept, and I wouldn't be worried about poisoning. At least,' he hesitated, 'I wouldn't be *that* worried. I might casually ask for a rundown of the ingredients, just to check there was no arsenic or cyanide, that sort of thing.'

Thea nodded, feigning seriousness. 'I *do* sometimes get *Healthy, Hearty Food* and *The Poisoner's Handbook* confused at work. But I think, on the whole, it's a great idea. Me, cooking: you, eating.'

'It's a date, then.' His eyebrows rose, as if his own words had surprised him, and he quickly added, 'Not a *date*, date, or anything. Just that . . .'

'A repayment, of sorts,' Thea said, rescuing him. 'You made me breakfast, and I'd like to make you dinner in return.'

Ben nodded, his Adam's apple bobbing. He was embarrassed, she thought, and for once in her life she wasn't, though she didn't quite understand why not. 'Thanks,' he said quietly. 'I'd better walk Scooter, or he'll pull off the lead and find some furrow to hole up in, and I won't find him for hours.'

Scooter was gazing up at Thea while she stroked his nose, looking as if the last thing on his mind was hiding somewhere on the wild Cornish clifftops. Still, she said, 'Of course. See you tomorrow, then.'

'Yeah. Looking forward to it.'

She watched them stroll towards the road in the soft evening light, Scooter's fur hauntingly pale. The air was cool and pleasant, and she could just make out the distant shapes of fishing boats on the blue water. As dusk slunk over the land and sea, she knew those smudges would become glimmering lights in the gloom.

She wished, now, that she'd gone with them, exploring the countryside in the setting sun. She would feel safe with Ben and Scooter. But she didn't want to use him as a sounding board for her worries when he'd already done so much for her, and it was clear he was embarrassed about the date slip-up.

Thea went inside and got her pre-made lasagne out of the fridge, scanning the ingredients on the back. She would need to look up a proper recipe, get everything in beforehand. Maybe there was a deli somewhere nearby where she could buy proper Italian pasta and cheese. If there was, then it would be another reason why Port Karadow was the perfection location for her: she was finding more of those every day.

* * *

'If we make the sand a bit wetter here, then we could fix that part of it.'

'You mean the bit that's supposed to be the cliff, but now looks like a terrible landslide has occurred?' Meredith gazed up at Finn, who was standing, hands on hips, looking down at their sculpture.

'We just need to shore it up,' Finn said. 'The good thing about a sand sculpture is that it's easily fixable.'

'Because it's so soft,' Meredith replied. 'So it collapses *constantly*, but that's fine because we can just repair it for the fiftieth time? If this was stone, we'd be laughing.'

'If it was stone, then this wouldn't be a sand sculpture competition, would it? And stone takes years to carve. Just think of Michelangelo,' he said, and Meredith's face softened, something passing between them that Thea couldn't interpret. She turned away, fixing her focus on the other competitors, trying to work out how they were getting on.

They were back on the beautiful beach, though this competition was taking up a much bigger portion than the cook-off, each team needing a large space to work with. On one side of them, there was a group of intense-looking teenagers, making what looked like a secret garden. Thea could identify a tree and a bench, and was trying not to be too impressed because it was still early days. On the other side, there were four people who looked around the same age as their team – late twenties or early thirties. Meredith had been chatting to a tall, red-haired woman when she and Ben had arrived, and there was something familiar about the handsome man with dark blond hair, who seemed more focused than the other three. The other man on their team looked like he'd given up already, and was scanning the area where the food trucks were, his arms crossed.

'Daniel, are you even paying attention?' A slight, dark-haired woman asked him.

'Not really,' the man – who must be called Daniel – replied. 'Is Marcus Belrose's food truck here?'

'Worried about the competition?' the redhead said, giving him an affectionate smile. 'Don't be, honestly. I'm the one with the portable beach café. What if everyone wants barbecue food instead of a cream tea?'

'Most people probably want both,' Thea called, because she couldn't help it. 'I know I do.'

Their whole team turned to look at her, and she dipped her head, embarrassed.

'That's good to know,' the redhead said, smiling. 'We're serving cream teas all afternoon.'

'You are?'

Meredith knelt beside Thea. 'This is Charlie,' she said. 'She runs the Cornish Cream Tea Bus, the big glossy double-decker up there. I can confirm that her scones, her *everything*, are delicious.'

Thea looked at the gleaming red bus parked between a burrito stall and a retro Citroën van selling coffee. The tables outside it were busy, a queue snaking out of the doorway.

'Our friends Hannah and Noah are running it while we're doing this,' the dark-haired woman chipped in. 'I'm beginning to understand why they were so eager to volunteer.' She sat back and held up her sand-caked hands. 'I am never, ever going to be free of this stuff. I'm going to be finding it in my underwear for *weeks* after this!'

'A hazard of living in Cornwall,' Finn called over. He was crouched next to his bit of their less than impressive sculpture. 'Maybe the eight of us should join forces? We could produce something a lot more impressive with double the troops.'

'Not sure that's allowed,' Ben murmured. 'But even if it is, you think we'll actually be able to make something that looks like what we intend it to?'

'Nope,' Daniel said. 'Not a chance. I say we quit while we're nowhere close to ahead.'

'Not yet,' Finn replied. 'I'm not giving up yet.'

Thea wondered if Charlie, Daniel and their friends had also looked up photos, just like she had, and had imagined – again like her – that they might be able to get somewhere close to those designs. But, she was both disappointed and heartened to see, she couldn't work out what they were trying to create, either.

Their offering was supposed to be a place nearby called Charmed Cove. Meredith had said she would take Thea there one day, so they could go swimming. Finn had suggested a layout that included the cliffs and the sea, a house halfway up the hill that he said was his aunt's place, a large, flat rock on the beach, and people swimming. It had sounded ambitious from the start and, now that they were halfway through their two-hour timeframe, it was proving impossible.

'Our swimmers look like Morph from *Hartbeat* got too close to the open fire,' Thea said. She was the one who had tried to make them, so she was allowed to criticise them.

'My house could be a house, or a caravan, or a shed, or maybe just a box.' Ben shrugged, appraising the lump of sand he was working on.

'We need to get the main shapes and placement right, then we can focus on the detail.' Finn wasn't deterred in the slightest. He had his shirtsleeves rolled up to the elbows, and his blond curls were tight in the heat.

They were all covered in sand, and Thea was glad she'd worn her shabbiest vest top and shorts over her swimming costume. She'd tied her hair away from her face, but her neck felt hot below the bun that had slipped down over the course of the afternoon, and was now hanging at her nape. Ben was somehow remaining unflustered in a T-shirt with a San Francisco motif on the front and navy cargo shorts, though his hairline was dark with sweat.

It was too hot to be doing this, Thea decided, so she allowed herself to be distracted. 'What are you making?' she called to their neighbours. Daniel had given up completely, sitting on the sand and typing on his phone, while the others kept going.

'It's a scene from *Estelle*,' the dark-haired woman explained. 'With the big spooky mansion, and the clifftops, and the ghost.'

'I love *Estelle*,' Meredith said. 'Finn's aunt Laurie has got a small role in the next series. I think she's due to start filming in August.'

'Really?' The sandy-haired man, who Thea sort-of recognised, looked up. 'Laurie Becker? She's your aunt?'

Before Finn had a chance to reply, Meredith's eyes widened. 'Oh my God, you're Sam Magee! And you're – you're Delilah Forest! They're actors in *Estelle*,' she said to Thea.

Both sand sculptures were temporarily forgotten – Thea thought with quite a lot of relief – as everyone introduced themselves, they discussed *Estelle*, and Finn and Sam talked about Laurie's upcoming role in the series. Thea tried not to fangirl over the actors who, now she knew what they did, seemed to have a slightly unreal glow about them, even though they came across as down-to-earth, no airs or graces in sight.

'This is shit isn't it?' Delilah – Lila – said to Thea. 'Not the best way to spend a summer afternoon.'

'I don't mind the beach part,' Thea admitted, 'but this feels like too much hard work for something we're definitely going to fail at.'

'Exactly,' Lila said. 'Sam's intent on finishing ours, but the rest of us would be happy to give up – except I suppose I have to be a *little* bit loyal to my beloved boyfriend.' She blew Sam a kiss and he returned it with a smile.

'How about we get Finn and Sam to do both our sculptures,' Ben suggested, 'while the rest of us melt into the background and go for a cream tea instead?'

'I like your man's thinking,' Lila said to Thea.

'Oh no,' Thea rushed, 'he's not my—'

'High five!' Lila held up her hand, and Ben, rather than join in with Thea's protestations, hit it with his own.

'Right,' Daniel said, standing up and dusting down his legs, 'cream teas all round, then? Maybe that'll fuel us through to the finish line.' He headed in the direction of the bus, and Charlie watched him for a moment, before scrambling up and racing after him.

'This was the right pitch to have,' Meredith said, sighing happily.

Thea returned to her pitiful sand people, though she was at a loss as to how to improve them, while Sam kept working industriously away and Lila lay on her back and stared up at the sky, humming a tune that Thea couldn't recognise.

Charlie and Daniel returned with trays laden with cream teas in gingham-patterned cardboard boxes, and English Breakfast tea in takeaway cups, and by the time everyone had gone to wash the sand from their fingers, then dug into the delicious, warm scones – the jam sweet and sticky, the clotted cream decadently thick – the time on the clock had almost run out.

'Thank you so much,' Thea said to Charlie and Daniel, wiping the jam from her fingers with a napkin. Everyone agreed that it was just what they needed, and both teams turned back to their sculptures, even though it was clear that whatever visions they'd had at the beginning, the outcomes would fail to get anywhere close.

'It's like an episode of *Bake Off*,' Thea suggested, her mind now firmly on superior baking. 'One of those ones where it's thirty degrees inside the tent and they have to make something with ice cream or tempered chocolate.'

'Sand doesn't melt,' Finn said.

'But it's not doing what we want, is it?' Meredith replied. 'We should have got one of those really extravagant sand castle buckets and made a settlement of little castles.'

'Not sure the judges would have gone for that,' Finn murmured, moving over to where he'd started to create a sunbathing figure, partly hidden by a parasol. It was currently an indistinguishable lump, and Thea was tempted to ask him how he was going to mould a parasol when they were struggling with something as abstract as a cliff.

They soldiered on, but even Finn's enthusiasm seemed to wane, slipping through his fingers like all those grains of sand.

'I can't get this to work,' he announced, after a long time fiddling with his parasol person.

'Have any of us been able to get *anything* to work?' Charlie called over, laughing.

'Well, the boat, over there—' Finn pointed, and Thea followed his finger to where the boat had clearly had its own mini sand-slide, and now looked like a small mole hill. 'Fuck.'

'I haven't got anything to work either,' Ben said, shrugging.

'I'm having a nightmare trying to make sand look like sea,' Meredith added.

'My ghost looks like a person covered in a white sheet,' Lila said, 'if that person had crouched into a ball, and the sheet didn't have any creases in it.'

'So a blob, then?' Daniel said, and Lila grinned.

'And you know what's *really* hard?' Thea piped up.

Everyone turned to her. 'What's that?' Finn asked.

She lifted clumps of sand and let it run through her fingers. 'Making sand look like a bloody beach, which is *literally* what it is.'

There was a moment of silence and then Ben started to laugh. It was quiet to begin with, but he soon got louder, leaning over and pressing a hand to his stomach. It wasn't long before Meredith joined in, and then Charlie and Lila on the other team, and after a big, heaved sigh, Finn started laughing too, rubbing a sandy hand over his face.

Thea's own laughter came on a wave of satisfaction. She stretched her legs out and lay back on the sand, as Lila had done earlier, staring up at the blue sky, a few, meek clouds drifting across it as the wind picked up and added another complication to their task.

Both teams gave up after that, and when the competition ended and neither of their efforts got a mention, none of them were surprised, or even – she was sure, now – bothered.

They sat next to their two failed sand sculptures, clapping the intense teenagers who had won with their secret garden, and Lila and Sam went to get iced coffees from the Cornish Cream Tea Bus, which they all accepted gratefully.

'I shouldn't have taken Crumble and Scooter to Laurie's house,' Finn said. 'They would have done a better job than we did.'

'Not my Yorkipoo Marmite,' Charlie replied. 'He would have destroyed all of our attempts. It's best that he stayed on the bus.'

'Marmite would have destroyed the entire beach,' Daniel pointed out. 'No sand sculptures would have survived his curiosity. That dog could wreck an entire country fair – and almost has, in the past.'

'Hey,' Charlie said, laughing. 'You're right, though,' she admitted with a shrug.

Meredith looped her arm around Finn's shoulder, bringing their heads close. 'It was fun, and that's all that matters.'

'I suppose,' Finn said. 'Though the cream tea was the best bit.'

Charlie gave a sitting-down bow. 'My work here is done.'

'It's not an afternoon I'm going to forget in a hurry,' Thea said. 'My friend Esme will be impressed – and envious – that I've taken part in a sand sculpture competition *and* met some genuine, prime-time actors.'

Sam gave her a sheepish smile, and Lila blew her a kiss, her eyes twinkling.

'I might not send her a photo of our finished design, though,' she added.

'Send her a photo of the secret garden,' Ben said.

'Ben! That would be lying,' she replied through her laughter.

'Aren't holidays about being the opposite of proactive?' Finn said. 'Do some good day trips, sure, but in as lazy a way as possible.'

'Oh no.' Thea shook her head. 'Esme and I have a list of everything we were going to achieve. Walks, sea swims, festivals and fairs, trips to Trebah Garden and the Eden Project. None of it was going to be as much fun on my own, but it turns out that hasn't been a problem since you adopted me. And it's been really lovely to meet you all,' she added, smiling at the other team, who had begun to pack up their things.

'It's been a fun afternoon,' Charlie said. 'And great to meet you, too. I'd better go and give Hannah and Noah a break.'

'And I need to call the hotel,' Daniel said. 'See how Sunday lunch service has gone.'

There were goodbyes, heartfelt thanks for the cream teas, and Lila insisted on giving them all a hug, her sweetly floral perfume engulfing Thea. 'Come and see the bus in Porthgolow if you have time,' she said. 'Sam and I are filming at the moment, but we get occasional days off, and the bus will be open all summer.'

'I'd like that,' Thea said. 'Thank you.'

Once they'd gone, Finn flopped back on the sand, his creativity exhausted. Ben lay back on his elbows, and Thea tried not to look at the band of flat, tanned stomach that was visible where his T-shirt rode up.

'I think we've adopted each other,' Meredith said, returning to their earlier conversation. 'It's not exactly a chore, hanging out with you.'

'Likewise,' Thea replied, drawing patterns in the sand

with her toe, hiding her elation at Meredith's compliment. 'Anyway, now I've been to a cook-off, taken part in this competition, met some celebrities and had an unpleasant encounter with a landlord.'

'What?' Ben's voice was sharp. 'While you've been in Cornwall? Was this somewhere you were looking at for the bookshop?'

She hadn't meant to say that: why had it come out?

'Yes,' she murmured, less defiant now. 'That was the appointment I mentioned to you the other day. I was feeling pretty down about it, but then Meredith and I went to Padstow, and you were so kind the other night, when we were walking home from the restaurant.'

'Who was it?' Ben asked. 'The landlord.'

'He was called Jamie Scable. He's got an empty building on Main Street, a little way down from Cornish Keepsakes. It wasn't perfect, but I've got a budget to stick to, and a lot of my ideas overspill it. But he didn't . . .' She took a deep breath. She wouldn't let the feelings from that day overwhelm her again. 'He didn't think it would work.'

'What? He didn't think your bookshop would work?' Ben's voice was quiet and steady. Finn shot him a glance.

'He said it was a pie in the sky idea,' Thea admitted. 'That it wouldn't last more than a few months, and then he'd have to start the whole process again: the paperwork; the effort of finding someone else to rent it to.'

'What the hell does he know about it?' Finn asked. 'He's a landlord, I assume, rather than your business advisor?'

'Exactly,' Thea said. 'Anyway, I can't let him put me off. That can't be the only available commercial property around here, and as you say, it's not up to him.' She took a sip of her iced mocha, aware of the three pairs of eyes on her. 'The only thing is, it's really hard, I've discovered, when it's your absolute dream. A part of me has always found it difficult to believe it could actually happen, I suppose. So then, when people throw doubts at you, it's easy to catch hold of them.'

Ben scooted closer to her. He had some grains of sand stuck to his cheek, in the stubble that was mostly brown but sometimes glinted gold in the sunlight. His eyelashes were long and glossy and, as they were sitting facing the sea, the sun setting off on its daily descent towards the horizon, she could see so many colours amongst the soft brown of his eyes: green and amber, flecks of blue.

'But the way you spoke about it the other night,' he said quietly. 'You *do* believe in it, don't you? Despite what this guy, Jamie, said. You really believe that you can find the perfect place and set it up, run it the way you've been imagining? You can picture yourself doing it?'

'Oh yes,' she said instantly, because she had fantasised about it so often: helping a grandmother pick out books for her grandchildren who were coming to stay; offering suggestions to a woman who had just finished the best romcom she'd ever read and wanted more like it; even those tricky customers who knew the cover was blue and that it was a thriller, that the title contained the word 'Girl' or 'Woman' or maybe even 'Night', and being able to whittle down the possibilities and find it for them. She had imagined it so many times, played through so many scenarios, that she sometimes got a shock when she remembered she was still a library assistant. 'Yes, I believe in it,' she said again. 'I can picture myself doing it.'

Ben nodded. His legs were drawn up, his wrists resting

on his knees. His forearms were tanned, with a light dusting of brown hair, and her mind tripped back to what Meredith had said in Padstow. She wished, for just a second, that he had taken his shirt off while they were pretending they could make sand sculptures.

'Well then,' he said, bringing her out of her less-than-appropriate reverie. 'If you believe in it, then you should believe in yourself, too. Fuck Jamie Scable, and anyone who's against you. They're not worth a second of your time.'

# Chapter Thirteen

When the time came for them to leave, Thea found she didn't want to. It was close to four o'clock and the heat was, if anything, more intense. The light was bright, the sun caressing her skin, and the water looked blue and inviting. She wanted to take off her top and shorts – she had her costume on underneath – and go swimming. The make-up of the crowd on the beach had changed, families disappearing to go back to holiday homes or caravans, teenagers and groups of older friends taking their place.

'We need to head off,' Meredith said. 'We're going to Laurie's house for dinner, though how we're supposed to fit anything in after that cream tea, I don't know.'

'We can blag it,' Finn said. 'Want a lift? Laurie's coming to get us as soon as I call her, and I'm sure she'd drop you off.'

Ben glanced at Thea. 'I think I'll stay for a bit,' he said. 'Thea?'

She grinned. 'It seems a shame to waste such a perfect afternoon.'

'OK then,' Finn said. 'I'll ask Laurie to bring Scooter, as long as you don't think he's going to get in the way? Three's a crowd and all that.' He raised his eyebrows, and Ben laughed.

'No, that would be great, thanks.'

When Laurie arrived, Ben went with Finn to get Scooter, leaving Thea to say goodbye to Meredith.

'Have a lovely time,' she said, her grin like a cat's, her cheeks rosy from their afternoon spent in the sun.

'I'm sure I will,' Thea said. 'It's scandalous that I've been here a whole week and I've not done any reading on the beach yet.'

'That's what you'll be doing, is it?' Meredith asked. 'Reading your book?'

'I might go for a swim,' Thea said, 'but I don't know if Ben will be up for it.'

'He loves swimming, as long as the water's warm enough. Enjoy yourselves,' she added, leaning in for a suncream-scented hug. 'Ben's a great guy.'

'I know that,' Thea said lightly. She didn't need anyone else adding weight to the time they were about to spend in each other's company, because she was doing that very well all on her own.

Ben returned from the car park with Scooter on his lead, and a jug of Pimm's and two glasses. Thea had removed her T-shirt and shorts, and was lying on the beach towel she had brought with her.

'Hey.' Ben's gaze flickered down the length of her body, the blue and white polka-dot one-piece she was wearing, then back to her face. 'I didn't know if you fancied a drink, but this seems like an afternoon for Pimm's, and the queues were relatively short, so . . .'

'I love Pimm's,' Thea said. 'And we deserve it, after all our hours of hard work.' She grinned and Ben laughed.

He knelt on the sand, pulling his own beach towel out of his rucksack and laying it out alongside Thea's. 'So much hard work,' he agreed. 'All those impressive, intricate sand sculptures that came off so well. I'm almost sad it's over, that all we have left to do is lie here and enjoy the beach.'

Scooter turned in several small circles, then lay down at their feet, his head on his paws. Ben took the metal bowl out of his bag, and poured water into it from a bottle he had with him. Then he did the thing that Thea had been wishing for and also dreading: he pulled off his T-shirt.

She swallowed, suddenly in desperate need of the Pimm's to quench her dry throat, as she let her eyes wander from his tanned arms to his toned chest, the dusting of brown hair that trailed towards the waistband of his shorts. His muscles were defined but not obscene; he looked healthy and fit, almost tailor-made for this perfect, early-evening beach scene. His skin glowed in the amber sun.

He noticed her looking, and glanced away self-consciously.

'Shall I pour?' Thea asked, holding up the jug.

'Go ahead.'

They clinked glasses, and Thea took a moment to appreciate the sweet drink that tasted entirely of summer. 'This,' she said, lying back and resting her head on her folded-up T-shirt, 'is bliss.'

Ben copied her posture. 'One of the very best things about being in Cornwall,' he agreed. 'The Lakes are great in summer, but Cornish beaches are something else. I'm glad you're getting a taste of how good it can be, especially after your knock-back the other day.'

'It wasn't that bad.'

'It sounds like the guy was brutal,' Ben said, his voice hardening. 'Which, in any situation, is unnecessary. You can't let it stop you.'

'I won't.' Thea studied his profile while he gazed up at the sky. And then, because she didn't know how to deal with the emotions rushing through her, or how to say thank you again, in a way that would convey the extent of her gratitude, she said, 'Do you fancy a swim?'

'Yeah, I really do.'

'Great.' She pushed herself up. 'Is Scooter coming in?'

He grinned. 'No, would you believe that he hates the water? He can stay and guard our stuff, can't you Scoot?'

The dog barked, and the moment Ben was off his towel, moved to lie the full length of it.

'Typical.' Ben rolled his eyes. 'Come on, then. Let's go and see how cold this water is.' He held out his hand, and Thea only had a moment's hesitation before she took it, and let him lead her down to the shoreline.

Despite the sun, the water was freezing. They coaxed each other to get past the breakers, Thea shivering as first her calves, then her knees, then her thighs were submerged in the frigid sea, and then Ben said she had to dive, fully, under the water.

'No way,' she said, shaking her head. Her 'no' had about five Ns at the beginning.

'I'll go first,' Ben offered.

'Be my guest.' She gestured expansively, and so he did, taking a deep breath and then disappearing under the water, popping up only a few seconds later, closer to Thea so she got sprayed with water. She yelped.

'F-fucking hell,' he stammered, wiping his hand over his face and blinking.

'Like that's encouraged me to do it,' Thea said, trying not to notice how his eyelashes were even darker, how they enhanced the colours in his eyes.

'You have to now I've done it.'

'I can see goose pimples over your whole torso,' Thea said.

'And you want some too,' Ben replied. 'Admit it.' He grinned, and he looked so carefree, all of a sudden, despite the obvious chattering of his teeth, that she couldn't bear to disappoint him.

'Fine.' She took a deep breath, like he'd done, and plunged beneath the surface. She needed even less time than Ben to realise what a bad idea it was.

'Oh-oh my God,' she said, bouncing up again, realising *she* was closer to *him*, now. 'That is r-ridiculously cold. God.'

'It's like an ice bath,' Ben said, his voice steadier now as he bobbed closer to her. 'How can it be so hot, and the water be so cold?'

'I don't know,' Thea replied, closing the gap even more. 'I guess it's the Atlantic, so it's . . . it comes from all around.'

Ben grinned, and she huffed in frustration.

'What I *mean* is that it's not a sheltered cove, where the water sort-of stays put, in a little eddy, and gets baked by the sun. This water flows in from hundreds of miles away. Cold currents, undertows, all that stuff. I'm not an oceanography expert, but—'

'I get it,' Ben said, his eyes bright. 'I know what you mean.'

'Stop pretending you don't, then.' She flicked water at him.

He blinked again, startled, then flicked some back.

Thea let out an involuntary squeak, then pushed her palms along the surface, sending a whole wave of water right into his chest.

'Fucking hell!' Ben looked around him, as if checking no small ears were nearby. 'That was a low blow, Thea.'

'Had enough?' she asked, smiling.

'Yes, I have.' He gave an exaggerated wince. 'I can feel things beginning to turn blue.'

'And we don't want our Pimm's to get warm,' Thea added.

'Strange how we're complaining about the water being cold, but if our drink is anything but, we're going to be annoyed.' He held out his arm and Thea moved towards it, until she was in front of him. He put his hands loosely on her waist, steering her as they bobbed in towards shore. She was thinking how good it felt, that simple touch: how it was starting to turn her insides to liquid, when Ben's grip tightened and he pulled her under the water with him. It was just for a second, but she was unprepared so she came up spluttering.

She whirled to face him, but couldn't help softening at the grin on his face. 'Y-you sod,' she gasped. 'You absolute—'

'Sorry.' This time when he took hold of her waist, he pulled her forward, not down, until they were pressed together. Thea didn't know what to do with her hands, but after a moment she put them on his shoulders. She couldn't look away from him: from the intense look in his eyes. 'I shouldn't have done that.'

'No,' she murmured. 'No, it was – I deserved it, for the splash.'

'Probably,' he said, his voice quiet and low.

Thea felt suspended in time, as well as in the sea. She could see individual droplets on Ben's skin, the pink of his cheeks beneath his tan more intense with the water reflecting the sun up at their faces. She wondered if her expression was as heated as his, if he was thinking that the moment felt like a dream, that it was heavy with possibility and promise, that it could lead to—

'Sorry!' The shout came at the same time as a beach ball splashed right next to them, making them both jump, and lose their grip on each other.

'No worries,' Ben called, throwing the ball back to the group of girls it had come from.

He turned back to Thea with a wry smile, and held out his hand. Thea took it and followed him towards the sand, her feet soon finding the seabed. She felt a momentary pang as she lost the weightlessness of the water, and then, when it was only up to their knees, Ben let go of her. She fell slightly behind, marvelling at his lean, strong back, and wondering how many times she would replay the moment in the water before she got bored of it. She realised there were other pairs of eyes – a lot of them female – following his progress up the beach.

They lay on their towels, Scooter only slightly stubborn about relinquishing Ben's to him, and let the sun dry them. They sipped their Pimm's while Thea gave Ben a full rundown of her encounter with Jamie Scable and then, because she didn't want to sully such a glorious afternoon, told him about the first time she had been to Port Karadow, aged ten: the way she and her dad had snuck out of the B&B like absconding teenagers; the copy of *Tiger Eyes;* the fish and chips.

'My mum's very highly strung,' Thea explained, 'so a headache is always a migraine, a problem is always a crisis, an opportunity is always a once in a lifetime chance.' She laughed, because it was easy to view her mum's behaviour with equanimity when she felt so far removed from it.

'What about your dad?' Ben asked.

'He's the opposite. Quiet and modest, prefers getting things done without making a fuss.'

'So you're more like him, then?'

'I think so,' Thea said. 'Mum wanted me to be her mini-me, and I think she's still disappointed that I didn't live up to it, to the name Theophania: that I'd rather read a book than go onstage, or run a PR company, or become a superstar in whatever field I choose.'

'That must be hard,' Ben said. 'But you're taking control, doing your own thing. Doesn't she realise that opening and running a bookshop is pretty fucking impressive?' He laughed and sipped his drink, orange slices bobbing on the surface.

'I haven't done it yet,' Thea pointed out. 'It's not glamorous enough for her, but I accepted that a long time ago. What about your parents? Are they still around?'

'Alive and well and living near Ullswater. I speak to them quite often, but haven't been back since I moved here. I'm hoping they'll come and stay as soon as the house is in a fit state.'

'You don't fancy a visit home?' Thea asked.

Ben shook his head. 'Not right now.' There was something about the way he said it, the tightness that crept into his voice, that suggested going any further down that line of enquiry would dampen their perfect afternoon. And to her, it was pretty much perfect. The hilarity and good-natured bickering of the sand sculptures, meeting Charlie and her friends, the delicious cream tea, followed by this: talking to Ben, soaking up the sun and drinking Pimm's, the views of the water and the man beside her a feast for the eyes. That moment in the sea, that had set off all kinds of sensations inside her, none of them remotely unpleasant.

She lay back on her towel and sighed contentedly, deciding that if she did nothing else on this holiday – if every day was her and Ben on the beach, with sand between their toes and sun kissing their skin, slowly finding out about each other – then it would be one of the best holidays of her life.

'Should we be getting back, do you think?'

'Mmm?' She had been close to dozing, the backs of her eyelids orange as the day produced another Instagram-worthy sunset. They'd had two jugs of Pimm's between them, and even though Thea knew they kept the concentration low at these mobile bars, she was feeling the effects. 'I suppose so.' She opened her eyes and gave Ben a lazy smile.

'Come on.' He pushed himself onto his knees and pulled his T-shirt over skin that had bronzed easily. He looked so delicious – almost as edible as the cream tea earlier – that Thea didn't know if she could stand it. He held his hand out.

'OK,' she said, taking it, letting him pull her to standing. They were close, him looking down at her, her gazing up. 'Thanks,' she murmured.

'No problem.' They were the same words he had said to her, over and over again, the day he'd fixed her bed, made her breakfast, taken her on a hike. But there was so much more warmth in them now: understanding, knowledge and friendship, from their shared time and conversations. He was smiling at her, reaching out to brush sand off her forehead . . .

'Do you think we could do this every day?' she whispered. 'Come to this beach, talk and swim and sunbathe? I was going to read my book, but I haven't even opened it.'

'Sorry about that,' he murmured, but he didn't sound sorry. Thea realised how kissable his lips were, and how much she wanted to take a step forwards, into him, so he had no choice but to wrap his arms around her or lean down to meet her upturned face with his. 'We can do the beach again another day, if you want.'

'I'd love that,' she said. 'I'd love to do this again, with you.'

He nodded, swallowed, and then, to her utter disappointment, took a step back. 'We should get going. Get home, drink about three litres of water.'

'Go to bed,' Thea added.

She'd meant it entirely innocently, because her limbs suddenly felt heavy, and she was imagining laying her head against her soft pillow, closing her eyes while the gentle sound of the sea lulled her to sleep. But when she met Ben's gaze there was an inferno burning in it, a flash of fire so hot that, for a moment, she was worried she might melt. But then he looked away from her, she saw his Adam's apple bob, and then he was all business – rolling up his towel, packing away Scooter's water bowl, helping Thea find her shoes, which were half-buried in the sand.

They strolled back to the twin cottages, the beach sounds receding into the distance.

'I've been meaning to ask,' she said. 'What's next for your cooking? Now you've got your second-place accolade, are you going to try anything else?'

'I'm going to spend an afternoon with Marcus Belrose in his beachside food truck,' Ben replied. 'The one he's running at weekends.'

'Wow! Really? That sounds like . . . fun.'

He laughed. 'You don't sound convinced.'

'It's just that he seemed very . . . intense. Quite an exacting boss.'

'I'm sure he is, but his food's the best, and I get the chance to learn from him for an afternoon. I'm not sure if I want to do anything with it other than improve my own cooking skills; I don't have any grand plans of giving up the day job to become a chef, or anything like that. I just want to get better.'

She nodded. 'When are you doing it?'

'Friday after next.'

'My last day,' Thea said.

'I know.' There was a pause, and then he added, 'I want to go out and get some fish before then, because Marcus said I could bring whatever ingredients I want, and I want a chance to practise. I'll go out with the guy I mentioned to you, Finn's friend, and I wondered if you'd like to come?'

'I'd love to,' she said. 'I have a feeling I'd enjoy being *on* the water a lot more than I enjoyed being *in* it.' *Apart from that one moment*, she thought, but didn't say it out loud.

Ben grinned. 'And to think, Meredith and Finn go swimming every day, even in February. The world's thickest wetsuit wouldn't convince me it was a good idea.'

'Ugh.' Thea shuddered. 'Just the thought of it is making me feel cold.'

They reached the cottages, Scooter sitting in front of Ben's door as if he was never planning to move again.

'I think he might want some dinner,' Ben said. 'Thanks for a great day, Thea.'

'Thank *you* for a great day. I'm not even sad that I didn't read any of my romance novel, which shows you just how good it was.'

'I'm flattered.' He paused for a moment, then bent to kiss her on the cheek. She could feel how hot and tight her skin was, despite the care she'd taken with the suncream all day, and his lips felt like a soft, cool balm against it. She might have hummed with pleasure, but it was too late to do anything about that.

'Night Thea,' Ben said.

'Goodnight Ben,' she replied. 'Sweet dreams.'

They went to their respective front doors, the gentle echo of wood hitting the frame almost synchronised as they both stepped inside, and shut out one of the best days Thea had had in a long, long time.

# Chapter Fourteen

Trebah Garden, with its swathe of impressive and unusual plants cut into a valley that ran down to the Helford river, was enchanting. From the moment Thea stepped through the door from the ticket office into the garden, she felt as if she was in a tropical paradise, immersed in a riot of colour and scent. She had been disappointed on the drive over, to the south-east side of the county, that it was one of those strange summer days where the sky was hazy, more grey than blue, and the temperature was stifling rather than deliciously warm.

But Trebah shone despite the pall, and she stopped frequently to read signs next to plants with vivid flowers, or trees that stretched high into the sky and looked as if they came from some far flung corner of the earth. She was wearing a long summer dress, her legs cool beneath it, and sturdy, flat sandals. On top of that, though it hardly went with her outfit, she had Ben's blue *Lakes for Life* baseball cap on.

She'd found it on her doorstep when she'd stepped that morning, his van gone from its usual space. There had been a yellow Post-it note stuck to it, the words, *Don't get burnt* written in a bold scrawl in black Sharpie. That gesture, along with everything that had happened yesterday, made her feel cherished, sending a tingling warmth through her that was similar to the way the Pimm's had made her feel.

She'd only known him a week and a day, but that meant she was over a third of the way into her holiday. She had packed a lot into it already, but she felt a low-level panic that it wasn't going to be long enough. She had made friends here, and she wanted to spend more time with them – with Ben, especially.

She walked down a rocky pathway nestled beside a trickling stream, that ran from the top of the gardens, all the way down to join the larger pools at the bottom, admiring the lilies, watching blue tits and great tits bounce in the trees overhead, enjoying the day despite its dullness.

She was startled by her phone ringing, the quiet tone sounding out of place in this paradise.

She hurried to take it out of her bag, and saw the name *Alex* on the screen.

'Hey,' she said.

'Thea,' he replied, as cheerful as ever. 'How did it go with your property viewing?'

His words reminded her that he hadn't called her afterwards, had seemingly forgotten all about her meeting, no doubt tied up with Esme and the festival.

'Not great,' she admitted. 'But it's just a stumbling block.'

'Why wasn't it great?' he asked. 'You could have called me, you know.'

‘I got caught up with other things,’ she said, which was true.

‘Of course.’ He sounded as understanding as always, his voice soothing, but Thea felt slightly on edge. She walked to a bench nestled amongst some vines, and sat down. She was still high up, and the spot gave her an incredible view of the gardens stretching out before her, the pond with the white, Monet-style bridge that was on all the promotional material looking like a miniature far below.

‘Landlords aren’t always sympathetic,’ she said, ‘and it made me realise that I need to be more forceful next time: ask all my questions, lead the conversation. I was thrown off by how abrasive he was, but I believe in myself, I believe in my bookshop, and if he doesn’t want me to rent his property, then he’s not worth my time anyway, is he?’ The words, mostly Ben’s, sounded good when she said them aloud.

Alex took a moment to reply, eventually saying, ‘Good for you, Rushwood.’

Thea could picture him sitting at a spare desk in the library, skinny tie undone and shirtsleeves rolled up, taking a break from the festival bustle. It had started on Saturday, so they would be right in the swing of things.

‘Really good for you,’ he said again, and she could tell he was slightly surprised. Alex had always supported her, helping to build her confidence, showing her where her business plan was solid and where it needed more detail. He’d also been there for her the one time, recently, when she’d needed backing up: when she’d found herself in a situation she couldn’t think her way out of. She would always be grateful for that, but she wondered if, because of it, he would always see her as someone who needed help. Was he shocked that she could do this next part without him?

'I need to look at some other places,' she continued. 'If I can't win Jamie Scable over – and after our last encounter I'm not even sure I want to – then I need to widen my search.'

'Exactly,' Alex said with conviction. 'A building isn't just about the bones, it's about the whole shebang: your relationship with the owners, the location, the legacy. I'm proud of you, Rushwood. Keep me updated, OK?'

'Of course,' she said. 'Thanks for calling.' They said goodbye and hung up.

For the first time ever, she felt slightly patronised by him: all his *Well dones and Good for yous*. She wondered if that was more about her than him: if her outlook, her attitude, had shifted slightly since being in Cornwall. She left the bench and headed for the heart of the garden, the forest of prehistoric-like gunneras she'd read about on the website, already looking forward to the beach, with its cool breeze and ice-cream hut, at the end of the trail.

Ben's van was still missing when she got back, and she felt a pang of disappointment, even though they hadn't arranged anything. She felt decadent opening a bottle of Prosecco early on a Monday evening, and ran water in the deep bathtub, adding coconut bubblebath from the bottle on the side.

The bathroom was at the front of the house, next to the master bedroom, and she opened the window, letting in the sea-scented breeze and the sound of the waves. The hot water and bubbles soothed her walk-weary limbs, and she sipped her Prosecco, then laid her head back and closed her eyes.

She didn't know how long she'd been like that when the harsh sound of tyres on gravel broke through the quiet. She listened to the engine cutting out, then heard the van door open, feet landing on the ground, and a familiar voice saying, 'Come on Scooter.' Ben sounded weary, and she couldn't help wondering where he'd been all day. '*Now*, Scooter!' he urged. 'I don't have time for this.'

Thea climbed out of the bath and wrapped a large, fluffy towel around herself. She tiptoed to the window, pushed it further open, and peered out.

The sky had turned a hazy violet, and the sea was flat and dark, devoid of sparkle. The outside light had come on, and she could see Ben below her, standing with his hand on the open driver's door, staring into the cab. His dog, presumably, was refusing to leave it. She let her gaze linger on his broad shoulders, remembering how he'd looked without his T-shirt on, and tried to push the image out of her mind.

She shifted slightly, knocking the window with her shoulder, and it creaked, sounding stupidly loud in the quiet evening air. Ben turned and looked up, his brow creasing. She hadn't even tried to move away: she knew she wouldn't make it, and her scrambling to hide would have looked even worse.

'Hey,' he said.

'Hi,' Thea replied. 'I had the window open, so I heard you come back. Is Scooter being unhelpful?'

'He gets like this when he's pissed at me. Today hasn't been a lot of fun for him – or me, for that matter – and I haven't been able to give him a proper walk, so he's punishing me.'

'What have you been up to?' Thea was fully aware that her shoulders were bare and her hair was dripping, but she couldn't seem to extract herself from the situation.

'I've been at the wholesalers, trying to sort out building materials for the next stage of the work. It's been a frustrating day, and now I have to go to Sylvia's.'

'The Old Post House?'

'The very same.' He sighed and rubbed his hands down his face. 'I've just picked up a voicemail from her. She says there's something creaking in the eaves. She asked if I could go around tomorrow, but I don't feel comfortable leaving her there tonight if there's something seriously wrong. The whole place is a nightmare, but I—' he stopped, as if he'd only just realised he was shouting up to a half-naked woman. 'Never mind.'

'Do you want some company?' She'd only had a few sips of Prosecco, and now he was here, she wanted to spend time with him. Besides, she'd found Sylvia and the Old Post House intriguing, and wouldn't mind having a proper look inside.

'At Sylvia's?' He sounded confused.

Thea shrugged. 'She did say you could give me a tour, and if anything needs fixing – if it turns out you need an extra pair of hands, or something, then . . . I could be those hands.'

'You're sure?'

'Give me five minutes to put some clothes on, and I'll join you.'

He leaned against his van, stretching his neck to the left and then right. 'My instincts are telling me to turn you down, that I should leave you to your bath, but I'm not going to say no to the offer of your company.'

'You're not?' She bathed in the glow of pleasure that accompanied his words. He nodded, his weariness evident, and she smiled at him. 'OK then. Five minutes, tops. Don't go without me.'

'What do you think is wrong?' she asked, once she was in the passenger seat of Ben's van, and he was driving along the coast road towards town.

'I have no idea,' he admitted. 'It could honestly be anything, the way that building is falling apart. I know she's leaving in a few weeks, but that doesn't seem soon enough.'

'It's so good of you to look out for her,' Thea said. Scooter was on the bench seat between them, and she imagined she could sense his sulkiness at not having been given his walk, at having to stay in the van even longer.

'I bet I'm not the only one she calls,' he said with a quiet laugh. 'But when she does call me, I like to go. She's getting in touch because she needs something – even if that something is just another person to talk to – or talk *at*, depending on the mood she's in.'

It didn't take long to get there, the beautiful old building coming into view as they crested the hill, a looming shape in the darkening sky, with just a single light on in an upstairs window.

'It's a stunning place,' Thea said as they got out of the van. 'I know it's not in the best health, that it's covered in ivy and dust, but it's quite grand, isn't it? It's not that big, but it's majestic, almost, in a way that modern buildings aren't.'

Ben stood next to her, Scooter sat at their feet, and they looked up at the Old Post House together.

'There are quite a few big, modern houses nestled in the countryside around here,' Ben said. 'You know those new-money mansions, glass fronted or built with peach-coloured bricks, with turrets and outdoor kitchens and anything else the owner has enough money to get an architect to design. Some of them are hideous; just because you *can* do something, doesn't mean you should. That's why I fell for Oystercatcher Cottage. It's old, it has character – all those beams and original fireplaces. It felt solid and . . . I don't know,' he shrugged. 'Honest, somehow. This place is the same.'

'I totally get that,' Thea said. 'It's been around for a few hundred years, so it's like a wise old owl in building terms.'

Ben laughed. 'The wise old owl of buildings. I like that. Sadly, quite a few of its feathers have fallen out, and it needs serious medical attention.'

'And I need you two to stop getting all misty-eyed and romantic and come and investigate this scrabbling noise.'

Thea jumped. She hadn't heard Sylvia open her window.

'Coming!' Ben called up, then flashed Thea a grin before heading to the doorway. She joined him, waiting while he found the key to the front door. She felt a swift, sudden breeze whip past the back of her head, her hair lifting and falling in its wake. She clamped her lips together to stop a squeak from escaping: she didn't want to think about what that was.

Ben opened the door and flicked on the downstairs light, and Thea walked in after him. She stepped around him, and then stopped. The lightbulbs were weak, probably ancient, and bathed the room in a sickly yellow glow. But, despite that, the Old Post House presented itself to her in all its wise old owl glory.

There was the solid, dark furniture she'd seen through the window, and several shelving units standing up against various walls in the large, open space. The staircase ran up the centre like a sturdy, elaborate pillar. She could see items that had been discarded: envelopes and greetings cards, pots of pens and rolls of parcel tape, as if the post office had been closed in a hurry. There were a couple of doors leading off the back of the space, a kitchen or storeroom – a bathroom, possibly – and everything was covered in dust, so thick in some places that it looked like cotton wool. A couple of posters were still partly attached to the walls, listing prices for sending parcels that must be a couple of years out of date, and the weak glow from the light bulbs left the corners in shadow.

'It's incredible,' she breathed.

'It needs a lot of work,' Ben said. 'Including . . .' She felt his warm palms on her shoulders, moving her gently forward.

'What? What's wrong?'

He pointed behind her and she turned, looking up at the large wooden beam over the front door. 'This,' he said, 'is no longer stable. Best not stand under it for too long.'

'Oh. Oh, right.'

'What are you doing down there?' Sylvia called. 'Having a tea party?'

Ben gestured to the staircase, and Thea clutched the wooden handrail and started walking up it, feeling the treads shift beneath her. 'Are these safe—' she got out before something dive-bombed her, something fluttery and small that flew at her face then swerved off into a shadowy corner. She shrieked and spun, and Ben's arms came around her, his hand pressing her head gently against his chest, shielding her. She was too terrified, too panicked, to enjoy the moment.

'Fuck,' he said emphatically. And then, 'Are you OK?'

'W-what was that?' she stammered. She could feel Ben's heart pounding against her ear.

'I told you!' Sylvia called down. 'There are *things* in here!'

After a moment, Thea felt composed enough to release herself from Ben's embrace, even though she didn't want to. He gestured for her to go forwards again, and she took the last few steps hesitantly, emerging onto the top floor, which was mostly open plan like downstairs, but a lot more homely.

To her right, was a bedroom. A large bed with a wrought-iron frame stood up against the wall, a patchwork quilt laid neatly over the sheets, a single bedside table with a lamp that was already switched on. To her left was the sitting room, which had an open fireplace and a couple of armchairs, their green fabric faded, a round coffee table between them.

The kitchen was along the back wall, with a row of cupboards and a gas hob, a modern, shiny microwave. A door at the back of the bedroom led, she assumed, to the bathroom. The big windows at the front of the building would let in so much sunlight, and show off the stunning views of Port Karadow. Right now, however, they were letting in a whole lot of dark, though Thea could just make out the sea in the distance, the last slice of sunset a deep red line marking out the horizon.

'Nice of you to join me,' Sylvia said. 'I see you've had a taste of what I've been enduring for the last few days.' She was sitting in one of the armchairs, wearing a pale blue dress with buttons down the front. She looked, Thea thought, far too put together for this building that was so obviously falling into disrepair.

Ben gestured to the other chair, and Thea sat down, still a bit shaky from the horrible encounter on the stairs. What *was* that?

'Hi Sylvia,' she said, her voice wobbling slightly. 'Sorry we took so long.'

Ben glanced at her, his brows lowered, then crouched in front of Sylvia's chair. 'We got here as soon as we could,' he said calmly. 'Are you doing OK?'

'Fine, Benjamin. I'm always fine, as you well know. Except for all this . . . fluttering.'

Ben sighed and dropped his head. 'Bats,' he said, making the word sound like a death sentence. 'How long have you had them?'

'How the hell should I know?' Sylvia said. 'I don't have night vision cameras set up, as I think you can probably tell.'

'That was a . . . a bat?' Thea put her hand to her hair, thinking of the waft of air she had felt outside.

'Yup,' Ben said. 'And that makes things a whole lot more complicated.'

'Why?' Sylvia asked. 'Just get old farmer thingamy to come by with his shotgun.'

Ben chuckled, holding onto the arm of Sylvia's chair as he balanced on his haunches. 'There are so many things wrong with that suggestion.'

'Name them.' Sylvia folded her arms and pinned him with a steely gaze.

'Firstly,' Ben said, 'bats are protected. You can't just shoot them, you need to get someone to come in and extract them in a humane way, find them somewhere else to go. Secondly, it would take a world-class sharpshooter to take down bats going about their business in the dark, and even they would need something a lot more precise than old farmer thingamy's shotgun. Thirdly . . .' He rubbed a hand over his eyes. 'I think the first two are enough, actually.'

Sylvia narrowed her eyes. 'So what do you suggest I do?'

'You need to call your daughter, Sylvia. Move out of here as soon as you can. Then the council can deal with the bats.'

Thea's heart squeezed at the gentle tone Ben was using, but there was weariness there, too. Perhaps it was the fact that he couldn't fix things for Sylvia, couldn't make the bats or the disrepair go away with a snap of his fingers, and allow her to leave the building in the way she so obviously wanted to: handing it over to the council in a good state, because doing anything less would damage her pride.

Thea glanced around her. Its state was a long way off good, but that didn't stop her being enchanted by it. It was unusual, she thought, for an old building to be so open, but perhaps when it was built, that was considered the best way for it to serve its purpose: the staircase up the middle as much a feature as functional; the large spaces upstairs and down more versatile than smaller rooms, and so light, too, when the sun flooded in in the afternoons. Even in its current condition, it was magnificent. She tried to picture it once it had had the attention it deserved.

While she'd been daydreaming, Ben and Sylvia had been talking quietly, and now she heard him say, 'You're sure you're going to be all right?'

'Of course, Benjamin. Now I know it's bats and not flying phantoms come to drag me to hell, I'm much less likely to throw myself out of the window to hasten their task. And how about you, Theophania? How is your vacation panning out?'

'Oh it's lovely, thank you, Sylvia. It's got a lot better since that first day.'

The old woman's flinty gaze slid between her and Ben. 'I don't doubt it.'

'Will you call your daughter?' Ben asked. 'I'll talk to the council about the best way to get rid of the bats, but only if you speak to Marie about coming to get you sooner than planned.'

'Marie will do everything in her own time. She won't listen to me.'

Ben pushed himself up to standing. 'I'm not sure I believe that. Give her a call. For me, OK?'

'OK,' Sylvia muttered. 'Now, be off with you. That gory new drama is starting on Channel Four in a moment, and I don't want to miss it.' Ben leaned down and gave the old woman a quick kiss on the cheek. Thea stood and walked over to her, wondering if she should do the same. 'Off you trot,' Sylvia said, answering her silent question, but at the last minute she gripped Thea's hand, squeezing it tightly before letting go. 'Thank you for coming,' she added, the harshness ebbing from her voice.

'Of course.' Thea wasn't sure what else to say, considering she had done nothing except squeal when a bat flew at her.

She followed Ben down the stairs, on high alert for any more nocturnal creatures.

'You go out and I'll follow,' Ben said. 'I need to lock up, anyway.'

'You mean if this big old beam starts to fall, you're going to hold it up like Atlas holding up the heavens so I can escape?'

'I really hope it doesn't come to that,' he said, amusement in his voice. 'I'd end up flattened. Go on.'

Thea hurried outside and Ben followed, retrieving the key from his pocket and locking the door. He stood, gazing into the darkened space for a moment.

'OK?' Thea asked.

He nodded. 'If she hasn't called Marie by this time next week, I'm going to do it for her.'

'Stage an intervention?'

'Yeah. She needs to be safe, not stuck out here on her own when her mobility isn't great. It's not an ideal home, this building, as lovely as it is.'

'No.' Thea looked up at it. 'I can see that. Great as a post office, though. Perfect for something like that.'

'That's what it was built for,' Ben said, walking around to the driver's side of the van. Thea climbed into the passenger seat, stroking Scooter who was snoozing, his nose tucked under a paw.

As they drove back through night-dimmed Port Karadow, Thea's mind was on overdrive. Now she had seen inside the old post office, as dusty and animal-infested as it was, she had the beginnings of an idea that didn't want to be dampened, however much reason she flung at it.

* * *

'I've got a bottle of Prosecco on the go,' she said when Ben pulled up in front of the cottages. 'And I have sausage rolls, from the Trebah Garden café. I don't think they really do takeaway, but they let me buy some. It's just a thought, but you're probably too tired.'

'No, that sounds great,' Ben said. 'If you don't mind giving me twenty minutes to shower? I don't want to come into your cottage like some kind of ancient dust monster.'

Thea glanced at her clothes. 'I could do with dusting myself down too.' The Old Post House's grime, it seemed, was quite clingy.

Inside Sunfish Cottage, she put the oven on to warm the sausage rolls, and the bottle of Prosecco back in the fridge door so it could chill. She changed into a jersey dress, and switched the lamps on in the living room. All the time, her brain was busy replaying their trip to the Old Post House – minus the bats. The generous rooms upstairs and down, the huge, light-attracting windows. All those shelves lined up against the walls.

The knock came twenty-five minutes later, and she opened the door to find Ben standing there in a black T-shirt and jeans. He looked freshly showered, his hair a few shades darker than usual.

'Can I bring Scooter in?' he asked. 'I don't think he'll put up with being left on his own again.'

'That's fine.' Thea stood back to let them in. 'Pets are allowed here, though I haven't brought one – obviously.'

'You're not a dog person?' He hovered in the kitchen doorway while she got the sausage rolls out of the oven.

'I'd love one, but my landlord doesn't allow pets. One day, though.'

'When you've got your bookshop?'

'Hopefully. What sauce do you want? I have ketchup, mayonnaise or barbecue.'

'Ketchup would be great. Shall I?' Ben pointed to the breakfast bar.

'I thought we'd eat in the front room.' She'd put the bottle of Prosecco in a bucket, her glass and a fresh one alongside it in preparation.

She brought the food in and they sat down, Scooter whining until Ben said, 'I've just fed you,' in his gentle, patient voice. The dog stared balefully at him, then lay on the floor, managing to squeeze himself between the tea chest and their feet. His fur was soft against Thea's toes.

She and Ben were close on the sofa, and the air seemed to fizz between them. She reached over and picked up the bottle, filling both their glasses.

'Thank you for this,' Ben said. 'And for coming with me to Sylvia's. It felt easier, somehow, with you there.' He held his glass out, and she clinked hers against it.

'I can't believe there are bats,' she said, once they'd both taken a sip.

He groaned, long and low, and she felt it all the way to her toes, her nerve endings sparking with interest. It wasn't *exactly* how she should be reacting to his obvious frustration, but it was such a rumbly, delicious sound.

'What does it mean, apart from someone having to get a specialist in to deal with them?' she asked, forcing her thoughts away from the direction they were heading in.

'They will have caused some damage to the structure,' Ben said. 'Their . . . guano does that. I don't have a whole heap of experience with bats, but that's what's happened in the couple of places I've worked on that were affected by them. And we have no clue how long they've been at the Old Post House. Sylvia needs to move out, but when she hands the building over to the town, she'll be handing over a huge problem.' He shook his head. 'The place needs so much work, and it should have happened long before now. With Sylvia, it's just that . . .' He put his glass on the table and leaned forward, his elbows on his knees.

'What about her?' Thea asked gently.

'She should have been looked after,' he said. 'She and Eric did so much for this town, and that building will still mean a lot to her, even once she's moved away.'

'But when she leaves, won't the council – or whoever she's giving the building to – make the repairs? If they're getting it for free, then they could do that, couldn't they?'

Ben turned to face her, bending his leg so his knee was on the sofa cushion, inches from her thigh. 'The risk is that they'll accept it, but won't invest the money needed to refurbish it properly, and it'll fall further into disuse. Anisha, who you met at the cook-off, is on the planning team, and I know she'd fight as hard as she could, but so often councils' hands are tied: they have to spend their budget on whatever the local councillor thinks will get them more votes at the next election. Is an old post office going to be top of their agenda?'

'It's so sad,' Thea murmured.

'It's not the best situation,' Ben agreed. 'I want to do everything I can, but I can't fix the bat problem without investing weeks of my time, not to mention getting this specialist in.'

'And you can't do all that for free. Even if you weren't trying to get your own house ready, you can't work for nothing.'

He sighed and slumped against the back of the sofa, his gaze on Thea. 'Nope. Sometimes, I wish I hadn't made the move.' He shook his head, his hair lifting with static as it rubbed against the fabric. 'No, that's not true. I have flashes of regret, but those are nothing compared to the long stretches of satisfaction. I can't say I'm properly content yet, but that's because I'm not getting on as much as I'd like to be.'

'Why did you move?' she asked. 'Did work run out in the Lake District?'

'No.' He laughed gently. 'It was always busy: people moving in, doing up homes and holiday cottages. Like here, I suppose. No, it was a personal thing.' He sipped his Prosecco, and when he put his glass down, Thea topped them both up. 'It was time to move on. I made the right decision.'

Thea nodded. 'It's not surprising that you're stalling with the building work.'

'Why's that?'

She gestured towards where the curtain fluttered in front of the open window, giving the impression there was someone lurking behind it.

'If I had that view outside my house, I'd never get any work done.'

He smiled. 'That was, partly, the point of buying Oystercatcher Cottage. I've always liked being near the water – I think I mentioned – and this was my chance to live within sight of it. I bought young in the Lakes, with help from my parents, admittedly, but because I was newly qualified I was able to get a complete wreck and do it up. It was good training, and a big achievement early on that gave me the confidence to run my own business. Then the market exploded, everyone wanted a second home up there, so when I came to sell – it was ridiculous. It meant I could get Oystercatcher.'

'Do you always work on your own?'

'Mostly.' Ben took a long swallow of Prosecco. 'I hire contractors if I need to: electricians, gas engineers and plumbers for particular jobs. Everything else, I try and get done myself.'

'A lone wolf,' Thea said, smiling.

'A bit more than I should be, perhaps. With the Old Post House, that whole situation, I'm definitely out of my depth.'

'You could talk to Anisha,' Thea suggested. 'See what she says. They might have some kind of plan to do it up anyway, in which case you can just warn her about how much work it needs, and the bats.'

He nodded. 'I'll do that.'

'It's a beautiful building,' she went on. 'It's full of history, isn't it? Especially as the remains of the post office are still there. It's as if it's never really moved forwards. I love buildings like that. I wanted to explore so many with Esme while I was here. You know, all those National Trust and English Heritage houses, with creepy taxidermy and horrible legends that the guides try and make more palatable.' She ran her finger up the side of her glass, collecting the condensation. When she glanced at Ben, he seemed mesmerised by the movement, and she could almost feel the tiredness radiating off him.

'Have you heard about the old lighthouse?' he asked.

She shook her head. 'I didn't even know there *was* a lighthouse. I haven't seen one.'

'It's a bit further down the coast,' he explained. 'It's not in use any more; one of those buildings that's been completely abandoned, partly because it's out on a spit and gets cut off by the tide. If you're interested in places full of history, there's nowhere better. It's pretty bloody spooky, though.'

'You've been?'

Ben nodded. 'Finn took me, soon after I moved here. His aunt knows all about it – they used shots of it in a television drama recently, I think. Maybe even that one that Sam and Delilah are in – *Estelle*?'

'Could you take me?' Thea asked, the reminder of Sam and Lila, and the chance of seeing another piece of Cornwall's unvarnished history, setting her pulse racing.

'We'd have to time it right, but yeah, I can take you.'

'And can we get inside? I suppose we probably shouldn't, but . . .'

He gave her a slow smile, and she could see her own excitement reflected in his eyes, temporarily banishing his exhaustion. 'I think, for the sake of getting the most out of your holiday, we could bend a couple of rules and go inside. It's not as if I'm short of tools.'

'Great,' Thea said. 'I mean, thank you. I'd love that. A lot.'

'Me too.' He sat up and finished his Prosecco. 'I feel bad throwing you into the path of bats, taking your food and drink, and then abandoning you, but if I stay here much longer, you'll have a snoring man and his dog in your living room. It's far too comfortable in here, and I'll be a dead weight once I'm asleep. I should go.'

'Of course.' Thea stood up when Ben did, watching as he gently shook Scooter awake and gestured towards the door.

As they said goodbye, Thea realised she wouldn't have minded if she'd ended up with them asleep on her sofa: Ben and his dog made her feel safe. That, and the fact that the more time she spent in Ben's company, the less she felt she'd had enough of it.

# Chapter Fifteen

Of course the sea was choppy the day Ben had picked for them to visit the abandoned lighthouse.

It was Wednesday, midway through Thea's holiday, and she hadn't done anything about her bookshop since her meeting with Jamie Scable. Or, at least, she hadn't done anything practical about it, but her conversations with Ben had reignited her confidence, and that felt like progress.

'The seat belt's a bit temperamental,' he said now. She was on the bench seat in his van, Scooter between them, and was wrestling with the belt as she had done the other evening. 'You just have to yank it, then it should be fine. Sorry, I've been meaning to get it fixed.'

'It's usually only you and Scooter in here though,' Thea said, finding that when she did what he said, the seat belt came out easily. 'What's the great smell? I hadn't expected a builder's van to smell so . . .'

'Delicious?' Ben chuckled. 'It doesn't, as a rule. You'll have to wait and see.'

'Oooh, so you're not *just* showing me around the lighthouse? There's more to today?'

He glanced at her then turned back to the road. 'You'll just have to wait and see,' he repeated, an amused note in his voice.

Thea couldn't take her eyes off the sea, the way the waves crested long before they got near the shore. It was still blisteringly blue, but the sun's heat was tempered by the strong wind, and she was pleased she'd put factor forty suncream in her bag. She was wearing frayed jeans and a red T-shirt, a thin hoody over the top, and her trainers. She didn't know what an abandoned-building appropriate outfit was, but Ben's T-shirt and jeans, along with his scuffed, solid-looking work boots, made her think she'd got it right.

'Is it going to be safe?' she asked, peering past Ben's profile to gaze at a rock formation sitting close to the cliffs, the churn of water around its base like the inside of a washing machine. 'It's quite rough today.'

'It's mostly safe,' Ben said. 'As long as we're careful, there's a fairly good chance we'll make it back in one piece.'

Thea swallowed. 'OK. That's . . . I mean, great . . .'

He flashed her a grin over Scooter's head, before turning back to the road. 'I'm joking. It's going to be fine. The tide's out, and the walkway's wide enough when it's low. I wouldn't take you if it wasn't safe: I'm not about to put you in danger.'

'I didn't think you'd do that,' Thea rushed. 'I just . . .' her gaze returned to the froth, and she thought of the bit in *Pinocchio* where he was eaten by the whale. But then Ben turned off the main road and, although they were moving towards the sea, the view of the coastline was obscured by a dense cluster of trees. Ben drove the van with ease, even as the road got narrower. Branches clawed at the windows, one talon shrieked along the glass, and Thea was suddenly in a horror film rather than a disaster movie.

'Not long now,' Ben said, in the same soothing voice he used with Scooter. She needed to get a grip: she was the one who had told Ben she was desperate to visit an abandoned building.

The greenish light disappeared all of a sudden, and the blue of the Atlantic opened up before them. Off to the left, beyond what looked like a concrete boat launch, a short, pebble beach and a stone pathway, a cream lighthouse rose up towards the sky. It was weather-worn; dirty and unloved, but the glass panels at the top, criss-crossed with leading in a traditional diamond pattern, the huge bulb visible through the panes, still shone out. She had always thought lighthouses had a distinctly art deco vibe, and this one was no different.

'It's beautiful,' she said. The inlet was tiny, part of a remote stretch of coastline, with no houses or other buildings overlooking it. It was certainly forgotten.

'Beautiful, or . . .?' Ben scrutinised her. 'Do you want to go back? If you don't fancy it now you've seen it . . .'

'No, no, I do! I promise. It's just – wow. Talk about living history.'

'That's what's so great about it, but – look, if it makes you feel safer.' He took out his phone and leaned towards her, so that she could see the screen. Scooter slunk down on the seat, unbothered by his master's intrusion, and Thea watched as Ben opened WhatsApp and typed a message to Finn.

Taking Thea to the lighthouse. If not back in 24 hours send search party.

'You didn't need to do that,' Thea said, laughing, as three dots appeared on the screen.

'Finn always replies quickly,' Ben said. 'It's a wonder he gets any painting done – unless he does it with his teeth.'

Finn's message flashed up on the screen.

Abandoned building seems a weird choice for a love nest, but if that's what she's into . . . Have fun and stay safe! ;)

Ben whipped his phone back, muttering, 'Fuck's sake.'

Thea thought how much younger he looked with the tinge of a blush covering his tanned cheeks. She put a hand on her stomach, which felt full of butterflies.

'He's an idiot,' Ben said, without much conviction. He busied himself getting out of the van, clipping Scooter's lead on, hefting a rucksack onto his shoulder. 'Got everything you need?' he asked her over the bonnet.

She held up her own, smaller rucksack. 'I think so.'

'Let's go, then.'

They walked to the edge of the pebble beach and Ben jumped onto it, Scooter loping easily down next to him. Ben held out his hand and, even though Thea didn't need help, she took it.

'Thanks,' she said, and they fell into step as they crossed the pebbles, quickly reaching the spit of land that would take them to the lighthouse. It reminded Thea of the invisible pathway in an *Indiana Jones* film; precarious and potentially deadly.

'It's not as wide as the walkway to St Michael's Mount,' Ben said. 'But that's got National Trust funding, whereas this place . . .' he gestured around them.

'It's been left to fend for itself.'

'Exactly. But that's better, in some ways. It's a piece of untouched history.'

'Why hasn't anyone done anything about it?' Thea asked as they began walking across the path. There was a few metres' leeway on either side of them, the water here lapping rather than churning, as it was around the base of the lighthouse, but she still felt exposed and was glad to have Ben beside her.

'Same reason I'm worried about the Old Post House, I guess. It's not exactly tourist material, when the road down here isn't built for multiple cars and you can only reach it at low tide, and then they'd need to do a whole lot of work to refurbish it. It's in a state. I hope you're not scared of spiders.'

Thea shuddered. She was. 'Are there a *lot* of spiders?'

'There are a lot of spiders,' he confirmed. 'Mostly in the corners, though. You'll be fine.'

'Does Scooter eat spiders?'

'Not when there's ham on offer,' Ben said. The dog stared up at him, as if he understood every word. 'Look.' He stopped walking, and Thea did the same. They were close to the lighthouse now, and despite her trepidation, she was eager to see inside.

'What is it?'

Ben took her arm and gently pulled her closer to him, then he pointed into the distance, towards the horizon. 'See them? You can just about make them out.'

'Where am I looking?'

'Here.' He bent his knees so that his head was next to hers, then, with a finger, angled her chin so she was looking in a slightly different direction. 'See them?'

'Are they . . . Oh my God! Dolphins?' She had never seen them in the wild before.

'They're a bit far out to see clearly, but you can spot their fins, right?'

'I can see them!' She was breathless. 'Wow, Ben.'

'Pretty great, huh?'

'*Very* great. Thank you.'

'No problem. I told them to pop by, just for you.'

Before she could reply, he had moved on, and she missed the way he'd been sheltering her from the wind.

'They've not even bothered to secure it this time,' he said, as Thea joined him at the base of the lighthouse. A padlock was hanging loosely from the lock, and it only took Ben a moment to wrench the door open. It looked solid, but it gave a loud screech when he pulled, the hinges rusty from years of disuse.

She expected a musty smell: damp and dirt and years of dust, but although it wasn't as fresh as the sea air, it also wasn't as bad as she'd anticipated.

'Wait here a sec,' Ben said.

'What are you worried about?' Thea asked, as he and Scooter stepped inside. 'Ghosts? Vampires? Criminals?'

'Killer spiders,' he murmured. Thea didn't know what to say to that, so she was quiet until he came back, peering out of the doorway with a smile on his face.

'Fine?' she asked.

'Fine,' he repeated. 'Come on in.'

The interior of the lighthouse was everything she'd expected, and also not. The majority of the space was taken up with the stairs that twisted up the middle, winding up and up to the top of the building. There were a couple of windows on the ground floor, letting in swathes of golden, summer light, highlighting a wooden table and a couple of old, rickety dining chairs.

'Is this where the lighthouse keepers stayed?' she asked.

'Mostly on the floor above, I think. But the majority of the furniture's gone, now.'

'And where are we going?'

'To the top, of course. Do you want to go ahead of me?'

Thea tipped her head back and looked up. She could just about make out the huge bulb. 'I think you should go first.'

'OK, but keep close behind me. The handrail's still pretty solid, but if you feel unsteady, grab on to me.'

Thea nodded, and when Ben started climbing, she followed closely behind. Scooter had gone on ahead, as if he knew the place well and the steepness of the stairs didn't bother him. They stopped at the first floor, and Ben pointed out the meagre living quarters in the circular room. There was a curved counter up against the wall, and a small sink, but she couldn't imagine the plumbing still worked. The floor was bare, dusty boards, the only real sign of human life a noticeboard pinned to the wall, a couple of torn scraps of paper still secured to it.

'God.' She swallowed. 'How long has it been since the lighthouse was active?' She peered at the bits of paper, but they were too faded to make out what might once have been on them.

'About forty years – that's what Finn told me.' Ben waited until she'd seen all she wanted to, then started moving again. She followed him up, past another equally barren floor, and then to the very top, where the huge bulb took up most of the space.

The glass around them was floor to ceiling, only a narrow circular walkway around the central light, and Thea was consumed by the sensation of being so high up, with nothing surrounding her but the dizzying views. There must have been a gap between a pane and its leading, because there was a shrill whine of wind cutting through the space.

'Wow.' She stared out at the writhing, choppy sea, the streaks of cloud racing across the sky. 'Imagine if someone turned this into a house, and got rid of the bulb. Imagine having these views all the time!'

'You'd have an isolated lifestyle though,' Ben said, putting his rucksack on the floor. 'It's not easy to get to, and you'd be cut off half the time: no way to get out if there was an emergency. I couldn't have been a lighthouse keeper.'

Thea thought she saw him shudder, then he was opening his bag and taking out a red and blue tartan blanket, laying it on the floor. It was too wide for the space, bunching up against the glass on one side, and the bulb on the other.

'What's this?' she asked. 'Lighthouse picnic?'

'I thought we could. If you're happy to stay up here?'

'It's an incredible place,' she said. 'It doesn't feel entirely safe, with these huge windows, but I think . . . I don't mind that.' She didn't want to admit that the reason she could deal with her fear was because she was with him.

'The glass is secure,' Ben said. 'It has to be, considering how exposed to the elements it is. It's not as precarious as it looks.' He got out several Tupperware boxes, which Scooter sniffed at approvingly, and some paper plates, paper napkins and two plastic glasses. Then he produced a bottle of sparkling wine, and a bottle of ginger beer.

'You didn't have to do this.' Thea sat down as he flourished an arm at the blanket. She opened one of the boxes, a tantalising, savoury smell wafting out as she saw two Scotch eggs nestled inside. 'But I'm very glad you did. You didn't make these, did you?'

'I did.' Ben sat next to her, opened another box, put a few cold sausages and slices of beef on a plate, and put it to the side of the rug. Scooter didn't wait, and while he ate, Ben poured water into his metal bowl. 'I also made the potato salad, and the sandwiches. The brownies though,' he pointed at another box, 'they're not mine. I'm not great at baking.'

'I might forgive you,' Thea said, as he filled her plate with the home-made food. 'Seeing as you made the rest of it.'

'Very considerate of you.' He poured her a cup of sparkling wine, and himself a ginger beer, and they clinked their plastic glasses together.

'To abandoned lighthouses and slightly spooky picnics,' Thea said, then took a sip. 'This is really lovely.'

'It's from the Camel Valley.'

'You don't expect me to drink it all by myself, do you?'

He shrugged. 'I'm driving, but we can put the stopper in. Anyway, I just . . . I thought you should have the whole experience.'

Thea laughed. 'Do you and Finn have a luxury picnic when you come here, then?'

Ben grinned. 'No. The one other time I've been, he sketched the view, because it's quite a unique perspective, especially if you look back towards the shore.'

She nodded, seeing how right he was. The pathway leading to land reminded her of the yellow brick road, even though it was concrete, and she could see the blue of Ben's van gleaming in the sunlight, surrounded by the verdant green of the trees that were thick along the shoreline. The pebble beach looked almost magical, with every stone seemingly a different colour, the sea bursting against them in frothy peaks. She felt impossibly removed from the scene, even though they'd walked through it only half an hour before.

'It looks strange,' she said. 'Almost like we're watching it on TV.'

'You don't often get to see it like this, unless you're on a boat.'

'Look how tiny your van is,' she said.

'A pocket van. No wonder I've been struggling to get my work done; I can only fit pencil-length planks of wood in it.'

Thea laughed, and picked up her Scotch egg. 'The coating is so crunchy,' she said, when she'd tried it. 'Usually it's soft.'

'That's because I made them this morning.'

'What time did you get up?' she asked, as he poured her more wine.

'About five thirty. I don't sleep once the sun's up. Not without curtains, anyway.'

'You should really get some curtains,' she said, pointing a serious finger at him. 'Part of your remodel, I presume? And you made these in your building-site kitchen?'

'I cleared a small corner to cook in,' he admitted. 'And yeah, I will do. But curtains feel a long way down the list.'

'Would you . . .' she hesitated. 'Would you consider getting someone else in to help you?'

'I don't – it's not my usual style.'

'But if there's some kind of block on it, for you? If you're finding it hard, working on your own place, then perhaps you should.'

'I've renovated all my previous places,' Ben said, a hint of defensiveness in his voice. 'My first house – the one I told you about – it was even worse than this.'

Thea smiled. 'Even worse than an abandoned lighthouse with killer spiders and at least three ghosts?'

'Why three?'

'Three is a good number for everything,' Thea said. 'Three ghosts seems right for this place: it's three floors, isn't it? Or is it four?' She giggled. She'd only had two glasses of wine, but it was so light and bubbly, and it had gone straight to her head. 'I think we should put the stopper in this.'

'It's in my bag.' Ben gestured to where his rucksack was resting against the wall, just behind Thea.

She turned and peered into its dark depths, seeing nothing, then put her hand inside. The first thing her fingers closed around was very familiar. 'Oooh. A book!'

'Thea, don't—' Ben said, but it was too late.

She looked at the paperback, taking in its broken spine and the curled-back corners, the cover tatty and ripped along the bottom, as if it were a much-loved tome he'd had for ages. But it wasn't the state of the book that was making her mind buzz with questions.

'Oh,' she said, rereading the title. 'I'm sorry, Ben.'

He didn't reply, and when she risked a glance at him, he stared straight back, not ducking his head or looking away. There was resignation in his expression, and also – she didn't think she was reading too much into it – sadness. Definitely sadness.

'I'll put it back,' she murmured, hurrying to replace the book, to find the stopper she'd gone in there for in the first place, though the title of Ben's reading material, *Trusting Again After Betrayal*, was already seared into her mind.

'No.' He wrapped his fingers gently around her wrist. 'I mean, you can. But you don't have to.'

Thea nodded, her lips pressed together. Scooter was lying stretched out around the glass bulb, his jaw resting on his front paws, his pale eyes fixed on his master.

'Do you want to talk about it?' she asked.

Ben huffed out a laugh. 'Not really. But also . . . maybe? I don't know.'

'Well, look,' she said, taking his empty glass and the bottle of wine. 'You can have *one* of these, can't you?'

He put his hand over the glass. 'I don't ever drink if I'm driving.'

'OK.' Thea bit her lip. She knew it was the right thing, but he sounded so serious, on the edge of stern.

'Sorry,' he said. 'Sorry, Thea. Let's forget about it – the book, I mean.'

'How can I forget about it when it was in such a terrible condition?' Her smile was short-lived. 'Though I suppose I can't blame you for taking your anger out on it, if . . . uhm . . .'

He sighed. 'It was my girlfriend, Allie. She's the reason I've got it. Or, not just her, but also my best friend – ex-best friend, Damien. They're both equally responsible. But the book was my sister, Julie's, idea. I wouldn't usually go for something like this.'

'Has it helped, though?' Thea asked quietly.

He shrugged. 'I don't know.'

She listened to the wind whistle through the crack in the leading, and Scooter's gentle, squeaky snores now that he was dozing, his head on Ben's ankle.

'Your girlfriend cheated on you with your best friend?' she whispered, once she'd let his words sink in.

'It sounds very soap opera, doesn't it?' She could tell he was trying to make light of it, and completely failing.

'It sounds terrible. I'm so, so sorry.' She rubbed his arm, her palm tingling against his warm skin. She could feel his eyes on her, but she didn't look up. 'That's the reason you're in Cornwall, then?'

'That's why I'm here,' he admitted. 'This is my fresh start. It's helping a lot more than any book could.'

# Chapter Sixteen

Thea found the stopper and put it on the bottle of sparkling wine. She was discovering that being near Ben, and finding out something so fundamental – not to mention heartbreaking – about him made her feel untethered enough, without any more alcohol.

'Ready for the horrendous cliché of it all?' he asked. He was sitting with his back against the glass, his knees drawn up, elbows resting on them.

Thea winced. 'Go on, then.'

'I went out to a job, came back an hour later because my customer had changed his mind about a design feature and I needed a specific tool, and found them . . . together.'

'Oh God,' she whispered. 'Seriously?'

'And not even in our bed, but in the, uh . . . kitchen. Scooter went racing up to them – he was really fond of Damien – and then, it was almost comical, the way they reacted to being found out. I was shell-shocked.'

'What did you do?' It came out as a scratch, as if her throat was clogged up.

'I left. Went to my sister's. She lived about half an hour from me, with her husband and three kids. I stayed in her box room and it was chaos, but what I needed right then: to be distracted.'

'Did they try to get in touch with you? Your girlfriend or Damien?'

'Oh yeah. They gave me all the obvious excuses: *It just happened; our feelings crept up on us; we never meant to hurt you*. And once the shock had gone, I wasn't really surprised. Allie is an interior designer, she loves the finer things, and Damien – he designs video games, he's done really well for himself. I'm not saying it's all about money, just that their views, their tastes, are much more aligned. They always got on well, but I never thought . . .'

'You never thought that two people you loved would betray you in such a horrendous way? That is entirely understandable.' Thea had found her voice again, her words propelled by anger.

Ben looked at her. 'I was naive.'

'You trusted them. That's not the same thing.'

How could anyone do that to him? He was such a genuine person: so quietly thoughtful and generous, hardly any ego, and objectively so good-looking that Thea sometimes caught herself doing a double-take, just to see if he really was that handsome. As she'd got to know him, she realised his attractiveness went so much deeper than his hazel eyes and carved jawline: his tanned, toned physique. Then, to hear this? She shook her head.

'I felt like a fool for not realising,' he went on. 'And because it was Damien – we went to school together. I was with Allie for three years, but I'd been friends with Damien for twenty. I've struggled with that, more than anything.'

'That's not surprising,' Thea said. 'Not at all. A friendship, especially one you make when you're young, goes so deep, I think. Of course his betrayal traumatised you. And if you've chosen Cornwall because you wanted to move away – physically and emotionally – but you haven't come to terms with what they did, then perhaps that's what's blocking your work on the house?'

He shifted around so he was facing her, his knee brushing hers. 'You think that might be it?'

She nodded. 'We have a lot of self-help books in the library.'

Ben shook his head. 'That came from you. You're not just quoting some relationship guru. Have you been cheated on?'

'No,' she said. 'Not cheated on.'

'There's something, though.' He moved again, so he was sitting cross-legged. Scooter planted himself between them, sniffing the crumbs on their empty plates before he lay down. 'Something happened to you, that's given you some insight?'

'Oh, I—' she started, wondering how much to tell him, realising he'd given so much of himself to her, opened himself up, that it was only fair she do the same. 'I was bullied a lot, at school. I've always been bookish, unpopular. I had my hair pulled and my notebooks stolen, but then there was a girl, Genevieve, who I was friends with for a while – close friends, I thought, in the first year of secondary school. But it turned out she wasn't a friend at all.'

'What happened?'

'She told me that there was a boy who liked me. He was called Chris, he was in the year above, and I had never even *considered* he would be interested in someone like me – he was one of the cool, handsome boys, a bit like you.' She gave Ben a quick smile, but his expression remained serious. 'I wouldn't have believed it – I knew where I stood in the school pecking order – except that Genevieve swore it was true, and encouraged me to talk to him. In the end, he asked me out, and Genevieve helped me get ready for our date. I was supposed to meet him at the cinema, but—' she swallowed. Even now, the memory had enough power to hurt her, her skin prickling uncomfortably.

'He didn't show up,' Ben said. His voice was hard, like flint.

'No. I waited for over half an hour, though I think I realised a lot sooner that Chris wasn't coming. Then I spotted him and his friends across the road, in the pizza place, sitting at a window table and laughing at me. It took me a moment to notice that Genevieve was there too. It was as if – I don't know – she wanted to make sure I knew where I stood: that I knew she was popular, and I wasn't.' She was cross with herself. It had been almost half her lifetime ago, and she still felt the horror and humiliation of it.

'Fucking cowards,' Ben said through gritted teeth. 'You shouldn't have had to go through that.'

'I know it was a long time ago, and after that, Esme sort of – I wondered if she was taking pity on me at first, but then we became firm friends. But still, there's a part of me that hasn't really shrugged it off, and it means I can be pretty judgemental about people. I feel like I have to assess, even as I meet someone, whether their friendliness is genuine. It makes me more guarded, shyer than I want to be.' She looked out at the acres of blue sky. She felt so removed from the real world, in this place that was like a fantasy, but some of this still wasn't easy to say. 'And these things don't just happen at school. There's bullying, belittling going on all the time.'

She thought back to a day as warm as this one, a little under a year ago, when it had felt like nothing bad could happen, but she'd been followed after leaving the library. She could still remember the pure, almost blinding fear as she'd realised what was happening, as she listened to the boys' laughter, tried to make out the whispered words that were deliberately too low for her to hear. The flashback came with an accompanying chill, and she didn't want to linger on it.

'Thea.' Ben reached over Scooter and took her hand, his touch banishing the last of those unwelcome memories.

'You were right,' she said. 'I haven't been betrayed in that awful way, like you have, but I do know what it's like to be seen as a fool, to have someone treat you as if your feelings don't matter.'

Ben nodded, his Adam's apple bobbing. 'I'm sorry that happened to you. Nobody should be treated like that.' He shook his head. 'I wish those boys at school, that Genevieve girl, could see you now.'

Thea laughed. 'I don't. I never want to go back there, but thank you.' She squeezed his hand, enjoying the contact. 'Esme helped me through the worst of it. And now I've got good friends, her and some other colleagues at the library;

Alex, who has helped me so much with the business plan for my bookshop, who has been there when I needed him.' It was Alex who had come to her rescue the year before, when she'd felt so vulnerable and alone, terrified of what was going to happen next. He'd diffused the situation, made her feel safe again.

'Alex is a close friend?' Ben asked.

'Quite close.' She should be honest about what had happened, but a part of her was still ashamed that she hadn't been braver. And then there was the way her feelings for Alex had shifted after he'd intervened. Those weren't things she could tell Ben right now – even though his mere presence was making her see her affection for Alex in a different light: as gratitude, rather than something deeper. All of it seemed too complicated, too self-indulgent, to explain to him in this moment.

He huffed out a breath. 'Why can't people just be kind to each other? What do they get out of being cruel, of belittling others? I know with Allie and Damien, they say their feelings took over—'

'That's so lame, though,' Thea said. 'Such a pathetic excuse. If they'd started to develop feelings for each other, Allie should have broken things off with you before they acted on it. They should not have sullied your kitchen counter – which I expect you built, and therefore deserved much better treatment – with their naked asses!'

Ben jolted in surprise, his cough turning into a splutter, which turned into laughter.

'What?' Thea had been proud – and also a little surprised herself – of her speech. 'What is it?' Ben's laughter was infectious, and soon she was laughing too. They woke up

Scooter, who stood and did several laps around the lighthouse bulb, barking excitedly.

When they had calmed down, Ben opened the last Tupperware box, and they bit into the chocolatey, gooey brownies he had bought from Sea Brew in town.

'These are amazing,' Thea murmured. 'And they go well with the wine.' She had a third of a glass left, the bubbles mostly flat, now, and she held it out to Ben. 'One sip won't hurt.'

He rolled his eyes, then took a sip and followed it with a bite of brownie. 'That's really good.'

'See? Champagne and chocolate beats champagne and strawberries every time.'

'I think you're right.' He handed her glass back.

He sighed again, though this time it sounded more content than annoyed. They swapped smiles, and the air in the room suddenly felt charged.

Thea knew Ben so much better than she had done when they'd arrived at the lighthouse, however long ago that was. It felt as if they'd been there for hours. She glanced at her watch and saw that it was after three. It *had* been a while, actually.

'Ben,' she said. 'How long does the pathway stay accessible? I don't know much about tide times, but I was wondering if—'

He whipped around, boxes scattering as he kicked them in his haste to turn, and then, stillness. All the hairs went up on Thea's arms as she noticed the tension in his shoulders, then followed his gaze, back towards the pebble beach and the van: their route away from the lighthouse.

'Fuck,' Ben said.

Scooter whined and let out a single, sharp bark.

'Fuck, fuck, fuck,' he said again, as if he hadn't made the point firmly enough before.

Thea had to agree. Because in front of the stony cove and the glossy trees and the pocket van, where before there had been a straight, narrow path, there was only churning, twirling water. There was no walkway left: the sea had swallowed it whole.

She should have panicked. At the beginning of the holiday, she knew that's exactly what she would have done. She thought back to that first, lonely walk, and how she'd funnelled all her annoyance and trepidation about her solo holiday into those few hours. Not any more, though: not since sand sculptures and cook-offs and meeting Jamie bloody Scable. And not since Ben.

'Looks like a bit more than a paddle,' she said lightly, watching the frothing waves where, earlier, there had been concrete.

'Fucking hell,' Ben said, pressing a closed fist against the window. 'I checked the tide times yesterday. I knew how long we had. I should have been paying attention.'

'We got distracted. These things happen.'

'They do?' She could hear that he was angry, and his eyes flashed as he turned to her. 'Getting stuck in an abandoned lighthouse because you're not smart enough to set an alarm on your phone? Think this has happened to a lot of people?'

'No, of course not. But that makes it unique.'

'When you say *unique* like that, you actually mean *horrible*.'

'There's nothing about this situation that feels particularly horrible,' Thea said. 'Not unless there's a huge storm coming in, or at this time every day a prowling monster with the ability to swim comes out of the forest in search of human blood, or the killer spiders all wake up and starting scuttling about—' she shuddered. 'Actually, let's not joke about that last one.'

Ben dropped his head, running his hand over the back of it. His hair was cropped short there, and Thea knew that if she ever got to touch it, it would be that delicious combination of soft and slightly prickly.

'Come on,' she said, 'it's not that bad. There are still two brownies left. There's more fizz, more ginger beer – more water for Scooter?'

'Yeah, there's more water.'

'We have a blanket, it's a beautiful day. How long until the causeway reappears?'

Ben glanced at his watch. 'This isn't fully high tide yet, though it's on the way in, but that means . . .' he grimaced. 'It'll be hours until we can cross again.'

'Right. And there aren't any . . . working facilities?'

'The plumbing uses a rainwater cistern. Finn and I checked it out last time we were here. There's a working toilet, but it's not . . . it wouldn't even get one star on TripAdvisor, put it like that.'

'I might be sharing my private moment with some of the spiders?'

He mirrored her smile, but it fell quickly. 'Thea, I'm so sorry. This was meant to be fun.'

'It *is* fun,' she said. 'It's an actual adventure, being stuck here. Unique in a good way.'

He leaned his head against the glass. 'I don't think you mean that.'

'I have tissues and hand sanitiser, and there's a half bottle of wine that you can share with me, now. And, if you want details about my humiliating school years, then I can regale you with stories for hours.'

He sat up straighter. 'I don't want to hear about how shitty people have been to you, unless – do you really want to talk about it?'

'No.' She sighed. 'Not really. But do you know what will make this a whole lot less fun?'

'What's that?'

'If you spend the next few hours moping because you feel guilty about landing us in this situation.' She burrowed in her rucksack, finding her tissues and hand sanitiser. 'I'm going to be brave and find the toilet. Please, *please* don't berate yourself too much for what's happened.'

His eyes followed her as she stood. 'First floor,' he said. 'Do you want to take a stick, to ward off spiders?'

'I'll kick them, it's fine.' She sounded braver than she felt. She took a deep breath. 'Right, if I'm not back in five minutes, please come looking for me. But sing, or something, so I know you're not a ghost.'

'Understood.'

Thea gave a quick nod and went in search of the ancient, and quite possibly traumatising, facilities.

When she returned to the top of the lighthouse, a lot less traumatised than she had anticipated but definitely missing the high spec bathroom in Sunfish Cottage, Ben had filled the two glasses with fizzy wine, and had laid what looked like a grey hoody over the blanket. He was tussling with Scooter, who clearly thought the extra layer of comfort was for him.

'Have you forgiven yourself?' she asked.

'I have, but I haven't stopped being sorry.'

'I've accepted your apology,' she said gently. 'I guess, now we're here, we need to make the most of it. And also,' she went on, sitting back down, 'now I've confessed about my school days, I feel like I should tell you something else.'

'What's that?'

She held her glass up, and he clinked his against it.

'The thing is,' she said, 'I didn't exactly warm to you, the first time we met.'

Ben gave her an awkward smile. 'I didn't show you my best side. I was pretty mean to you.'

Thea shook her head. 'I didn't think you were mean. But you seemed like one of *those* guys. One of the popular, unapproachable ones. With your – your . . .' she gestured at him, and he frowned. 'Oh come on, don't be deliberately obtuse.'

'I'm not being,' he protested. 'What are you talking about?'

'Ben!' She raised her eyes to the ceiling, which reflected the light and the water, the movement of the waves dancing patterns across it. 'You were basically monosyllabic when we met, apart from making that comment about me taking selfies and losing my soul—' she was gratified to see him wince at that, '—and you're way too handsome, with that jawline and your physique, and I thought: *I am not going to speak to him. He'll give me this one, disparaging assessment and then pretend I don't exist, and that's fine.* I really thought it was fine.'

'That is . . .' he wiped a hand over his mouth. 'That is a lot. I'm sorry about the selfie comment. I get stuck, sometimes: I get inside my head and a gloom descends, and sometimes I can't snap out of it. It's happening less and less, the more time passes since Damien and Allie, but I shouldn't have taken it out on you. I'm sorry I said that. The rest of it, though . . .'

'What about the rest of it?'

'Am I really unapproachable?'

'You mean, are you really intimidatingly handsome? Yes, that is entirely true.'

He shook his head, took a long swallow of wine. A cluster of seagulls flew past, cawing and screeching, and Thea wanted to stand up, to walk to the other side of their circular holding cell, because it felt exposing, admitting that to him – even though it was true. Instead, she sat and waited for his response.

'Thea,' he said.

'Ben.'

'Thea.'

She smiled. 'Ben?'

'I never wanted you to feel uncomfortable.' He was the one who looked uncomfortable now. 'What can I do, to make it up to you?'

'Oh, it's fine now. I've seen you try and make a house out of sand, and obviously there's this ultimate move of stupidity.'

The side of his mouth kicked up. 'You mean going on about how easy it is to get cut off here, then totally failing to pay attention to my own warnings?'

'Exactly. I'm much more comfortable now I know you're completely fallible.'

'You know,' he said, then paused to take a sip of his drink. 'I could easily blame you for this predicament.'

'You could, but it would be both shameless and rude. How could you possibly justify it?'

'Because you distracted me,' he said. 'You're very distracting.' He said it in a soft voice that did funny things to Thea's insides, and she stared at his free hand, resting gently in his lap. His tone was much less certain when he added, 'You listened to me. Finn and Meredith have heard my sob story, and I'm lucky that I've made friends in Port Karadow, but it's usually such a hard thing to talk about. I didn't find it hard, talking to you.' When she raised her eyes, there was a rawness in his expression that she felt all the way through her.

She took his hand. 'I'll listen any time you want.'

Ben wrapped his long fingers around hers, and Thea wanted to take a mental snapshot of the moment. The sensations running through her were far more important than the image, and, she knew, even harder to hold on to.

# Chapter Seventeen

The light changed around them as the afternoon slipped into evening. They stood up to stretch their cramped limbs, and looked out at the view. The sea had gone from a swirling green-blue to a dark, intense navy, the foaming crests starkly white against it. Thea knew there was no point checking the causeway, because it was still hours before it would emerge again, but she didn't mind. She couldn't think of anyone she would rather be stuck in a dilapidated lighthouse with.

'What are you grinning at?' Ben asked, after he'd pointed out two cormorants flying north to south, their flight streamlined, black bodies glossy against the turquoise sky.

'I was thinking that, of all the people I could have been trapped with out here, you're the one I would have picked.'

'Why?' He nudged her shoulder. 'Because of my intimidating good looks? I can see how they would be a selling point.'

Thea laughed. 'No, not that reason, or not that specifically: the view *is* stealing some of your thunder. But it's easy with you – like you said earlier. I was imagining what it would be like to be stuck here with Esme, or Alex.'

'The guy who helped with your business plan?' He cleared his throat. 'And I'd win over both of them? Even though we've not known each other that long?'

'You're so calm,' she said, trying to explain exactly how she felt. 'So . . .' She couldn't help running her eyes over him: the way his T-shirt clung in all the right places; the set of his jaw; the quiet focus in his gaze. 'So . . . solid.'

'Well,' he replied, 'you're also the person I would pick to be stuck here with. I messaged Finn what had happened, and he sent me about twenty different laughing GIFs, followed by a text asking if we were OK.'

Thea grinned. 'I think being trapped here would stress him out.'

'I think you're right.'

They turned back to the window, the turquoise sky dissolving to pink in front of their eyes.

'Look,' Ben said. 'The first star.'

Thea followed his gaze, and saw it: a tiny, bright diamond winking in the vast expanse. She shuddered, not sure if it was because the temperature had started to drop, or because it was so stunning: the endless waves, the pearly pastel cloak of dusk. She felt Ben's arm around her shoulders, drawing her closer. She leaned into it.

'If we'd got out before the tide came in,' she murmured, 'we wouldn't have seen this.'

'No,' he said. 'It's a good silver lining.'

They watched the sky darken, the sun slip, quicker than Thea expected, towards the water. It was beautiful, but at least sixty per cent of her focus was on where she and Ben touched: her right side, his left. His hand rested loosely against her arm, his fingers tracing the shape of her elbow, drifting down towards her wrist and back up again. She felt as if she was being ignited, burning brighter and brighter as the sun also seemed to be, turning from yellow, to amber, to red as it descended.

She heard Ben inhale, felt him move his arm away, and was about to say something when he turned towards her and slipped a strand of her hair behind her ear.

'Thea.' His voice was gravel.

'Yes?' It came out as a breathy whisper, and she would have laughed at herself if she wasn't so desperate to hear what he was about to say.

'Can I kiss you?' There was no hesitancy, no drop of his eyes from her face to the floor. He took her hand and squeezed it, as if she hadn't heard him.

'Please,' she said, and when he closed the gap between them, she tipped her face up, and a moment later his lips were brushing against hers. They moved softly at first, then boldly, his hand pressed against the small of her back, holding her in place.

It was such a good kiss, one that took over her mind and sent shockwaves of sensation through her, and when she gripped his shoulders, the extra contact made her feel as if she might combust from all the sparks firing inside her. Ben, it turned out, was as confident and determined about kissing as he was about everything else. It made Thea feel trembly in the best possible way.

When they broke apart, she felt completely undone by him. They were standing next to the lightless bulb in an abandoned lighthouse, surrounded by a churning sea. It was the perfect metaphor, because to her, Ben felt like a lighthouse in a storm: he was solid and steady, and he burned so brightly.

He took her hand, led her to the blanket and sat down, tugging her gently so she was next to him. He pressed his palm against her cheek, and she leaned into his warmth. Now the sun was slipping away, their temporary prison was getting chilly. But Ben, it turned out, had a way of combating the cold.

He brought his head close to hers. 'I'm regretting getting stranded a lot less, now,' he murmured.

'It seems like there are even more silver linings,' she agreed. This time, she was the one who closed the gap between them.

They kissed like teenagers, Ben pulling her closer, somehow managing to wrap the blanket around her while his mouth stayed on hers. Thea loved her warm cocoon of desire and sensation, and she wanted to be even closer to him. But his hands didn't stray anywhere other than her back and her arms, occasionally cupping her jaw, and she laced her hands around his neck, finally sliding her fingers into his soft, prickly hair, and kept them there.

Eventually, he pulled back. 'We have to stop.'

'Because your dog's eyeing me like I'm some kind of intruder?'

Ben laughed softly, reaching out to stroke Scooter's fur. 'No, because this isn't – it's not the right place.'

'I know,' she said quietly.

He leaned against the glass, holding his arm out so Thea could settle herself in the crook of it. She wondered if part of her had been wanting this to happen since the moment Ben had invited her here. Not the stranding, of course, but the kissing. She pictured Alex, with his twinkly eyes and easy charm, and tried to feel an inkling of regret about what had just happened. She couldn't.

'What are you going to call your bookshop?' Ben asked, his words vibrating through her as her head rested against his chest.

'I don't know,' she admitted.

'What?' He sounded surprised.

'It's mad, isn't it? It's been my dream for so many years, but I have no clue what to call it. The Port Karadow Bookshop – if I end up here, of course. Thea's Reads? I want something unique and memorable, but whenever I try and come up with a good name – and even though I love words – my mind goes blank.'

'Because you care about it so much.'

'I do care,' she said, as drowsiness slipped over her like an extra blanket. 'I care a lot. I love that you understand.'

She was woken by Ben shaking her gently, whispering that it was time for them to go. Her immediate concern was that she'd dribbled on his T-shirt, but when she looked up at him, his features lit by moonlight, now, instead of the fiery sunset, his smile was warm.

'We've got a causeway again,' he said. 'Better not miss this one as well.'

'Of course not.' She extracted herself from him and they put everything – the Tupperware boxes, the empty bottles

– back in their rucksacks. Scooter had been dozing, too, and Thea conjured an image of Ben watching guard over them both, shooing away any giant spiders that tried to get close. The thought made her smile.

Walking back across the causeway, the moon a bright, surreal guide, was one of the strangest, most breathtaking things Thea had ever done. Ben led the way, his arm behind him, his hand out towards her – not to hold, she didn't think – but as reassurance. She could grab it if she needed to.

The drive back to the cottages was quick, the roads empty, and the whole time Thea had to resist pressing her fingers against her lips. They still tingled from all their kissing, from the slight scrape of Ben's stubble. He parked the van in its usual place, and she wondered what would happen now. It was really late, and even though part of her was crying out for Ben to come inside with her—

'We should probably get some sleep,' he said softly. 'Seeing as we're back quite a lot later than I'd planned.'

Thea nodded, smiling. 'Thank you. I don't think it's a day I'm going to forget in a hurry. I really enjoyed it.'

'I did too, despite my monumental slip-up. Maybe we could catch up again, in a couple of days?'

'I'd love that. I owe you a lasagne.'

'You don't owe me—'

'I want to,' she rushed, and he nodded.

The awkwardness between them felt sweet: tender, somehow, and when she got out of the van, Ben walked her to her door, even though it was only a few metres away.

She unlocked it, then turned, noticing the way Ben was looking at her, his brow slightly furrowed. She reached a hand behind his neck and pulled him towards her, giving him a soft kiss, letting her mouth linger against his.

'See you soon,' she said. She went inside, leaving him standing there, a whisper of a smile on his lips.

Sleep came easily, but didn't stay. She kept waking, her mind replaying the view from the lighthouse, how the causeway had disappeared without them noticing; their first kiss, the seconds of anticipation before Ben's lips brushed against hers; his question about her bookshop name, and Alex, with his cheerful smile and encouraging words, the way he'd shown up just when she'd needed him, a white knight in a suit and tie instead of armour.

Thea tossed and turned, the sheets tangling around her legs, her bedroom much warmer than the top floor of the lighthouse. The one thought she kept returning to, was that she hadn't had a name for her bookshop when Ben asked. Did he think she was fickle, that her plans were unrealistic after all? The idea that he might think less of her wouldn't leave her alone.

She woke up mid-morning, her eyes gritty, and forced herself into the shower, then downstairs for breakfast. She spent the day drifting around the cottage, reading but not focusing, looking out of the window and wondering where Ben was, and what it would be like between them from now on.

On Friday, she got up early and drove to the Eden Project. It had been on her and Esme's list: a must-see attraction. The huge domes replicating Mediterranean and rainforest ecosystems held her attention for a while, but Ben and the bookshop kept slipping into her thoughts to distract her, and she went in search of fresher air.

Outside in the gardens, she bought herself an iced tea and sat on a bench close to a vine-strewn pergola. There was only one person she wanted to talk to when her thoughts were so tangled – and she couldn't speak to Ben about her feelings for him – so she got out her phone, navigated to the right number, and waited.

'Thea?' Esme said. 'I haven't heard from you for ages!'

'I thought you'd probably be too busy to talk,' Thea replied. 'Today's the last day of the festival, isn't it? Has it gone OK?'

'It's been great. Most of the events have been sold out, and we've had excellent footfall for the walk-in sessions. Just a couple more to go, and then . . . freedom!' She sighed. 'How are you, anyway? Thanks for the photos of Trebah – it looked beautiful. What else have you been up to?'

'Avoiding coasteering,' Thea said, and Esme laughed.

'I don't blame you. Even I wasn't entirely sure about it when we added it to the list. What *have* you done?'

'I'm at the Eden Project. You'd love it here, Es. There's so much going on, and it's all so well organised.' They both laughed this time. 'And something rather . . . unusual happened.'

'Oh?'

'I got stranded in a deserted lighthouse. Only for a few hours, but—'

'All by yourself?' Esme squealed.

'No! Not by myself. With Ben.'

'Ben?' She sounded confused, then said, 'Oh my God! Mr Irascible Hash Browns? You got stranded in a deserted lighthouse with *Mr Irascible Hash Browns?* Holy hell, Thea!'

'It was OK actually.'

'You . . . you . . .' Esme was spluttering now. 'You had a thing, didn't you? You're having a *thing*? Romance is in the Cornish air, and I'm missing it. Tell me everything!'

'Don't you have a festival to finish?' Now she had her friend's undivided attention, she found she didn't want it.

'No festival is as important as this. You like him?'

'We've been getting on well,' Thea said carefully. 'We're starting to be friends. But then, you know . . . forced proximity, and the sense of danger, being trapped there, surrounded by the ocean. It's not a whole thing. It was one kiss. Two, possibly.' *And the second one lasted a really long time*, she didn't add. 'Anyway, it wouldn't have happened if you'd been here. I never would have gone looking for other people.'

'Are you blaming me for your holiday romance?' Esme asked. 'Or crediting me with it? You're so confusing sometimes.'

'How's Alex?' Thea asked.

There was a slight pause, then Esme said, 'He's Alex, same as always. Stop changing the subject.'

'I've come to the end of the subject.' Thea shifted on her bench as a man wearing a beige flat cap and carrying a bag of birdseed sat on the other end. She was wearing Ben's *Lakes for Life* cap again. She'd felt a small thrill when she put it on; it had made her think of those scenes in books when girlfriends wore their boyfriend's shirt after spending the night together, even though her thing with Ben was nothing like that.

'No you haven't,' Esme said. 'Are you going to see him again?'

'He's in the cottage next door, so it seems likely.'

Esme made an exasperated noise. 'Are you *planning* to see him again?'

Thea chewed her lip. They had one week left together, and after that, she would be going back to Bristol. She was no further on with her bookshop premises, hadn't done anything to explore any options beyond Jamie Scable's shop on Main Street. It had been the most important aspect of this trip for her, and she'd achieved nothing.

'I'm just going to see how it goes,' she said to Esme. 'But this is a holiday, isn't it? If anything happens between us, it's only a bit of fun. Anyway, he's as cool as they come; not my type at all. It could never be anything long term.' It was a total lie, one that made her feel uncomfortable all the way to her core. If her future in Cornwall was assured, then she would be viewing him as a significant part of it, all her caveats about why it couldn't work between them suddenly gone. But she couldn't tell Esme that, because Esme didn't know about her plans to move here, and she didn't want to say anything that might arouse suspicion. 'Listen, I have to go. I'm on this tour and it's about to start.'

'Fine, but call me later, OK? There's something I want to ask you. Love you lots.'

'Love you back,' Thea said absentmindedly, and hung up.

'What tour's this you're on?' the old man asked, proving that he'd been listening to her side of the conversation. 'Any good?'

'There's no tour,' she admitted. 'I made it up so I could end the call.'

'Ah.' The old man tapped the peak of his cap. There was a robin standing on the path in front of him, head cocked, clearly waiting for him to throw more seed. 'Good thinking. I tell my neighbour I've got a pie in the oven, but I can't cook for toffee and I'm worried one day she'll ask for a slice.'

Thea smiled. 'Make sure you always have an apple pie in your freezer, then if you need to you can cook it and pretend you made it.'

The man chuckled. 'You've got a plan for everything.'

'Not really,' she said, because she had no plan for the things that mattered: what to do next about her bookshop, the fact that Esme didn't know anything about it, her and Ben. 'Enjoy the rest of your day,' she added, getting up and walking away, leaving him to his eager robin.

Except, she thought, as she strolled back to her car, she *could* do something about the bookshop. She could stop avoiding the difficulties, and be proactive. She took her phone out again, scrolled through the contacts to a name that gave her a little shock of revulsion, and pressed the 'call' button. He answered after one ring.

'Jamie Scable.' He sounded jaunty and confident. Those were the things Thea would have to be if she wanted to succeed.

'Hi Jamie,' she said, glancing back at the transparent domes and deciding she could be as bold as the flowers she'd seen inside them. 'It's Thea Rushwood. I want to come and have another look at your commercial property in Port Karadow. When are you available?'

# Chapter Eighteen

Jamie Scable agreed to meet Thea on Sunday. She knew it was a power play, but she didn't mind. The shop on Main Street felt like unfinished business, and she wanted to tick it off her list, one way or the other.

When she got back to Sunfish Cottage Ben's van was outside, the sinking sun turning the windscreen pink, reflecting the view as if it was a painting. There were lights on in his house, and with no curtains over the windows, she had to resist the urge to peer inside.

She was at her front door, key in hand, when she felt something nudge her leg. She looked down and saw Scooter, then turned around. Ben was standing next to his van, his hands in his shorts pockets. His smile was wide, and she had to force herself not to run up to him.

'Hey,' he said, then cleared his throat.

'Hi.' She saw his gaze flit down, landing on the *Lakes for Life* cap sticking out of her bag. 'I was at the Eden Project today. Your hat saved me from sunstroke.'

'Good time?'

'Great, thanks. What I really needed to do to escape this heat was go somewhere even hotter.'

He laughed. 'It's pretty impressive, though.'

'Oh, it is! I wasn't complaining. Just . . .'

'I know.'

Thea felt the apprehension, the uncertainty, thickening the air between them, and decided it was ridiculous. 'What are you doing tomorrow?'

He rubbed the back of his neck. 'My grand plan is to tile the bathroom, so you're going to struggle to come up with anything that will tear me away.'

'You *should* be tiling your bathroom,' she said, mock-scolding.

'And while I'm doing that, what will you be doing?'

'I'm going coasteering,' Thea said, and enjoyed the way Ben's eyes widened and his lips parted in surprise.

'But you're—'

'I'm not really,' she said, 'I just wanted to see your face.'

He frowned, his annoyed confusion so adorable that she doubled over laughing. He folded his arms, feigning irritation. The posture emphasised his biceps, showed off his strong forearms. Thea swallowed.

'How about I help you with the tiling, then we can have my incredible home-cooked lasagne?'

'You want to spend the last Saturday of your holiday helping me tile my bathroom?'

'I've done tiling before.' She had added a splash-back behind her bathroom basin, and it had taken most of a morning, but he didn't need to know that.

'I'm not questioning your ability,' he said. 'Just your sanity.'

'The weather's meant to break.' She waggled her phone. 'Tiling and lasagne doesn't sound a bad way to spend a grey day. We could throw in a film night for added excitement.'

He raised his eyebrows. 'You're sure?'

'I'd like to,' she said. 'Really.'

'OK.' His frown cleared, and it was like the sun coming out from behind clouds. 'I'd love that, too. See you tomorrow, then?'

She nodded and smiled, and wondered how this was supposed to end. Would they stand there, grinning at each other until darkness fell? She couldn't do that, so she walked forward, leaned up on her toes and kissed him. He tasted of coffee, and his initial hesitation, followed by the pressure of him returning the kiss, made her want to drag him into her cottage. Instead she stepped back, said, 'See you tomorrow,' and went inside before he could reply.

She closed the front door and leaned against it, touching her fingers to her lips. This holiday was turning out to be a lot better than she'd imagined, in some very unexpected ways.

Her lasagne construction the following morning – making the béchamel sauce from scratch, preparing the vegetables, creating a tomato rich ragù – had gone surprisingly well. Everything tasted delicious, and the kitchen wasn't a bomb site at the end of it. She'd agreed to go to Ben's after lunch, and was looking forward to being let into his inner sanctum for the first time, even if it was – not a bomb site – but a building site.

The sun was trying to put on a good show, but the clouds had gone from small and unassuming first thing, to hulking shapes edged with grey. She didn't think it would be too long before the blue was obliterated, and she got her first taste of Cornish rain. Anticipation bubbled low in her stomach, and that, combined with the seesaw of confusion about her feelings for Alex versus her feelings for Ben, only served to heighten her agitation.

Alex, she was sure, didn't know how fond of him she was, but then, since being in Cornwall, she had begun to realise her affection was more about how comfortable she felt with him, along with gratitude for all the ways he'd helped her. It certainly didn't compare to her feelings for Ben. He, of course, knew there was something between them, because those kisses hadn't simply been to pass the time while they were stranded.

The strength of the connection between them had surprised her: she had never been kissed like that before, as if he was trying to communicate through his touch all the things he didn't quite know how to say to her. Just thinking about his soft, hesitant smile made parts of her tingle, and it was a long time since she'd felt like that.

She was wearing jeans and a pale blue vest top, had tied her hair in a plait, and put on blusher, mascara and lip gloss. The lasagne was in the fridge, ready to cook later, and she had nothing else left to do. She quickly checked her phone, then stepped outside.

The wind pushed her back into her doorway, and she gripped the frame until the gust passed. The tumultuous weather was definitely on its way. She locked the door and walked over to Oystercatcher Cottage. She could hear barking inside, the echo of a summer hit playing on a radio.

Before she'd lifted her hand to knock, the front door opened to reveal Ben, a picture of scruffy perfection in a paint-stained black T-shirt and grey shorts, his toolbelt low on his hips. He looked edible, and Thea clamped her lips together to stop herself licking them.

'You know,' he said, his body filling the door frame, 'we could go back to yours instead, give up on the tiling.'

'Work before play,' she replied, sliding past him, her shoulder brushing his chest as she passed. 'Wow.'

His living room looked like an actual building site. The only furniture was a workman's bench and the large tool chest she'd got a glimpse of before. The rest of the space was taken up with boxes of tiles, shrink-wrapped laminate boards, cans of paint and sealant. There wasn't even a carpet.

'Where do you relax?' she asked.

'You sound horrified.'

'No wonder you nearly fell asleep on my sofa the other day.'

'I have a bed upstairs.'

She looked at him. 'Good to know.'

His blush was instant, and she hid her smile. She'd never played seductress before – the idea of it generally terrified her – but there was something about the way Ben treated her, as if he understood her, and believed wholeheartedly that she could do anything she put her mind to, that gave her the confidence to tease him. She felt, in general, a lot more confident than she had done when she'd arrived in Cornwall.

'Where's the bathroom?' she asked.

'What?' He looked flummoxed.

'Isn't that where we're doing the tiling?'

'Oh yeah. Yes. Of course.' He ran his hands down his shorts and turned in a circle, as if he had no idea where he was or what he was supposed to do, then gave her a sheepish smile. 'I get the feeling that it's going to be quite hard to concentrate with you here.'

'Why's that?' She grinned. 'Because I'm hopeless at tiling?'

He shook his head, returning her smile. 'You know why.'

'I do,' she said softly. 'We could give it a try, for a little while, at least?'

Ben set her to work on the opposite side of the room to him, telling her it was for the best if they wanted to be remotely productive. The cottage was a mirror image of hers, the bathroom at the front, next to the master bedroom, and she thought it was funny, seeing the room in its rawest state, knowing what it could look like after a bit of imagination and some elbow grease had transformed it.

Music from the radio drifted up the stairs, and Thea concentrated as best she could, after Ben had showed her how much adhesive to put on the wall, how to set the tile in the right place. He'd cut them all already, so she just had to fix and move, fix and move. The grouting would come afterwards.

'I've been thinking about what you said.' Ben's words broke the quiet.

'Which thing I said?' Thea was trying to move a tile that she'd put on wonkily, gripping the corners so she could pull it off again.

'About me stalling on this place because I haven't let go of what happened back ho—' He stopped, and Thea glanced behind her. Ben was staring at the wall. 'Back up north,' he finished.

'You might have just proved your own point,' she said. 'It still feels like home?'

'It doesn't. It feels so distant, after only a few months. I can barely remember what my old place looked like, even though I lived there for years.'

Thea moved from kneeling to sitting cross-legged, then picked up her next tile. 'You're stuck in a vicious circle,' she said. 'You won't feel properly at home here until this place is finished, but because it's not you're a bit lost, so you're struggling to focus on it. Do you think that . . .' she bit her lip. 'Do you think talking to Allie or Damien would help? Do you feel like there's something left to say there?'

'No,' Ben said immediately. 'No way. They made their choice; I just have to leave them to it.'

'OK. And you've got friends here, now,' Thea said. 'Finn and Meredith, and Sylvia. But you can't expect to leave your whole life behind, plonk yourself down in a brand new place and feel settled right away. Have you got work set up?'

'Not really,' Ben admitted. 'I was always going to give myself a few months to get the cottage done first. I factored that in with the house sale and my savings. But it would help.'

'You're doing stuff for Sylvia.'

'Not anything serious, and that's not paid.'

'People always need builders,' Thea said, thinking of her conversation with Mel. It didn't sound like she'd been in touch with him yet – if she was even planning to. 'That might make you feel more at home, too. You're adding building blocks to your new life. Putting it together piece by piece – like starting a house-build from scratch!'

Ben chuckled. 'You're pleased with that analogy, aren't you?'

'Very.' She pressed another tile to the wall, realised it was the most uneven one she'd done so far, and tried to remove it. 'Crap.'

'Having fun over there?'

'Tiling isn't easy, you know.'

'I know.' Ben kneeled next to her and used his chisel to dislodge the wonky tile. 'It took me years to get the hang of it. You're doing great.'

'If you pat me on the head, I don't know what I'll do, but it won't be pleasant.'

Ben sat down, leaning his back against the shiny new bathtub. It was deep, with curved edges and gleaming taps in the middle. It could easily fit two people, one at each end.

'Did you ever confront Genevieve, or those boys?' he asked.

'What?' Thea placed the tile she was holding carefully on the pile.

'After what they did to you, did you ever speak to them about it? I know you were a teenager, that it was probably the last thing you wanted to do, but did you ever get . . .' he winced. 'Closure? It's something they mention in that book.'

'I didn't,' Thea said. 'I avoided them as much as possible. I didn't think anything could come of it except more humiliation. And then Esme told me it wasn't worth it, and I started spending time with her, instead. The shame and hurt faded, and I was glad to put it behind me.' What had happened the previous summer felt a lot rawer, because it was much more recent, but then, too, she'd just been pleased it was over.

'That's how I feel,' Ben said. 'I was an idiot for not realising what was going on, for not spotting the signs – because they must have been there. But if I try and talk to Damien or Allie, the anger I'm starting to let go of will come back with full force. I don't want to feel like that again.'

'I get that,' Thea said, picking at a bit of glue that had stuck to her finger.

'But?' Ben asked.

'What happened to me at school – it's so far in the past. And it *has* changed the way I look at things sometimes, even now. But for you, it's all fresh, and it was a big enough trauma that you moved to the other end of the country because of it. I just wonder if talking to them would help? Even if you know nothing can be done, telling them how it's affected you – I don't know.' She shrugged. 'Don't listen to me.'

Ben was tapping his chisel against his knee, and Thea could see a jagged cut, mostly healed, running across the skin there. Her fingers itched to slide over it, to soothe it somehow, even though it probably didn't hurt any more.

'You're quite hard to ignore,' he said eventually.

'I'll be more careful what I say, then.'

'No, Thea—'

'I'm joking. Sorry. This is . . .'

'Had enough of tiling?'

She nodded.

'Me too.' He glanced around the room. 'Give me half an hour to finish this row and get everything tidied away.

I would say you could relax downstairs, but I'm aware of how unlikely that is. Shall I join you at yours?' He ran a hand through his hair, and dust drifted down onto his T-shirt.

'What about a shower?' Thea asked.

His eyes widened. 'I can have one later on tomorrow, after the grouting's set.'

'You can have one at mine, if you like. And I'll take Scooter with me now too, if that would help?'

'OK. Thank you.'

He stood and held out his hand, and Thea let him pull her to her feet, their eyes locking.

'I'll see you in a bit,' she said, the last word catching in her throat.

She hurried down the stairs, where an expectant Scooter was waiting for her, and, before she had a chance to think too much about Ben being naked in the brightly tiled bathroom at Sunfish Cottage, she called to the dog and stepped outside.

The wind was stronger, and the sky was filled with a giant inkblot of dark cloud, blocking out the sun. It was dramatic enough on its own, but the sea below was a riot of white horses, flecked and frothing, tumultuous and angry. She could hear waves crashing brazenly against the rocks, and though it wasn't raining yet, she could tell it wasn't far off. She turned to check Scooter was following, then hurried to her cosy cottage.

Ben knocked on the door almost an hour later. Thea's gaze went straight to the pile of clothes, fresh towel and wash bag he was holding.

'Sure this is OK?' he asked.

She stepped back to let him in, feeling the wind whip around him and reach out to her with its cool fingers. 'Of course. Upstairs, the door at the end of the corridor. Help yourself to shampoo and whatever else you need.'

'Thanks.' His attention went to Scooter, who was lying on the kitchen floor. 'Making yourself at home, I see.' The dog raised his head and barked, and Ben laughed. 'Of course you are.'

'Red or white wine, or beer?' Thea asked. This, she realised, felt like a proper date. Hikes, abandoned lighthouses and tiling – even though one of those had included some epic kissing – were not traditional dates. Cooking a homemade meal, producing wine, sharing them in the elegant living room of her holiday home: there was no escaping what this meant.

'I'm happy with wine, if you're having it,' Ben said. 'Whatever you fancy.'

'OK. Red will go with the food, so I'll open that.'

'Great. Shall I?' He gestured to the stairs.

'Go for it.'

Thea prepared a salad to go with the lasagne, opened the wine and poured herself a small glass, leaving the rest to breathe. As she kept herself busy, Scooter followed her every movement with his pale gaze. She tried not to listen to the creak of the floor as Ben moved about above her, the slight squeal of the pipes as he switched the water on, the gush as it came out of the rainfall shower head. She would not think about him standing there naked, all muscles and tanned skin, the water dripping off the planes of his body, his glossy eyelashes. She would *not*.

'I'm not thinking about him,' she told Scooter, and the dog tipped his head on one side, in the ultimate *I do not believe you* gesture. She slumped onto a stool. 'I'm *not*.'

She took a sip of wine, let out a long, calming breath, and was plunged into darkness.

# Chapter Nineteen

Thea heard an exclamation of surprise from upstairs, followed by the sound of the shower turning off. It wasn't an electric shower, but the sudden outage must have surprised Ben as much as it had her. She put her hand out and took a couple of tentative steps forward. Her foot hit something, and the gentle snuffle told her it was Scooter, though the dog clearly wasn't as alarmed as she was.

She edged round him, felt the door frame against her palm and stepped into the living room. The cloud cover meant there wasn't any moonlight, no red dots or digital clocks on anything because they'd all been wiped out by the power cut.

'Ben?' she shouted, edging towards the stairs.

She heard the bathroom door open. 'Thea?' he called down. 'Are you OK? What happened?'

'I think it must be the storm. I didn't do anything to trip a switch, though I suppose we should check, just to be sure.'

'Under the stairs? That's where mine is. Do you have a torch?'

'I have my phone.' She crept over to the coffee table, where she'd last seen it, and fumbled about for it. The relief as she felt its smooth surface was immediate. She unlocked it and switched the torch on, glad of the weak light it let out. She swung it in the direction of the cupboard, and its glow found Ben, coming slowly down the stairs.

Thea froze, and a voice inside her head said that now would be a great time for the power to come back on, because he had a blue towel wrapped around his waist, and that was it. Seeing him like this felt a lot more intimate than it had at the beach, where they had been surrounded by other people. Now it was only her, gazing on all his lean, tanned muscle, and she felt as if the red wine had sucked every ounce of moisture out of her mouth. She swallowed, then tried to clear her throat as he came to join her.

'In here?' he asked, his hand on the knob of the small door set into the wall beneath the stairs.

'Yes,' she scraped out. He smelled of her coconut and pineapple body wash, which she loved because the fresh scent woke her up every morning. On him, it was like the most moreish cocktail.

Ben pulled open the door, and the light from Thea's phone illuminated his broad, muscled back. She drank it in all over again: his wide shoulders tapering to a narrow waist, everything strong and smooth and—

'Can I have your phone?' he asked. She held it out to him and he took it, oblivious to the storm of sensations she was experiencing.

'You're right, no tripped fuse. It must be the weather.' He shut the door and turned to her, his bare chest pale in the glare from her phone.

'No lasagne then,' she said. 'No film either, unless . . . I might have enough battery on my iPad for us to watch one. But we'd have to huddle up.' Her eyes slid back to his chest, and this time it was Ben who cleared his throat.

'I should put some clothes on,' he murmured.

Thea nodded vigorously. 'Yes. Yes, I think that would be a good idea.'

Somehow, they had moved closer. His hair was damp, and it sent water droplets sliding tantalisingly down his skin.

'Thea.' He sounded breathless all of a sudden, as if he'd hefted a whole floor's worth of laminate boards up a very steep slope.

'Hmmm?'

'I think we should . . .' Their eyes held, and even though the light was faint and weirdly distorted, Thea thought she saw at least fifteen emotions pass across Ben's face. Then he closed his eyes, looking pained.

'This might be a good time to test how well you've fixed my bed?' Her voice came out a lot smaller than she'd intended, and she clenched her hands into fists. She wanted to be confident in this moment.

Ben's eyes shot open, and she saw him swallow. 'That's the best idea I think anyone's ever had,' he said quietly, but she knew, from the way he was looking at her, that he was going to turn her down.

Shame started as a creeping coldness in her stomach, spreading up and down and outwards. She dipped her chin. 'But you don't want to.'

His touch was light, but she let him tip her chin up to meet his gaze.

'It's Sylvia,' he said. 'If the power's out in the whole town, and she's stuck in that rickety old place in the dark, the storm howling—' As if to back him up, rain spattered violently against the windows. 'Let me call her.'

Thea loved how thoughtful he was, but it didn't entirely banish the sting of his rejection. He took her phone upstairs, so he could see the way to finding his own, and she leaned against the sofa. Scooter was lying next to the coffee table, his breathing loud and even, sleeping through the crisis.

She expected Ben to return fully clothed, but he came back still wrapped in the towel, carrying both phones. She was about to make a quip about him torturing her, but he handed her phone back and then, his hand gently around her wrist, pulled her onto the sofa with him. Thea went to put some space between them but he tugged her closer, bringing his arm around her so she was pressed against him, her back to his bare chest.

'Ben?' She turned to look up at him, and he gave her a soft kiss that sent waves of sensation all the way to her toes.

'Let me check Sylvia's all right,' he said. 'With any luck the power cut hasn't extended that far, and she's fine. Then, instead of putting my clothes on, we can work on taking yours off instead. If you want to?' His smile was as gentle as his kiss, and had an equally powerful effect.

'I want to,' Thea said, and waited, wishing silently, while Ben phoned Sylvia's number. They listened to the dial tone as it rang. And rang. And rang.

Ben groaned.

'Your clothes on, then?' Thea said, trying to hide her disappointment.

'I need to make sure she's all right.'

'Of course. But I'm coming too. No way am I leaving you to go there all alone, especially if the power's out.'

Ben pressed his forehead against hers. 'It won't take long.'

'It's fine. These things happen.'

Ben's heavy sigh suggested he was as pleased about the turn their night had taken as she was.

It was an unsettling feeling, driving through a town where not even the street lights were working. The summer storm was raging, the wind screaming and the rain coming in determined waves, battering the van from all sides. The sea road felt precarious, even though Thea knew she was safe with Ben at the wheel. Their headlights carved a path through the darkness, picking out the sheeting rain, tiny pockets of light appearing when there should have been a whole, twinkling galaxy of them.

'Those must be generators,' Ben said, slowing for a turn and peering ahead, trying to see through the hurried back and forth of the windscreen wipers. 'People who have back-ups when the power goes. This is town-wide.'

'It's mad,' Thea muttered. 'There are hardly any lights, anywhere. It feels like the end of the world.'

'Hopefully not if I keep the van on track,' Ben murmured, patting the steering wheel.

It didn't take long for them to reach the Old Post House, and Thea scrambled out of the passenger seat, then almost climbed back in again when she was assaulted by the torrent. They were both soaked in seconds.

The building was in darkness, a hulking, imposing shape, until Ben's impressive torch – a proper one that made their phones seem like toys – lit it up. He banged on the door with his fist, shouted Sylvia's name, but they couldn't make out any sounds or movement above the raging storm.

Ben pulled a set of keys out of his pocket, and Thea took the torch from him, pointing it at the bunch so he could find the right one. He put it in the lock, his fingers slipping as the rain pelted them remorselessly. Eventually he got the door open, and he ushered Thea inside before following her and pulling it closed behind them.

The sound of the storm dimmed, but there was an echoey drip-drip-drip from somewhere, and the timbers creaked, protesting against the wind. As Thea swept the torch in an arc, dust motes danced in its beam.

'Sylvia?' Ben's voice was quieter now, more hesitant as he walked towards the staircase, and Thea felt a jolt of fear. Why wasn't she answering? What were they about to find?

'Ben, should you—' she grabbed his arm.

'I need to see,' he said, his voice tight.

She wouldn't, *couldn't*, let him go up alone.

She didn't know how to explain it. Ben was one of the strongest, most in-control people she'd ever met, but her urge to protect him, to shelter him from anything bad, was overwhelming. She stayed close to him, the stairs creaking menacingly below their feet. Ben reached the upper floor first, and came to a sudden stop.

'Sylvia?' His voice cracked, and then he said it again, more urgently. '*Sylvia?*'

Thea joined him on the landing and swept the torch around the open plan space. There was a figure in the armchair, exactly where Sylvia had sat the other day. But now she had her eyes closed, her skin was ghostly in the torchlight, and it didn't look as if she'd heard him.

'Sylvia?' Ben shot across the room and crouched down, shaking the old woman's arm. 'God. No, please don't let her be—'

'Good *Lord* boy! What's all this?'

Ben reeled back, landing with a *thunk* on the hard floor. Thea almost jumped out of her skin.

'You're OK,' he said, with obvious relief.

'What did you think had happened?' Sylvia reached up and took something out of her ears. They were AirPods, Thea realised, and let out a burst of hysterical laughter.

'You weren't answering your phone,' Ben said. He pulled himself up so he was crouching again, and Thea saw him rub his tailbone. 'And when we got here, we called up, but—'

'With the telly not an option, I thought I'd catch up on Lucy Foley. *The Paris Apartment*, this one is. It's very sinister, and the narrator is ever so good. I spent a lot of time in Paris back in the day, and she gets the feel just right.'

'Good to know,' Ben murmured, and then, giving Sylvia's hand a quick squeeze, he stood up and pulled out his phone.

'What are you doing?'

'Calling Marie. You can't stay here.'

'I bloody well can,' she shot back.

'Nope. Not happening. This place is no longer safe for you – for anyone – and we need to get you out of here. You can take a bag now, then come back and get your other things when the storm's over.'

Before she had a chance to protest, Ben walked into the kitchen area, his phone to his ear.

'I bet you like all this dominant stuff,' Sylvia said to Thea. 'All this *I won't take no for an answer, listen to me because I'm a big strong man* rhetoric.'

'That's not how he is,' Thea said. 'And I'm sure you know that, really. Besides, I think he's right. It's pretty precarious being here without any light or electricity, and with the bats, now, too. Do you really like it?' She gestured around the space.

The older woman didn't reply, and Thea could see that she was being scrutinised, Sylvia's eyes missing nothing, despite the elongated shadows, the pockets of darkness contrasting with the torchlight, the storm that hadn't abated.

'*You* do,' she said eventually.

'What?' Thea blurted.

'You like this building,' Sylvia repeated. 'I can see it in your face. You're fascinated by it. If you were local, I'd think you were gearing up to ask the council what they intend to do with it now I'm being booted out.'

'Nobody's *booting* you,' Thea said weakly, her mind racing with questions. How did Sylvia know? How had she divined that, ever since Thea had come with Ben to investigate the noises that turned out to be bats, she had been thinking about the future of the Old Post House. Wondering . . .

'What would you do with it?' Sylvia asked. Her hands were resting on her Kindle Oasis, the device she must have been listening to her Lucy Foley book on.

'A bookshop,' Thea said. 'I'd open an independent bookshop, with different sections, including a romance section, and a coffee machine, and big, comfy armchairs.'

Sylvia returned her gaze, and Thea thought she looked . . . triumphant? No, that could only be wishful thinking. 'Well then,' the older woman said, 'what are you waiting for? The place will be empty after tonight. Bag yourself the building and that handsome, thoughtful man over there, and you're destined to have a life as happy as me and my Eric.' She nodded, satisfied, then called over to Ben, asking him how long she had to pack a bag before Marie arrived.

Thea was stunned. Was Sylvia a witch? Did she have a magical ability to reach in and grasp hold of Thea's thoughts and dreams? Or were all her desires written plainly on her face, and the old woman just happened to be able to see them in a building with no power, their features lit only by torchlight? Because turning the Old Post House into her bookshop, having Ben as a big part of her new, idyllic life living by the sea in Port Karadow, had, over the last few days, become the ultra-HD version of her dream. What, she wondered, had this place, and these people, done to her?

Marie arrived half an hour later. She was a taller, wider version of her mother, and no nonsense in a cheery sort of way, ignoring the storm and the creaks of the old building as she bustled about, collecting Sylvia's things.

'We're exchanging next week,' she explained, once Ben had made the introductions. 'Then Mum'll have her own annex. Until then, she'll have to put up with close quarters.'

'These headphones are going to be a godsend,' Sylvia said, waving her AirPods. 'Your Barry has the loudest voice of anyone I've ever met, and it would be all right if he spoke sense occasionally, but it's usually just rugby-related claptrap.'

'Better than being in this place,' Ben said. 'I'm surprised we haven't been set upon by a whole horde of bats, considering it's not really a night for flying.'

'Are you scared of a few winged creatures, Benjamin?' Sylvia asked, letting him help her to her feet, then leaning on him as she made her slow, unsteady way towards the stairs.

'I just think tonight's got enough of a horror film vibe already.'

'There's a ghost,' Sylvia said. 'Comes and stands by the window sometimes, looking out at the harbour. She seems lost, rather than vengeful. You'll have to make sure she's next to a good section, Theophania, when your bookshop's open. Uplit, possibly. Not Thrillers.'

'What's this?' Ben glanced behind him to look at Thea.

She opened her mouth to explain, to tell him it was a silly, fanciful idea, when Sylvia said, 'Your girl wants this place for a bookshop. I can't think of anything more appropriate, frankly, and I know Eric would be chuffed to bits. He loved a bit of the old Sherlock Holmes, a smidgen of Dickens. All those David Jackson thrillers, more recently. Turn this place into a bookshop, and I can't think of one person who'd be unhappy about it.'

'No,' Ben murmured, and Thea wished she could see his face: could ask him what his immediate reaction was.

Marie got the car open and put Sylvia's bag in the boot, and then, the moment they opened the door of the Old Post House, Ben rushed her to the passenger side and helped her in. The rain was stronger than ever, the wind still howling in anguish. Marie hurried to the driver's side of the car and got in, but before she'd driven away, Sylvia tapped on the window, and her daughter opened it.

'Thank you, Benjamin,' Sylvia said. 'For everything you've done.'

He nodded, swallowed. 'Don't be too much of a nuisance for Marie.'

'Nuisance isn't a strong enough word for what I'm going to be.' They exchanged smiles and Sylvia put a hand on Ben's arm, seemingly oblivious to the downpour. 'Look after yourself, and that girl.' She gestured to Thea. 'I'll expect updates on the bookshop too!' she called over, and Thea waved a hand in acknowledgement.

Then Marie pressed the button, closing the window, and, with a quick wave, drove Sylvia away from the Old Post House, the red glow of the tail lights vanishing, leaving behind the unnatural darkness and the rain.

'Get in the van,' Ben said. 'I'll check it's locked.'

Thea climbed onto the bench seat, wishing she had a warm, furry dog to cuddle up to, but they'd left Scooter at Sunfish Cottage, not convinced that it was safe for him to come. Everything was damp and cold, and she had to wipe the fogged-up windscreen to see Ben huddled by the door, then running over to climb in alongside her.

'Are you happier now that Sylvia's left?' she asked.

'Much.' He sighed. 'Though I would have been even happier if we hadn't had to do it like this. She's lived here for decades, so many years with Eric, and to have to rush her out of her home in the dark, in the middle of a storm . . .' He shook his head.

'She's lucky she had you looking out for her.'

'And what about you?' Ben leaned over to wipe a raindrop off her cheek.

It felt so good when he touched her: even that one, tiny gesture. She felt desire, a longing that was getting fiercer, but also comfort and certainty. She couldn't remember the last time she'd felt that with another person.

'Me?' she asked.

'What Sylvia was saying, about you turning this place into your bookshop. Have you really been considering it?'

'In a fanciful, flighty way,' she admitted. 'It hasn't been anything more than that, really. Or it wasn't, until we came to investigate the bats, and I saw what it was like inside. But I have no idea how Sylvia picked up on it. Tonight, I was mostly thinking about the storm and the bat guano and the spiders – I'm sure I saw one in a corner, though maybe it was the ghost. *Ugh*. How she realised I actually *like* the place, I have no idea.'

'She's very perceptive,' Ben said, starting the engine and turning the van around on the gravel. 'She stays quiet, then reveals what she knows at the worst possible moment, so she can torture you.' He paused, then said, 'You could see it as your bookshop, despite the bats and spiders?'

'I mean, it would have to be fixed up a *lot*. But maybe bats eat spiders, and that part would fix itself?'

'It's like the old lady with the fly,' Ben said. 'The bats eat the spiders, which is good, but they also destroy the roof, which is bad. And they need to be protected, so it's not remotely easy to clear them from the building and repair the damage they've caused.'

'That is *nothing* like the old lady with the fly, except for the spider part,' Thea said, laughing. She felt a surge of joy, despite the storm and how cold and wet she was – and knew it was because of this man: a man who, just over two weeks ago, she hadn't even met.

'You know what?' Ben said, brushing his hand over hers, then returning it to the steering wheel.

'You're about to tell me that I'm right, and that your comparison was woeful?'

'I'm about to tell you that you're right, and that the Old Post House would make a really great bookshop.'

'You think?' She had to clear her throat, to remove the lump that had formed there.

'It's obviously a long way from being fit for anything at the moment, but if we could petition Anisha and her team, somehow get the work paid for, give it a major overhaul, then it could really work. When it was the post office, it was the heart of the town, and isn't that where a bookshop should be?'

'You honestly think I could do this? That it's not a stupid, outlandish idea?'

Ben shook his head. 'You can do anything you set your mind to, Thea, and I think that building is perfect. So much better than a commercial box on Main Street.'

'Thank you,' she said. She hoped that, despite the driving rain, he could hear the sincerity in her voice.

They were quiet after that, Ben focusing on steering through the storm. Thea's thoughts tumbled over each other like crashing waves. How had Sylvia known what she'd been thinking? Did Ben really believe she could set her sights on the Old Post House instead of a small, manageable building like the one on Main Street? It would be a much bigger undertaking, a huge challenge, but could the finished result be worth it?

The windscreen misted up and Ben turned the heater up to the max, trying to clear it. They were both soaked, and Thea could feel the cold working its way into her bones.

The whole day felt overwhelming. So much had happened, somehow, though the shifts were as much in her mind as anything: how she felt about Ben, her understanding of him and her desire for him growing; the idle daydream of inhabiting the Old Post House becoming a tangible, spoken possibility. The power was still off, and she wanted Ben with her, in Sunfish Cottage. She wanted to show him how she felt: how much he meant to her.

He turned onto the driveway and pulled into the space outside Oystercatcher Cottage, then shut off the engine.

'Are you coming inside?' she asked.

His smile was lopsided. 'If you'll have me?'

She laughed. 'I can't tempt you with my lasagne: it's currently raw, in a fridge that's no longer cold, and I have no way of cooking it.'

'You don't need a lasagne to tempt me,' he said softly, then pushed open the door.

They ran through the rain to Sunfish Cottage, and before she'd got the key in the lock, Ben leaned towards her, his lips inches from hers. 'Shall we—'

'Thea?'

At first she thought she must have imagined it, her name a creation of the wind and rain, but then Ben squeezed her shoulder and she turned, blinking through the downpour to where two figures were emerging from a car she hadn't even noticed was parked next to hers.

She ran her hand over her sodden face, opened her mouth and closed it again.

One of the figures laughed and took a few steps towards her. Her hood was pulled up, obscuring her features so, until she was closer, Thea didn't quite believe it.

'Surprise!' she said, in a singsong voice that was achingly familiar.

Thea looked from her friend, to the other hooded figure, to Ben, then back again. 'Esme?' she said, shouting to be heard over the storm. '*Alex*?' For quite possibly the first time in her life, she wasn't happy to see either of them. 'What on earth are you doing here?'

# Chapter Twenty

Thea's walk into Port Karadow on Sunday morning was more of a stomp. How had things gone so wrong in such a short space of time? Less than twenty-four hours ago she'd had Ben in her cottage – naked, in her shower – they were going to eat her home-cooked lasagne and then, hopefully, kiss each other like they'd done at the lighthouse and see what happened after that: frankly, she'd been expecting a lot. Instead, they'd lost power, spent the evening at the Old Post House – albeit rescuing Sylvia, so that couldn't be considered a waste of time – then she'd found Esme and Alex on her doorstep and her night with Ben had disintegrated.

She sidestepped a large puddle, not wanting to add soggy feet to her woes, and replayed in her head Ben's reaction when he'd realised who the man accompanying Esme was. His face had been inscrutable, as it so often was, but Thea had seen his shoulders drop, then his chin tilt up, as if he was resolved to an outcome he didn't want.

'I'll leave you to it,' he'd said.

'No, it's fine,' she'd rushed. 'Come inside. Scooter's there anyway. I can't make tea, but there's wine.'

'I could murder a glass of wine,' Esme had said, skipping towards Thea and putting her arms around her, despite the rain still falling. 'But tea would work, too.'

'All the power's off,' Thea had explained. 'Throughout the town. Come on, we're drowning out here.'

She'd ushered everyone inside. Esme had gone easily, Alex following quietly behind, and Ben had been reluctant. She was sure he'd only agreed because she still had his dog. Scooter had greeted them eagerly, though he'd been hesitant around the new arrivals, and Ben had whistled, bringing the Australian Shepherd to his side.

'Ben,' Thea had said, the introductions with an extra layer of awkwardness in the dark, 'this is Esme and Alex, my friends from Bristol. Alex and Esme, this is Ben. He lives in the cottage next door, and he's been showing me around Port Karadow.' She didn't know how else to introduce him, and in the gloom it had been hard to gauge his reaction. She'd bitten her lip, praying silently that Esme wouldn't reference any of their conversations about *Mr Irascible Hash Browns*.

'It's lovely to meet you,' she'd said, pushing down her hood to reveal her short blonde hair. 'I've heard so much about you.'

'You too,' Ben had replied, as they'd shaken hands.

'Good to meet you,' Alex had said when it was his turn. 'Glad you've been looking out for Thea.'

'She doesn't need looking out for,' Ben had replied, stealing her thoughts, 'but we've been having fun. It's been good to get out and about when I've been so focused on renovating my house.'

'That's what you do, is it? Great stuff.'

'They're beautiful cottages,' Esme had said, squinting as she'd tried to make out details of the living room in the dark. 'I'm gutted I missed the first two weeks of this.'

'I'd better get back,' Ben had said. Thea hadn't wanted him to leave, but what could she offer him? A conversation in the dark with her and two people he didn't know? It was a strange situation, and she wasn't sure how to fix it. She'd followed him to the door.

'I'm so sorry,' she'd said. 'I had no idea they were coming.'

'It's fine. You'll be OK without power?'

'Of course,' she'd said. 'Will *you?*' She'd thought of the piles of building materials in his house, ready to trip him in the dark; the lack of comfort. Did he really have a bed, or was he sleeping on a mattress on the floor?

'I'll be good,' he'd said, and turned to go. Thea had grabbed his wrist, pulling him back.

'We'll catch up soon, though?'

'If you'd like to.'

'You know I would. Esme and Alex being here doesn't change anything.' She'd tugged on his wrist and he'd lowered his head, giving her a quick, chaste kiss. Then he was gone, hurrying down the path with Scooter.

When Thea had gone back inside, she'd tried to make her questions sound interested and happy, rather than accusatory.

'You didn't call me back yesterday,' Esme had explained. 'I was saying to Alex how glad I was that the festival was over, and that I was still gutted I'd missed this holiday, and he said why not come down. There's nearly a week left, and it made so much sense. It is *so* good to see you – and to meet Ben. The only rubbish thing is that the power's out.'

'You could have told me,' Thea had said. 'Even though I didn't get back to you, you could have tried calling me, or sent a message. It's such a surprise! Not a bad one, but . . .' She had glanced at Alex, his presence making her even more uncertain. Did Ben think there had been anything between them? It was only recently that Thea's feelings had crystallised, separating out her gratitude for Alex and her desire, her growing closeness to Ben – all the myriad other things she felt for him. She hadn't taken the opportunity at the lighthouse to explain it to him: she didn't think she'd need to after tonight, showing him with actions rather than words. Of course, now that wasn't going to happen.

'It's great though, isn't it?' Esme had said. 'We can do some of the items you've got left on the list.'

'But what if I've got plans? I didn't expect you to come, so . . .'

'We can do them together, can't we? Shall I get some wine?' She had turned on her phone torch and made a sweep of the room. She found the kitchen and went in search of drinks.

'There are only two beds,' Thea had said to Alex, because he'd been standing in the living room in his dripping coat, looking lost.

'Uhm,' Alex had said. 'Well, I suppose we could just—'

'It's fine.' Esme had come back with the bottle Thea had opened earlier, and three glasses. She'd glanced at Alex and said, 'I can bunk in with you, can't I Thea? Let Alex have the other room?'

Thea had nodded, because what choice did she have? She'd been too tired, too bored of the dark to argue. The other bed was made up, and her bed was big enough that sharing with Esme – at least for one night – wouldn't be too torturous. Except that she'd been expecting to share her bed with someone else that night. Despite Esme knowing about Ben, and seeing them arrive at the cottage together in his van, she hadn't been able to read the room.

They'd settled themselves on the sofa, and while Esme and Alex had told Thea all about the festival, her mind kept drifting back to Ben. When they'd finally gone to bed, Thea had lain on her back, Esme breathing softly beside her, and tried to quash her irritation that all her plans had been disrupted – first by Esme not coming with her, and now by her turning up unprompted, with Alex in tow. She'd still been awake when the power had come back on at two a.m., the oven and some of the lights pinging back to life, so she'd had to get up and sort it all out.

Then, this morning, when the sun had revealed a world that remembered nothing of the night before, save for a few puddles and damp pavements, neither Esme nor Alex were anywhere to be found. Thea had hoped to use her imminent meeting with Jamie Scable as an opportunity to finally tell Esme about the bookshop, but they were gone, leaving a note on the kitchen counter next to their unwashed mugs, and plates covered in crumbs:

> We tried to wake you but you were dead to the world. Gone out for a short explore! Back soon. E & A. xx

What had they come here for if not to spend time with her? What was Alex doing here at all? She could understand Esme wanting to claw back some of the holiday she'd paid for and missed out on, now that the festival was over. But why bring Alex, too?

Thea had thrown out the lasagne, which she didn't trust to be OK after sitting in a warm fridge for hours, got ready for her meeting, and now here she was. Stomping. She knew she needed to calm down before she got to Main Street. She knew she should be enjoying the sunshine, but everything was upside down.

She'd messaged Ben when she woke up, finding the other side of the bed empty, glad of a moment to herself.

Hey. You OK? Sorry about yesterday. Xx

His reply had come thirty minutes later.

I'm fine. What about you? How are you feeling about this morning? You are in charge of this, T. x

She had smiled and rolled over, happy thoughts overtaking her for a second before she remembered who else was in the house. Not two weeks ago she would have been overjoyed to have Esme here. Now, she and Alex were a complication she wasn't sure how to deal with.

Main Street was bright and shimmering, as if the rain had washed everything clean. There were a few tree branches that had obviously been dislodged by the wind, but she couldn't see any damage to any of the buildings. The door of the empty shop was open and Jamie was waiting inside, his hands in his suit pockets, staring at the floor. The smile he gave her was polite but empty, not getting close to his eyes.

'Hello again,' she said. She was going to stay positive, whatever happened.

'Miss Rushwood.' He held out his hand. 'Good to see you again.'

*Is it, hell*, she thought. 'I'm looking forward to having another chat with you,' she said. She was reminded what a good size the space was, how clean and well-positioned in the town, but her thoughts kept returning to the Old Post House. It had endless dust, a bat problem she would have to combat before any renovations could start, and it was a huge project. She'd be mad to consider it.

Jamie Scable stood back to let her walk further into the empty shop.

'Are facilities included in the price?' she asked. 'Electricity and water?'

'They are.'

'What about deliveries? I'm assuming most of the buildings here have deliveries to their doors?'

'There are loading bays at the top and bottom of Main Street, which most of the businesses use. Obviously it's pedestrianised, so you can't have lorries and vans driving up to the door during opening hours.'

'No, of course. Understandable.'

She walked to the back of the space and breathed deeply, settling her pulse. She was relieved that he was being reasonable. Not warm, exactly, but she hadn't expected that. He was answering her questions, at least.

'What are the issues that come up with your other tenants? As I'm coming from out of the area, it would be good to know what challenges I could be facing.'

'My tenants are very happy,' he said, giving her a shark-like smile. 'So much so that – well, there has been a development, since the last time we met.'

'Oh?' She could already guess that it wouldn't be good.

'I've had several other people show an interest in the property; demand for commercial venues is high in the sea-side towns, and Port Karadow has put itself firmly on the map over the last few months.'

'That all sounds great,' Thea said slowly.

'For me, certainly. But it does mean I'm going to have to put the price up. I have to be competitive.'

Thea resisted rolling her eyes. 'By how much?'

'Two hundred a month. That's the going rate right now.'

'It's not been updated on your website, or any of the literature you sent to me.'

'It's a fast-moving situation, love.' He shrugged, as if it was out of his control, as if he wasn't doing this deliberately. Did he really have other interested parties, or was he taking her for a sucker?

Thea nodded, an icy resolve settling over her. As much as she hadn't wanted to dismiss this place entirely – not without finding out whether the Old Post House was even a possibility – she wasn't going to be treated like this. She was worth more, and she knew that Ben thought so, too.

'That's such a shame,' she said, keeping her voice even. 'Luckily, there's somewhere else that's much more suited to my needs.'

Jamie's brows rose in surprise. 'Care to tell me where?' he asked casually. 'I know most of the available properties in this area, and I'm not aware of any others on the market. I'm sure I could be competitive, if the other place is currently more appealing.'

Thea could see his smile wavering, that he was uncomfortable being on the back foot. 'Its appeal is about so many more things than just the price,' she said. 'And it's a private arrangement, so I don't want to bother you with it. Thank you for your time, Mr Scable – I won't waste any more of it.'

He nodded, taken aback, and she held out her hand. His grip wasn't anywhere near as strong as Ben's, and had none of the same warmth.

'Very sorry we couldn't help each other,' he said.

Thea stepped outside. 'I'm not,' she murmured.

She walked up the hill and went into Sea Brew, then took her takeaway latte down to the harbour, where the sun was dusting everything in a soft, golden glow, the boats swaying on water that was so much calmer than it had been last night. In contrast, Thea's mind and stomach were churning, her chest tight.

She was proud of what she'd done, telling Jamie Scable – with all his judgement and bullying tactics – that she didn't need him, but she would have felt a whole lot better if it had been the truth: if she had another property secured, rather than just a distant, fantastical possibility that was somehow both too good, and too difficult, to be real.

The main problem was, she realised, as she gripped her cup in trembling hands, that she didn't want to look anywhere else. She loved Port Karadow, with its harbour and beaches, the strong sense of community she'd got a taste of. She had let herself imagine it as her home. But now, the only option she was left with might be a non-starter. And, even if renting it from the council *was* a possibility, taking on somewhere that needed a complete renovation had never been a part of her plan.

She took the lid off her cup and blew on the hot coffee, looking out at the idyllic view. She felt like she was flailing, failing, and she needed someone to talk to. Alex was here, in Port Karadow – the man she had always turned to when she wanted to discuss her future – and there was Esme now, too. Would she have some words of wisdom for her, if Thea admitted everything? But, she realised, it wasn't either of them she wanted to tell.

The high, bright sun added an extra layer of charm to the twin cottages, and Thea's insides warmed at the sight. She hadn't been her best self with Esme and Alex last night: she'd been cold and soggy, her plans had been upended, and she had been caught entirely off-guard. Now she'd had time to process their arrival, she could make up for her less than cheerful welcome.

Ben's van was parked outside and she glanced at Oystercatcher Cottage, remembering the way he'd wrapped his arm around her on the sofa, wearing only a towel, while he'd called Sylvia's number. It had been such a confident gesture: unconscious, almost, as if they were already intimate with each other. The thought sent a pleasant shiver running through her. She turned her attention to Sunfish Cottage. Were Esme and Alex back from their walk?

She took a couple of steps towards Ben's house, then heard footsteps behind her.

'This bit of the coast is really wild,' Alex said, slightly out of breath as he trudged up the hill. Esme looked invigorated, her short hair blowing in the wind, her walking boots covered in mud. Alex was wearing a pale blue shirt and grey trousers, and his boots looked even newer than Thea's had been, as if he'd bought them in a hurry, specifically for this trip.

'It's magnificent, isn't it?' she called.

'I could spend days walking along here,' Esme said as they reached her. 'Have you been swimming yet? Tried surfing?'

'Surfing was never on our list,' Thea said, laughing. 'And the water is a *lot* colder than you'd expect. I bet it's even chillier after last night's storm.' The sea was much calmer, but a few white horses still flecked the surface.

'It could do with a bit more signage, though,' Alex added. 'More robust barriers in some of the hollows. There are deathtraps all the way along.'

Thea agreed with him about the barriers, but if there had been more, would she have been able to go into that crevice with Ben? See those incredible seabirds? 'It's the rugged outdoors,' she said lightly. 'Not everything can be risk-managed.'

Almost every sentence out of her friends' mouths, every new discovery they made about Cornwall, reminded Thea of Ben. He was stitched into the fabric of her time here, impossible to remove. She loved it, but it also made not seeing him harder.

'Shall we get a coffee?' Esme asked. 'I'm parched after that. Where have you been, anyway?'

'We can sit outside,' Thea said, her thoughts trying to catch up. 'I just nipped into town for a – a coffee.'

'And you're already desperate for another one?' Her friend laughed.

'Sure! Sunny Sundays were made for coffee.' It was too awkward, and she knew she needed to sit down with Esme and tell her everything. She looked longingly at Oystercatcher Cottage, then moved towards her own front door. 'What do you want to do with today?' she asked. 'What are you dying to do while you're here?'

'Give you a proper hug in the daylight, for one thing,' Esme said. 'Come here. It's so good to *see* you!'

'You too,' Thea said, wrapping her arms around her friend. 'And you, Alex.' She stepped out of Esme's embrace, and into his. 'It's so lovely to have you both here.'

'Great to be here, Rushwood,' Alex said, squeezing her tightly.

All she could think about was how he didn't feel anything like Ben, and instead of relaxing into his hug, she felt herself stiffen.

She lifted her gaze, looking over Alex's shoulder, and saw Ben standing in the doorway of his cottage, Scooter beside him. She stepped away from Alex and waved.

'Hi, Ben,' she called, her pulse thrumming as he walked to his van.

'Hey,' he replied. Then, without another word, he opened the van door, let his dog jump up and followed him into the cab, then slammed it closed behind him.

Thea watched as he backed out of the space, and then, wheels spinning in what seemed a very un-Ben-like manoeuvre, he raced down to the road and turned onto it, driving away from the cottages at speed.

'OK?' Esme asked, squeezing Thea's hand. 'We need to catch up so you can tell me what's going on.'

Thea gave her what she hoped was a warm smile, even as her insides felt like they were crumbling, and followed her friends inside.

# Chapter Twenty-One

The three of them drank coffee outside Sunfish Cottage, enjoying a day that seemed to be apologising for the extreme weather of the night before with endless sunshine and a soft, caressing breeze, then they strolled into Port Karadow.

Even as they caught up, as Thea heard about Michael Morpurgo's triumphant event, and she regaled them with details of her time in Cornwall so far, she couldn't help worrying about Ben. What had he thought when he'd seen her and Alex embracing earlier? What had he done when he'd got home, after their night had been interrupted? What would have happened if Thea's friends hadn't turned up: where would she and Ben be now?

'This is a gorgeous town,' Esme said, stabbing at some peas with her fork. 'I'm so glad we decided to come, though I'm sorry it wasn't as welcome a surprise as we thought it would be.' The pub they'd found was bustling, and they'd had to sit inside because the tiny patio was rammed, groups of friends and families spilling across tables to make the most of the limited space.

'I guess you'd got used to being on your own,' Alex added. The look he gave her suggested he was silently trying to ask how her bookshop plans were progressing.

'But she's not been on her own,' Esme pointed out, and now it was her turn to give Thea a deep, meaningful look, because Alex hadn't been involved in their conversations about Ben. Thea clearly remembered their last one: desperate to get Esme to change the subject, she'd told her that Ben wasn't long-term material, definitely not her type. She cringed, felt a flutter of worry, because she hadn't been expecting these two parts of her world to collide.

'That Ben bloke seemed nice,' Alex said. 'A little bit surly, but then he hadn't been expecting us either.'

This, Thea decided, was exhausting. She wanted to tell Alex that she'd kissed Ben, that she liked him very, very much; she wanted to explain to Esme that she was going to move here and open a bookshop. These secrets, these undercurrents, were all her fault. She didn't want to tell her best friend about her future plans in a crowded pub; that conversation needed to be approached carefully, with a whole lot of tact. What she could do, however, was address Alex's comment about Ben being surly.

'Ben is a sweetheart,' she said. 'He's helped me find my feet here. He's been fun to spend time with, and I think he could be a . . .' her gaze drifted to Esme, then away. 'A real friend, even once my three weeks is up. We're going sea fishing tomorrow.'

Esme's face lit up. 'Sea fishing?'

'I can find out if there's room for you both on the boat, if you like?'

'I would love that,' Esme said. Alex nodded, though he didn't look quite so keen.

Thea was torn. Now her friends were here, she wanted to spend time with them, but she was also desperate to speak to Ben, to see him on her own. Would he mind if she invited Esme and Alex on their pre-arranged boat trip? Did he think that, now they were here, Thea didn't need him any more? She had to explain to him that that wasn't the case at all.

Later that evening, she left Esme and Alex in front of a *Mission Impossible* film they'd found on ITV3, telling them she'd be back soon. She hurried to Oystercatcher Cottage and, taking a second to notice Ben's van was gone, knocked on the door anyway. When there was no response, she sent him a message.

Hey. Is fishing still on tomorrow? Xx

His reply came almost immediately.

Yes. Your friends can come too, if they want? There's enough space.

Amazing! Thank you. Hopefully we can talk afterwards? Xx

Great. Looking forward to it. Bx

She went back inside to her friends and the action film, and decided that things were looking up.

The following day Thea dressed in black shorts and a pink T-shirt, tied her hair in a ponytail, and checked she had suncream and a waterproof jacket in her rucksack. She finished off her outfit with Ben's cap, pulling her hair through the hole in the back.

'Where did you get that?' Esme asked. She was also in boat-trip-appropriate clothing, leaning on the sofa, sipping a coffee.

They had decided to keep the sleeping arrangements as they were, as it didn't seem fair to make Alex sleep on the sofa when she and Esme could easily share a bed. Thea couldn't help wondering what Ben's bed was like, whether his bedroom was as unfinished as the rest of his house, and if she'd get a chance to see it.

'Ben gave it to me,' she said now, touching the brim.

Before Esme could reply there was a knock on the door. Thea pulled it open to find Ben standing there, wearing green shorts, sturdy boots and a navy T-shirt with a print of the *Casablanca* poster on it. For a second Thea was mesmerised by him in all his tall, tanned perfection, and by the image of Humphrey Bogart adorning his chest.

'Hello,' she managed.

'Hi,' he said. 'Ready?'

'Yup. Good to go.'

He touched the brim of her cap, as she'd done herself only moments before. 'This is a good look on you,' he said gently.

'Better than pink, peeling skin, you mean?' She laughed self-consciously.

He shook his head. 'It makes your eyes look huge,' he said, then took a step back, as if trying to escape his own words. The silence stretched between them, and Thea was trying to work out how to reply when Esme filled the gap.

'It's so kind of you to let us come with you.'

'No problem,' he said. 'You can help me catch some fish. I need to practise cooking them before Friday.'

'Ben's working with one of the top local chefs in his beachside barbecue truck,' Thea explained.

'A whole food truck dedicated to barbecue?' Alex asked. 'It sounds brilliant.'

'We can all come and cheer you on,' Esme said, as they collected their things, and Thea met Ben's gaze. She wondered how he felt about that, and hoped she'd soon get a chance to ask him.

Two hours later, the small boat – owned by one of Finn's friends, Stan, and called *Endeavour*, which was ironic because their trip was definitely trying – bobbed on a calm sea that twinkled like a frosty pavement. They were out far enough that the land had disappeared, and it would have been disconcerting if it wasn't so breathtaking. Their fishing lines were secured on the deck, so they didn't have to stand and hold them, and trailing over the stern and down into the water. Stan was looking over the bow, shouting something about tides and catches that Thea didn't understand, and she should have been having fun, but was failing spectacularly. She wasn't the only one.

'This is a fucking peach of a day,' Stan called, when he'd got to the end of his monologue. 'Get a load for your barbecue, Benny boy.'

Thea was sitting next to Ben and didn't see him cringe, but she thought he must be, because he was as far from a *Benny boy* as it was possible to get.

'Check your lines for a bite,' Stan went on. 'Keep on checking. How's your mate doing?'

Thea was tempted to tell him to ask Alex himself, but Alex was leaning over the side, his face almost as green as his life jacket was yellow. Esme was crouched next to him, rubbing his back in small, soothing circles. They had been fifteen minutes into the journey when seasickness had overwhelmed him, and now they'd come to a stop, and the boat was bobbing *and* turning slowly, she could imagine that he felt a lot worse.

'I think he's still . . . unwell.'

'Maybe we should go back,' Ben said. He didn't sound exasperated or annoyed, though she could imagine he was feeling both.

Alex raised an arm in the air. 'No no,' he called, his voice rasping. 'I'll be fine.'

'I don't know, though,' Esme said. She turned to look at Thea. 'He's *really* green.'

'I'm fine, Es,' Alex said. 'Give me a few more minutes, and I'll be right as rain.'

Thea and Ben exchanged a look. 'I'm so sorry,' she whispered.

'Don't worry. I can go to the market and get what I need. Their catches will be bigger than the few we've got so far.' He gestured to the cool box, where their three modest fish were lying in ice.

'But you wanted to do it this way,' she said. 'To make a good impression on Marcus.' Thea knew it was a big deal for him, and this wasn't helping in the slightest.

'It was just so I could practise,' he replied. 'It doesn't matter in the scheme of things. Besides, we've made it out here, you've seen what it's like, and I—'

'Bite!' Stan called from where the rods were idling.

Ben grabbed Thea's hand and pulled her carefully across the deck to the straining line. 'We'll get this one in, then we'll head back,' he said, as Thea positioned herself in front of the fishing rod and began slowly turning the reel.

Stan chuckled. 'We've been out here about five minutes.'

'I know,' Ben said, 'and I'm sorry it's been a mostly wasted trip, but we need to get Alex back on dry land. I'll still pay you the full rate.'

'I'm OK,' Alex called, but his voice was weak.

Thea looked at his hunched figure, at Esme's obvious concern, and chewed her lip. She felt Ben move behind her, then he bent and whispered in her ear. 'We'll take him home in a moment, but let me do this.'

'Do what?'

He brought his left arm around her, so he could grip the fishing rod. 'Keep you steady. You reel the fish in.'

Thea laughed. 'Do you really need to help me?'

'I'd feel a lot better if I did.'

'Because you're worried that I'm inexperienced and I'll throw myself overboard?'

'Exactly,' he said. 'And also, it's quite a nice place to stand.'

She didn't disagree with that. She loved the way his body sheltered her from the wind, the way his arm brushed her side. They felt close again, even though their lifejackets were air bubbles between them.

'Are you guys focusing on the fish, or what?' Stan called.

'Or what,' Ben whispered into Thea's ear, then said loudly to Stan, covering her giggle, 'one hundred per cent on the fish.'

'I believe you,' Stan said in a way that made it perfectly clear he didn't.

Thea reeled the line in, gasping in delight as it revealed not one, not two, but three shimmery mackerel. Ben helped her pull them over the side of the boat, and Stan unhooked them.

'Big enough for your barbecue, Benny Boy?' he asked.

Thea looked at the wriggling, writhing fish, and felt Ben's fingers drift down her arm. 'We don't have to keep them,' he said. 'I'll go to the market.'

'I just . . . I don't—'

'Let's throw them back,' Ben said. 'Thanks, Stan.'

'You're the boss.' Stan threw the fish over the side, and with a flash of silver they were through the blue glitter of the surface, swimming down into the depths.

'Thank you,' Thea said quietly. 'I know it's hypocritical. I like eating fish, but—'

'I get it,' Ben said. 'Really.' He gently lifted the peak of her cap, and the sea breeze slipped in to caress her hot cheeks. 'It's very different, seeing it like this.'

'It's been a beautiful trip, though,' she said. It would have been peaceful, romantic, even, if it weren't for Stan's constant commentary and the sound of Alex retching over the side.

Ben grinned, and she realised how much she'd missed it: the change in his face when his smile took over. 'Maybe I should charter a boat for the two of us?'

'Really?' Did she have time? Could she escape Alex and Esme for half a day? She knew it was an uncharitable thought, that she should be doing everything she could to make their few days here perfect, but it was clear Alex wouldn't want another boat trip, and he could do something with Esme while she spent time with Ben.

'Let me have a word with Stan when we're back in the harbour,' Ben said. 'Speaking of which . . .' He glanced over Thea's head, his brows creasing. 'We should get back. Alex must be feeling pretty rough.'

'I know.' Thea sighed. 'I'm really sorry.'

Ben dismissed her apology and went to talk to Stan, while Thea trod carefully across the deck to where Alex was slumped. 'We're going home now,' she said.

He turned to her, his blue eyes watering. 'You're sure you don't mind?'

'It's for the best,' Esme said. She was holding Alex's hand, a water bottle between her knees, poised to give it to him when he asked for it.

'This wasn't supposed to be a horror trip,' Thea added. 'It was meant to be fun.'

'I expect me hauling my guts up hasn't been the best soundtrack,' Alex replied, then shut his eyes as the boat bobbed jauntily.

'I meant for *you*,' she said. 'We're going to get you back on dry land and get some fluids into you. Give you a chance to rest.'

'That would be great,' Alex said. For a moment his bleak expression brightened, but then, as the engine began to chug, he turned back to the side and retched again. Esme rubbed his back and Thea winced sympathetically, then decided he wouldn't appreciate being crowded, not when Esme was already looking after him.

Ben was sitting on one of the small plastic seats on deck, looking far too big for it, his tanned legs stretched out in the sunshine. Thea sat next to him, deliberately pressing her knee against his. It was a small boat, and the engine was loud, but she still felt wary about saying anything too personal.

'Do you feel prepared for Friday?' she asked.

'As I'll ever be. I'm nervous, but I don't want to pass up the opportunity of getting to cook with Marcus.'

'I can't wait to come and watch you – and taste your food, of course. I know it's going to be amazing.'

'What about you?' he asked. 'You've got less than a week left.'

Thea shifted on the hard seat, then felt Ben's arm go around her waist. She leaned into him, and was instantly more comfortable. 'I was going to ask you about the Old Post House. Do you really think the council will let me rent it?'

'I honestly have no idea, but there's no harm in making enquiries. I can talk to Anisha for you, if you like – or give you her number? I'm sure they'd want it to have a purpose, instead of sitting there, getting more and more run-down.'

'The thing is,' she said, 'it needs so much money spending on it. And my business loan will cover standard set-up costs: getting stock in, any furniture and tech I need – shelves and the payment system – and some initial marketing. There's so much to do even if the premises are perfect, so to factor in a whole-scale renovation on top . . .'

'And the bats. Don't forget about them.'

'How could I forget the bats?' She laughed. 'But I don't have to go through with it, if it doesn't look like it'll work out.'

'Exactly,' Ben said, his tone as light as hers. 'It's just an idea to explore. If it doesn't come to anything, no harm done. More properties will come up in Port Karadow: it's a busy town, things are always changing.'

'Right.' She nodded, resolute.

Beside her, she saw Ben do the same. It seemed that he had decided, as much as she had, that her future lay in this particular town. He wanted her here. The realisation made her giddy.

She took in the endless stretch of glistening ocean, the scents of saltwater and fish, the wind caressing every bit of exposed, sun-warmed skin. It was blissful and magnificent, and she knew she felt that way because of the trip – even if she didn't have the stomach for fishing, and Alex didn't have the stomach for being on the sea – but also, perhaps predominantly, because of Ben. His hand was still on her waist, and she could feel the heat of him through her T-shirt. She loved the expression *all at sea*, and right now it felt entirely appropriate, in the most thrilling, anticipatory way.

When they got back to the harbour, Stan lined *Endeavour* up with the stone wall, and Ben leapt off to tie the boat to its mooring, before helping Thea's friends onto dry land. Esme led Alex to the nearest bench, and he slumped heavily onto it. Ben held his hand out for Thea, steadying her as she stepped off the boat.

'I'll finish things up with Stan, then I'll come and join you.'

'I'm going to get Alex some more water,' Thea said. 'Meet you at the bench in five minutes?'

'Sounds like a plan.'

'Thank you for today,' Thea called to the boat owner. 'Sorry we cut it short.'

'No worries,' Stan said. 'Bit of a damp squib, but that's your problem, not mine.'

Thea surveyed the harbour side, wondering where the closest place to get water was, when she felt Ben's fingers on her arm. She turned around.

'Do you think . . .' His words trailed away.

'Do I think what?'

'That you could get away for a bit this evening? Lock your friends in a cupboard, or something?' He gave her a sheepish smile, and Thea laughed.

'I'm sure I can do something a bit less drastic than that. And I'd love to come and see you.'

'Good. Me too.' He nodded, then turned back to Stan while Thea hurried up the hill towards Main Street.

She bought bottles of water and three baguettes, because she was starving and she thought Ben and Esme might be too, though she didn't think Alex would be up to eating anything for a while yet.

She could see the bench from the top of the hill, could see that Ben had joined the others, and that he and Esme were talking. She felt a flicker of unease, as if they were a small herd of unruly ponies and it was her job to corral them. As she got closer, her unease deepened. Esme was gesticulating wildly, and Ben had his arms folded tightly across his chest.

'Hey,' she said, as she got closer.

Alex turned tired eyes on her, and Esme's expression was a strange mix of alarm and defiance. Ben looked closed off, cold: nothing like he'd been on the boat.

‘What’s going on?’ she asked as Ben stood up. She held out a bottle of water to him, but he shook his head.

‘I have to get back.’

‘What? Why?’

Ben shot a quick glance at Esme, pressed his lips together, and then, without saying anything else, turned and strode away, radiating hostility as he went.

‘Ben?’ Thea called, but he didn’t turn around. She wanted to go after him, but then she looked at Esme and knew there was a fire to put out here, too.

She slumped onto the bench and handed Alex a bottle of water.

‘Uh, Thea?’ Esme said. She sounded confused, rather than contrite, and Thea’s stomach clenched in anticipation.

‘What is it?’ she asked quietly, and though she couldn’t quite work out how it had come about, she had an inkling of what might have been said.

‘Are you *moving* here?’ her friend asked. ‘To open a *bookshop?*’

Thea closed her eyes for a beat, then steeled herself. Here it was, then. The time to explain herself had come, and it looked like Esme would be first.

# Chapter Twenty-Two

This, Thea realised, as she, Esme and Alex walked slowly back through Port Karadow towards the twin cottages, was the problem with keeping secrets.

She needed to tell her friend about the bookshop; she wanted to hear what had happened between her and Ben, so she knew just how bad it was, and she wanted to go to Ben and fix things. She was fluttery with panic: worried that, by the time they got back to Sunfish Cottage, the house next door would be empty, Ben would have moved on again, and she would never get another chance to talk to him.

But Ben wasn't here, and Esme was, and she knew she had to tell her everything. She took a deep breath, and said, 'You know when we first met, when we were just getting to know each other, I told you my dream was to run a bookshop by the sea?'

'Of course,' Esme said. 'And *I* told *you* that I wanted to move to Las Vegas and open a bookshop there, working during the day and watching the shows at night? It was part of the reason we became such good friends so quickly: we both love books.'

'And also that you sort of . . . rescued me,' Thea added, because that was part of the fabric of their relationship.

'I just helped you see that you were worth way more than how you'd been treated. But anyway,' Esme glanced at her, 'carry on.'

Thea nodded. 'OK, Alex?'

He was keeping step alongside them, but he still looked pale. 'I'm OK. I'm sorry this has happened, though.'

'It's not your fault,' Thea said. 'It's not anyone's fault except mine.' She shook her head. 'So. My dream. My bookshop by the sea. I've been planning it for years. Putting away some of my salary each month in a separate account. I'd like to move here – to Cornwall, for sure, but to Port Karadow if I can. Alex has been helping with my business plan, with some of the practicalities I was clueless about. And while I've been here, I've looked at a couple of possible locations for it.'

There was silence from her friend. The cries of seagulls, sounds of cars driving through the town, the hollow clunk of boats in the harbour, filled the space she left. And then, 'So it *is* true. You've been secretly planning this all along?'

'Not *secretly*,' Thea tried. 'I just didn't want to tell you until I was sure—'

'But you told Alex. He's been helping you.'

'He surprised me when I was working on my business plan, then coaxed it out of me. I asked him not to mention it to you.'

'I'm sorry, Es,' Alex said.

Esme shook her head. 'You were *going* to tell me though, right Thea?'

'I was going to tell you on this holiday,' Thea said. 'I thought having all that time together, away from the library, would give me a chance to explain everything. Then you could have come to the shop viewings and helped me decide.'

'You could have told me before,' Esme said quietly. 'Then none of this would have happened.'

'I wanted to, but it always felt like there was so much in the way of it actually being real. If I'd told you and then it fell apart, I would have been mortified.'

'Why?'

'What?'

'*Why* would you have been mortified if it didn't work out? Do you think I would have laughed at you? Or do you think I might have sympathised, then helped you find a way around whatever the problem was?'

'I know you would have helped,' Thea said, feeling chastised.

'And I know you know it, but sometimes you don't *act* like you know it. And then to tell Alex but not me! A girl could get very hurt, especially when she discovers her best friend has been planning to move away for years.' She huffed. 'You realise we're going to have to come up with an iron-clad plan for staying in touch: for visits and FaceTime and probably letters, too, once you're living here?'

Relief flooded Thea's system at Esme's teasing tone, at her acceptance. She looked over at her friend. The confusion was gone, but she still seemed uncomfortable.

'We'll come up with the most foolproof plan possible,' Thea said. 'And I know it was wrong to confide in Alex and not you, but Alex had all the goods: the financial knowledge, experience about which formal, business-y questions to ask.'

'I am pretty hot at business-y stuff,' Alex said, his voice still sandpaper.

'You are.' Thea squeezed his arm. 'I am so, so sorry Esme – that I didn't tell you myself.' She swallowed, knowing she needed to ask the next question, but also dreading it. 'Was it . . . Ben?'

Esme sighed. 'We were just chatting. I said how pretty the harbour was, that it was a lovely town, and he said I'd have to come and visit you lots once you'd moved here. And I was dumbfounded. I thought – I thought he was confused, but I was worried, because it also sounded so plausible, and I went on the defensive. Even when Alex tried to talk me down.'

'I could see it all going wrong,' he chipped in. 'It was like a slow-motion car crash and I couldn't stop it.'

They had reached the clifftop path, the wind buffeting their hair, the twin cottages up ahead. They looked so shiny, so welcoming, as if they knew how beautiful they were and how well situated, with their sea views and the easy walk into town. But what they signified to Thea, right now, was a conversation with Ben that she knew wasn't going to be easy.

'So you thought Ben had got the wrong end of the stick, somehow?' she asked Esme.

'Right,' Esme confirmed. 'And I remembered what you told me on the phone a couple of days ago: that whatever you had with Ben it was just temporary, a bit of fun. I didn't— All I said to him was that *I'd* spoken to you, and you hadn't given any indication of staying: that what you and he had wasn't serious.'

'Shit,' Thea whispered.

Esme stopped and turned to face her. 'I shouldn't have said it. It wasn't fair on him, or you, and I didn't really mean to – I blurted it out. But I just felt defensive! I wanted to show him – I wanted him to realise that you'd told *me* the truth, not someone you'd only known for a couple of weeks. I wanted to believe that was true.'

'I tried to tell her,' Alex said.

'But by then, Ben was angry, I was angry, and—'

Thea rubbed her forehead. 'I shouldn't have kept any of this from you, and I should have told Ben the truth, too: about how much I like him.'

'I can talk to him again, explain what happened?' Esme suggested.

'No, it's OK. I need to speak to him.'

'I bet he'll be fine, once it's all out in the open,' Esme said. 'When he knows it was just a misunderstanding.'

'Maybe,' Thea murmured. But his trust had been betrayed before, and he might think she was no better than Allie and his best friend: hiding the truth from him, pretending they had something special, when she was really planning to go back to Bristol after her three weeks was up, and not come back.

She gazed at the two white cottages nestled in harmony overlooking the coastline. She wondered if she could bring back the harmony between her and Ben, or if it was irreparably damaged.

* * *

'You go,' Esme said, when they got back to Sunfish Cottage. 'I'll sort Alex out.'

'I just need to rest,' Alex assured them. 'I'll be fine after I've shut my eyes for half an hour.'

'OK then.' Thea hovered in the doorway. Now she was within shouting distance of Ben, she felt too nervous to move.

'Go on.' Esme squeezed her hand. 'Go and make up with Mr Irascible Hash Browns. And apologise from me, too, once you've kissed and made up.'

Thea nodded, determined, and walked along the path between the houses.

The afternoon was heading towards evening and the light was intense, as if someone had turned up the saturation levels. The sky was turquoise, contrasting with the amber sun, and it was so beautiful it took her breath away. Or it could have been her apprehension doing that: the thought that Ben wouldn't want to talk to her.

As she got close to his front door, she noticed it was ajar. She was about to knock anyway when she heard Ben's voice, raised in a way that was entirely unfamiliar.

'I don't *care* Damien,' he said. 'Why are you even calling me? I'm out of it – you should be happy about that! Move on like I've done.'

A chill worked its way down Thea's spine at the mention of the familiar name.

'There's nothing else to say,' Ben went on, his voice tight. 'You made your decision – you both did – and there isn't anything to talk about. Except, you know what the worst of it is? It's *you*, Damien. With Allie it was bad enough, but we've known each other for decades, and it turned out my friendship meant fuck all to you. That's the bit I've struggled to get my head around. How could you do it? Look—' There was silence, and Thea assumed Damien was talking. 'No, I don't want an answer. There isn't anything you could tell me that would make it better. Just leave me alone now, OK? It's done.'

Thea sucked in a breath at the anger in his voice. She ached for him, having to talk to Damien so soon after what Esme had told him. The ache quickly turned to guilt, because she was the one who was really responsible.

'Hello?' She pushed the door inwards, not giving herself time to think about whether this was a good idea or not.

Scooter appeared, whining and pressing his nose into her hand, and she could sense his disquiet. A lump thickened her throat and she swallowed it down.

'Ben?' She was louder this time, warning him that she was here.

He wasn't in the would-be living room, so she turned towards the kitchen. Through the open doorway she could see the bare bones of a room, the counter tops and cupboards in place, but the doors missing. She didn't know how he cooked a microwave meal in here, let alone food up to the standard he enjoyed making: the Scotch eggs they'd had at the lighthouse. Perhaps that was why he was so keen on the barbecue event at the end of the week.

She stepped into the room and saw him, and the lump in her throat returned. He was sitting on a small stepladder, his knees drawn up and his head in his hands.

'Ben?' This time it came out as a scratch, but she was close enough that he heard her.

He looked up, his hazel eyes burning into her like twin flames. His expression wasn't happy or relieved, but it wasn't impassive, either. It was almost glittering with anger.

'Why are you here, Thea?'

'I came to see if you were OK, and to apologise.'

He shook his head. 'I don't want an apology.'

'You don't? Because I know Esme said some things, and—'

'I just want you to go, please.'

Scooter nudged her more forcefully, as if telling her not to give up. Thea didn't want to, but it would have been a lot easier if she hadn't contributed to his dark mood.

'What if I don't want to go?' She folded her arms, then unfolded them, conscious of coming across like a stubborn schoolgirl.

Ben narrowed his eyes, and she thought she might, with a bit of gentle pushing, be able to break through his scowl.

'I'm not in a chatty mood,' he said. 'Not after everything that's happened today.'

'I know I'm mostly responsible for that.'

'You're partly responsible, but not entirely. I just need to reassess a few things. Like it says in that book: cut your losses and move on. A lot of it I'm not sure about, but those things make sense.'

'I hope you're not talking about me, because I'm not ready to lose you, Ben.' She took a step forwards, Scooter a shadow at her side. 'I know we've not known each other long, but—'

'But we're just having a bit of fun, aren't we?'

Thea grimaced. 'When I said that to Esme, I didn't—'

He waved her words away. 'Ordinarily I would say it's none of my business what you say to your friends about me, but when there's such a disconnect between what you've led me to believe and what's real . . .'

'But I've been honest with you! Everything – the bookshop, my plan to move here – all of that is true.'

'So you haven't told Esme about *any* of it? I'm supposed to believe that you've been honest with me, and not with the best friend you've known since school? That's the point she made, and it's pretty valid. Why bother telling me the truth, when in less than a week you'll be gone and none of it will matter?'

'You really think I'd do that to you?'

Ben rubbed his eyes. 'I don't know what to think any more. I thought I knew you, understood the kind of person you were, but then Esme turned up – and Alex, too: the man you've spoken about with such affection, who's been there whenever you needed him – and since then . . .'

'Alex has been a good friend,' she said, defensiveness creeping into her voice, mainly because she knew Ben had a point. 'He's been kind to me, he's got me out of some difficult situations, and I admire him. But it's never been anything more than that, and it's never going to be. Is that what you're really angry about?'

His laughter was brittle. 'I'm angry about being lied to. I don't really know how you feel about Alex, or how true any of this bookshop stuff is. I don't know anything, any more.'

'I promise you, Ben, I haven't lied to you. I didn't tell Esme my plans because I didn't want to look like an idiot in front of her if it all fell through. I told you because . . . because as soon as we started spending time together, you said you believed in me: that I could do anything I wanted.

I was more honest with you at the lighthouse than I've been with anyone in a long time.'

Ben held her gaze, but he didn't have a comeback. Thea felt herself softening, limbs tingling, as she remembered how kissing Ben made her feel. From his expression, she thought part of him was back there, too.

'If you really, genuinely care about me,' he said in a low voice, 'why did you downplay it with Esme? And are you and Alex really only friends, or have things got especially awkward now he's turned up and you have both of us to deal with? Tell me something that helps me make sense of it, Thea.'

She opened her mouth but nothing came out. She hadn't heard bitterness from him before, and it shocked her, showed her just how angry he was. She'd hurt him, and that was on top of all the pain Damien and Allie had caused. It was as if she'd stepped into a minefield and was prancing about, certain of standing on one.

'*Ben.*' His name came out as a whisper. 'I didn't want to make Esme suspicious. I was trying to change the subject, because I wanted to tell her about the bookshop face to face. I downplayed how I felt about you, because if I hadn't, it would have led to her asking about us, about . . . our future: how it was going to work when I was back in Bristol. I couldn't get into it with her then, and since she's been here, there just hasn't been a chance.' She took a deep breath. 'And I *promise* you, Alex and I are friends, nothing more. There was a time when I would have been interested maybe, but—'

'Of course.'

'No! No, Ben. I'm only telling you this because I want to be completely honest with you. Since we started spending time together, I haven't stopped thinking about you. You showed me that what I once felt for Alex wasn't *anything* compared to my feelings for you, and we've only known each other a couple of weeks. I understand, after Allie and Damien, I know you must feel—'

'You have no idea how I feel!' Ben stood up quickly, his foot slipping on the step so the ladder crashed into the wall behind him and made them both jump. He blinked, shocked, then ran a hand over his mouth. 'You don't know how I feel, Thea,' he said, much more gently. 'If you did, then you wouldn't have messed with my head like this. I thought I understood what was going on with us.'

'You did – you do. Everything that's happened between us, everything I said, was real.' But in that moment, she didn't know how to prove it to him. She thought she was getting some of the anger he wanted to aim at Damien, too. It wasn't lost on her that part of the reason he was questioning her was because she'd been lying to Esme, deceiving her best friend, and that was exactly what Damien had done to him. It was a mess that she had created, and right now she didn't know how to fix it. 'I'm so sorry,' she said. 'I can see how wrong I've got this. But I like you a lot, Ben. I want to be with you.'

'For four more days?' He sounded weary, now, his shoulders slumped as he leaned against the cupboard opposite her.

'You know I want it to be a lot longer than that. Would you just—'

'Can you go now, please?' He'd been looking at the floor, but with his plea he raised his head. She saw so many things in his expression: hurt and anger, sadness, but not indifference. For a man who often came across as impassive, his emotions tucked firmly away, she didn't think he could quite manage it when it came to her.

'OK,' she said quietly. 'I'm going to leave, but you know where I am. I don't want things to end like this. I care about you, Ben.' She walked slowly out of the room, feeling his eyes on her. It was an effort not to turn around, but she managed it. She stroked Scooter, then opened the front door, stepped outside, and closed it gently behind her.

She stood on Ben's doorstep and stared at the sky, the blue starting to deepen as the sun slunk through it, heading for the flat line of the horizon. The view here, regardless of the weather, was always breathtaking, somehow timeless and short-lived all at once. She didn't want to go back to her cottage, where Esme and Alex would be waiting to hear how it had gone. She wanted to hold onto the image of Ben in his unfinished kitchen, to work out how she could fix things between them.

She understood why he was upset, but she wasn't going to give up. All their conversation had done was confirm that she didn't want to lose him, that she cared about him even more than she had realised. She would give him space, then try again.

Eventually, she turned away from the mesmerising seascape. The one good thing that had come out of this disastrous day, was that it had forced her hand with Esme; there were no secrets left between them, now. What she had to do next was get Anisha's number from Meredith, so she could ask about the possibility of renting the Old Post House. Her stomach churned with a mixture of discomfort and anticipation.

It felt like all the threads of her life were tied up in knots at her core, and she was going to have to work slowly and methodically to undo them. She hoped her thread with Ben wasn't tangled to the point where she would have to admit defeat and snip it, rather than untie it and pull him close to her again.

# Chapter Twenty-Three

Esme was sitting on the sofa, reading *The Greek Escape* by Karen Swan, but she put it down as soon as Thea walked in.

'How did it go?' she asked.

'Not great,' Thea admitted.

'You told him it was all a misunderstanding, though?'

Thea perched on the edge of the sofa. 'I did, but he's been hurt recently, by someone else, and I think I've just exacerbated things. I hope that if I give him time, he'll realise I was telling him the truth, that I haven't been leading him on.' She shook her head. 'How's Alex?'

'Sleeping,' Esme said. 'Which means it's just us for a while. I want to know *everything* about your bookshop, the places you've seen while you've been here, and then, if you wanted, we could talk about Ben? I don't know if I can do anything, but I'm here to listen if you want to tell me about him. I could crack open one of the bottles of wine we brought with us, and you could spill the lot.'

Thea smiled, her nervous energy receding a little bit. 'I would love that,' she admitted. After all that had happened between her and Esme recently, Thea wanted nothing more than to reconcile properly, to put all their niggles behind them. 'You get the wine, I'll get the glasses.' For a couple of hours, at least, she would try and put thoughts of what to do about Ben to the back of her mind, and focus on her friend.

Thea stared at the building that, for the last few days at least, she had imagined could be her bookshop. She huffed out a laugh. It looked like something from a horror spin-off of *Bridgerton*. With the sun coming up behind it, the facade was still in shadow, though the promise of honey-coloured stone showed through the ivy, and there was a bird – a goldcrest, she thought – chirruping in the foliage. She'd come out early, sleep proving difficult after everything that had happened the day before.

She heard a whistle behind her, thought she was being summoned, and spun to find a man in sunny yellow shorts and a blue T-shirt, his dark beard greying, walking a sleek black dog that might have been a lurcher. It was snuffling in the bushes at the edge of the space in front of the Old Post House.

'Sorry, I—' she started, but Ben's words about apologies came back to her, and she swallowed the rest of her sentence. 'Lovely day, isn't it?' she said instead.

'It's looking like a grand one,' the man concurred. He was in his late forties, Thea guessed. 'Are you from the council?'

'What? No! I just came to look at the building. You can tell it's empty now, can't you?'

'Probably breathing a sigh of relief,' he said with a grin. 'I expect Sylvia's driving her daughter around the twist.'

'At least she hasn't got to deal with the bats any more,' Thea said.

'There are bats here?' In reply, Thea gestured to the building, with its foliage cloak and the worn windowsills, and the man laughed. 'Fair point. Do they do a lot of damage then, bats?'

'If they stay in a place long enough, their . . . guano, their, uhm, poo, can cause some erosion. But there's a lot of structural damage that has nothing to do with them.'

The man put his hands on his hips while his dog continued snuffling. 'It does need a lot of work, but we shouldn't let it become the spectre on the hill.' He pointed behind him, at the attractive view of rooftops that led down to the picturesque harbour, the water shimmering as the sun rose up to meet it. 'It's part of this town's heritage, and it needs to be cherished.'

'Is that why you asked if I was from the council?'

'Sylvia's gifted it back to the town, hasn't she?'

'I think so,' Thea said. 'I don't know all the ins and outs, because I don't live here, but that's what I've heard.'

'So someone needs to make a few decisions. We have a post office in town now, in the corner shop, but it could be useful again. What it shouldn't be is a bloody second home. We don't want some fancy-pants Londoner finding their way around the listed building regulations and turning it into a modern playpen they only visit for two weeks every year.'

'OK then.' Thea bit back a smile and the man's stern features softened.

'Sorry, I do tend to get on my high horse. I've lived here all my life, and wouldn't go anywhere else. These towns are in danger of losing their integrity. Port Karadow still has some left, and the council works hard to keep the locals and tourists happy, but I'm worried they'll fall short here, because it's such a big job.' He sighed, then gave her a sunny smile. 'Anyway! I'd best be off. Pronto gets bored if he has to stay in one place for too long.'

'Nice to talk to you,' Thea said. 'Enjoy the rest of your walk. Bye, Pronto,' she added, to the dog who hadn't paid her a second of attention.

She felt a pang of longing for Scooter and his easy affection, and that led her thoughts to Ben, and the pang intensified. She wondered how long she should leave it until she tried to talk to him again. How long did he need to calm down? Or – maybe that was doing him a disservice, and he didn't need to calm down. His feelings were valid, and she had to respect them, but that didn't mean she couldn't plead her case again before she left.

*Before she left.* That thought was the least pleasant of them all.

She walked up to the Old Post House, which she imagined was looking sullenly down at her like a teenager – she'd met enough of them at the library, conveying a *So what?* attitude with only their eyebrows and the sulky set of their mouths. They were churlish. It was a good word.

'Are you a churlish building?' she asked the Old Post House. Only the goldcrest replied, but its high, liquid trill didn't sound remotely ill-mannered. Thea patted the stone. 'You have potential,' she whispered, then turned away.

It was just before eight on Tuesday morning, and she had crept out of the house with her reusable water bottle and her *Lakes for Life* cap, which had, over the last couple of weeks, become a talisman as well as protection from the Cornish sun. Esme had still been asleep when she'd left, so Thea had written a note and left it in the kitchen, saying she'd be back later.

Her calves burned as she descended the steep hill, discovering little pockets of the town away from the main roads: narrow alleyways with painted gates at the ends, leading to tiny courtyard gardens with colourful plants in terracotta pots; a high stone wall with a row of carved ducks sitting on top of it; a homemade wooden stand with a chicken-hut roof, selling fresh eggs and home-grown vegetables. With every new discovery, Thea fell a little bit more in love with Port Karadow.

Turning onto Main Street, she saw that the door to Sea Brew was open, and she picked up her pace.

She walked through the open doorway into the compact, sunny space that smelled of coffee and freshly-cooked pastries, and saw that Max was behind the counter. She'd seen him in here a couple of times, and at the cook-off, where he'd been an enthusiastic judge. He was tall and broad-shouldered, with dark curls and green eyes, and a chequered apron over his navy T-shirt.

He gave her a warm smile. 'Hi, how can I help?'

Thea took off her cap and put it in her rucksack. 'Could I get a latte please, and one of your sausage rolls?'

'Sure.' He turned to the gleaming coffee machine, and Thea soaked up the sound of beans crunching, the enticing smells wafting around her. 'Are you on holiday?' he called over his shoulder. 'I've seen you a few times, I think.'

'I am,' she said. 'For nearly three weeks, now.'

He laughed. 'Can't get enough of the place?'

Thea smiled. 'Something like that. It's a beautiful part of the world.'

'It's unbeatable, in my opinion.' He turned to face her, wiping his hands on a tea towel while the coffee machine drizzled two shots into a tall glass. 'Quieter in the winter months, obviously, but you want that after the summer surge. You wait an hour, once all the holidaymakers have had their lie-ins, and I'll be non-stop until three.'

'You get enough custom over the winter, then?'

'Oh yeah. There are a lot of shops and businesses along here, the boat owners who always want something a bit stronger than the instant in their cabins, and winter seaside holidays are becoming more popular. People want to prove that they're made of hardy stuff, that they can do the long hikes despite the wind and sea spray, then I reap the rewards because they need good coffee and hot snacks to defrost. Incidentally, would you like yours warming? I'll do it in the oven if you have time: the microwave destroys the pastry.'

'I've got time,' Thea said, leaning against the counter. 'I want to pop in and see Meredith – she works at Cornish Keepsakes.'

Max's face lit up. 'I know Meredith. I know them all, next door. She'll be there soon; she's always in early, cooking up schemes to sell hampers and keep Adrian in line.'

'Oh great,' Thea said. 'Thank you.'

'Go and take a seat by the window if you fancy. You've got your pick; it's mostly takeaways until nine.'

'Thanks.' Thea went to sit down, even though she felt restless now she'd decided what she was going to do. She didn't have Meredith or Finn's numbers, despite the time they'd spent together, and hadn't felt able to ask Ben. This had seemed like her best option for finding Meredith, though, as a familiar figure stepped into the café, just as Max was approaching with her order, she hadn't realised it would be quite so easy.

'Hi Max,' Meredith said. Her gaze followed him to Thea's table, and her smile widened. 'Thea! How are you? How's the holiday?'

'Good and bad,' Thea admitted. 'Complicated, too, it turns out.'

'Bookshop stuff?'

Thea nodded, thanking Max as he put her coffee and sausage roll down.

'No worries, hope you enjoy it.' He sauntered away, and Meredith took his place next to her table.

'Want to talk about it?'

'I'd love that, if you have time. I actually came here to ask you a question.'

'Ooh. Colour me intrigued. Let me order, then I'll be with you.'

Ten minutes later, Thea finished explaining her predicament: Ben's fear that the Old Post House wouldn't be prioritised because of the challenges it posed, the idea that it could, potentially, be the end of her property search.

'Anisha loves a challenge,' Meredith said. 'So I wouldn't rule her out of being behind a project to renovate it. But it would help if there was a solid future for it.'

'So you think I should ask her, then?'

'What harm could there be in asking the question?' Meredith grinned. 'Finn *survives* on asking questions: if he wants to know about something, he just barrels in and tries to find out. In this case, you need to be more Finn.'

'Right: *Be more Finn*. I should be able to manage that. Do you think I should aim to set up a meeting, or . . .'

'What about tomorrow morning? I'm meeting Anisha for coffee, so you could gatecrash and see what the response is.'

'That sounds easy.'

'It's an informal conversation,' Meredith said, then wrinkled her nose. She was wearing a yellow sundress with a strawberry pattern, her skin freckled. She looked so suited to summer, and Thea felt a brief flutter of envy. 'They might already have plans for it, though,' she continued. 'So . . . I don't know, best not to get your hopes up.' She rolled her eyes. 'Sorry, you must realise that.'

'I'd rather have too much information than not enough,' Thea said. 'Thank you, Meredith.'

Meredith sipped her drink and glanced out of the window, where a blonde woman was lifting the shutters of the ironmongers opposite, then turned back to Thea, a smile bunching her cheeks. 'You must have been spending time with Ben, if you've been discussing Sylvia's old place with him.'

Thea sagged in her seat. 'That's where things have got complicated.'

'Oh no! How come? I heard Finn talking to him on the phone yesterday, and he said something about Ben needing cheering up, but I assumed it was house woes. Did something happen between you?'

'It did,' Thea admitted. 'It almost did, anyway. But I made a mistake, and now he's pissed off with me. I understand why, but I want to make it right between us.'

'He's had a hard time of it,' Meredith said. 'Has he told you what happened before he moved here?'

Thea nodded. 'It sounds awful. I honestly can't imagine going through something like that, being betrayed by your partner *and* your best friend. And now, he thinks I've been lying to him too. I haven't, though.' She rubbed her forehead. 'I want another chance to explain, but giving him space makes more sense than forcing him to talk it through before he's ready.

'Right now, I want to focus on the Old Post House, on talking to Anisha. Once I know if it's a possibility, I can work out what to say to Ben. One thing at a time, hey?' She ate her last mouthful of sausage roll, thinking that if she *did* end up in the Old Post House, then the walk up the hill to get there would justify having at least one of these every other day.

The thought of creating daily rituals in this beautiful seaside town made her insides dance with excitement. Still, she thought, as Meredith got out her phone to message Anisha, she was a long way from that. *One thing at a time*, she told herself. She hoped a methodical plan of attack would pay off eventually.

After Meredith had left to go to work, and Thea had thanked Max, ordered another two sausage rolls to take back to Esme and Alex, and bought a bag of the home-made dog biscuits that were in a jar next to the till, she strolled down to the harbour.

Being by the sea, she had come to realise over the last couple of weeks, automatically made every single day just that little bit better. Could she really end up living here, running a business here? Her excitement was a physical thing, flowing through her like a second bloodstream, and she had to force herself to walk slowly, to take everything in, on her way back to Sunfish Cottage.

She was no longer adrift with Esme, and that had quieted some of her unrest. She felt a sense of clarity, her thoughts almost as clear as the water that filled the harbour and flooded out to the open ocean. Anisha would be honest about her chances for the Old Post House, and if it didn't work out, she would come up with another plan. That, and Jamie Scable's property, weren't the only options.

Clarity and simplicity, the two things that were driving her right now, had been brought into sharp focus by Ben, and the straightforward way he dealt with things. Not everything in life was black and white, but sometimes you simply had to pick one of two options: yes or no; left or right; this one or that one.

That morning's walk, seeing the Old Post House again, spending time in the coffee shop, and Meredith's encouragement, all suggested that if she wanted to live in Port Karadow, to open a bookshop here and fulfil her lifelong dream, then she could. She just had to follow the correct path, choosing yes or no at every turn, to get there.

Getting back to Ben might not be as simple, but right now she was focused on the first part of her plan. Without her future in Cornwall secured, Ben might not even consider trying again. She wanted something to show him, something to make him proud of her, and, even though this was for her, she didn't think it would hurt that – if she was successful – he'd been a part of that success: taking her to the Old Post House, telling her she could do anything she set her mind to.

The sun rose higher in the sky, bathing Port Karadow in a soft, shimmering light, and Thea walked back to the twin cottages with her sausage rolls and her dog biscuits, ideas swirling in her head that was, once again, protected by Ben's *Lakes for Life* baseball cap.

# Chapter Twenty-Four

'Are you sure you don't want us to come with you? To be your wing people?' Esme bit into her toast and swivelled from side to side on her stool.

'I love that you want to be my wing people, and ordinarily, I would say yes,' Thea said. 'Alex, I wouldn't have got to this stage without you, and Esme, it means so much to me that you're happy I'm doing this. But . . .' She took a deep breath. 'I need to do this bit on my own. I think it's right that I do.'

'You're going to ace it, Rushwood. You know that, don't you?' Alex was next to Esme, leaning back on the breakfast bar.

'I don't *know* that, but I'm going to give it my best shot. And, if they end up saying yes and want me to write some sort of proposal on top of my business plan, I would love your help with that.'

'Of course,' Alex said. 'Whatever you need.'

'There are so many things the two of you could do: go to the beach, visit Trebah Garden or the Eden Project. Drive all the way to Tintagel. You should make the most of being here.'

'I've always wanted to see Tintagel,' Esme said. 'Do you fancy it, Alex?'

'Sounds good. The weather's meant to hold.'

'There you go, then.' Thea nodded. 'Sorted.'

'And you,' Esme said, standing up, 'are going to knock them dead, OK?'

'Well, I hope not. It'll stop my sales pitch in mid-flow if they all expire on the spot.'

Esme rolled her eyes, and Thea grinned.

She checked her appearance in the mirror by the door, and felt the nerves clawing at her. She was wearing a loose black dress with a bold bee print, had dried her hair so that it hung in a glossy curtain, and put on mascara and lip gloss. She hoped the look – calm, professional, but not remotely corporate – would survive the walk into town. She had a brisk breeze in her favour, cutting through the day's heat.

'Right, I'm going.'

Esme and Alex came to see her off at the door, which was possibly a bit over the top, but Thea appreciated their support. She walked across the gravel and out towards the road, then turned to give them a final wave. Alex had his arm around Esme's shoulder, and she was laughing at something he was saying.

Her gaze shifted to Oystercatcher Cottage, and she noticed the bag of dog biscuits she'd left on the doorstep yesterday had gone. Did that mean Ben was softening towards her, or that Scooter had pounced on them when Ben had taken him for his walk? It felt odd, having no interaction with him, as if they were strangers again: ships passing in the night. Still, now was not the time to think about that.

When she got to Sea Brew, the cheery location of the meeting that could change her life, Meredith was waiting for her, Max smiling from behind the counter.

'I've ordered pastries for the table, then I thought we could get our own drinks,' Meredith said, hopping from one foot to the other.

Thea squeezed her arm. 'Are you OK? You seem really nervous.'

Meredith nodded. 'I'm OK. I just . . . ever since we went to Padstow, I've been thinking how wonderful it would be to have a bookshop in town. Somewhere to go and browse, rather than looking at thumbnails on Amazon and worrying that the cover will be bent when the book arrives.'

'The *worst*,' Thea agreed.

'And also, I really like you, and so does Finn. And, despite how things are between you and Ben, I know he likes you a lot, too, so we all want you to stay, to take over the Old Post House, open a bookshop where authors can have events, and you can hold open mic poetry readings – if you're into that. It would be *so* lovely, and it feels like the future of the whole town, its happiness, is resting on this meeting, and—'

'Way to pass those nerves over to me,' Thea said, laughing.

'And also, Anisha is bringing her boss, Andy.' Meredith's words finally dried up, and she bit her lip.

'What?' Thea whispered.

'Nish only messaged me half an hour ago. She said it made sense to bring him in now, as it would cut out a level of negotiation, or something. I'm sorry.'

'Is he . . . nice?'

'Yes,' Meredith said. 'Nice and fair and – he'll listen to what you have to say, I think. I don't know him that well, but when we organised a Christmas pageant last year, he was part of it, and he's always seemed like a good guy.'

'Right. OK. That's . . . great, then. It's not like I'm having to present my business plan to a whole committee, is it?'

'Exactly,' Meredith said. 'Though I did sell this as an informal chat, so I'm sorry if you feel unprepared.'

'It's fine,' Thea said quickly. 'Without you I wouldn't even have this chance.' It was true, but it didn't stop trepidation snaking through her like an icy wind. It had been bad enough when she was going to put her case to Meredith and Anisha – and she'd *met* Anisha. Now there was the big boss man to impress. Thea was used to local council managers, of course, but this was one she didn't know, and she'd have to be her best, most confident self, and—

'Let's sit down,' Meredith said. 'Latte?'

'Please.' While her friend went to order, Thea got out her trusty business plan, the purple folder smart but not dour, and pressed her palms on top of it.

She could do this. She *had* to do this. She just needed to stop the insidious thoughts that had started to creep in, whispering that everyone was judging her, that when Andy and Anisha arrived they would focus on the things she didn't get right, on every time she stumbled over her words, rather than the positives.

On a logical level she knew they wouldn't be meeting her if they weren't interested in her idea, but those thoughts were so hard to ignore. She imagined Ben sitting beside her, remembered his calm confidence in her plan, his quiet belief in her, and straightened her spine.

Meredith sat beside her and said Max would bring their drinks over, and that was when Anisha walked through the door, looking elegant in a dusky pink business suit and cream blouse. She was followed by a pleasant-looking man with short brown hair, dressed in a white shirt and dark trousers. He greeted Meredith warmly, then turned his attention to Thea.

'Hi, I'm Andy Sparks,' he said. 'I work with Anisha in the planning team at Cornwall Council.'

'Lovely to meet you,' Thea said, standing up and shaking his hand. 'I'm Thea Rushwood. I've got a proposition – or, it's more of a discussion about . . . I'd like to talk about the Old Post House, if I could?'

'That's what we're here for,' Andy said kindly. 'Let's sort out drinks, then we can make a start.' He headed to the counter, and Anisha took the window seat opposite Thea.

'Lovely to see you again,' she said. 'When Meredith told me about your idea, I was delighted. A bookshop seems ideal for that location, and it would be a huge benefit to the town. Now, just be confident with Andy, make out like you've got everything sorted even if you haven't – we can work on the details later – and convince him that his *only* choice is to turn that building into Port Karadow's new independent bookshop. He's always wooed by a firm plan, because he wants an easy life, minimum confrontation and a happy ever after for this town. Show him that's what he's getting, and he'll bite your hand off.'

'Right,' Thea murmured, the word hard to get out past the lump in her throat.

'It's all good.' Anisha gave her a warm smile. 'I know you've got this. Ready?' she asked, as Andy came back to their table and sat down, clasping his hands in front of him.

'Right then Thea,' he said. 'What's this grand proposal of yours?'

Thea pulled her spine straight once again and tapped her business plan, got another reassuring smile from Anisha, and explained her lifelong dream to a bunch of near strangers.

'So that's it,' she said, the words coming out in a rush as she reached the end of her speech. She had veered off course, from the facts and statistics in her plan – the way having a bookshop in the Old Post House would be in keeping with the building's origins, and how she'd protect and cherish it – and into why *her* vision specifically would be such a great addition to the town, and the almost limitless ideas she had for it. 'Oh,' she said, remembering something quite crucial. 'Aside from all of that, the building has bats.'

'We know about the bats,' Andy said. He was rubbing his cheek, looking slightly deer-in-the-headlights. 'You can apply for grants to help with their humane removal, and any refurbishments that might be needed because of their . . . tenancy.'

'Really?'

'Yup. It wouldn't cover all the work that's needed, but if this goes ahead, then the council would be your landlord, and therefore responsible for upkeep. And it's a listed building, of course. There's a lot to consider.'

'There is,' Anisha said, giving Thea a quick smile. 'But we do want the Old Post House to have a purpose again, to be an integral part of the town, and what Thea's proposing certainly has merit.'

Andy chuckled, and his gaze, when it found Thea's again, was warmer. 'Yes, indeed. Merit and depth. This isn't a fly-by-night plan from an enchanted holidaymaker.'

'No,' Thea said, feeling a rush of pride at the compliments. 'I mean, I *am* an enchanted holidaymaker, but one who's been planning this for years. I came here when I was little, and I always thought Port Karadow could be the perfect location, for me and my bookshop. Now I've spent some time in the town, I know it is. I don't want to look anywhere else.'

'And this is your business plan?' Andy tapped the purple folder. 'A written version of everything you've said today?'

'That's right.' She offered it to him.

'Could you email it to me?' He looked at Anisha. 'We can take it to our team meeting tomorrow, Nish. What do you think?'

'That's an excellent idea,' Anisha said. 'It makes sense to make a quick decision. The sooner we have a direction, the sooner we can start work on the restoration.'

Andy tipped his mug back, swallowing the dregs of his coffee. 'Wonderful,' he said. 'What an unexpectedly productive morning. Thea, it has been a pleasure. We'll be in touch in the next couple of days, and if you could email your plan to me by lunchtime, that would be a great help.'

'Of course.' She stood as the others did, shaking hands and saying goodbye. As Anisha followed Andy out, she gave Thea a quick wink.

When they were gone, Thea turned to Meredith and said, 'Holy shit.'

'Holy shit indeed. You were *great,* Thea – you knocked it out of the park! There's no way they'll say no.'

'Except that it's going to cost an absolute fortune to restore the building, and they can't afford it.'

'But it's their responsibility, and they have a duty to everyone in the town to manage its upkeep. It's not big enough to be a museum, and if they have someone like you looking after it, making a feature out of it and also giving it a purpose, then some of the responsibility is off their hands. They'd be mad to turn you down. You've got this, Thea. We should celebrate!'

'I can't,' she said. 'Not until I've heard back from them. Do you know if their meeting is in the morning, or the afternoon?'

Meredith laughed. 'I'll message Nish. Let's have a drink this evening anyway, as a distraction if not a celebration. I'm sure Finn would want to come.'

'That sounds great,' Thea said, but she deflated slightly.

'You could, just casually, ask Ben if he wanted to come, couldn't you?'

'I could,' Thea admitted. 'I don't know if he'll say yes.'

'No harm in trying though, is there?' Meredith squeezed her arm. 'At the very least, I'm sure he'd want to hear your news.'

'There isn't really anything to tell, yet.'

'Not *yet,*' Meredith said. 'I'll see if I can book us a table at the Happy Shack again. Now I've been there, I don't want to go anywhere else.'

'Isn't it always booked up?'

'At the weekends, definitely, but this is mid-week. Besides, it doesn't hurt to ask. If you don't, then you'll never know.' She said it pointedly, and Thea laughed. She couldn't let herself feel excited quite yet, but if she was honest, she didn't think that meeting could have gone any better.

They were back with the stunning views and friendly ambience of the Happy Shack, out on the terrace again because, Meredith had explained, there had been a last-minute cancellation. It felt strange being just the three of them. Thea had checked with Meredith and then called Esme, to see if she and Alex wanted to join them, but they were still up in the north of the county, and Esme didn't think they'd make it back in time. While that eliminated the potential awkwardness of bringing her old friends and her new friends together, the empty chair at their table still felt conspicuous, because Ben hadn't answered Thea's message.

'Thank you for this,' she said. 'For coming out with me again, especially now that I'm the enemy.' She held her wine glass out, and was about to clink it against Finn's beer when he pulled his bottle back.

'What do you mean *the enemy*?'

'You know: me versus Ben.'

'That's not how it is,' Meredith said, as Finn rolled his eyes.

'I spoke to Ben earlier,' he explained. 'I invited him, and he gave some pathetic excuse about having to sand down a worktop, as if the piece of wood would turn to dust if he didn't do it this evening. You were both invited; he's choosing to stay away.'

'Because of *me*,' Thea said. 'I don't want him to feel like his friends have abandoned him.'

'I'll make sure he knows we haven't abandoned him,' Finn replied. 'I'll go around to his place tomorrow and be so in his face that he throws me out.' He gave Thea a soft smile. 'Don't worry, I won't let him give up on our bromance. He's just working through some things.'

Thea rested her chin on her hand. 'I've hurt him, though.'

'If he *is* feeling hurt,' Meredith said, 'then it's because he cares about you, and surely that means there's hope?'

'Agreed.' Finn nodded. 'What I've learnt about Ben is that he's good at putting up emotional walls, as well as real ones. So many, in fact, that it's like a pass-the-parcel of walls. You get through one, and there's another one waiting, without even a sweet inside to keep you going. But, at the risk of sounding like a beauty advert, he's worth it.'

'So you think I might be able to get through to him?'

'I do,' Finn said.

'And he's got his barbecue thing on Friday,' Meredith added. 'He's really focused on that, probably nervous, and I think if you're there, showing your support . . . I don't know.' She shrugged and sipped her wine. 'It wouldn't hurt.'

'That's a great idea,' Finn said. 'Does he know about your meeting today?'

'No.' Thea sighed, just as a huge dish piled high with fresh seafood – cod goujons and dressed crab, mussels and half a lobster, the spread garnished with watercress and lemon slices – was brought to their table. Chunky granary bread and golden pots of butter came on a separate plate. 'Bloody hell,' she muttered.

'Feast fit for a king,' Finn said, handing out the plates that were stacked on the end of their table. 'Why didn't you tell Ben about your meeting?'

'Because I wanted to see if he would reply first, so I sent him a message, inviting him tonight, and he never got back to me.'

'The blue ticks of doom, though?' Finn raised an eyebrow.

Thea nodded, thinking how much Ben would have loved this platter.

'He doesn't help himself,' Finn said. 'I'm going to send him a photo, so he knows what he's missing.'

Meredith laughed. 'That's cruel, Finn!'

'No, it's what he needs. Pose behind it, Thea.'

'No, I—' she tried to slide out of the way, but Finn waved his hand at her, gesturing for her to move back.

'Sometimes you need to be cruel to be kind. And I promise I'll go around tomorrow and check he's OK, but right now he needs a bit of tough love, because he's missing out on a lot.'

After a bit more coaxing Thea moved back behind the huge plate. She didn't want to be part of the teasing, but she trusted Finn when he said he'd follow it up with kindness.

'There,' he said. 'Perfect.' He typed on his screen, and Thea looked out over the dark, glistening water. The sky was a rich blue high above, while the setting sun lit up the horizon like molten gold.

'We'd better dig in.' Meredith handed out chunks of bread, and Thea gave them each a pot of butter.

Finn held his phone screen out to the two of them. There was the photo of Thea, smiling but not entirely comfortable, the right side of her face turned orange by the sunset. She read the message underneath and her heart contracted.

We're all missing you, buddy. How are we meant to get through this monster without you? Hope you're doing OK. Call me if you want to talk. F.

'You're a sweetie, Finn,' Meredith said, squeezing his hand.

Thea's smile warmed, and he gave her a quick nod, then put his phone away. 'Come on,' he said. 'The three of us can at least give it a good go, and what we don't finish we can ask to be put in dogfishy bags.'

Meredith laughed. 'That sounds gross.'

'We'd better try not to leave any, then. Up to the challenge?' Finn held up his beer bottle and they all clinked.

Thea thought that this night, with the gentle chatter of other diners, the evening breeze dusting their bare skin and a feast laid out before them, was almost perfect. Add one council decision and an honest chat with Ben that led to him forgiving her, and it would have been one of the most blissful nights of her life. Still, she thought, as she sipped her wine and smeared butter onto the home-made bread, there was still time for those stars to align. In the meantime, she would enjoy everything she had, every moment of this delicious – this *congenial* and *scintillating* – evening, and keep a small section of her heart reserved for hope that those other stars might, one day, slide into place.

# Chapter Twenty-Five

Thea got back to the cottage full of fresh seafood and wine, her cheeks aching from laughing so much. As she lay in bed that night, her mind buzzing too much to fall asleep, Esme breathing gently alongside her, she thought how glad she was that Finn had found her sitting outside on her first day here, and struck up a conversation with her.

The next day she woke to grey dawn light, its usual, golden hue nowhere to be found. Her stomach felt heavy, and not because of the chocolate puddings they'd indulged in after their fish platter, but because it was her penultimate day in Cornwall. Even if things went well at the meeting Anisha and Andy were due to attend, she would still be leaving on Saturday morning. She had her job to go back to, then a potentially complicated process of arranging renovations and setting up a brand new business while she was miles away.

'Penny for them?' Alex said, turning on the coffee machine when she wafted into the kitchen, the sky still dull, the sea a greenish-grey. She could hear the gentle patter of the shower overhead, but the low thrum of the waves was still there, a backdrop to everything.

'Bookshop stuff,' she said, sliding onto a stool.

Alex got out plates and a packet of pains au chocolat.

'You thought your pitch went well, though?'

'It did – I'm sure of it.'

'And this has led to you worrying about . . .' He rolled his hand, and Thea grinned.

'My plan was simple,' she said. 'I've budgeted enough to go without any salary for four months, then with a reduced one for another three. I'd estimated that was how long it would take me to set everything up with a straightforward location, then start to make some money from the business. Everything is variable, of course, and depends on rent, outgoings. They're only ever going to be estimates, but still.' She shrugged.

'Ah.' Alex pushed a plate towards her. 'I get it. Now you've set your sights on the charming character property, and it's blown your plan out of the window.'

'Exactly. I don't know how long it will take to renovate the Old Post House, but it's going to take a while. I want to be close by, to be fully involved, but I also don't want to fritter away more of my savings than I have to. I can't be jobless for six months.'

'Some people might say that managing the refurbishment of a historic property and turning it into the bookshop of your dreams *was* a job.'

'Yes, but only I can pay me, because there isn't anyone else.' She remembered her first, terse exchange with Ben, when he'd told her he wasn't being paid for the job next door, but didn't explain that was because it was his house. She smiled, pushing pastry flakes onto her finger.

'You seem particularly happy about your predicament.' Alex gave her a tentative smile. 'Esme mentioned that you and Ben haven't managed to reconcile your differences yet.'

Thea shrugged. 'I understand why he's upset. I just want him to give me one more chance to talk to him. Just *one*.'

'I could have a go,' Alex said quietly, 'but I've discovered, over the years, that interfering in other people's affairs of the heart doesn't always go well. It's best to focus on yourself when it comes to these things.'

'And what *is* your status when it comes to affairs of the heart? Anyone special in your life?' She felt comfortable asking this, now that the affection she felt for him had revealed itself to be entirely platonic. But Alex squirmed in his seat, as if she'd asked him to show her his underwear.

'It's a bit—' he started, just as Esme bounded into the kitchen.

'I can smell the chocolate from upstairs. I hope you've saved one for me.'

'Of course.' Alex went to open the oven. 'Take a seat and I'll bring it over.'

'Thanks, Alex.' She gave him a goofy grin, and he returned it.

Thea narrowed her eyes at them, her cogs beginning to turn when Esme broke into her thoughts. 'Shall we all go into town today? Take your mind off imminent, life-changing phone calls?'

'That would be great,' Thea said.

'When will you hear?' Alex asked.

'Anisha and Andy have a meeting with the wider planning team this morning,' Thea said, and suddenly she couldn't eat another mouthful of pastry. 'Once they've given me their verdict, then, whatever it is, it'll give me a reason to talk to Ben. I'll be going there with an apology *and* some concrete news. Hopefully it'll be positive.'

'Of course it will be,' Esme said. 'But until we hear, I think you should show us around this town that you've fallen in love with.'

Thea finished her coffee and stood up. She couldn't bear the thought of showing her friends the delights of Port Karadow, only to find out that she was back to square one in her quest to move here. But that wasn't going to happen, she told herself. She just had to put it out of her mind until she heard from Anisha. That couldn't be so hard to do, could it?

In the flat, sun-free day, Port Karadow still managed to shine. The shops along the cobbled streets were colourful, their summery bunting, sweets and postcards creating a holiday atmosphere that sucked Thea in. Esme seemed equally charmed, insisting on buying chocolate orange fudge for them to munch as they walked along, then stopping in front of every shop window and deciding which item in the display she'd buy, and making Thea and Alex do the same.

Then, although spending time in an ironmonger's wasn't top of Thea's wish-list – and she thought it probably wasn't Esme's either – when Alex coaxed them inside, they discovered an old-fashioned treasure trove. It was full of tools Thea couldn't name and light bulbs she wasn't sure would ever find a light to pair with; of garden ornaments and endless trays of screws and nails, picture hooks and key rings in every size and shape imaginable.

She got lost in a sea of kitchen utensils: potato peelers and mandolines, grapefruit and cheese knives, egg timers and garlic presses. She found a sleek barbecue set with rubber, easy-grip handles, the blades and tongs shiny steel. She thought she could give it to Ben, perhaps leave them on his doorstep like she had done with the dog biscuits, as another peace offering.

'Planning on becoming the grill queen of Bristol?' Esme asked. Alex was behind her, holding several reels of different coloured rope, the threads intricately braided.

Thea grinned, eyebrows raised, and he gave her a mulish look.

'These will come in very handy,' he said.

'For what?' she asked lightly.

'All sorts.' He refused to elaborate.

'I've told him that if he leaves them lying around, I'm just going to braid them all together,' Esme said.

'Why would he leave them lying around the library?' Thea laughed.

'What's with this?' Esme asked quickly, pointing at the barbecue set.

'I thought I'd get it for Ben,' she admitted. 'For his barbecue on the beach thing tomorrow.'

'You think he won't have the right tools?' Alex asked, incredulous. 'He's a builder, isn't he? Having the right tools for any given job will be his first rule.'

Thea sighed. 'You're right. I just . . .'

'You need to talk to him,' Esme said. 'He doesn't want a

pair of *Infinite Grip Tongs*, he wants you to lay all your cards on the table.'

Thea nodded and put the barbecue set back. She eyed a stone ornament of a cat reading a book, thinking how lovely it would look beneath the Old Post House window, then reminded herself she didn't have it yet. She followed Alex back to the wall of rope, where there were at least ten different colours and thicknesses, and tried to concentrate while he explained his reasons for purchasing each one and Esme disappeared to look at garden lighting.

Once Alex had paid for his haul of goodies, they crossed the narrow street to Cornish Keepsakes.

'If you come out of here with fewer than three candles,' Thea said to Esme, 'I'm going to be both disappointed and shocked.'

'I wouldn't want you to be either of those things,' Esme said as they went inside, then set about smelling every one. There was no sign of Meredith, just a very tall teenager standing behind the counter, his black hair glossy in the sun coming through the window.

Thea was examining a cream tea hamper, wondering if they could carry it back to the cottage between them, when her phone rang.

She took it out of her bag and turned to face the shelf while she answered it. 'Hello?'

'Thea? It's Nish.'

Thea's swallow turned into a cough. 'Hi, Nish,' she managed. 'How are you?'

'I'm good! I was wondering if you were free to meet? How about down by the harbour in an hour? I'd be there sooner, but I'm coming from Bodmin.'

'The harbour in an hour sounds great,' Thea said faintly, wondering if it would be rude to ask for a clue. Before she could decide, Nish had said goodbye and hung up, so she turned anxious eyes on Esme and Alex and told them the news.

Her two friends exchanged a look.

'Right then,' Esme said. 'Nothing else is going to help you right now, except book chat. There isn't a bookshop we can browse, because that's the whole point of all of this, so we'll have to make do with talking about them.'

'If you say so,' Thea said. She was struggling to do anything other than replay Nish's words in her head, seeing if she could divine any answers from her tone and the exact phrases she'd used.

She let her friends lead her out of the gift shop, into Sea Brew for a coffee, and then down to the harbour, where the breeze was fresher and the seaside smells reminded her what she would be winning if the news she got in the next hour was what she was hoping for.

She and Esme were arguing about which Sally Thorne book was best, *The Hating Game* or *99 Percent Mine*, when a familiar figure appeared in her eyeline and all words deserted her.

'I told you,' Esme said, 'you can't beat the kiss in *99 Percent Mine*, even though *The Hating Game* got all the attention and the film adaptation.'

'Thea?' Alex prompted.

'Nish is here,' she said, the announcement coming out in a Darth Vaderesque scratch.

'Shit,' Esme said, twisting around on the bench. 'Good luck, then.'

'Thanks.'

Thea got up and, leaving her half empty coffee cup behind, went to greet Anisha.

'Hello,' the other woman said with a bright smile. 'Sorry about the grey day.'

Thea returned her smile. 'If you're controlling the weather too, then you're the most advanced council in the country.'

Anisha laughed. 'I wish! Do you want to hear how our meeting went?'

Her eyes were gleaming, and Thea thought it could only be good news. 'Yes please.'

'There was overwhelming approval for your proposal,' Anisha said. 'Everyone thought your business plan was excellent, and that if you were that thorough, thoughtful and passionate about your bookshop, then you'd be the right kind of tenant for the Old Post House. Not to mention that a new independent bookshop is exactly the kind of business we'd like to see here. The area needs some new life, and I'm hoping we can do that – fill the gaps in the town and on Main Street – without bringing in the chain stores.'

Thea nodded along, trying to absorb what Anisha was telling her. 'I looked at a property on Main Street,' she admitted. 'The landlord and I didn't see eye to eye.'

'Well, his loss.' Anisha folded her arms. 'There are some great private landlords in this area, and some who, in my opinion, need to take a long, hard look at the way they do business. But it's worked in our favour, because the Old Post House is yours, if you're happy with the amount we're proposing?' She told her, and Thea nodded. It was less than she'd anticipated. Anisha left a pause, and she knew she was supposed to fill it.

'Yes,' she said eventually. 'Yes please. Oh my God, really?'

'Truly,' Anisha said. 'There are things to work out: we'll have to sit down, plan out the refurbishments and the timescale. The council will fund the structural work, but it's likely you'll need to arrange the grant for the bat removal, and pay for the interior work once any core damage has been fixed. It's not entirely straightforward, but we would like to offer it to you on a long-term lease, if we can agree on the conditions.'

'That sounds wonderful,' Thea said, the words coming out as a garbled rush. 'It all sounds ideal, and I'd – I can sort out the bats, of course. I can do whatever you need me to.'

Anisha shook her head. 'It's not all on you. We'll be your landlord, after all. I'm taking responsibility for it, since I've been working on the town's regeneration.'

'We'll be working closely together?' Thea asked.

'Absolutely.'

'Excellent!' Thea resisted the urge to hug her. 'That is *excellent*.'

'Good.' Anisha's smile was wide, but Thea could see she was keeping her professional hat on, too. 'You're heading back to Bristol on Saturday?'

'I have to be at work on Monday,' Thea explained. 'But I can get the ball rolling, hand in my resignation, plan the move.' She exhaled, realising there would be so many things to do in the coming weeks and months, but she couldn't summon an ounce of reluctance or trepidation, even though she knew it would be the biggest challenge of her life. She was getting her bookshop, in the town she'd fallen in love with.

'I'll schedule a Zoom meeting for us some time next week,' Anisha said. 'You don't have to motor back and forth for our discussions, unless you're planning on being down here anyway.'

'That sounds perfect.' Thea wondered if she could find a flat or house in town to rent on a short term basis. 'Thank you so much, Anisha. This has changed my life.'

'Well, we're incredibly pleased, too. To be honest, Sylvia's place was in danger of becoming the Port Karadow white elephant, but with your proposal and the kick up the backside Andy and I gave the planning team, the future is looking rosier. It's serendipity.'

'One of my favourite films,' Thea said.

They shook hands, Anisha promised to be in touch, and then Thea was alone, standing near the harbour wall. The sun was still failing to break through the cloud, but she had enough sunniness inside her to power a whole town's worth of solar lights. She took a deep, calming breath, then raced over to her friends.

'Good news, I'm guessing?' Esme said.

Thea nodded, still struggling to take it all in. 'The Old Post House is mine. I'm getting my bookshop. Here, in Port Karadow.'

Esme jumped up and down, and Alex grinned at her. 'We knew you could do it.'

'Thank you,' she said breathlessly. 'Thank you both, so much. For believing in me, for helping me. For not being mad at me.' She looked at Esme, and Esme smiled back.

'If you get a place without a spare room for me to stay in, then I *will* be mad. I'm going to miss you so much, but this is – it's the best news, Thea. It's everything.'

Thea could hear the emotion in her friend's voice, and it almost set her off. Instead of crying, she pulled Esme into a hug, then felt Alex's arms come around them both. They stayed like that until Alex cleared his throat and stepped back, and Thea looked up, following his gaze.

She watched Stan's boat, *Endeavour*, come to a stop against the harbour wall, Ben standing on deck and staring at the three of them, a frown clouding his handsome features.

# Chapter Twenty-Six

It was Thea's last full day in Cornwall, and her life had changed. She had the premises for the bookshop of her dreams, and was a signature away from leasing the most beautiful, historic building in Port Karadow. Still, she couldn't stop thinking about Ben.

She had approached him the day before, hoping to tell him about her conversation with Anisha, but he'd turned his back on her to talk to Stan, and that simple gesture had told her all she needed to know. He still believed she'd been dishonest, and had no interest in reconciling with her. The realisation that he'd gone out on Stan's boat again – presumably to get fish for his barbecue – had made her feel even worse, because she and her friends had been the reason that first trip had been a disaster.

When Meredith had called her that evening to congratulate her, then to plan their attendance at the barbecue, Thea had been reluctant.

'I don't want to put him off,' she'd explained.

'Please come,' Meredith had said. 'You'll be in the crowd and he can ignore you if he wants to – he'll be busy working alongside Marcus – but I think he'd still be touched if you were there. He won't have forgotten it's the last day of your holiday. And you need to tell him you're moving here. It might make all the difference.'

Thea didn't think anything would make a difference now, and the last thing she wanted to do was put Ben off his stride at such an important event, but she didn't want to stay inside and mope on her last day.

Esme wasn't in the bed when she woke up and, assuming she was in the bathroom, Thea put on her dressing gown and pushed the bedroom door open. She would go and make a cup of tea, soak up the beautiful view so the memory could keep her going until the next time she was in Cornwall.

She stepped onto the landing, keeping her movements quiet in case Alex was still asleep, then noticed his door opening. Thea watched as Esme emerged, wearing her summer pyjamas. Her friend closed the door gently, turned around, and gasped when she saw Thea, her eyes widening in surprise.

'T-Thea,' she whispered.

'Esme?' Thea's thoughts were sluggish, as if they were browsing through all the unlikely, absurd reasons Esme might be coming out of Alex's room rather than alight on the obvious one. 'Are you and . . . and—'

Esme exhaled. 'Can we have a chat?' she asked. 'Let's . . . take coffees out to the cliff. There's a bench there, isn't there?'

'There is.' Thea had put her rucksack on it when she was mere minutes from the cottage on the way back from that first, demoralising walk. It was easier to think about that, to replay her holiday memories rather than hone in on what was happening, what she'd missed, even though it was right under her nose. She felt stunned – just like Stan had stunned those fish, she thought, as she went back into the bedroom to get dressed, leaving Esme to wait outside on the landing.

They sat side by side on the bench, the pale, early light and the soft breeze flooding Thea's senses. Ahead of them, beyond the patchy grass, was miles of blue. It was mesmerising, but right now she couldn't fully appreciate it.

'Lovely morning,' Esme said brightly, then blew on her coffee.

'Very.' Thea had no idea what else to say. She didn't have to wait long for her friend to fill the gap.

'So, here's the thing,' Esme said. 'The reason that Alex came with me to Cornwall, rather than me coming on my own—'

'I think I've worked it out,' Thea cut in. She sounded frosty, so unlike herself, and she didn't quite understand why.

Esme nodded, her head down.

'Why didn't you tell me?' she asked, more gently. 'Didn't you think I'd understand?'

Esme sighed. 'I didn't know *what* you'd think. Since last summer, when those guys harassed you and Alex came to your rescue, you've spoken about him with such fondness. I thought maybe your feelings for him went beyond friendship.'

Thea took a moment to organise her thoughts into words. 'I did feel grateful to him, and I think I *was* confused for a while. He's so kind, so steadfast. He's safe, and you know how much I like safe.' She laughed gently.

Esme nodded. 'I do. And that's partly why I didn't want to say anything. I didn't want how I felt to come between us.'

'It wouldn't have come between us. Don't you think we know each other well enough that we could work through *anything*?'

'Does that anything include you moving here to open up a bookshop?' Esme's tone was light, but Thea knew she was putting her in her place – and that she deserved it, too.

'You're right. I'm sorry.' She paused, then said, 'How long have you been together?'

'Officially?' Esme glanced at her watch. 'Nineteen days.'

'Just after I came down here.'

Esme swivelled to face her. 'We didn't plan it this way – waiting until you'd gone. But I've liked him for ages; I've always felt this chemistry, this possibility, between us. Then, when we were working on the festival prep, staying late, going through the risk assessments or whatever, it just . . . happened. It turns out he's liked me for a while, too. But neither of us knew how you really felt, and we didn't want to turn up here holding hands or anything.' She dropped her gaze. 'I was waiting for the right time to talk to you.'

Thea swallowed as embarrassment crawled through her. It had been right under her nose, and she hadn't picked up on it. And they'd felt as if they needed to keep it from her, to protect her as if she was some kind of delicate flower – perhaps with her own crush on Alex – and treat her with kid gloves.

It was a huge shock, this new knowledge, and it made her realise how Esme must have felt when Ben had mentioned the bookshop to her. It also gave her a better understanding of how Esme's retaliation – telling him that there was no way Thea was moving to Cornwall, that she saw Ben as a bit of holiday fun – would have upended everything he thought he knew.

She had caused so much confusion in such a small space of time: she should be grateful that Esme was still talking to her, rather than indignant that Ben wasn't.

'Are you and Alex staying on in Cornwall?' she asked. 'Is that part of the reason he came with you?'

Esme shifted uncomfortably. 'We've got a little place near Falmouth, just for a few days next week. Work let me shift my leave forward, because of the festival.'

Thea nodded. 'You've been sharing the bed with me.'

'I know,' Esme said. 'But I couldn't exactly suggest that I bunk up with Alex: not without telling you what was going on.'

'You should have told me as soon as you arrived. I wouldn't have minded, honestly. I'm really happy for you.' She tried to sound enthusiastic, but wasn't sure she managed it.

'And I'm happy for *you*, Thea. Your bookshop – it's such an achievement. Are you going to speak to Ben again, before you go? At his event this afternoon?'

'I'm not sure. Meredith and Finn want me to go, but I'm worried I'll distract him. And even if I do get to talk to him afterwards, it's my last day: I'm going to be back in Bristol until I can arrange to come down again, to start sorting out the Old Post House.'

'I think you should go this afternoon,' Esme said. 'If his other friends are there, it won't be like it's just you, giving him a laser stare and putting him off his game.'

'I suppose not.'

'If part of the reason he's upset is that he thinks you don't really care about him, then staying away will just compound that. If you show him you *want* to be there for him, that you know how important this event is to him, then won't that work in your favour? He can't stay mad with you for long.'

'He could stay mad with me for ever.'

Esme shook her head. 'No. Not with Thea Rushwood: it's not actually possible. And think how hard you've worked to make your bookshop a reality. You knew Port Karadow was the right place, and even when Jamie whatsit tried his best to dissuade you, you didn't give up, did you? If you like Ben as much as I think you do, then isn't it worth the effort to sort things out with him, too?'

Thea gazed at the water. She could see an inflatable yellow speedboat cutting through the waves, and what looked like a fishing boat further towards the horizon, nothing more than a pale smudge amongst the glittering blue.

'He's worth the effort,' she said. 'But I need to clear my head first, so I can think about what I want to say to him.'

'I get that.' Esme squeezed her arm. 'What do you want to do?'

'I'm going to go for a walk, I think. It'll give you a chance to tell Alex there's no need for subterfuge any more.'

Esme nodded. 'OK. Thanks, Thea.'

'And later, I'll take you to the Old Post House. Maybe after I've spoken to Ben?'

'I'd love that.'

They walked back across the road, towards the cottages. Ben's van was outside, and Thea wondered whether he was nervous about the afternoon with Marcus, or felt calm and in control. She wished she'd been able to support him in the run-up, offering to taste his dishes, distracting him from any anxious thoughts. It had only been a few days since they'd spoken, but she felt as if they'd missed out on so much.

She pushed open the door of Sunfish Cottage and Esme went in search of Alex. Thea glanced at her phone, hoping that Ben might have seen her sitting on the bench and sent her a message, but her screen remained free of notifications, and she put it on the side table and went to get her walking boots.

'See you in a bit,' she called towards Alex's bedroom door when she was ready, not wanting to think too hard about what was happening behind it. She was happy for them – of course she was – but she couldn't help feeling envious: she could have been like that with Ben if she hadn't been so thoughtless. She hurried out of the cottage and closed the door behind her.

She walked towards town, unsure of her destination but with a vague idea that she might head to the crevice Ben had shown her, where the seabirds whirled around the cliffs. She thought that might put things in perspective. Could she tread that precarious path all on her own?

A car horn blared as she was striding along the clifftop, and for a moment she thought it was Ben, her heart leaping at the possibility. But when the car pulled up alongside her, its hazards flashing as it drew to a stop, she saw it was Anisha.

Thea bent down at the open window. 'Hey!'

'Glad I caught you,' Anisha said. 'For you!' She held out a set of keys. 'I shouldn't really be doing this, but I thought you might like to have a look around your new property, so you can take it all in, now you know it's yours, and before you head back to Bristol.'

'Really? That's so kind, thank you!'

'As long as it doesn't make you change your mind.'

Of this one thing, Thea was certain. 'Don't worry, I love it – warts and all.'

'Great. I can't make Ben's event this afternoon because of work, but I'll message you later and find out where you are, so I can pick up the keys. Or – actually – give them to Meredith, and she can give them back to me.'

'Perfect,' Thea said. 'Thank you again. This means such a lot.'

Anisha grinned. 'Enjoy!'

Thea waved her off, then stood for a few moments looking at the view. Maybe whirling, frantic seabirds and a terrifying drop weren't what she needed right now. Maybe she needed to look around her new bookshop, her decades-long dream made real, with nobody peering over her shoulder. There, she might be able to process the news about Esme and Alex, come to terms with the fact that Ben wouldn't be a part of her future, and most importantly, start thinking about this town, this life, as hers.

Then she would go to Ben's event, try not to think of herself as an unwelcome distraction, and enjoy the last afternoon of what had been a life-changing holiday: perhaps even toast this new, miraculous chapter she was about to embark on with her friends. She wondered if Ben would clink glasses with her, or if she'd sullied their friendship, and the possibility of more, too much even for that.

She pushed the thought away. Now was the time to be positive, to put negative thoughts to the back of her mind.

She had achieved a lot, and she was going to revel quietly in it, to share her triumph with some spiders and sleeping bats. She gave a quick, involuntary shudder, then lifted her chin.

With the sea sparkling to her left, Sunfish and Oystercatcher Cottages behind her, and the wind spurring her on, Thea set off again, striding along Port Karadow's clifftop path towards her future.

# Chapter Twenty-Seven

As she walked, Thea soaked up her surroundings. The bright, cheery town, the way the buildings – some of them pale, some brightly coloured – looked like an assorted box of sweets, shiny and enticing in the June sunshine, and how that contrasted with the wildness of the craggy coastline, the blue-green expanse of the sea. She wanted to remember it all, to save it in her mind until the next time she was here, knowing a photo wouldn't do it justice.

She walked along the harbour front, busy with tourists eating ice creams and throwing bread to seagulls already fat on discarded chips; past a family where the smallest, welly-clad boy was being held up by his dad to look through the telescope pointing out to sea. She got wafts of holiday aromas, of coffee and fried batter and the sharp scent from the fishing boats. It made her think of Ben and his barbecue event, starting later on the beach, and her stomach tightened with nerves.

She cut up the alleyway that led to Main Street, then took the smaller, less obvious path that snaked between houses, its steeper trajectory leading to the Old Post House's hilltop position. She still couldn't decide whether to go with Meredith and Finn, or stay away.

She wanted to try and talk to Ben one more time before she returned to Bristol, but she didn't want to make that afternoon's event about her. Ben was so often in the background, so the fact that he was putting himself on show meant he really cared about this, and she didn't want to ruin it. Perhaps she could do something with Esme and Alex, then try and speak to him that evening.

She slid her hands into her pockets, looking for her phone, and found only the key Anisha had given her. She heaved herself up the last, steepest part of the hill, and the Old Post House came into view: neat chimneys first, then the tiled roof, then the rest of it in all its tatty, charming glory.

'Hello,' she said to the building, then looked behind her, checking nobody had overheared. But, it seemed, everyone was milling about the town centre, and she supposed there was no real reason for tourists to come up here since the post office had closed – unless they were taking the hiking trail she'd been on when she discovered it. She would have to come up with a marketing campaign to start her off: *The views and books are worth it* – something like that, only infinitely catchier.

She was musing on the wording, wondering why her vocabulary had chosen to desert her when she wanted to call on it most, as she took out the key Anisha had given her and unlocked the door. It creaked inwards, its hinges in need of a good oil, and as she stepped into the gloomy interior, she heard something scuttling in a corner. She shuddered, hoping the spiders here weren't big enough to be quite *that* loud. She closed the door gently behind her and the whole frame shook, dust particles dancing in the air.

As Thea walked further into the room, golden light filtered through the admittedly grimy windows, touching everything with a warm, gentle glow. Her excitement built as she took it all in, the confirmation that – beyond the broken shelves and dented counter where the till used to be, through the dust and disuse – there were the makings of a wonderful bookshop. The staircase would have to be checked for stability – *everywhere* would have to be checked for stability – but once it was solid, she could have sections on the upper and lower floors, and make use of the whole building.

She did a small circuit of the downstairs space. The back corners, furthest from the sea-facing windows, were the creepiest. The shadows here were as thick as the dust, and there was a wonky bookshelf, bare apart from a small cluster of cuddly toys, the gleaming plastic eyes of a koala bear and a puppy staring out at her from their huddle. 'Ugh.' She patted her pockets again, thinking that she would be able to see things better with her phone torch.

Again, she came up with only the key to the building, and as she tapped her back pockets absent-mindedly, a memory flashed into her head: putting her phone on the side table at Sunfish Cottage before she pulled her boots on. The thought of Esme and Alex behind the bedroom door had made her hurry out without pausing, and she realised she didn't have her phone with her. The thought was slightly disconcerting, but not enough to make her give up on her tour.

She climbed the stairs gingerly, each tread creaking. The upper floor still held the remnants of Sylvia's life, a few pieces of furniture that she must have decided she didn't want. Thea wondered what it would be like to live here; to be trapped in the upstairs space like Rapunzel, and have most of your conversations through the open window.

She moved to the front of the building, because it was the views she really wanted to see. The windows were cleaner up here, the frame Sylvia had pushed up to get people's attention clear of grime.

Beyond the glass, the sight didn't disappoint. Port Karadow stretched ahead of her, a field of rooftops and squat chimney stacks, sliding down by degrees like the seats in a theatre circle, the glistening blue of the sea in the harbour the curved, faultless stage. It was magnificent. She could see how Sylvia had been reluctant to give it up: not just because this had been her home with Eric, but because she had a view that not many other people got to see.

Thea pressed her palms against the rough wood of the windowsill. She wished she had her phone with her, so she could take a photo through the glass. There was movement behind her, something shifting or scratching, and she shivered. At least there was a plan to get rid of the bats humanely. The spiders? She didn't know what would happen to them. She imagined some kind of gentle fumigation, all the arachnids exiting the building like in that terrifying scene from *Arachnophobia*, and suddenly the glitter of the sea, the bright sunshine, was calling her.

She stood up straight and stretched her arms to the ceiling, then glanced at her watch. An hour and a half until Ben's barbecue session with Marcus. Could she really miss it, when it meant so much to him, and she had come to realise that he meant a lot to her? She turned away from the window, the floorboards creaking, then the creak turned to a judder and there was a crashing, wrenching sound, so loud and close that Thea put her hands over her ears, the whole building shaking around her.

The walls were trembling, and she could feel vibrations beneath her feet, the tearing sound going on and on, assaulting the quiet stillness of her visit. Dust and cobwebs fell from the ceiling, and she squeezed her eyes and lips closed, even as her breathing sped up. She wanted to lean against a wall, because her legs were shaking along with the building, but leaning no longer seemed like a safe option.

After what felt like long, long minutes, the groaning and splintering stopped, and the shudder settled to nothing. Thea could sense the upheaval it had caused, the shrill sound of birds outside – the goldcrest probably hadn't enjoyed having his foraging disturbed – and the squeaks and scuttles of things, *creatures*, inside. She dusted herself down and took a couple of tentative steps. It was definitely time to get out of there.

It wasn't until she was halfway down the staircase that she realised the doorway looked very different to how it had when she had come in. It had felt dark, overshadowed, when she stepped inside, and she remembered the heavy wooden beam Ben had shown her: the one he had thought was unsafe.

Thea tiptoed down the last couple of steps, her hand lightly touching the handrail, and realised the beam had proved Ben right. One side of it had fallen, and it was covering the doorway at a jaunty angle, like a hefty no-exit barrier.

She grimaced. It would probably have had to be replaced anyway, but she didn't want to have to admit to anyone that she'd managed to add to the building's problems with one, short visit. She walked up to it and pushed against it. If she could get the other side to come down, then at least it would be on the floor and no longer blocking the door. She pushed and pushed, but the beam felt as if it had grown out of the ground, it seemed so solidly in place.

Thea flexed her fingers as the first, tiny trickle of panic filtered through her bloodstream. But it would be all right, because even if she couldn't move the beam, she could slip behind it, and open the door far enough to get out. Except, she remembered, the door opened inwards, and there was less than a foot between it and where the beam now rested, as if it had been there for eternity. She went to grab the handle, to see just how far she *could* get the door open, and realised the fates had conspired to give her yet another challenge. When the beam had fallen, it had knocked the door handle off. There was nothing to grasp onto, nothing to pull. The doorway she'd come in by, she realised, as the trickle of panic turned into a stream, was not going to be the way she got out of this place.

Thea walked slowly around the ground floor of the building, fully aware, now, just how unstable it was. She tested the window frames, hoping for a loose one – one she could slide up and bend through, to get out into the fresh air. They were all wedged firmly closed.

At the back of the ground floor, next to the terrifying toy bookshelf, there was a door into what she presumed was an office or storage space. She hadn't tried it yet, worried that it might harbour some things she didn't want to face on her own. But she was out of options.

She pulled the handle and the door flung open. It was dark inside, but not too dark, and she found a small office with a desk and a long table, which she presumed had been used by staff for sorting the post. Its only window was above the desk, and it was only about the size of her head. Big enough to fit a mouse through, but not a whole Thea.

The tiny bathroom next door was similarly unhelpful, with a hardback-sized, frosted window, and Thea had to work hard to stop panic overtaking her reasoning. There had to be something she could do: some way of getting out. She felt in her pockets again for her phone, even though she'd established, she'd *remembered*, that she'd left it at the cottage.

Gingerly, she went back upstairs, hoping that the falling beam wouldn't have lined up a whole domino effect of collapses. She didn't want to go back to the front of the building, but that was where Sylvia had stuck her upper body out of a window and spoken to her and Ben, and it seemed like her best – her only – option.

She got her fingers under the frame and gently lifted it up. She was met by welcome fresh air, and the seaside sounds of waves breaking and seagulls, distant voices carried on the wind. Thea's pulse settled slightly, and she peered down. The ivy looked strong, but the drop was substantial, and she was quite a lot heavier than a goldcrest.

She lowered herself to the edge of the windowsill, felt the subtle shift of the building as she sat, and prayed someone – a hiker or a dog walker – would come past soon and rescue her.

Half an hour later, Thea was beginning to despair for herself and her future bookshop. Nobody had come past. This was an almost-forgotten corner of Port Karadow. No wonder Sylvia had leaned right out of the window and heckled passers-by so she could have some company. How would Thea attract customers if nobody walked along this road? How would she ever have customers if she never even got to open the bookshop, because she'd died alone inside the building she'd chosen, starving to death and then being eaten by giant spiders?

She cursed herself for so many things: for leaving her phone behind; for suggesting that she was going to take herself off for a walk, and for telling her friends that she wasn't sure she was going to Ben's event. Did Esme and Meredith think she'd decided to miss it? It had just started, and she fancied she could smell his delicious food. She wondered if he had struck up some kind of entertaining banter with Marcus Belrose. She couldn't imagine him doing that, but maybe that was because he'd been so taciturn with her the last couple of times she'd seen him. Perhaps, without her in his sights or his thoughts, he was as sunny as a person could be.

With her bum sore from sitting on the edge of the windowsill, and her throat parched – because she hadn't even brought a bottle of water with her, so quick was she to leave Esme and Alex to it – Thea slunk down onto the bare floorboards. She rested her arms on the sill, her gaze focused on the road outside. This way, she would be able to see her rescuer approaching. Because someone had to come past eventually, didn't they?

She sighed. She had wanted this place – badly, it turned out – and now the universe was laughing at her. She was going to be trapped here for ever, without selling a single book to a single, happy customer.

If it was possible to die from self-pity, then it might turn out to be the way Thea went. She leaned her head on her arms, gazed out at sunny, sparkly Port Karadow going about its day without her, and prayed for a lost tourist.

# Chapter Twenty-Eight

The worst thing was, Thea thought, as she stared at the scene she had come to know so well over the last couple of hours, that she could see the passage of time marked by the sun: the way it moved overhead, the shadows elongating before her eyes. She had more things to add to her pity party now: mainly the fact that she had briefly fallen asleep, and was sure that a whole horde of people – probably an entire hiking party, with crampons and sensible hats and flasks of water – had been past while she had been dozing, mouth slightly open, possibly catching spiders while she failed to save herself.

*Enough*, she thought. She could get out of here. She *could*.

She left her upstairs viewing post and, her limbs stiff, her hip and elbow sore from her awkward snoozing position, went back downstairs. She tried the beam again. It was wedged as tightly as it had been earlier: steadfast and solid. *Just like Ben*, she thought. She gripped it with both hands, planted her feet wide apart, and pulled. There was the tick-tick-tick of wood shifting, but nothing more promising than that.

'Fuck it.' She walked to the window where, less than three weeks before, she had peered into the building for the first time. The glass was latticed, and she knew that breaking one of the panes would get her no further than sticking her hand outside. She went back to the beam and tried to move it again. It groaned, as if to say, 'Enough now'. But it *wasn't* enough. She had to get out of here. She had roughly twelve hours, maybe sixteen, to find Ben and tell him she was sorry. To explain that she had picked this place, that she was coming back here to live, to start a new chapter of her life. She had to—

What was that? A sound cut through the stillness of the sunny afternoon, and it was close – nowhere near the beach or harbour. The sound of an engine.

Thea abandoned the beam and raced back upstairs, forgetting to be careful about where she put her feet, and hurried to the open window. She couldn't see anything yet, there was no sign of a car. Maybe it wasn't anyone: maybe it was a generator somewhere nearby, or a low-flying plane, or – no. *No.* The blue van appeared at the crest of the hill and then came, tyres screeching, into the space in front of the Old Post House.

The doors opened and there was a flurry of movement and noise, so different to the hours Thea had just spent by herself. She saw Meredith get out of the passenger side, Finn come out of the back of the van, and there was Ben, in a white cotton shirt and jeans, Scooter at his heels.

Ben went straight to the front door, but Meredith looked up, gasping when her eyes landed on Thea, who had stuck her head and shoulders out of the window and was trying very hard not to sob with relief.

'You're here!' Meredith shouted.

Ben stepped back and looked up at her, and Thea felt a charge as their eyes met, almost as strong as when the building had vibrated.

'Are you OK?' he called up. 'We've been calling and calling, but—'

'I left my phone at Sunfish Cottage.' It came out as a croak. 'I came here to look around, to see my new—' she swallowed. 'The beam fell down.'

Ben put his hands in his hair. 'On *you*?'

'No,' she said quickly. 'I was upstairs. But you were right: it's very unstable. Or it *was*, anyway.' She tried to laugh, but no sound came out.

'We need to get you out,' Ben said, approaching the building again.

'The beam's stuck in front of the door,' Thea called down. 'I can't move it from in here, and the door won't open wide enough for even a bat to get through.' She heard the clunk as Ben pushed the door and it connected with the solid weight of the beam.

'Fuck,' he said.

Finn smiled up at her, his arm around Meredith, who was looking slightly panicked. Scooter was with Ben, barking and whining as his owner tried to make headway.

'You doing OK, Thea?' Finn asked. She frowned at him, unsure why he seemed so pleased about the situation.

'I'm thirsty, and dusty, and there are some pretty humungous spiders in here.'

'Finn, Meredith?' Ben called. 'A little help, please.'

The couple stopped staring at Thea and went to help, and she thought she should see if there was anything she could do from the inside. She went carefully down the stairs, wincing whenever Ben banged the door against the beam and bits of plaster fell from the ceiling.

'This fucking thing,' he said.

'There's no way it's going to budge,' Finn added. 'Not like this.'

'We need to get the door off,' Ben said, and for the first time since she'd realised she was trapped, Thea's heart skittered with relief. 'Hang on.'

'Ben's going to take the door off!' Finn called. 'I was hoping he'd scale the ivy and rescue you that way, but we can't always have a Disney ending.'

'If he gets me out of here, it'll be better than a Disney film,' Thea called back, and Finn and Meredith both laughed. She waited for Ben to join in, to say something in response, but there was nothing, and her panic returned more forcefully than before. What if he was going to get her out and then walk away? His one act of kindness, then they would go back to being strangers.

She heard the whirr of an automatic drill, murmuring from Finn and Meredith, and pressed herself as close to the door as she could, which actually meant she was pressed up against the beam.

'Ben?' she called.

'Hang on, Thea. I'll have you out of there in a couple of minutes.'

'I want to say something first,' she rushed.

'This'll take two minutes,' Ben said again. There was a short pause and then he added, 'Are you hurt?'

'No, no, I'm fine. And I've been here for – I don't know how many hours, and no giant spiders have got me yet. But I want to say something. *Please.*'

'Now?' He sounded bemused, but his voice had softened. The buzzing from his drill stopped, quiet settling over their corner of Cornwall once more.

'I don't want you to get me out of here and then just leave,' she said. 'I know that sounds horribly ungrateful, because you've come to rescue me, but I don't – I need to say some things.'

'What things?' He sounded closer, and she looked past the beam and saw him, peering at her through the misty glass of the door between them. She could see what a good face he had: the best face, really. She had missed spending time with him.

'I'm so sorry,' she said. 'I'm sorry that I said those things to Esme. That I wasn't honest with her about how I felt about you, that I dismissed what we had. I promise that I never thought of you as temporary, because even before I met you, I was planning on moving to Cornwall.'

'Right,' Ben said, his tone giving nothing away.

'And I'm sorry I wasn't completely honest about Alex from the beginning, that I gave the impression that there was something between us. But there never, *ever* was. Not before, and not since he's been here.' She paused, waiting to see if he'd fill the silence. He didn't, but his eyebrows rose slightly, and she knew she had to go on. 'My feelings for Alex were more about being comfortable, feeling safe. Mostly, I was grateful to him.'

'Grateful?' Ben asked. 'What for?'

Thea swallowed. 'Last summer, at the library, there was an . . . incident.'

'What kind of incident?'

'There were these guys – they must have been teenagers, though they weren't exactly small. They'd been hanging about, making a nuisance of themselves. We'd asked them to move on, but they said they were doing research for college projects. There wasn't much we could do, because they weren't causing damage or offending anyone, and I'm sure they were just trying to amuse themselves.

'But then I ended up leaving late – I'd been working with some local schools on an anti-bullying campaign, of all things . . .' She cleared her throat. Even now it was hard to go through it again: not because she was still afraid, but because she was ashamed.

'What happened?' Ben asked, his voice echoing against the glass.

She noticed that he'd pressed his fingers against one of the lower panes, and for the first time, she felt an inkling of hope. It was ironic that he was listening to her when, now more than ever, he could walk away and she wouldn't be able to follow.

'I locked up the library,' she continued, letting the memories crowd in. 'It was dusk, and I thought I was alone. It was a lovely, warm summer's evening, so I knew town would be busy, but by the library it was quieter. They walked out of the shadows – the same boys who'd been inside, messing about all day. They didn't want to hurt me, I don't think, but they were intimidating, walking close behind me, saying things too low for me to hear, then laughing. One of them tugged on my handbag strap, but when I turned around, they backed off. When I walked faster, they kept up with me.' She closed her eyes. 'My flat's twenty minutes from the library, and it's a quieter, residential part of town, so there were no restaurants or pubs I could duck inside. I felt helpless, panicky. I didn't know what to do.'

'Alex turned up?' Ben guessed, and Thea nodded.

'He was as laid back as usual. He told the men to leave me alone, but in a way that wasn't threatening – there was no challenge for them to rise to – and after a few, uncertain moments, they just walked off. Proving, I suppose, that they weren't ever going to do anything to me. But since then I've felt so grateful, so warm towards him, and so I – I guess a part of me thought—'

'You don't have to say anything else,' Ben said.

'I want to.'

'You've already said enough. I'm the one who didn't listen.'

Thea didn't know what to say to that, and in the space where she should have replied, the drill started up again. She deflated. So that was it, then. She'd opened her soul to him, and he wasn't interested. She rested her forehead against the beam, feeling it vibrate under Ben's ministrations towards the building.

She heard murmuring, then Ben's voice, whispered but forceful. 'I want to get her *out* first. I'm not doing it through a bloody door!'

She heard the tinkle of hinges falling to the ground and the door listed sideways, a fresh blast of sea air reaching her through the gap. She saw Finn shuffle into place, gripping the door so it didn't fall unchecked. Ben crouched down, and the drill whirred again. Thea felt the beam, rough and warm beneath her palm, and wondered how long it had been in place, secured above this doorway, before her footsteps had brought it crashing down.

There was a crack, another metallic clink, and then Ben and Finn were moving the door out of the way, and it was Ben who came back and held his hand out for Thea to take, so she could slip past the beam, step over the debris that had come down with it.

Scooter whined, and Finn crouched down and held the dog's collar.

'Careful,' Ben said, his warm fingers wrapping around her hand the moment she pressed her palm into his. She dropped her gaze, navigated her way over the fallen plaster and wood, past the beam, through the narrowed doorway, and was suddenly out in the sunshine.

'Thank—' she started, but Ben pulled her forward, wrapping his arms around her and bringing her flush against his chest. It was sudden and unexpected and very, very welcome. She slid her arms around his waist and rested her cheek against the soft cotton of his shirt, the heat of his skin beneath turning her relief into something else, something that made her stomach pulse low down. But she couldn't think those thoughts, so she forced herself out of his embrace.

'Thank you,' she said. 'I didn't think anyone would come. I thought Port Karadow had become a ghost town at the worst possible moment.'

'Everyone was at the beach,' Meredith said, hugging her. 'Watching Ben's triumph.'

'It would have been a triumph, if he hadn't left halfway through.' Finn gave Thea her third hug, then released her so that Scooter, who had been wagging his tail madly, could bounce up on his hind legs and lick her cheek.

'Scooter!' Ben admonished. 'I thought I'd trained him out of that.'

'Some things bypass all the rules though, don't they?' Finn said, grinning at his friend.

'What do you mean?' Thea asked. 'Why did you leave early, Ben?'

He winced. 'You didn't turn up, and when Meredith came to collect her food, she said she couldn't get hold of you. I wasn't surprised that you weren't there: not after the way I'd behaved. But when you didn't reply to her messages or calls, I started to get worried.'

'He made me go to Sunfish Cottage,' Finn added, 'to see if you were there. Your friend Esme answered the door, but she said she didn't know where you were. She'd been busy all afternoon, apparently.' Finn's raised eyebrows made it clear he knew exactly how Esme had been busy.

'Esme and Alex are together,' Thea said.

Ben frowned. 'They are?'

She nodded, her cheeks burning. She thought of all the humiliations that had piled up on her over the last few days; the misunderstandings and missteps. She glanced behind her, at the open doorway and the fallen beam. The mistakes.

'I was worried about you,' Ben said again, forcing her attention back to him. 'I wanted to apologise to you, anyway, before you went home. I understand why you weren't there this afternoon, but a small – I suppose arrogant – part of me hoped you might still come.'

'I hadn't decided,' Thea admitted. 'I didn't want to distract you. Obviously, the decision was taken out of my hands.'

'I wanted you to distract me,' Ben said, with a hint of a smile. 'I've missed you, and I've behaved like a dickhead. I've *been* a dickhead. Yesterday, at the harbour, when I turned my back on you – I was pathetic, and I'm so sorry.

'You had already explained everything, and I didn't listen. I was still angry about Damien: the way he'd betrayed me, the way they'd both acted, so when Esme told me what you'd said to her, and I added that to the way you'd been talking about Alex . . . I decided that it was going to happen again. Despite the way you were around me, the way we got on, I didn't think it was real. Too good to be true, I guess.' He shrugged, then glanced at Finn and Meredith, who were standing there, grinning at them both. 'Do you have to be here?' he asked.

'You wanted our help,' Finn said.

'And you brought us in your van,' Meredith added. 'We deserve to see this.'

'Romantic declarations are my speciality,' Finn went on. 'If you want me to—'

'No,' Ben said firmly, then turned back to Thea. 'Meredith told me you got this place? That it's going to be your bookshop?'

'If I haven't completely destroyed it before we can even get the bat man in.'

Ben's smile kicked up a notch. 'You won't have. That beam was on a countdown, anyway. I'm so fucking glad you weren't underneath it when it fell.'

'Or Sylvia,' Thea said, suppressing a shudder.

There was a moment of quiet contemplation, all of them trying not to imagine the worst. Then Ben took a deep breath and said, 'Thea. I am beyond happy that you're moving here, and – despite the way I've behaved the last couple of days – I wondered if you might like to try that film night again? I could cook the lasagne this time. I could—'

'Have another shower at my place?' Thea finished, and Ben glanced at Meredith and Finn, his cheeks colouring. Then he turned back to her, and his smile became a grin.

'That, too. If you'll have me?'

Thea's heart thrummed, and her fingers itched to touch him: his hair or his hands, or the collar of his shirt, so she could tug him closer. 'Yes please,' she said. 'I would really like to have you.' She reached up on her tiptoes, and as his hands came around her waist, she threaded her fingers around his neck, into his hair. Then his lips were on hers, giving her what was, undoubtedly, the best kiss of her life. So what if they had an audience? She would happily declare her feelings for Ben to the whole of Port Karadow, hold an event at her new bookshop solely to talk about how much she liked him. She tuned out the whistles from her new friends, and Scooter's barking, and gave her mind over to just feeling: Ben's lips, the soft hair at the nape of his neck, the way his body fitted so well against hers.

When they broke apart, breathless, eyes latching onto each other as if they couldn't give up contact altogether, Ben's smile was as wide and confident – as *unequivocal* – as she'd ever seen it.

'You gave up your barbecue gig to come and find me?' Thea asked, remembering the story he had been in the middle of telling.

He nodded. 'I needed to make sure you were OK.'

'Well, I wasn't, entirely, but thanks to you – to all of you – I am now. Very OK. More OK than I've been in a long time. How was Marcus Belrose?'

Ben grinned. 'He wasn't OK.'

Finn tutted. 'He'll get over it. He'll have to, because before this afternoon even kicked off, he'd asked Ben to come back, to make it a more regular thing.'

'I'm not sure that offer's going to stand, now,' Ben said.

'I bet it will,' Meredith chipped in. 'Marcus's bark is worse than his bite. Adrian says he's a decent guy, and I'm sure he'll give you another chance.'

'He won't want to pass up on your talent,' Thea agreed, letting Ben take both her hands in his, feeling a delicious thrum in her veins at being so close to him, knowing that the hard, jagged edges that had been between them had been, if not fully smoothed out, then at least shaved down, paving the way for more softening to come. 'But what about your house renovations?'

Ben scowled, but it wasn't a serious scowl: it couldn't put a dent in his obvious happiness. 'I'll get there eventually.'

'I could always help with the tiling, next time I'm down.'

'Now that,' Ben said, 'is an offer I can't refuse.' He walked around the van and held the door open. Thea climbed into the passenger seat, Finn and Meredith not seeming to mind that they'd been relegated to the back. 'Except I'm hoping that the next time you're here, I will have made a lot of progress.' He opened the driver's door and Scooter jumped up, settling himself in the middle as Ben climbed in behind him.

'Oh?' Thea said. 'Why's that?'

Ben shrugged, started the engine and then turned to her, his hazel eyes so full of hope and desire that Thea felt as if she was in an unstable building once more, her whole body trembling. 'I'd really like to impress my girlfriend when she visits,' he explained. 'I can't have her coming to stay in a building site, can I? Not when you'll already have this one to deal with.' He gestured to the Old Post House.

'Oh, I don't know,' Thea said. 'I seem to remember you telling me you had a bed, and maybe that's all you'll need?'

'Maybe it is,' he agreed.

Their gazes held, and a silent promise, a charge, passed between them, before Finn interrupted from the back of the van.

'I've changed my mind. Can you let me and Meredith out here? We want no part of these shenanigans, Benjamin Senhouse. Where's the repressed, untalkative guy I've come to know and love?'

Ben drove down the hill, Port Karadow a picture postcard of Cornish summer below them, all sun-warmed buildings and blue, inviting sea. 'I don't know,' he said mildly, reaching past Scooter to put his hand on Thea's knee, his touch both soft and sizzling. 'Maybe he's finally happy again?'

There was silence after that, but it was a shared, contented silence, and Thea put her hand over Ben's, looked out of the windscreen at her new home, and decided she was quite pleased that she'd decided to take the plunge and, despite all her misgivings, have a solo holiday in Port Karadow after all.

# Chapter Twenty-Nine

The September light in Cornwall had a different quality to the June sunshine.

Thea stood outside the Old Post House, revelling in the gentle warmth and the way the sun seemed to polish the houses. She felt a sense of peace descend on her, at the fact that the back and forth of the last few months was over, that she could call herself a resident of Port Karadow, finally. If she was honest, the relief was entirely secondary to the excitement, the thrill of all that lay ahead of her, even if a lot of it would involve uncertainty and brain-ache and hard, hard work. At the end of it, there would be a bookshop. *Her* bookshop and, if she did it well enough, the town's, too.

That was what she wanted more than anything, for her business to be embraced by the town, just as the post office had been when Eric and Sylvia were running it. She wanted her bookshop to be as integral: as loved, and as visited. After all, what better way of earning chips, ice cream or a sausage roll from Sea Brew than by walking up the hill to buy a book first? There would be so many benefits to visiting it, and she was going to make sure people were aware of all of them. Already, the Old Post House looked completely different to how it had done in June. Most of the changes were structural, on the inside, but now the honeyed stone was hidden by scaffolding rather than ivy.

An engine noise assaulted her senses, and she wondered if this would be the team the council had hired, or her very own, personal builder. Neither outcome would be horrible, though one was a lot more preferable than the other. Her smile widened when she saw that she'd hit the jackpot, the blue Ford van coming to a stop in front of the Old Post House.

Ben got out, Scooter following close on his heels, and they both greeted her warmly – the dog with a bark and a lick, Ben with a hug and a kiss – even though it had only been a few hours since they'd seen each other.

'So,' Ben said, his smile easily reaching his eyes, 'it's looking good, right?'

'So good,' Thea agreed. 'They've already done a wonderful job. I can't believe it's nearly ready for me to start work on the interior.'

'I could have done this, you know. Foreman of a larger team. I wouldn't have let you down.'

'I know you wouldn't have,' Thea said, her tone gentle, because they'd been over this already, 'but it wasn't up to me. The council already had contractors they worked with, and anyway, I didn't want you here, working so hard throughout the summer. Also, you really didn't need another thing distracting you from your home renovation. And now you've got enough other work to be going on with, with Mel's holiday properties and the extension on Finn's aunt's place, it's not like you need it.'

'I guess not,' he said. 'And listed buildings can be a nightmare.'

Thea nodded. There had definitely been a few of those so far, but the team were great, and Anish had been practical and unflappable throughout. 'Anyway,' she went on, 'now that I'm here for good, I want you at home in the evenings, to spend time with you at weekends. I don't want to upset our equilibrium.'

Ben grinned. 'We've got an equilibrium already, even though you've officially been living in Cornwall for three days?'

'I think we have. Don't you?'

Ben's eyes turned serious. 'I do. Oystercatcher Cottage already feels a lot better with you in it.'

Thea smiled. 'Well, I love being there. And it's funny, isn't it, how many of the little touches – the built-in bookshelves, the art deco reading lights either side of the bed, which is *so* solid, by the way, and that atmospheric photo of the abandoned lighthouse in the front room – are exactly what I would have put there.'

Ben rolled his eyes and pulled her close, bending to kiss the spot just below her ear. 'I know you're pleased about that,' he murmured, 'but you can't embarrass me. I'll give tours if you want, telling anyone who'll listen that I designed it all with you in mind.'

Thea closed her eyes, overwhelmed all over again at his thoughtfulness, his commitment to what they had; at knowing he saw a future for them, just like she did.

Since she'd gone back to Bristol at the end of June, they'd spoken daily, and without planning it properly, somehow set up a schedule whereby every two weeks, either she travelled back to Cornwall – usually tacking on a Friday or Monday, or both, so she could meet with Anisha and the construction team, or the bat man, or the historical buildings conveyancer – or Ben came to Bristol.

The three out of four weekends that he stayed in Port Karadow, Ben joined Marcus Belrose in his food truck on the beach, and for one of those three, Thea was there, often with Meredith and Finn, eating his incredible food and catching up with her friends. Thea spent time up here at the site, seeing how the work was progressing, and Anisha kept her updated when she wasn't in Cornwall. When Ben came to Bristol, they spent lazy hours in her flat, talking about the future while she methodically packed up her life, or they went into town, sometimes just the two of them, sometimes with Esme and Alex.

Two months of only spending time together every other weekend might have seemed like an unsteady foundation for Thea to move in with Ben, but he'd suggested it early on, saying it was practical more than anything: he had a house, he had the room, and it would allow Thea to hold onto more of her savings while she was setting up the bookshop and had no income. She could see the sense in it, but she was also reluctant to move too fast too soon, to mess up something that seemed so perfect.

But as July became August, as Thea's notice period at the library neared its end, and as her thoughts turned more towards Cornwall, Ben's argument became a lot more personal: he wanted to be with her, and there was no point in them living separately when they could be together. Then, a couple of weeks ago, when she was in Port Karadow at the end of August, had come the point of no return.

They'd been walking back to Oystercatcher Cottage after a night spent with Meredith and Finn at the Happy Shack, the sun flickering like a flame above the horizon, the stars and moon already so bright that they barely needed a torch to find their way back, when Ben had stopped, turned Thea to face him on the clifftop path, and kissed her.

'What was that for?' Thea had asked, high enough on their wonderful night without his touch sending her into the stratosphere.

'Because I can't quite get over that you're here, and that you'll soon be here for good. And also because I love you, Thea Rushwood. Move into Oystercatcher Cottage with me. Please?'

Her lingering doubts had already been trailing far, far behind her by that point, and she'd been wondering when to say those three, short words to him. With Ben's admission, his eyes looking green in the moonlight, his face more serious than she'd seen it in a long time, those last, lingering doubts had fizzled to nothing.

'Yes please,' she'd said, exhaling. 'I would love to move in with you. Not only because you do a mean house renovation, Ben Senhouse, but also because I can't think of anywhere I would rather be when I move here, and because I love you, too. Very, very much.' His smile had competed with the moon, his kiss had tasted of the Happy Shack's divine chocolate pudding, and when they'd got back to the newly-finished bedroom at Oystercatcher Cottage, their focus hadn't been on sleeping.

But despite all that, it wasn't until she'd brought her suitcase and a couple of boxes, being uncharacteristically ruthless about which books to hold onto and which to donate to other readers, because this house was Ben's, first, (though theirs to share equally, he'd assured her on multiple occasions) that he'd admitted his secret.

They'd been sitting at the breakfast bar, eating a pile of Ben's creamy mash topped with Cajun-spiced chicken that Thea was already addicted to, when she'd asked him outright: what about the floor-to-ceiling bookshelves in the living room, the vanity mirror in the bedroom with dressing-room lights around it, the Velvetiser in the kitchen for making perfect hot chocolates? These all seemed like Thea-shaped touches, not things she would have imagined Ben thinking about or wanting for himself.

He'd glanced at his plate, a smile denting his cheeks, and when he'd looked up she'd sensed no shyness or embarrassment. 'Ever since that weekend, when you got trapped in your bookshop, and we . . .'

'Kissed and made up,' Thea finished, though the truth was that on her last night in Port Karadow, in the bedroom of Oystercatcher Cottage, which *did* have a double bed in it but not much else, they'd done a lot more than kiss.

'Exactly,' Ben said, the reminder of that night heating his expression just as it was Thea's blood. 'Well, after that, my design plans for this place changed slightly.'

'You mean you started thinking about it with me in mind? Anticipating that I'd be living here with you?' She'd laughed, because that had been too soon, surely.

But Ben didn't join in with her laughter, and she'd realised he was serious. 'Yes,' was all he'd said, and Thea had felt a flood of happiness, of rightness and contentment that, even back then, when their relationship had only just got over a big hurdle, and was as fresh and new as the five a.m. sun, he'd wanted a future with her.

And now, standing in front of what would soon be her bookshop, that future had become the present.

'No sign of any bats?' Ben asked, pulling slowly away from her, so they could both look up at the Old Post House.

'Nope,' Thea said. 'Mr Parker's methods have done the trick. Since he gave us a bat-free bill of health, there hasn't been a single flap of vampiric wings.'

'Good to know,' Ben replied, and she could hear the smile in his voice.

Mr Parker the bat man had been efficient and focused, but his eccentricities – including singing old music hall songs while he worked, something his small team seemed inured to – had made Thea both warm to him and question her choice of specialist. But, it turned out, he loved bats and old buildings, and was dedicated to protecting both.

After the first day, Thea had felt comfortable enough to leave him and his team of experts to it, and it hadn't been long before their work was declared a success. Now the building team were ensuring the refurbished roof had no holes to encourage them back, and she had full confidence that they were doing a good job.

Soon, the Old Post House would be reborn as Thea's bookshop.

'What about the name?' Ben asked. His tone was gentle, but it gave her a burst of anxiety, because they had spent *hours* talking about this incredibly crucial element, and she still hadn't decided. It was actually happening, and she didn't have a clue what to call it.

'Same as ever,' she said.

'That's a strange name for a bookshop.'

She turned towards him, and before he had a chance to escape, she tickled his ribs. She had discovered that he was *very* ticklish there, and an assault had been known to make him yelp. He twisted away from her, but she moved quickly, and when the foreman drove into the space in front of the building, followed by two more vans, Thea had her boyfriend backed up against the hedge, trying to protect himself while she tickled him mercilessly. It was not the most professional greeting, but Thea knew Mike, a burly man who always had a pencil behind his ear, well enough now, that she was sure he wouldn't mind.

'Any issues, boss?' he asked her, tipping his head in a nod. Anisha was really who he answered to, but Thea liked being seen as important.

'No,' she said. 'I'm just finding it hard to stay away, now it's so close to being done.'

'A few more weeks, and all being well it'll be time to hand it over.'

'Really?' Excitement was a solid lump in her throat. 'That's . . . thank you.'

'All credit to the team,' Mike said. 'We're finishing the floor today, so if you want to come back tomorrow, I can give you the tour.'

Thea glanced at Ben, and could see her own happiness mirrored in his eyes. 'I would love that, thank you.'

She knew she needed to let them get on, so after saying hello to Mike's team, she and Ben left them to it, getting into his van.

'Where to?' he asked, his hands on the steering wheel, Scooter trying to climb onto Thea's lap. 'Lunch in town?'

She shook her head. 'No, I don't think . . .'

'Home, then? I could knock us up some killer sandwiches, then finish the tiling in the downstairs bathroom.'

'Tiling? I could help with that.'

Ben grinned. 'You'd have a job fitting in there with me, but I think . . .' He stared out of the windscreen, looking thoughtful. 'I think we could make it work, one way or another.'

They drove through Port Karadow, the September sunshine dusting it with an extra layer of beauty, although Thea knew that, even on the greyest days, it had so much to recommend it. Despite only being here for a few weekends since her solo holiday, she was on friendly terms with so many of the locals already: Anisha and Nick, Finn's aunt Laurie, Max in Sea Brew, and Adrian in Cornish Keepsakes. She and Ben had agreed to go to dinner at Marie and Sylvia's house next week, and Thea was expecting to have to take photos of the Old Post House with her, to satisfy the old woman's inevitable questions. But she didn't mind at all: she already felt part of the community, and she hoped, more than anything, that she could pay everyone's kindness back with her bookshop.

The sea sparkled to their right as they hit the coast road, the blues vibrant, the grass along the clifftop thick and wind-blown, and soon the twin cottages came into sight. Thea noticed a car parked in front of Sunfish Cottage, and wondered who the latest holidaymakers were, and what had motivated them to choose Port Karadow in September. She put her hand on Ben's knee.

'OK?' he asked.

'More than,' she said. 'I was just wondering who we're having next door to us.'

'That's the good thing about being next to a holiday cottage: there's so much variety. Some guests are better than others, obviously, but on the whole I like it. There was one woman, a few months back, who I took a particular fancy to.'

'Oh, really?'

'Yup. Pretty glad she picked Mel's house for her vacation.'

'Quite an eventful one, I seem to recall.'

'Some might almost say life changing,' Ben said, and they looked at each other and smiled.

He drove into the space in front of Oystercatcher Cottage, reversing the van so that the windscreen faced the coastline, the view different every single day, but always breathtaking. It was a sight Thea could enjoy out of her bedroom window, now: her and Ben's bedroom window. She shook her head. How had she got this lucky?

'I know,' she said suddenly, the idea coming to her in a flash of inspiration.

'What?' Ben asked, turning to face her.

'How about . . .' She paused, feeling a second of uncertainty before it was wiped out by Ben's smile and his hazel eyes, the way he was looking at her with anticipation, and a warmth she would never take for granted. 'A New Chapter?'

Ben's lips parted, his breath hitched, and then he leaned over and kissed her, the touch of his mouth against hers sending a thrill through her, as it always did.

'Perfect,' he said. 'I think it's perfect.' There was something else in his expression now, too. Admiration.

Thea had to agree with him. Everything was pretty much perfect.

# Acknowledgements

In the sometimes-lonely world of book writing, I am lucky to have so many people who support me, and so many people who have been instrumental in turning my words into the paperback or ebook you're holding right now, or the audiobook you're listening to.

The biggest thanks to Kate Bradley, my shining light of an editor, who has understood me and my books from the very beginning, and who helps make my stories as good as they can possibly be.

Huge thanks to my wonderful agent, Alice Lutyens, whose energy and encouragement is so inspiring, and who makes me feel like I can achieve anything.

The HarperFiction team have always looked after me so well, and this time around has been no different. Thank you to Chere Tricot, Lynne Drew, Susanna Peden, Sarah Munro, Namra Amir and Sarah Shea. Thank you to Charlotte Webb for the wonderful copyediting skills, for finding all those errors and niggles that I couldn't, and to Penny Isaac for proof reading.

I am in *love* with this cover! I don't know how they can get better every time, but they do. Created by the always amazing Holly MacDonald, Caroline Young and May Van Millingen. Thank you for these blissful designs that make my books look so desirable and, in this case, so completely summery.

I couldn't do the lonely days without the chat, hilarity and help of writer friends. Most notably Kirsty Greenwood, Sheila Crighton, Pernille Hughes, Katie Marsh and the Book Campers.

My mum and dad's support of my writing means so much to me, and they also teach me about resilience; about facing the tough bits of life with humour and grace, and I am so, so lucky to have them. I wouldn't be here, writing my twelfth set of acknowledgements, if it wasn't for them.

Thanks to Lee, to Kate G, Kate and Tim, and Kelly.

A massive thanks to David, whose interruptions while I was writing this book were always welcome (when doesn't a writer want a distraction?), especially as quite a lot of them came with coffee. I couldn't ask for a lovelier, funnier, or more supportive husband. Also, as I write this, he is as hooked on *Bridgerton* series two as I am, so I may be able to convert him to romance yet!

Lastly, thank you to you – my readers. You make this job worthwhile. You get in touch to tell me how much you've loved my stories, and you chat to me online about books, more books and Henry Cavill. If you want to join in, come and find me on Instagram. When the real world is so difficult, books can be one of the best escapes, and I'm so glad mine have helped you disappear to glorious Cornwall for a bit. I hope *The Cornish Cream Tea Holiday* has been as summery and romantic as you were expecting.

# Cosy up with more delightful stories

## om Cressida McLaughlin

## All available now.